PRAISE FOR FARAH HERON

KAMILA KNOWS BEST

"An endearing cast led by a Bollywood-loving hero and a fashionista heroine set Heron's retelling of Jane Austen's *Emma* apart from the pack. Both Austenites and movie fans who fondly remember *Clueless* will be delighted." —*Publishers Weekly*

"There's nothing better than a book that warms your heart and your belly. This Bollywood-inspired retelling of Jane Austen's *Emma* is a fun, lighthearted binge from page one."—*USA Today*

"Heron's sensitive insights infuse this romance with both immense charm and emotional depth." —*Booklist*

ACCIDENTALLY ENGAGED

***Entertainment Weekly* Best Romances of the Year**
***USA Today* Best Rom-Coms of the Year**
NPR Best Romances of the Year

"Voraciously readable...fresh, warm, soft in all the right places...both its comedic and emotional moments sing. We dare readers not to devour it. Grade: A."—*Entertainment Weekly*

"An engaging read with authentic characters who continue to surprise you." —*USA Today*

"A mouth-watering romantic comedy...This book is undoubtedly what Heron would pull out during the Showstopper Challenge on a literary version of *The Great British Bake Off.*" —*BookPage*

"Full of heart and humor...Farah Heron balances the ingredients for a charming romance: a heroine finding her way, a swoon-worthy love, a complicated but loving family and a happily ever after." —Shelf Awareness

"*Accidentally Engaged* does what all good romance novels do best: It's full of emotion, fun, and family, with that ultimately satisfying HEA that will settle in your stomach like a home-cooked meal." —*Vulture*

ALSO BY FARAH HERON

The Chai Factor
Accidentally Engaged
Kamila Knows Best

YOUNG ADULT TITLES

Tahira in Bloom
How to Win a Breakup

FARAH HERON

FOREVER

New York Boston

Forever
Hachette Book Group
1290 Avenue of the Americas, New York, NY 10104
read-forever.com
twitter.com/readforeverpub

First Edition: May 2023

Forever is an imprint of Grand Central Publishing. The Forever name and logo are trademarks of Hachette Book Group, Inc.

The publisher is not responsible for websites (or their content) that are not owned by the publisher.

The Hachette Speakers Bureau provides a wide range of authors for speaking events. To find out more, go to www.hachettespeakersbureau.com or call (866) 376-6591.

Library of Congress Cataloging-in-Publication Data

Names: Heron, Farah, author.
Title: Jana goes wild / Farah Heron.
Description: First Edition. | New York ; Boston : Forever, 2023.
Identifiers: LCCN 2022057840 | ISBN 9781538725450 (trade paperback) | ISBN 9781538725467 (ebook)
Subjects: LCGFT: Novels. | Romance fiction.
Classification: LCC PR9199.4.H4695 J36 2023 | DDC 813/.6--dc23/eng/20221208
LC record available at https://lccn.loc.gov/2022057840

ISBNs: 9781538725450 (trade paperback), 9781538725467 (ebook)

Printed in the United States of America

LSC-C

Printing 2, 2023

This one is for my mom and dad, who took me on a life-changing Tanzanian safari when I was twenty, and then again (with my husband and kids this time) when I was forty. We are so lucky to always have those memories together.

CHAPTER 1

Five Years Earlier, Washington, D.C., USA

J ana Suleiman was perfect. Or, at least, that's what everyone had assumed her entire life. And they assumed that perfection came easily for her. In reality, Jana had found it incredibly hard to live up to those almost unattainable expectations. That didn't stop her from trying, though, because being a high-achieving, righteous, moral, and principled person was all she knew.

But after waking up incandescently happy for the first time in her memory, Jana wondered if she should have shed her perfect image a long time ago. Because right now, doing something a little unexpected, a little out of character, and a little bit *bad* felt soooo good.

It was extremely early in the morning to be having this epiphany, but Jana was jet-lagged and a bit sore from the exuberant activities the night before (really, from a week and a half of the best sex of her life). She admired the toned, naked back of Anil Malek, the person who had been the catalyst for this discovery that her comfort zone was way too stifling. Lazily rolling onto her side, she wrapped herself around him tightly.

"You woke me up," he said, voice raspy with sleep. Despite his words, Jana knew he wasn't complaining. Their "relationship" was only in its infancy, but they both knew there was *always* something better to do together than sleep.

"It's not early. The sun's up. I'm still on London time, anyway. I don't have to go into the office today. What do you want to do?"

She and Anil had been traveling together for twelve days now and were currently in Washington, D.C., Anil's hometown and the base for the agency where Jana worked. This was technically a business trip for Jana. She'd been working the last few months on opening a new maternal health clinic in Tajikistan. When Anil Malek turned up there to visit an old friend who happened to be Jana's boss, no one, least of all Jana herself, expected Anil would join her on the next leg of her trip to London. Or that they'd start a hard-and-fast fling while there. Between her meetings, she and Anil went to museums, galleries, and antique shops during the day and spent their nights in bed in a tiny London hotel room.

Now Jana would be in D.C. for a month, settled into an extended-stay hotel where she assumed Anil would be spending a lot of time, too—since his actual home was a few hours away in Virginia. She'd never had a more fulfilling, more satisfying, more *fun* business trip in her life. She kissed the back of Anil's neck softly.

In one smooth motion, Anil rolled over and lifted Jana on top of him. She loved it when he did that. He was a big man...big and built. He could lift her in his arms with seemingly no exertion. He could pin her against a wall and devour her. And he had. Many times.

Jana adjusted herself so she was straddling his firm stomach, ignoring the twinge of pain from her protesting hips. It was no wonder—she hadn't asked so much of her body quite like this since...well, since ever.

Resting her hands on his shoulders, she leaned down and kissed him briefly. His hands skimmed her thighs and landed on her hips. That ever-present mischievous twinkle in his eyes was there. It was amazing that someone like this—someone so...*alive*—wanted to be with Jana Suleiman, the woman who always played it safe.

"Well, we could always take in one of the Smithsonian museums," he said. "Or a park?"

Jana shook her head. "We did the British Museum and the Victoria and Albert in London...I'm about done with shrines to colonization."

Anil laughed as his hands trailed up Jana's ribcage, sending a delicious shiver up her spine.

"Galleries? We could go shopping or take a tour of the historical sites." His wide hands were spread over her breasts now, thumbs teasing her nipples, making her back arch. He knew exactly what he was doing to her. "Or we could stay in," he suggested. "I'm sure we can find something to occupy our time."

She laughed, letting her head fall so her shoulder-length hair skimmed Anil's face. His hands slid up her back so he could pull her down for a thorough, all-consuming kiss.

Jana had never felt anything like this before. True, they'd had a lot of sex in the last few days, but that's not all this relationship was. They were very different people—he was clearly more of an extrovert and could talk happily to every person in a room, while Jana preferred to retreat to a corner or read a book at home. But when they were alone, it was so easy between them. They'd talked for hours about their work in the development field. About their goals of bringing grassroots-style microdevelopment to a larger scale, and about how lifting women and girls could help entire communities. Jana had never been so in sync with anyone else about development philosophies and politics or even history and art. And she never felt her usual awkwardness with him.

But it was when they were like this, skin to skin, in the tiny bubble they'd brought with them from Central Asia to London, and now D.C., that Jana felt positive she'd found her soul mate—the one person in the world who saw her actual self. And loved her for *her*.

Not that he'd said he loved her yet. Neither had she... but she was on the way there.

Leaving her comfort zone—doing exactly what no one would expect Jana Suleiman to do—was the best thing she ever did. She shifted again, this time reaching over to the nightstand and getting a condom out of the drawer. Everything for Jana fell into place when she and Anil were alone, so why waste that time at galleries or museums?

After a few more blissful days in D.C., Jana and Anil were in an upscale Mexican restaurant gorging on beef barbacoa and the best ceviche she'd ever had. She'd wanted a margarita, too, but all her recent flights had led to a small sinus infection, and her antibiotics didn't play well with alcohol. Jana had eaten amazing meals all over the world, and she was delighted that Anil was as big a fan of exploring cultures by eating as she was.

"I went to a restaurant on a beach in Cancún once that only served ceviche," he said.

"That sounds like heaven." Jana scooped some of the bright, citrusy diced fish onto a fresh tortilla chip.

"By the way," he said, smiling, "my mom called today to tell me how much she liked you."

Jana grinned. She'd been nervous about meeting Anil's parents at brunch the day before—it seemed too soon to get families involved in their relationship. But she was so glad she went. Anil's parents were warm, funny, and clearly so proud of his work. They'd asked Jana about her job and told the cutest stories about Anil as a child. Jana felt like she knew him better after seeing how much his family adored him.

"Your parents dote on you."

He nodded. "I'm the golden son. Only-child syndrome. Your mom must be the same with you?"

Jana shook her head. "No...I...Mom and I aren't really close. I haven't lived at home since I was eighteen—not for more than a few months at least."

"Must have been hard for her—her only child moving out not long after her husband died."

Jana shrugged. "Mom has a very busy social life. Don't get me wrong—she's *thrilled* when I'm home so she can show me off. But sometimes I think the *idea* of me means more to her than the actual person." That sounded so bleak. Jana regretted saying it almost the moment it came out of her mouth. Right after seeing his perfect little family, she wasn't sure she wanted to delve into her dysfunctional one. She changed the subject. "Your family must love having you nearby, though. You're about an hour-and-a-half drive to their place, right?"

He nodded. "Yeah, about that."

"Could I see your home sometime?" she asked.

"Of course, but it's really not much to see." He sighed. "I really should sell it soon. Not sure why I'm hanging on to it. It's a dull little house in an even duller little town."

The house seemed a bit of a sore spot for him. And she could guess why.

"You bought it with Nadia, right?"

He nodded but didn't say anything more.

Jana knew that Anil had been married before, but he didn't talk much about his ex-wife. There were no pictures of her in his parents' house. She had no idea how long ago the divorce was, or why the marriage ended. Which, fair. They were building something—and even if it felt so real now, Jana knew they had time.

"We should order more ceviche," Jana said. "They had shrimp on the menu, right?"

At the office the next day, Jana was editing a proposal to add a mental health day clinic to the health center in Tajikistan, when her phone buzzed with a WhatsApp message.

Unknown: Stay the fuck away from my sister's husband.

Jana stared at the message. What the hell? Was someone trolling her? Was this a bad joke? She wrote back.

Jana: Who is this?

Another message came through calling Jana a series of expletives and accusing her of sleeping with a married man.

Nausea built in Jana's stomach. Anil was *not* married…He had told her he was divorced…

Jana didn't know what to say. With blurry eyes, she texted back.

Jana: I think you're mistaken.

Unknown: I don't know what he told you, but Anil Malek is married to my sister. Not divorced. Not separated. Married.

Another screenful of profanity flashed on her phone. Jana blocked the number.

Could this be true? She'd been with Anil almost twenty-four

hours a day for two weeks now—save for when she was at work. She'd been with him on three continents. She'd met his parents. She'd slept wrapped around him every night.

But…what did she really know about him? He hadn't introduced her to any of his friends in D.C. this week. He clearly didn't want her to come to his house in Virginia. Wouldn't his parents have said something if he was married? What did he tell them about her? He hadn't introduced Jana as a girlfriend or a holiday fling…just a friend and colleague in his field. But that seemed normal to Jana—South Asian parents sometimes leaped too quickly from dating to marriage, and Jana assumed he wanted to wait until they were together longer before telling his parents the true nature of their relationship. But maybe he didn't tell them because he had a wife waiting at home.

What did Jana know about Anil Malek at all?

Jana closed her eyes. She knew she was falling in love with him. And maybe love was a little blind.

She picked up her phone again—not to call Anil, but to message Rasheed, the manager of the project in Tajikistan. The one who Anil had been visiting when this relationship started.

Jana: Rasheed, is Anil married?

It was the middle of the night in Tajikistan. Jana wasn't expecting an answer. But he responded.

Rasheed: Have you asked him that question?

Jana: Rasheed, please. I'm asking you.

She'd only known Rasheed for a few months, but she'd thought they were friends. Friendly, at least. She trusted him.

Rasheed: The answer is complicated.

Jana felt like she was going to throw up.

Jana: The answer is yes, then.

There was a long pause before Rasheed answered.

Rasheed: Yes, he's married.

Jana threw her phone onto the desk and ran to the bathroom, where she did throw up. Then she cried…for a long, long time.

Anil had many excuses when she confronted him later that night in her hotel room. He said his marriage was complicated. That he and Nadia were effectively separated. That it was long past over. But all Jana could think of was her phone lighting up with the worst names possible when Nadia's sister had messaged her.

Jana gritted her teeth. "Does her *family* know it's over? Does *she*?"

When he didn't answer, Jana asked Anil to leave. He tried to object again, begging Jana to let him explain, but Jana was done. She didn't want to hear it.

He finally left. And she threw up again.

That was the end of the best relationship Jana had ever had. The one that should have been forever. How pathetic. It had all been an illusion. He was *married*. And Jana was a fool. She'd stepped out of her comfort zone and taken a risk with the charming, charismatic, sexy man who'd looked at her like she was more than just perfect Jana Suleiman. Like she was a person who was worth getting closer to. And look what she'd gotten out of it.

Her eyes blurry with tears, Jana blocked Anil Malek from her phone. Thankfully, it had only been two weeks. They lived in different cities—countries, even—so it wouldn't take much to never see him again. She could avoid him professionally. She could put this whole mess…this *affair*…behind her and pretend it never happened. She'd learned her lesson. Comfort zones were comfortable for a reason.

After two more weeks, Jana's heart had mostly mended, but she was still throwing up regularly. When she saw two pink lines after peeing on a stick, she realized she wasn't quite done with Anil Malek after all.

CHAPTER 2

Present day, Toronto, Canada

D o you think airport security will confiscate samosas?" Jana's mother, Rashida Suleiman, called out the moment Jana walked into her mother's townhouse. Jana was balancing two pizza boxes, her purse, and her planner in her arms.

Jana frowned as she dropped the pizza boxes on the table near the door. "I don't know. I thought they only confiscated liquids. Samosas are solid." She really hoped security wouldn't take their samosas. Their already stressful holiday would be infinitely more frustrating for Jana if they didn't have a stash of her mother's samosas on hand.

"I'll make the filling dryer to be safe," Mom said from the kitchen.

Jana kicked off her job interview shoes and beige blazer, cringing when she noticed that the living/dining room had fallen into complete chaos while she'd been gone. The mess made her eye twitch, but what did she expect? Her daughter, Imani, and her mother were clearly still packing. They were all leaving to-morrow for a two-week vacation in Tanzania for a family friend's wedding in which Jana was a bridesmaid and Imani the flower girl. Jana was a seasoned traveler, but she was usually alone or with colleagues for overseas flights, not with her mother and four-year-old daughter.

The scent of daal and maybe kheema in the air told Jana that Mom was making more than just samosas. She took the pizza boxes to the kitchen, where she found her mom stirring a tiny pot filled with ghee, curry leaves, chilies, and spices.

Jana shook her head. "Why are you making all this? I told you I was picking up pizza tonight." Mom wasn't capable of making a small amount of food. "Airport security *will* confiscate daal. That's a liquid."

Mom poured the hot ghee and spices into the pot of daal. "This is all for the freezer. Won't we be happy to have home-cooked food waiting for us when we get back? I made two dozen samosas. That should be enough for the trip, right?"

Mom's cheddar-and-potato samosas, just one of her many Indian fusion recipes, were the only thing Imani would eat with no cajoling. "Hope so. Don't really want to be lugging more than that from hotel to hotel."

"How was the job interview?" Mom asked.

"It went well, I hope," Jana said, taking a handful of peanuts from the jar on the counter, then popping one in her mouth. She'd just come from her second interview at Think Canada for her dream job—working with Think affiliates to plan development projects around the world. Jana really thought she had a good chance. The executive director, Dr. Lopez, was a brilliant, kind man who reminded Jana a bit of her father, and she'd love to work with him.

She wanted this role so much. She desperately needed a change professionally. But best of all? She'd be doing it all from Toronto. No more traveling. She could be right here, at home, when Imani started junior kindergarten in the fall.

Mom smiled. "I told you my prayers would be answered. So great that Rohan found that job for you."

Jana's good friend, and the groom at the upcoming wedding, had learned about this position long before the job was publicly posted, which gave Jana the time to polish her resume and gather references.

Jana rubbed the back of her neck. "I may have made a mistake. I slipped and mentioned I'm a single mother, and he made some comments about how he values family. With all the short-term contracts on my resume, he probably thinks I'm a terrible mom."

Mom shook her head. "Nah. Divorce is common these days. This isn't like back home."

Jana gave her mother a raised-eyebrow stare. "Mom, I'm *not* divorced. I've never been married." Which is a fact she'd reminded her mother of countless times. She sighed. "The director also said he was looking for a dynamic, vibrant addition to a close-knit team." Jana wasn't sure anyone had ever described her as *vibrant*. Capable, brilliant, accomplished, yes, but not vibrant.

Mom shrugged. "So be vibrant."

"It's not like I can just flip a switch and be someone else." She peeked into the disaster of a living room. "What's the cyclone all about?" She'd finished her own packing the day before, but Imani insisted she wanted to pick her own clothes for the trip.

Mom snorted. "Your daughter is apparently having a fashion emergency."

Jana frowned. "Does it have to be such a *messy* emergency?"

"She's four, Jana," Mom said pointedly. "Things are allowed to be messy for four-year-olds."

Sometimes Imani seemed four going on fourteen. Jana went into the living room to her daughter, who was sitting on the floor in the middle of all the clothes and toys. Imani beamed at Jana and immediately started talking as if her mother had been with her all afternoon. That's just how Imani was. Jana had sometimes been gone weeks, and once even months, without seeing her daughter in person, and Imani would always carry on as if they'd never been apart. It killed Jana, though. She really hoped Imani wasn't masking distress about her mother being away so much.

"I don't understand why I can't bring *all* the dresses," Imani said, looking at the piles of folded clothes surrounding her. "Kamila Aunty said I need lots of pretty things for the wedding."

Jana squeezed into the few inches of clean floor next to her daughter and kissed the top of her head. Imani was wearing a zebra-print sundress, and her curly hair was escaping the French braids Mom had done in the morning.

"Why aren't you doing this in your room?" Jana asked.

"Nanima said to pack here because she's cooking."

"How many dresses do you have here?"

"Thirty-seven," Imani said with wide, solemn eyes. Imani was usually a cheerful, playful child. Her personality resembled her father's in many ways but especially in her extroversion and easygoing nature. But Imani took fashion and her dresses very seriously. Jana often wondered how exactly this outgoing and completely fabulous little person came from her uterus.

Jana reached for her planner and showed Imani the month spread with the days they would be gone colored in yellow. "Well...we'll be gone for sixteen days, but I don't think you need a fresh dress each day. And sometimes you might want to wear pants or shorts."

Imani looked scandalized at that suggestion. Jana laughed. "Okay, but you have new lehengas for the wedding events. How about eight dresses?"

Imani thought about it. "Ten?" she offered.

"Okay, ten."

"Can I bring more dresses when we go to Disneyland?"

Jana smiled. "We're going to Disney *World*, sweetie. It's in Florida...where Kassim Uncle lives in the winter, remember?" Well, they were going to Disney if Jana got a new job. Jana was waiting to buy the tickets, but as far as Imani knew, the trip was happening. "Did you pack pajamas?"

Imani's little face scrunched up in thought. "I need sixteen pajamas?"

Jana laughed again and scooped up her daughter and put her on her lap. After giving her a tight hug, she smoothed Imani's hair. "How about we finish packing together? Then after we clean up, we can eat pizza."

Imani jumped off Jana's lap and ran toward the kitchen. "There's pizza?" Jana winced as the clothes fell into even more disarray.

Jana resisted the urge to chase after her. First, she needed to tidy this mess.

The first leg of the trip, an overnight flight from Toronto to Amsterdam, was, well, long. And about as easy as one would expect an economy flight to be with a cranky four-year-old who refused to sleep on the plane. Or eat. Thank goodness for Mom's samosas, because Imani wouldn't eat anything the airline provided, including the cute kid's meal Jana had preordered. Jana finally managed to get her daughter to understand how to make the in-flight entertainment work, but then Imani was so delighted that there was so much *Peppa Pig* available that Jana doubted that the girl would close her eyes on the flight at all.

Traveling was usually effortless for Jana, since she went abroad for work so often, but she hadn't been on a trip with Imani before. At least not a trip as long, or as far, as this one. Hopefully things would be better once they got to Tanzania.

Jana was not looking forward to the actual wedding. At least she'd been able to skip the four-day bachelorette party extravaganza in Amsterdam first, thanks to that job interview at Think. Jana felt out of place during *normal* parties—a wedding where she would be on display as a member of the bridal party may as well be a den of snakes to an introvert like her. But after the wedding, they were all going on a safari trip through several national parks, and Jana was excited to show Imani the African animals that she'd recently become obsessed with.

And truth be told, Jana could use the vacation. She'd been job hunting for a month now, since her last contract position ended. It was the cycle of Jana's life—get a new contract to launch a development project somewhere in the world, work from home planning the project, go on site for a few weeks or longer to oversee the launch, then come home and look for the next contract. Jana loved that she could make lasting impacts in regions that needed it most, but the cycle was exhausting. The job at Think was *permanent*. And in Toronto, with little travel. If she got it, both Jana and Imani would have more stability. They could do trips like this more often, just like Jana had traveled with her parents when she was young.

But she wasn't sure that being in the wedding party would feel like a vacation. Jana had been quite surprised when Kamila had asked her to be a bridesmaid. Jana was actually closer to Kamila's fiancé, Rohan, and despite the fact that she and Kamila were friends now, they hadn't always been.

Jana knew she often rubbed people the wrong way. That her introversion and her, well...*awkwardness* around people were seen as curt or pretentious. But most of the time, she just didn't know what to say or how to fit in with others. It was like everyone spoke some social language that she'd never learned. She used to have a few close friends whom she'd known since university, but not since Imani was born. She was fine, though. Jana wasn't really a social person. She had Imani, and that was enough. She hoped to stay on the sidelines at this wedding. Be there to support Rohan and Kamila and get some good, quality alone time with her daughter. She needed this recharge.

But after getting no sleep at all on the seven-hour flight, Jana was sore, cranky, and tired by the time they landed. Imani was even worse. Mom had slept on the plane, so at least she had a bit of spring in her step.

They had a few hours to kill in Schiphol Airport in Amsterdam before their evening flight to Tanzania. The rest of the bridal party, who'd been in Amsterdam for a few days, was booked on the same flight to Africa, so Kamila had messaged her that they would all see each other in the airport. Jana would have preferred not to have to socialize while she was feeling like such crap. She didn't have much of a choice, though.

Jana, her mother, and Imani were navigating the busy hallway of the airport toward the gate for their next flight when Imani suddenly shrieked.

Jana instinctively reached for her daughter. She didn't know whether to drop to the floor, run for cover, or inspect Imani for injuries. Jana realized, in horror, what her daughter had screamed about the moment Imani broke free from her arms and started running.

Imani was leaping straight into the arms of her father. *Anil Malek.*

Ugh.

CHAPTER 3

W*hat* are you doing here?" Jana asked as she caught up with her daughter, who was now in Anil's arms and hugging him, her little legs kicking with joy. Imani was a complete daddy's girl.

Anil Malek flashed his always charming, never irritable smile at Jana. His charcoal gray T-shirt was stretched over his solid arms, and he had a leather bag hanging off his shoulder. Jana cringed when she saw #GROOMSPLATOON printed on his shirt. He was clearly here as part of a wedding party. Maybe it was someone else's wedding? Amsterdam was a popular bachelor party spot.

"Last-minute change of plans," he said. "I shuffled some meetings around and extended my project timetable so I could be one of Rohan's groomsmen. I hated missing the wedding of two of my closest friends."

Jana tried to ignore the pounding of her heart in her throat. Of course he did. The man was nothing if not adaptable. "And you didn't tell us because…"

He smiled at Imani. "I wanted to surprise Mini," he said, using the nickname he'd given Imani as an infant. He rubbed her back, then tickled her stomach. Imani shrieked with glee again.

"How wonderful!" Mom beamed at Anil. She was as happy to see him as Imani was. "Now you can all be together as a family for this trip!"

Jana didn't glare at her mother. There was no point. She did glare at Anil, though—not that he noticed. He was currently listening intently to Imani as she told him all about Peppa Pig's trip to Italy.

Jana couldn't be *that* surprised he was here. Months ago, when Kamila had asked Jana to be in her wedding party, she'd also asked Jana if it would be okay if Rohan asked Anil to be a groomsman. Rohan and Anil had gone to university together and had become close again since Anil permanently moved to Toronto to be near Imani. But when Jana looked at Anil's schedule on their co-parenting app, she saw that the timing of the wedding conflicted with his long-planned trip to D.C. to start a nonprofit there. So Jana confirmed to Kamila that she'd be honored to stand alongside her at her wedding, happily assuming that Anil would say no when Rohan asked him. Which he did. So this wasn't supposed to happen. Jana hadn't traveled with Anil Malek since that spring when Imani was conceived, and she preferred to keep it that way.

She looked away from him quickly. Even after so many years, looking at Anil too long hurt too much.

"C'mon," he said. "The wedding party is all at the gate. I saw that your flight landed so I came to find you." He plucked Imani's bag out of Jana's arm and started walking.

Jana fumbled with her own bag and followed Anil through the busy airport. Her heart was still racing, and her legs felt weak, but that could just have been because of the lack of sleep. Then again, Jana's body always reacted this way when she saw Anil.

Thankfully, she didn't see him often. In fact, they'd barely had face-to-face contact since their daughter was born, despite sharing custody. With the help of an excellent family lawyer, Jana had an ironclad co-parenting agreement hammered out that spelled out their fifty-fifty custody before Imani was even born. Their daughter usually switched back and forth between their homes each week, unless one parent was traveling. Neither parent paid child support, but they shared major expenses. They communicated and coordinated schedules through a comprehensive co-parenting app. The arrangement worked.

Jana and Anil had never really had a conflict about Imani, but that didn't mean any of it was easy for Jana. She loved her daughter fiercely, but she was not fond of the child's father. At all. Which was why she avoided him whenever possible. Mom was usually the one home when Anil picked up or dropped off Imani. She was a healthy, adaptable kid, so they'd rarely needed to have long conversations about parenting. A quick message was all that was needed to let Anil know that Imani hadn't slept well the night before, or that she'd been at the playground so she needed her hair washed before bed.

Now Jana wondered if avoiding the man for so long had been a mistake. Maybe she needed to desensitize herself so her body wouldn't react like this to seeing him.

"How was she on the flight?" Anil asked as they walked. He'd put Imani down and was holding her hand as they crossed the terminal.

Jana shrugged. "She didn't sleep much. Hopefully she'll pass out on the next one."

He chuckled at Imani, then glanced at Jana. "You both look exhausted."

Jana tried not to scowl at him. Of course, *he* didn't look exhausted. He looked great. It wasn't fair that he was fresh-faced and cheery while Jana probably resembled a used tissue. He'd had a full night's sleep in a hotel in Amsterdam and hadn't just gotten off a transcontinental flight with a preschooler with insomnia.

But he always looked this good. And it always annoyed Jana.

Anil wasn't particularly tall, but he was a large man—wide shoulders and big hands. He'd been wearing his hair either closely cropped or shaved completely off to combat his hairline for years, and Jana had been surprised at how much she liked that bald head back when they were together. Years of watching *Star Trek: The Next Generation* with her father had given her a bit of a bald fetish.

He *had* changed in the last five years, though. He wasn't as muscular as he used to be, and his waistline had thickened since becoming a father, but with his new dark-framed glasses, he gave off a worldly intellectual vibe now. The man still looked so much better than he had any right to look. Even now, years after their disastrous relationship, if Jana concentrated, she could feel the soft stubble on his head tickling her palms. She could remember how it felt to curl up on that broad chest. She wished the memories didn't feel so fresh. Honestly, her life would be so much easier if she weren't still so attracted to Anil Malek.

Not that she would ever admit that to anyone.

"I wish you'd told me you'd be here," she said primly. One rule they'd had since Imani was born was to always let the other one know where they were—down to what city, at least. It was necessary when they both traveled so much, and often in areas with political unrest or natural disasters. Anil leaving Washington and flying to Amsterdam without letting Jana know was against their arrangement.

"It was very last-minute," Anil repeated. "I only got here

late yesterday. And, like I said, I wanted to surprise Imani." He grinned at Imani again, then looked at Jana. "I want to be here for her first trip to Tanzania, and if I told you in advance, I knew you'd make...that face."

Jana tried to wipe off whatever face Anil claimed she was making. He was right, though. Although both Jana and Anil were born and raised in North America (Jana in Canada, Anil in the US), their parents, like many of the older generation in their South Asian Ismaili Muslim community, were originally from East Africa. Jana's parents and Anil's father were from Tanzania. The country was as sentimental for Anil as it was for Jana, and it was only fair he be there when his daughter saw it for the first time.

But still. She had not signed up for two weeks of traveling with the inconveniently handsome face of one of the small handful of men she'd slept with, and frankly, she was irritated at the bride and groom for springing this on her.

She had no idea how she was going to get through this trip now.

CHAPTER 4

"Mommy, can I have Daddy's gum for my ears?"

Jana blinked at her daughter. They were only one hour into the long flight from Amsterdam, and Jana could already tell Imani would be trying her patience again. Jana was sitting in a row with Imani on one side of her and Mom on the other. Kamila and Rohan were in the row in front of them, sitting with Kassim Uncle, Kamila's father. Anil, Kamila's sister, Shelina, and Rohan's brother, Zayan, were in the seats in front of Kamila. This arrangement worked well for Jana because she couldn't see Anil at all—not even the back of his head. It was less satisfactory for Imani, who wanted to be closer to her father.

"I have gum. Are your ears hurting?" Jana picked up her purse from under the seat in front of her.

Imani thought about that for a second. "No. I need Daddy's gum."

Jana pulled out a packet of mint gum and held it up.

"I like Daddy's gum."

Jana sighed. She reached between the seats in front of her and poked Kamila. "Can you ask Anil if he has gum?"

"What do you need, beta?" Jana's mother asked Imani, taking

off her large headphones. Mom had found a Gujarati soap opera on the in-flight entertainment and had been engrossed since takeoff.

"I want Daddy's gum," Imani said.

"I have gum," Mom said, unzipping her bag.

Kamila turned so she could see Imani between the two seats. "So do I. Three kinds."

"I want Daddy's gum," Imani repeated.

Jana looked at her daughter. Imani was rarely demanding, but...traveling was stressful for small children. And stressful for mothers who desperately wanted to pretend the fathers of those small children weren't hurtling through the air in the same airplane as her.

"Do you want to ask him yourself, Imani?" Kamila asked. "I can see if Zayan Uncle will switch seats with me, and then I can switch seats with you. Then you can sit with your daddy. I need to talk to your mommy, anyway. How does that sound?"

Imani beamed, nodding happily at the option of sitting next to her daddy. They ended up doing a lot more shuffling than that because Mom chimed in saying she wanted to sit with Kassim Uncle so they could discuss the Gujarati soap, then Rohan said he wanted to talk to Jana, too. After annoying every non-Hussain-Nasser wedding guest on the plane, Jana found herself sitting with Kamila on one side of her and Rohan on the other. Imani was two seats ahead with her father.

"You're mad at us, aren't you?" Rohan asked Jana once they were all settled.

Jana shook her head. "Why would I be mad at you? Imani is happy to sit next to Anil."

Kamila frowned. Completely in character, Kamila was wearing a pink shirt so bright Jana considered taking her sunglasses out of her bag. Uncharacteristic, though, was the fact that it was a *sweatshirt*, and on it was an illustration of Godzilla wearing a bridal veil. Kamila was normally a blouse or vintage dress kind of woman. She looked gorgeous as always, though, with her long, wavy dark brown hair pulled back in a ponytail and her lips painted a perfect fuchsia.

She immediately handed Jana a slightly paler pink T-shirt. "Here's your hashtag Bridal Brigade shirt."

Jana held up the shirt that was printed with the word #BRIDALBRIGADE. Jana had seen the rest of the bridal party wearing these in the airport. Shrugging, she pulled the shirt over the navy long-sleeve she was wearing. She'd agreed to be in the wedding, so if it meant wearing Day-Glo pink, so be it.

"That color is *stunning* on you. You should wear it more often," Kamila said. "You're mad we didn't tell you that Anil would be here, aren't you?"

Jana shrugged. "Did you see how happy Imani was at the airport?"

Kamila sighed heavily. "We were asking about *you*. Of course Imani's happy. She's such a daddy's girl. I relate."

Jana exhaled. "I'm fine. Don't even worry about it."

"I think I liked it better back when you used to tell me off all the time."

Jana rolled her eyes. "What's that supposed to mean?" Jana was trying to give her friend the benefit of the doubt and let Kamila be a bit of a diva for her wedding. But seriously, now it was a *bad* thing that Jana was being nice?

Jana and Kamila had grown up together, along with Rohan, Shelina, and Zayan, but when they were younger, Kamila and Jana had never been able to overcome their oil-and-water person-alities to be anything other than rivals. It was no wonder—both their families had pitted them against each other since birth. Jana regularly heard that she needed to be friendlier and more outgoing like Kamila, and Kamila heard she needed to be more ambitious and respectable like Jana.

But when Jana ended up back in Toronto pregnant and friendless, she and Kamila realized their rivalry was fueled only by their families. They'd been friends since, and Jana really appreciated Kamila's and Rohan's support exactly when she needed it. But Kamila and Jana were still incredibly different people, and sometimes the muscle memory of resenting each other for their differences came to the surface again.

Kamila stroked Jana's arm in a placating gesture. "It means nothing. You said before that you wouldn't mind if Anil was here, but you didn't look happy in the airport."

"Did something happen recently between you?" Rohan asked with concerned eyes. "I noticed the way he was looking at you at the gate." Rohan and Jana had always been friends, despite their age difference. As the two studious introverts in their group, they'd always had the most in common.

Had Anil been looking at her? Jana sighed. "I was tired. There is nothing between us. It's a little awkward—but it'll be fine once we get used to it."

"Maybe Anil joining us can be good for you. Now you can give him half the 'Imani duty' on the trip. You can let loose a bit. Go wild."

Jana rolled her eyes again. "My mother and most of my aunties and uncles are here." Not to mention that Jana wasn't exactly the *wild* type. At least not according to Kamila's definition of *wild*.

"I'm not talking about spinning around stripper poles or anything," Kamila said. "I mean, I don't know. Stay up late with us when we're talking. Get to know the others in the hashtag Bridal Brigade. Have an extra drink. Be a little less..."

"Me?" Jana said. She sounded bitter. She didn't mean to.

Rohan frowned. "I happen to like you."

"So do I," Kamila said. "Look, we're sorry we sprang an ex on you unexpectedly. But you said you'd be fine with him being here—and he was insistent that he wanted to surprise Imani. This trip is supposed to be fun for everyone."

Kamila was right. There was no reason why Anil's presence had to ruin her trip. Jana could be a mature adult—she could manage being around the man. But did Rohan and Kamila really think Jana would find thirty-plus people traveling together *fun*? She sank in her seat. "You guys know I'm not really wired to be social. I can't understand why you'd want me in the bridal party, anyway." There was mostly resignation, not anger, in the question.

Kamila put her hand over Jana's, squeezing. "Nope. We're not going to let you do this now, Jana. We asked you to be in the wedding party because we love you very much and can't imagine getting married without you with us. Imani, too."

Rohan shook his head. "And it won't all be wild parties. There will be no stripper poles or anything of the sort."

Kamila nodded emphatically. "We got that all out of our system in Amsterdam. Remind me later, Jana—we got you something in the red-light district. We had the *best* time there."

Jana raised a brow at Kamila.

Rohan looked amused at his wife-to-be but didn't ask exactly what the bridesmaids had been up to in Amsterdam. "Jana, no one will mind if you spend the whole trip at the pool with a book," he said. "Seriously. Do what you need to do to be comfortable."

Kamila grinned widely. "The pools at the hotels are gorge. Having Imani's father here will ease your burden a bit—you'll see. You can chill while he social butterflies with her."

It seemed Kamila was reverting back to her old meddling ways. She probably planned all this because she thought it would be *good* for Jana.

"It's okay that *people* aren't your thing," Kamila continued. "They never have been. But lately...I don't know. You've been different. You've always been reserved and private, and lord only knows what's going on in that gorgeous head of yours, but I don't think you're *happy*. Maybe with this trip you can focus a little more on Jana. Because a happy mommy would be the best thing for Imani. I promise."

Jana felt a lump in her throat. She wanted to object, to reassure Kamila that she *was* happy, but the words didn't come out. Imani was the best thing that had ever happened to Jana, and she was sometimes overwhelmed with how much she loved her little girl. That was enough. And if she got that job, she could have stability and be home for her daughter more, which was better than enough.

Jana needed to sidestep the happiness (or *not* happiness) issue for now. This was Kamila and Rohan's wedding, and Jana didn't want to be the Eeyore at her friends' celebration. "Honestly, guys, I'm fine. I'm looking forward to the trip."

"It's going to be amazing." Kamila picked up the remote control for the in-flight entertainment and turned it on. "Hey, the bridal party should all sync up a wedding movie to get in the mood." She scrolled through the Bollywood choices. "*Dilwale Dulhaniya Le Jayenge* or *Bride and Prejudice*?"

Before they could agree on a movie, Kamila's sister, Shelina, who was now sitting in the row in front of them, poked her head between the seats. "Imani wants to sit with her mommy."

Jana nodded. "Hopefully she's finally tired," Jana said. She looked at Rohan. "Do you all mind shifting around again?"

They did not mind, so another epic round of musical plane seats started up. After the move, Jana found herself sitting with Imani on one side of her at the window, and Anil on her other side. Because apparently Imani wanted to sit with both of her parents—and a window.

Jana pursed her lips. She could do this. This was a test of her ability to deal with Anil on this trip. She put on a pleasant smile and opened her e-reader. Imani was already engrossed in a show on the entertainment system.

"You still upset I'm here?" Anil asked quietly.

Jana did not put her reader down or look at him. "When did I say I was upset? Imani was thrilled to see you in the airport."

He chuckled low. "Imani was, but you weren't."

Jana sighed, closing the cover on her e-reader. Airline seats were so ridiculously tight that it was probably against the Geneva convention to be stuck next to an ex on one. Plus, he was...big. Maybe Jana should have splurged for business class. Or one of those blissful pod seats where she could be alone. "What exactly are you hoping I'll say here? I don't like surprises, and I was caught off guard, but it's fine. It's Rohan's wedding, and if he wants you in the wedding party, then who am I to complain?"

Anil ran his hand over his chin. "I'm sorry I didn't tell you I'd be here, but like I said, I wanted to surprise Mini. And..."

"And what?"

"I didn't want you to back out of the trip because of me."

Jana snorted. "I *wouldn't* have done that." She wouldn't have. She may have thought about it, but Kamila was her friend, and she'd made a promise to her. It *would* have been nice to be able to put up her defense walls before seeing him, though. Also, it would have been nice to get a full night's sleep first. Maybe wash her face. Brush her hair.

"This could be an opportunity for us to get closer," Anil said. "We can be friends again."

Okay, first of all, she was practically sitting on top of the man in these seats, so Jana wasn't exactly sure how much closer he wanted them to be. And also? When had they *ever* been friends? They'd been lovers...and then this.

Jana's eyes narrowed. "Anil, I'm too tired for this conversation right now. Can we just get through this flight?"

He smiled. It was funny—his smile had changed over the years she'd known him. Still devastatingly handsome, but less...mischievous now. He used to smile in a way that made everyone think they were in on an inside joke. He used to be so...playful.

Of course, he was still like that with Imani. But he seemed more...reserved now. Still social. Still charismatic. Maybe matured? Because he was older, of course. They both were. And being parents had to mature them.

Kamila had just said it was obvious that Jana wasn't happy. Jana had no idea if she was actually happy or not, and she had no idea how Kamila could know something about Jana's mental state that Jana herself didn't even know, but now she wondered about Anil. Was he happy?

As far as Jana knew, the man hadn't been in a serious relationship since Jana. Or rather, since his divorce. He moved to Toronto soon after Jana returned from the Tajikistan project, and then stayed so he could be close by for Imani, but was he happy in Toronto? Did he have regrets about becoming a parent unexpectedly? Did he wish things were different in his life?

Jana looked over at Imani, whose eyes had closed. "I think she's finally asleep."

"You get some sleep, too," Anil said. "We'll talk later." He rustled through his bag and handed something to Jana. It was a new pair of cheap fuzzy socks—the kind you could get at the dollar store. "I already gave Imani a pair of these. They don't give you socks on these economy flights anymore. I know you don't want to put your feet on these airplane carpets."

Jana chuckled. She most definitely did not want to put her feet down on this carpet. "Thanks," she said. She quietly took off her shoes and slid his socks over the ones she was wearing. She was too exhausted to think about why he'd brought her socks, and she had no doubt they *would* talk later. She was not looking forward to that conversation at all.

But right now, she just wanted to rest.

CHAPTER 5

The rest of the flight was uneventful. Once Imani had fallen asleep, Jana herself had a restful and comfortable nap. They were both awake when Mount Kilimanjaro came into view. The look on her daughter's face when she saw the enormous mountain was beyond priceless.

After landing, Jana and Imani went down the steep stairs off the plane hand in hand, and Jana took her first lungful of hot, dusty Tanzanian air. This was Jana's fourth trip to the country, and every time she set foot on East African soil, she felt simultaneous goosebumps and full-body contentment. Everything hit differently here. The air smelled different. The dirt was a different color. People seemed less hurried. Less intense. Jana traveled a lot, but Tanzania felt more like home to her than any of the other places she'd been to. Maybe the generations of her family who had lived here before immigrating to Canada was still deep in her DNA. She wondered if Imani would feel as connected to East Africa as she did.

After dealing with the chaos of immigration and baggage claim at Kilimanjaro Airport, the party was led to a small boarding area to wait for the chartered Cessna aircrafts to take them to Serengeti National Park. Despite sleeping for a good chunk of the flight from Amsterdam, Imani was cranky.

"Baby, you ate all the fruit bars. All I have are cookies," Jana said. She'd already turned down another one of Mom's cheddar-and-potato samosas, saying she wanted something sweet.

"But I want strawberry bars! Buy some!"

Jana tried to explain that this wasn't like the Toronto airport with fully stocked shops, but trying to reason with a jet-lagged four-year-old was as fruitless as Jana was right now.

"Do you want circus cookies, Mini?" Anil said as he rustled though his bag. He pulled out a snack packet of the pink-and-white frosted animal crackers his parents often mailed to Imani with presents. Imani loved them, but they were a rare treat because they weren't available in Canada. Or Africa, Jana assumed.

Jana was relieved he was two steps ahead of this meltdown, but it was also slightly disconcerting to see him so prepared. Like with the socks. Jana wasn't used to seeing him be a dad in action.

"Oh, I brought this for you," Anil said, holding something else out for Jana, too. It was a Clark Bar, a peanut butter and chocolate candy bar that Jana loved and that also wasn't available in Canada. Anil was leaning down and helping Imani open her bag of cookies before Jana could say thank you.

Soon, Mom, Imani, Anil, and the bridal party, or the hash-tag Bridal Brigade, as Kamila was still irritatingly calling them, boarded a small aircraft to take them to the Seronera Airstrip, the primary airstrip within Serengeti National Park. Rohan, Kassim Uncle, and the Groom's Platoon were on a second plane. Imani fell asleep immediately after getting buckled into her seat, so Jana stared out the window at the scenery during the one-and-a-half-hour flight.

The view was spectacular. Vast, open plains with sparse trees and wispy grasses as far as she could see. This was all surreal. For the last few months, Jana had felt like she was on the brink of...something. And this trip—while she'd been dreading the whole socializing part of this wedding and safari—it could be a catalyst for her.

The last few months had been chaotic. Stressful. But more than just feeling busy, she'd also been feeling...restless. Unsatisfied.

Relaxing, reading, and spending quality time with her daughter on safari would rejuvenate her right when Jana needed it most. And if she was lucky, she'd hear about that job soon after getting home. Everything would fall into place.

When the plane landed, a large safari van was waiting to take them to the hotel. The driver told them that wedding guests had been trickling in all day, including Rohan's parents and various aunties, uncles, and friends.

It was early evening by then, and the low sun was adding an otherworldly haze to the golden-brown terrain. Imani's eyes were glued to the window for the dusty drive, hoping to see some animals before they reached the resort. Jana had warned her that it was unlikely—this was just the road to the hotel, but the tour operators would know where to take them to find animals on their game drive scheduled in a couple days.

But suddenly the van slowed. They weren't near the hotel yet. In fact, they looked to be in the middle of nowhere. Jana checked out the window—why had they stopped?

"Mommy, look!" Imani was positively shaking with excitement, and everyone in the van had leaned over to the left-side windows. Three majestic giraffes were standing near the road. There was nothing else in view—just acres and acres of golden African savanna reaching out to the horizon, broken up by sparse trees, and these three tall giraffes welcoming them to Tanzania. They took Jana's breath away. She smiled, remembering the Swahili word for *giraffe* that her father had taught her. *Twiga*.

"Giraffe!" Imani yelled, pointing out the window.

"A Giraffe is called a twiga in Swahili," Anil said to Imani. He was across the aisle from Jana and Imani. "My mother collected giraffes and had them all over the house when I was a kid. Remember from when we visited Dadima and Dadabapa last summer, Mini? Dadima still has a few in their dining room."

Jana remembered those giraffes from when she'd gone to Anil's parents' place for brunch before Imani was born. She, of course, hadn't seen Anil's parents since then, but the memory of them being warm and welcoming to Jana that day hadn't faded. She'd thought they were lovely. Now she felt an emptiness in her stomach when she thought of that day.

Jana looked back out the window at the three majestic giraffes and said a silent thank-you for welcoming her family to Tanzania.

CHAPTER 6

Kamila and Rohan had picked a bustling, enormous, and luxurious resort in Serengeti National Park for their wedding. The sun had almost set by the time they arrived there. Staff members in vibrant African print clothes stood under the covered entrance built of dark wood and greeted them as they climbed out of the van. They handed them all warm, damp towels to wipe the dust off their faces, and cool glasses of mango juice.

Kamila was grinning ear to ear. "I can't believe we're finally here. You all thought I was nuts for wanting to get married on the other side of the world. You didn't think I'd pull this off, did you?" Kamila was looking directly at her sister, Shelina.

Jana had assumed that Kamila had picked an epic destination partially to upstage her sister, who had married Rohan's younger brother, Zayan, years ago in a lavish wedding at an estate in Ontario wine country. Jana didn't understand the point in competition. Both weddings seemed a waste of time and money.

Asha, Kamila's maid of honor, grinned, holding her glass of juice. "This place is even prettier than the pictures."

A beautiful woman approached them and introduced herself. "Kamila! I'm Elsie Mbame, the wedding planner."

"You're the genius who put this all together for me! I want to hug you!" Kamila did hug Elsie, before introducing her to the rest of the party.

Elsie had luminous dark brown skin, and hair in narrow braids reaching down her back. She was wearing a suit tailored to perfection in the same shade of pink as Kamila's sweatshirt. She motioned them all inside while porters unloaded the luggage out of the van and piled it all onto carts.

The lobby of the resort took up half of an enormous round room with a thatched straw ceiling. The walls, floor, and furniture were all dark wood, but bright splashes of color were everywhere—not just in the prints the staff were wearing, but also on the plump cushions on the chairs and sofas in the seating area, and in all the tribal wall art. Huge wicker ceiling fans gave the wide-open space a light breeze, and there was a bright tropical flower scent in the air. While Elsie and the front desk attendant sorted out the room assignments, Jana sat on a chair, pulling a sleepy Imani onto her lap. Jet lag was kicking Jana's ass. She wanted a warm tea and a bed as soon as possible.

"I can't wait to see my kids," Shelina said. Shelina's children had arrived the day before with their paternal grandparents and nanny, having skipped the Amsterdam stopover. "I texted them—they're all in the dining room. I can't believe they have 5G out here!" She laughed. "Oh my god, Jana, that picture your mom posted of you in the WhatsApp group is seriously adorable!"

Jana frowned. She avoided WhatsApp like the plague, but it was the social media platform that the aunties and uncles had chosen as their communication channel for this wedding. Why was Mom putting pictures of Jana there without telling her?

Bracing herself, Jana opened the app. After scrolling past

countless boomer memes, Jana found the picture. It was from the plane after Imani finally fell asleep. And after Jana had fallen asleep, too. Imani had never been a very contained sleeper, so it wasn't a surprise that the child was pretty much draped over Jana with her head on Jana's chest and her knees digging into Jana's side. Jana had no idea how she could have slept through that. In the picture, Jana had a bright blue sleep mask pulled over her eyes, and she was pressed into the person next to her—*Anil*. Jana's head was resting on his shoulder, and he, also asleep, was resting his head on Jana's. His mouth was open, and he was probably drooling onto her hair.

Jana ran her hand over her head, sick to her stomach. Why the hell had Mom taken this picture? And how could Jana have *fallen asleep* on Anil? Why had Mom posted the picture for all the aunties and uncles to see? Had Anil seen this?

Fuming, Jana looked up. Her mother was talking animatedly to some aunties and uncles. Anil was with the Groom's Platoon near the bar on the other side of the big room. She'd have to talk to her mother about this picture. Later, though. When Imani wasn't asleep on her lap.

Could you delete pictures from WhatsApp?

Ugh. She should probably let it go. It was just a picture. People would gossip more if she made a big deal of it. But she needed to make sure she wasn't in this situation again—maybe she should avoid Anil Malek as much as possible on this trip.

"Oh, there's Farzana Aunty," Shelina said, looking toward the lounge area on the other side of the space. "My goodness—look at her hair. Can you imagine wearing that shade at her age? She's probably having a midlife crisis. Would explain getting back together with her ex."

"What does age have to do with hair color?" asked Asha. Her

hair was currently her natural black on top, with vibrant purple curls peeking out from underneath.

"Sam Uncle is a total silver fox," Shelina continued, not seeming to care if anyone was listening. "Can't say I blame her."

"Who are these people?" Asha asked.

"Well," Kamila said, clapping her hands together as if she was going to spill some excellent tea. "Farzana Aunty is Rohan and Zayan's mother's youngest sister. She's the wild sibling. Ran away with her professor. Apparently, it was quite the scandal back in the day. He quit his job and they moved to California. She didn't talk to her family for *years*—except for Rohan's mom. He and Zayan used to go visit them every summer when they were kids."

"Zayan is excited to see him again," Shelina added. "He said Sam Uncle used to wake up early and have warm parathas and achar waiting for them every day."

"They lost touch with them?" Asha asked.

Kamila nodded. "The aunty and uncle *divorced*. Like, years ago—when Rohan was a teenager. Farzana Aunty moved to the UK without him."

Shelina tilted her head, stars in her eyes. "But now they're *back together*, and she's teaching in Toronto again, and their kids are *thrilled*. It's so romantic, right? Don't you think it's romantic, Jana?"

Jana had never thought Shelina was anything resembling subtle, but pointing out this couple with kids who just got back together while she was here with Anil and her daughter was even more on the nose than Jana would have expected. Did Shelina seriously think there was any possibility Jana and Anil would get back together?

Jana looked over to see the woman with fire-engine red hair talking to Rohan's parents and Jana's mother.

Jana's mother waved at her. "Jana, come," Mom said. Jana was completely not in the mood to meet some random aunty, but she got up anyway, leaving Imani on the chair and asking Asha to keep an eye on her.

She smiled at her mother and greeted Rohan's parents, Nadira Aunty and Jon Uncle. Nadira Aunty introduced Jana to her sister, Farzana Aunty. After the red-haired aunty shook her hand, she asked Jana about their journey from Toronto, and they chatted briefly about the flight. Jana liked the aunty so far. She had a kind, thoughtful face. And despite Shelina's opinion, the red hair looked fabulous on her.

"I met Farzana and Sam at Kassim's party last week," Mom said, holding on to Jana's arm. "Farzana is a child psychologist! So interesting, right?"

That *was* interesting. "Do you work in a clinical setting?" Jana asked.

"No, primarily research. And some teaching. I'm at York University."

"What's your research focus?" Jana asked. Jana had always been a bit of a psychology nerd and had seriously considered going into that field instead of development.

"Family structure and how it affects long-term development. Right now, I'm looking at children's outcomes after divorce."

"I told her all about Imani and how well she's doing, even though she's only home half the time," Mom said.

Jana frowned. "Imani *is* at home when she's with her father. Imani has two homes."

Farzana Aunty smiled. "A testament to good parenting. I love to see people put the needs of the child first despite a relationship breaking down." She leaned close to Jana. "The results from my current study haven't been published yet, but so far it's clear that children thrive if the parents co-exist well and have equal access to the child. It's so important for parents to put their differences aside for the sake of the child."

Mom opened her mouth before Jana could. "Yes! It's just like I told you last week—my daughter had the friendliest divorce! Did you see the picture I put on WhatsApp? They're still so close!"

Jana cringed. *Ugh.* Mom was apparently *lying* about Jana's marital status. Years ago, Mom used to tell people that Jana and Anil had been married when Imani was born, but Jana thought Mom had stopped doing that. Jana opened her mouth to correct her mother, but Mom was still talking.

"But of course, my Jana always does everything with such maturity! Not like other girls! She's never caused me any drama. None of these custody or money fights. And they've stayed such good friends. What did you call it when we talked last week?"

"Aspirational," Farzana Aunty said.

Jana looked up at Nadira Aunty and Jon Uncle, who were nodding happily despite being fully aware that Jana had never been married and, thus, could not have ever been divorced. She wondered how long—and how widely—this lie had been told in their social circle.

Jana exhaled. She wasn't about to embarrass her mother by correcting her now. That would be mortifying for them both. But it stung to see her mother was still so ashamed of her that she lied to her friends, and it hurt to see her aunty and uncle nodding along, clearly also ashamed of Jana's choices.

Jana had never hidden her marital situation—even after the professional backlash when her affair with Anil came out and Jana lost a job because of it. There was no point in hiding the truth—*she* was the one who'd turned down Anil's marriage proposal after she told him she was pregnant, and she was the one who walked away from him. She couldn't marry the man after he'd lied to her, so Jana needed to own that choice.

It was true that Jana wasn't like the other women in Mom's social circle. Jana was the disgraced one.

But she still couldn't let this lie stand. Anil was *at* this wedding, for goodness' sake. At some point someone was going to call Jana his ex-wife, and he would have no idea what they were talking about. Or he'd think they meant Nadia, his actual ex-wife. Jana would speak to Farzana Aunty alone later. She seemed like a kind, reasonable woman. And as a researcher in the field, she'd probably encountered lots of thriving kids whose parents had never been married.

Jana needed to change the subject right now. "I hope the rooms are ready soon. Imani needs to get to bed."

Farzana Aunty looked in the direction of the front desk. "Yes, I am dying to get out of these shoes. Sam's gone to ask now, but there's a line at the counter."

Jana glanced in the direction of the solid wood counter where there was a big crowd hoping to check in. It seemed a second van of travelers had arrived at the resort. Jana easily picked out the man who she assumed was Sam Uncle—based on his bright silver hair. But when he turned suddenly toward them, Jana's heart nearly stopped.

She was seeing things. Clearly delirious, thanks to jet lag, annoyance with her mother, and the weirdness of traveling with Anil.

Because Sam Uncle looked a hell of a lot like Dr. Lopez, the man who'd interviewed her in Toronto just a few days ago for the job at Think Canada.

Jana felt a hard thud in her chest as she took a step back

from the others. She quickly asked her mother to keep an eye on Imani and escaped before the man saw her.

With legs like rubber, Jana rushed down a hallway behind the check-in counter and found a little seating alcove decorated with elephants: Dark chairs carved into elephants. Elephant-print cushions. Even an elephant-print area rug. Jana sat and put her head in her hands, willing her heart rate to return to normal.

This wasn't possible. How—and, for that matter, *why*—was Dr. Lopez here?

"Are you all right?" a voice asked.

Jana looked up. Asha and her wife, Nicole, had found the little elephant corner. Perfect. Nicole was an ob-gyn...and while Jana was pretty sure this problem had nothing to do with her vagina, a doctor was a doctor. "Nicole, do the malaria-prevention pills cause hallucinations?"

Nicole frowned, then shone her phone flashlight into Jana's eyes. "Anything is possible. What are your symptoms?"

Asha looked around the room. "Are you seeing elephants? Because I'm seeing a lot of elephants right now."

"What about dizzy spells or headaches?" Nicole asked, putting the back of her hand against Jana's forehead.

"No. I thought I saw someone I knew. But it's impossible. He lives in Toronto."

"More than half of us at this wedding live in Toronto," Asha said. "Who do you think you saw?"

"The executive director for an organization that interviewed me a few days ago."

Nicole cringed, putting her hand down. "Seriously? Like, a job interview?"

Jana nodded.

"Ouch—that's awkward," Asha said, plopping on an armchair

with elephants on it. "It really is a small world. I once bumped into my literal next-door neighbor in Istanbul. This is a big resort, though. You can avoid them. If it's them. Which it probably isn't."

Jana shook her head. "I *can't* avoid him. I think it's Sam Uncle. The uncle with the red-haired aunty."

Nicole squeezed in next to Asha on her chair.

"Silver Fox Uncle?" Asha asked. "We can find out if it's him. Kamila had lunch with that uncle and aunty last month." Asha's text tone went off then. She checked her phone, then snorted. "Kamila just sent a dick-dick pic again."

Jana's eyes widened. "What?" How exactly did she ever think she'd fit in with this group? Were they twelve years old? "She sent you a picture of a *penis*?"

Nicole laughed. "Not a *dick*, a *dik-dik*. It's a small antelope native to this area. Kamila and Asha are adults, but they think penis puns are hysterical."

Asha held up the phone so they could see the picture of the, frankly, adorable Disney-worthy antelope. "Dik-diks are better than dicks, in my opinion. Let me ask Kamila about Silver Fox Uncle." Asha texted Kamila something, and soon Kamila, and the other two bridesmaids, Shelina and Yuriko, joined them in the tiny elephant room.

"What's the bridesmaid emergency?" Kamila asked. "Should I get Elsie, too? Do we need another doctor or a lawyer? Because I can grab Jerome or Marc."

Jana closed her eyes for a second. Did they *all* need to be here? Couldn't she have her little crisis in private?

There weren't nearly enough elephant seats for all six of them, so Kamila and Yuriko squeezed on an ottoman while Shelina took the last chair.

"Jana thought she recognized Sam Uncle," Asha explained. "She thinks he interviewed her for a job. What's the uncle's full name?"

Kamila shrugged. "I don't know. Rohan calls him Sam Uncle. I can ask Rohan."

Jana shook her head. "Don't worry about it. It can't be him. The man wasn't Indian."

"Neither is Sam Uncle," Kamila said. "He's from Mexico."

Jana frowned. *Crap*. Dr. Lopez had told her that his own focus had been Mexican and Central American development. "Why does Rohan call him Sam Uncle if he's not Indian? Zayan said he used to make parathas and achar for them!"

Kamila gave Jana a sideways look. "He calls him *Uncle* because he's married to Rohan's aunty. Or they *were* married, at least. Also, parathas are delicious, so not sure why Sam Uncle isn't allowed to make them."

Jana put her face in her hands. This was a disaster.

"I don't understand how you determine who is an aunty or an uncle," Yuriko asked. "I think it's different in Japanese culture."

"Everyone at least fifteen years older than you is an aunty or uncle," Nicole explained. "It simultaneously makes everything very simple and incredibly confusing."

"It's Lopez!" Kamila said suddenly, holding her phone up in the air. "I texted Rohan! His name is Samuel Lopez, and he's the director of an aid organization!" She frowned at her phone. "The cell service out here is phenomenal."

Jana let out an audible groan.

"I don't understand why this is a bad thing," Kamila said. "He's really cool. If you get a chance to talk, I'm sure he'll hire you. This is good!"

Jana shook her head. "No. It's not. This trip is two weeks! I can't be, like...*job interview* nice for that long." Jana put her face back in her hands. She needed this job, but how could Dr. Lopez hire his ex-wife's sister's son's fiancée's bridesmaid? Wouldn't he be accused of nepotism? Besides, now he'd have a front-row seat to discover Jana was the furthest thing from the vibrant team player he wanted. She was a usually frazzled single mother with drool in her hair who was annoyed to be traveling with her child's father, and whose mother was clearly ashamed of her.

"You're a delight," Asha said. "He'll love you even more after spending time with you."

Jana doubted that. "But Mom *lied* to him and his ex-wife."

"What did your mother say?" Kamila asked.

Jana sighed and lifted her head. "She told them I was divorced because..."

"She didn't want them to know your child is illegitimate?" Shelina asked. Kamila slapped her on the arm.

Asha cringed. "Ugh. Parents. I'm not surprised. You know my grandmother tells everyone Nicole is a man?"

"That's horrible, Asha," Jana said, giving Nicole a sympathetic look. Nicole's expression was blank.

Asha shrugged. "I mean, it's not like I'm ever running into those people in India, anyway. I don't care. And it's just my grandmother who's not accepting—it would be worse if it were my *mother*."

Jana sighed. She hadn't really thought about it that way. Her own mother didn't accept her.

Mom had always been delighted to tell everyone how proud she was of her successful daughter. Jana tried not to let it bother her too much that her mother had never really told *Jana* that she was proud of her.

When all the kids were young, Mom always joined in with the aunties and uncles as they one-upped each other with their children's grades, their scholarships, their Ivy League schools, their fellowships, and their advanced degrees. As the kids grew, the boasting was about jobs, promotions, and the important work they all did in the world. As a highly educated development professional with a PhD, Jana gave her mother plenty to boast about. That is, until the boasting turned to things like engagement rings, proposals, weddings, houses in the suburbs, and finally, babies.

Jana was a thirty-two-year-old unwed mother living at home. Divorce was more accepted in their South Asian Muslim community than it used to be—but having a baby out of wedlock wasn't. Jana knew that Mom used to tell people that Jana had once been married, but she had no idea her mother was still saying it—or that her closest aunties and uncles were in on the deception.

"Who cares if you weren't married when you had Imani?" Kamila asked. "This isn't Jane Austen or anything."

"*I know*," Jana said. "Mom lied, not me. Apparently, your dad and Rohan's parents are in on it."

Kamila shrugged. "So, I'll correct them. It's not a big deal."

Jana shook her head. "No. Please don't." She sighed. She needed more time to think this through before Kamila put her butt into the situation. "This job will be competitive. I'm worried that telling Dr. Lopez the truth now will make me stand out...and not in a good way. What if he thinks all Mom's boasting was to influence his decision? Or that Mom lied because I was trying to hide from my past? And if he discovers the *whole* truth about Imani's birth, he may not approve. I mean, it's one thing that Anil and I weren't married to each other, but I would rather he didn't know that Anil *was* married to someone else when Imani was conceived."

Jana didn't have an issue admitting that she hadn't been married to Imani's father, but she didn't exactly broadcast that Anil was technically an adulterer.

"Why should any of that matter at all for your job?" Kamila asked.

"Did you forget that I was once *fired* from a job because it *did* matter to someone?" Jana reminded Kamila.

Nicole cringed. "You're kidding. You *lost* a job because of who you had a child with? That's puritanical nonsense."

"Sam Uncle isn't like that, though," Kamila said.

"Do you know that for a fact? And like I said, development jobs are competitive. I have no doubt there are plenty of amazing non-home-wrecker applicants for this role. He could pick someone else over me for the tiniest reason." Jana paused, thinking. "The bigger issue is that he's going to discover that I'm not exactly the social team player he wants in his department. And my mother is going to be *mortified* if I correct her lie. I can't ruin her trip. The last time she came to Africa she was with my dad."

Jana's first trip to Tanzania had been when she was fifteen, and it was their last holiday before Dad died. It was a big trip like this one—Kamila's family and Rohan's family had been with them, too. Jana's father had always been an animal lover—and excitedly looking for big game with him in one of those safari vehicles was one of her favorite memories of Dad. Jana's father was a lot like her—the quiet one in the noisy world. When everyone around him was playing cards, or singing Bollywood songs, or gossiping, he was always happy on the sidelines. She'd found it so comforting—he belonged there with the others even if he wasn't like them.

Jana missed her father so much. And maybe in the back of her head, she'd been hoping that she would be able to feel as comfortable and content on this trip as he had seemed back then, despite being surrounded by people. But now she wondered if Mom had brought some extra emotional baggage along, too, because the last time she was here, her husband had been alive.

Mom was a widow, and she had only one child—Jana. And Jana was in the enormous wedding of Mom's two closest friends' kids. It was wrong that society had taught Mom that marriage and babies were necessary to consider her daughter a success, but Jana couldn't exactly blame her mother for being a product of her culture and her generation.

Jana rubbed her temples. She was much too tired to deal with this. She wanted a bed, not a crisis. "Ugh. I just want this to go away for now. I need to get some sleep."

Kamila nodded. "We got you, Jana. We can make this go away. I'll have Elsie make some changes to the schedule and keep you, your mother, and Anil away from Sam Uncle until you decide what to do. He won't even realize you're here at the wedding." She thought for a moment. "Elsie can probably keep you all apart for the whole trip. Let your mother have her little lie. Elsie has us scheduled down to the minute, anyway. Then if you get the job, you can explain that it was a misunderstanding and you were never legally married."

"And what about Anil?" Shelina asked. "He knows they were never married."

Asha shrugged. "Just tell him what's going on. He'll go along with it."

Jana winced. "No. I can't ask Anil to lie for me or my mother. It's out of the question."

"Why?" Shelina asked. "I thought you two got along?"

Yeah, they *did* get along... the way distant colleagues working on a joint project got along. Asking Anil to lie for her would change their dynamic, and Jana didn't want that.

When Jana said nothing, Kamila stood. "Let's go, ladies. I need to have a word with my wedding planner. I am positive she can fix this. Sam Uncle won't even know that Anil is Imani's father." She headed out of the elephant room and her bridesmaids followed.

Jana went with them, but she didn't see how this plan could possibly work. She should just go out into the Serengeti and fulfil her childhood dream of living with elephants.

When she got to the lobby, Jana practically walked right into her mother talking to Dr. Samuel Lopez and Farzana Aunty.

Shit.

In a last-ditch effort, Jana said a silent prayer that Dr. Lopez wouldn't recognize her.

"Dr. Suleiman, is that you?"

Double shit. The bridal party all scattered from the awkward situation, but Kamila stayed. Jana was incredibly proud that she didn't turn around and run straight out into the wild when Dr. Lopez said her name.

"Ah! How wonderful!" Mom said, briefly putting her hand on Jana's arm. "You've met my daughter!"

There was a beat of silence. Two beats. Jana had no idea if she was supposed to say how she knew the man.

Dr. Lopez finally smiled. "Yes! I had the honor of hearing your daughter speak a few years ago. I see why you're so proud of her," he said, grinning at Mom like Jana was his own daughter. It was disconcerting how much he reminded her of her father when he smiled. Or…maybe Jana was imagining it. She'd been thinking about Dad a lot today.

But also…wasn't Dr. Lopez going to mention that she was interviewing for a position in his organization?

He looked back at Jana, and she thought something passed over his face. A *Don't worry, I can keep a secret* look. "How delightful to see you here!" He pointed to the #BRIDALBRIGADE T-shirt she was still wearing. "And a member of the bridal party?"

"Yes!" Kamila said, because Kamila was always able to speak. "Jana and I have known each other *literally forever*. She's amazing. Such a great…person. And brilliant, too! She's in such high demand. Honestly, Jana Suleiman is an asset to any…wedding party."

Oh my god. That was as subtle as the color of Kamila's sweatshirt. Jana closed her eyes and counted to ten. Maybe if she clicked her heels together, she would disappear from this place and be absolutely anywhere else. Like…Siberia. She'd been there—it wasn't as bad as people expected. She didn't mind the cold. The mountains were nice. She loved the isolation.

Jana needed to say something—*anything*—or her friends would keep digging this hole. "Dr. Lopez! So nice to see you here!" Jana's hand fisted as she struggled for a way to get out of this conversation.

Fate stepped in, because Elsie then announced that the room assignments were ready. In the chaos of key cards being distributed and luggage being sorted, Jana was able to escape from Dr. Samuel Lopez.

She doubted it would be that easy for the whole trip, though.

CHAPTER 7

Jana cornered her mother out of earshot of anyone else as soon as she could. "Mom, why are you *still* telling people I'm divorced?"

Jana's mother frowned. "It's okay, beta. It's not important."

Jana tilted her head. "It *is* important because it's not true."

"What difference does it make?" Mom asked. "It was so long ago."

"It makes a difference because now that aunty who studies divorce will ask me questions!" And the aunty's partner was currently considering Jana for a director of research and programs position. But Jana couldn't say that to Mom—it would make everything even more awkward. Also, she'd hate to see what all the aunties and uncles would do to the poor man if Jana *didn't* get the job. They'd run him out of the family all over again. "Why did you even say it?"

"They were talking about their daughter's wedding and asked me what your wedding was like. It's not a big deal—just play along. Who could it hurt? Come on, beta...Do this one thing for me."

Mom had a pleading look in her eyes. And Jana had a lot of

difficulty not giving in to it. What would Mom do if Jana broke her bubble?

"Mom, did you forget that Anil is here at the wedding?"

Mom cringed. "I thought he wasn't coming when I met Sam and Farzana last week."

True. No one knew he was coming.

They were interrupted at that moment by Elsie, handing Jana and her mom key cards and telling them that their room was in the east wing and that their luggage was being brought there now.

It was late. Jana was tired. And Imani, who was still dozing in the armchair in the lobby, needed to be in a bed.

"Don't say anything more to anyone," Jana said. "We'll figure this out in the morning." Jana scooped her daughter into her arms and took her to their room. Mom was apparently staying in the hotel lounge to gossip some more. Hopefully not about Jana.

When she got to their room, Jana pushed out all her thoughts about Mom, Dr. Lopez, and Anil Malek so she could focus on getting Imani cleaned and into bed. Imani was both worked up and exhausted, and her nightly bedtime routine took longer than usual. When Imani was finally tucked in, Jana lay with her daughter, stroking her hair and humming softly to help her sleep.

Jana was so torn about what to do. She knew she should tell Dr. Lopez the truth, that she was never technically married. It was a tiny, inconsequential lie, but even a small lie was ill-advised when she wanted to show the man she had integrity and maturity and would be a good addition to his team.

But also . . . what difference could it make? This was her *personal* life—and it *shouldn't* have any bearing on her employability. And there was a possibility that Dr. Lopez's knowing the truth about Imani's conception could hurt Jana's chances at getting this job. Jana was confident in her abilities in her field, but Kamila's assurance to Dr. Lopez that Jana was in high demand wasn't anywhere close to Jana's reality lately.

Jana wrapped one of her daughter's curls around her fingers. She didn't think of herself as a particularly saintly person, but she was aware that others saw her that way—or at least they used to. It was partially because Jana was bookish, excelled academically, and had never been a party girl. But it was also because of her line of work. International development was a field for people who wanted to change the world. To level the planet's inequalities. It was also sometimes a field for people who took their faith seriously and who saw it as a higher calling. Jana wasn't particularly religious, but she was used to working with colleagues who were. And she was used to others projecting good and wholesome qualities onto people in development. But Jana's saintly reputation had been crushed like a dung beetle under an elephant's foot when Imani was born. She ran her hand over Imani's head, listening to her daughter's slow breathing.

It shouldn't have been a surprise that some in her field turned against her. She knew what her industry was like. But Jana had been a little idealistic—she'd honestly thought people wouldn't care about her personal life and would focus on her professional accomplishments instead. And most did. But not all.

When the major donor of a project learned Jana had had a baby with a married man, he threatened to pull funding if she continued to lead the project. Eventually, the board of directors decided that Dr. Jana Suleiman being the face of the project was more of a liability to funding than an asset, despite her skills, education, and experience.

Jana didn't know if Dr. Lopez would feel the same way as that donor. Signs pointed to no—Kamila and Rohan both said he was a good man. Jana could see that he was very professional. The fact that Dr. Lopez reminded Jana so much of her father didn't mean the man felt the same way as her mother did and how Jana assumed her father would have felt—that the circumstances around Imani's birth were a disgrace.

Jana watched Imani's long lashes fluttering as her lips pursed in sleep, then quietly got out of the dark wood bed and closed the mosquito net around it to keep her daughter safe. Mom hadn't come to the room yet. She was probably still chatting away in the lobby. Hopefully not telling any more lies about Jana.

Their suite was impressive. Two bedrooms—Jana and Imani's with two double beds and Mom's with a queen bed—plus a little sitting room. The decor was similar to the rest of the luxury hotel—tasteful and understated elegance with a definite African art theme. The walls were clean white, and the flooring was dark tile. It was all comfortably luxurious.

Jana had traveled so much for work but rarely stayed in places like this. She'd spent so much time working to lift people up economically that she felt guilty being surrounded by this opulence knowing the social challenges around her. How much could the money being spent on this wedding have helped the region? She'd bet they could have funded a new maternal health clinic instead. But this was Kamila and Rohan's wedding, and Jana knew they had picked this particular resort because it was known as a generous employer for locals, and it sponsored nearby development projects. Plus, Kamila and Rohan donated to projects in East Africa and in other areas. Tourism was an important part of the economy here, but Jana still felt a little strange.

A large gift bag on the dresser caught Jana's eye. She opened the note attached.

To Jana and Imani: Thanks for being a part of our celebration! Love having you on our team, and love you both to the moon and back! Kamila and Rohan

Inside were two backpacks. The little Lion King one was filled with a set of children's binoculars, baby sunscreen, some candy, some books about safari animals, and a tan wide-brimmed hat. The larger adult backpack was in a weathered gray canvas and had #BRIDALBRIGADE embroidered in pink on the lower right corner. It also contained binoculars, a tan hat, and sunscreen, as well as vitamin C tablets, bug repellent, electrolyte powder, some stomach medicine, Tylenol, lip balm, a bikini in Jana's size, and a kanga—an East African wrap made of brightly printed cotton. Plus, a full box of condoms. Jana snorted at the condoms. It was a thoughtful bridesmaid gift, though.

She read the note again. *Love having you on our team.* Dr. Lopez also said he was looking for a team player. Had Jana ever been that?

Dr. Lopez would be seeing Jana at her worst on this trip—at her lowest professional confidence and, honestly, her lowest social confidence. He thought she was a vibrant team player. Why would he hire *this*?

The last job Jana had interviewed for had gone to a woman who was young, bubbly, intelligent, and so nice that it was impossible for Jana to resent her. That woman *was* vibrant. Dynamic. She stood out.

There was a time, long ago, when Jana had thought she stood out—with her fellowship at Cambridge. Her scholarships. She'd pitched countless development projects over the years. Sometimes they worked, sometimes they didn't, but she'd never given up without trying. Jana may not have always fit in with others, but she used to excel at faking it. She used to *try*.

Maybe her personal issues with Anil were seeping into her professional life. She knew she was still much too bitter about him and the past. Seeing him here on this trip solidified it for Jana—it was long past time for her to get over Anil Malek. She needed to move on from her anger, bitterness, and her regret over what happened. Imani was only four. They had years of co-parenting left. And as their child grew, they would have to work together even more if they wanted her to continue to thrive.

Jana needed to move on. She couldn't be *vibrant* if she was always angry. But she didn't know *how* to get over it.

But maybe she didn't have to. Maybe she could fake it. Pretend that being around Anil was no big deal. Pretend to be confident and dynamic. Show Dr. Lopez that she was the right person for that job. And she and Anil really did have the aspirational co-parenting relationship that Mom claimed they had. Hell, maybe *pretending* she was over the past was the way to actually get over it. And now she had two weeks with Anil—this was the perfect time to put it all behind her for Imani's well-being and her own.

It was time to show everyone—including Anil Malek—that the last five years hadn't broken Jana. Most of all, it was time for Jana to show *herself* that.

CHAPTER 8

The next morning, Jana was greeted by a printed piece of paper that had been slid under the suite door while they slept. It was a revised wedding schedule. Jana assumed Elsie had rearranged everything so Dr. Lopez wasn't in the same activities as Mom, Jana, Anil, or Imani. Kamila hadn't been kidding when she said Elsie was a wedding planner with military-level organizational abilities.

According to the schedule, Jana and Imani's game drive through Serengeti National Park had been rescheduled for tomorrow morning. They would be with Mom, Anil, and the Bridal Brigade, while the Groom's Platoon (minus Anil) and Dr. Lopez would be going today. The rearrangement meant Jana and Anil would be together all day. Good. This was Jana's chance to pretend she was perfectly fine being around him.

After dressing, Jana and Imani headed for breakfast. The small private dining room had a buffet off to one side with fresh fruit and pastries, and a woman in a chef's jacket was making omelets and pancakes to order. There were also East African additions—like chapatti and Jana's favorite, mandazi, which were lightly fried triangles of sweet dough like beignets, except made with cardamom and coconut. Imani made a beeline for the elaborate pastries. Jana let her grab a few so long as she took fruit, too, while Jana was happy with chai, mandazi, and some mango slices.

They weren't alone for long. Soon, Kamila and Asha joined them, each with overladen plates. Kamila's was just fruit, though.

"Don't worry," Kamila said. "I am *not* buying into that whole bridal diet–culture crap, but if I eat all the croissants I want to eat, there's no chance of fitting into my lehenga." She looked at Jana's plate. "After the wedding, I will be eating mandazi only." She speared a piece of mango onto her fork, then moaned with appreciation as she put it in her mouth. "Oh my god. This is fine, though. Honestly, the mangoes here are better than..." She mouthed the letters *s-e-x*, presumably for the sake of Imani at the table. "Never mind the mandazi—I'm only eating mangoes from now on."

Imani was outraged, though. "But you have to eat cake at the wedding!"

Kamila smiled, then leaned in close to Imani. "I'll tell you a secret, Princess: one of the layers of my cake will have a mango filling. I'll eat that one. But don't worry—we got vanilla for your mother, too."

Jana frowned. Was that an insult? She knew vanilla was considered plain and basic in North America, but elsewhere in the world, it was a luxurious treat. Jana loved a quality, fragrant, almost floral vanilla.

"Good morning, ladies!" someone said behind Jana. Anil. Jana squeezed her chai mug. She could do this.

"Daddy!" Imani squealed so loudly that Dr. Lopez on the plains of the Serengeti probably heard her.

Anil smiled at Imani, then looked at Jana, clearly hoping Jana would invite him to pull up a chair. She *should* be accustomed to being around him by now. But no. The hair on her arm stood on end. Her stomach flip-flopped. It still felt so weird to have him in front of her—and in Tanzania, of all places.

Kamila suddenly stood. "We need to go check on the banquet hall. Elsie had some questions about table arrangements for the sangeet on Friday. C'mon, Ash." Asha smiled apologetically at Jana, then took her plate of food and followed Kamila out.

Imani beamed. "Daddy, now you can sit!"

Jana put on a smile. "Yes, join us."

Anil grinned as he sat in Kamila's vacated seat.

"How'd you sleep, Mini?" he asked. Anil was dressed in jeans and a linen short-sleeve button-up. Nothing fancy, but he looked effortlessly put together. He always did. Shirt never wrinkled. Pants always at the right length. No small coffee stains. No child scribbles on his clothes. Everything was tailored to fit right.

Jana used to be effortless—at least she used to think she was. Not anymore. Motherhood had changed her—but it was irritating to see Anil looking *better* than he used to look. She smoothed her hair behind her ears.

"Are you ready for our first game drive tomorrow?" Jana asked Imani.

Imani's little face scrunched with confusion. "Are we going to play games instead of looking at animals?"

Anil shook his head. "*Game* means big wild animals here."

"Do the big animals play games?"

"Oh, no. They're called game because..." Anil paused.

Jana looked at him sharply, hoping he understood her glare meant *Don't you dare tell our African animal–obsessed daughter that they're called game because humans like to shoot them dead.*

He ran his hand over Imani's head. "Because it's like a game to find them all. Did you bring that passport book I got you? The one where you can color in the animals when you see them?"

She nodded happily, then pointed to her backpack. "I didn't color giraffes, even though we saw three giraffes. Are we going to see more?"

Imani and Anil chatted about the animals they hoped to see on the game drive while Jana sipped her chai.

Kamila came back to the table then and smiled at Imani. "Elsie is decorating the room for the sangeet party. Do you want to help me put the wooden animals on the tables?"

Imani beamed. "Can I go?" She looked at Jana.

"I'll be with her," Kamila said.

"Okay. But don't get in anyone's way."

Imani jumped out of her seat in half a second and took Kamila's hand. "Can we put the elephant on Mommy's table? It's her favorite."

"I already picked out the best elephant for her."

Hand in hand, Kamila and Imani left the dining room. Which left Jana alone with Anil. Awkward.

"Do you think they all left us on purpose?" Anil asked.

Yes, Jana did think that. But she dipped a mandazi into her chai instead of answering.

"You still love mandazi," Anil said, more a statement than a question.

She raised a brow. When had she ever eaten mandazi with him?

He chuckled. "You don't remember. Not surprised. When we went to my mom's for brunch, she made them fresh. I think you ate a dozen. Seems like a lifetime ago now."

Jana blinked. Was he... *reminiscing* about those weeks? Neither of them *ever* brought up the two weeks they were together.

It was always like the giant elephant in the room whenever they spoke.

But maybe now that they were in Tanzania, Anil assumed elephants were fair game. Jana tried not to think about their affair. She remembered the sex—because as hard as she tried, she couldn't seem to wipe that from her mind. Probably because she'd had so little sex since then.

"That reminds me," he said. "Someone on the Toronto Aim High board had to step down. Would you be interested in coming back as a board member?"

Jana exhaled. More memories. Back in Tajikistan, they'd talked about their work at dinner one night and excitedly put together a business plan for Aim High, a nonprofit in the US for helping refugees start small businesses. It was invigorating, collaborative work, and Jana had been amazed at how Anil was completely on the same page as she was for the best way to build up communities.

But when she broke up with him, he launched Aim High in Toronto instead of D.C. Jana had told him he could do whatever he wanted with the business plan, but she'd still been bitter when his magic touch made it happen so easily. She'd worked with Aim High for a short time but left before Imani was even a year old. Partially because she found it too painful to be around Anil while everyone gushed over him. But also because she wanted to get back to her calling—development work in the global south. But then the job she left Aim High for fired her when that donor decided he didn't want to give any more money to a project led by a home-wrecker.

"Probably not." Jana needed to move this conversation to more comfortable ground. "So are you thinking we'll be *together* for all the game drives on safari?" There would be several vehicles; they didn't have to always be in the same one.

Anil rolled his eyes. "No. Don't do that, Jana. You always do that."

She crossed her arms in front of her. "Do what?"

"Make things more complicated than they need to be. I'm not the devil, you know. We can be in a car together."

Jana shook her head. "When did I say we couldn't?"

"You didn't have to say it. It's all over your face."

Jana's nose wrinkled. She was off to a terrible start. Anil could see right through her attempts at pretending to tolerate him.

"Look, I know this is strange," Anil continued, "but we're here for Imani, and for Rohan and Kamila. Let's not make this more stressful than it needs to be for anyone. I know you'd prefer I weren't here, but I am."

"I never said that."

"Yeah, but you're thinking it. We can be a team for once and make this a memorable trip for Imani."

There was that word again—*team*. Jana's lips pursed. She didn't growl angrily at him, because she had some restraint. But she wanted to. They had already been a *team* for the last four years, hadn't they? They'd been flexible when either of them needed to change their time with Imani. They'd easily agreed on which daycare, babysitter, and activities for Imani. They'd never argued about money. Just because Jana hadn't wanted to be around the man didn't mean she hadn't cooperated.

This was why she avoided him. He made it seem like she *wanted* to be miserable.

"Fine," Jana said. She speared a piece of pineapple and popped it in her mouth.

"Fine what?"

"Fine, we'll have an idyllic holiday together. We'll pretend we're a happy family."

Anil sighed. "Not pretending. We *are* a family, Jana."

Jana raised a brow.

"Seriously. We are. You and Imani are a family. Me and Imani are a family. Which makes all of us a family. If you ever stop hating me, we could be a *happy* family."

"You're being arrogant," she said.

A waitress came by the table, and Anil's expression instantly changed from glaring at Jana to cheerful. He chatted pleasantly about the weather and the breakfast spread with their server. He was always so charming. *Happy family.* It was impossible.

He stirred some cream into his coffee after the server left, his expression blank again. "I'm here. Maybe it wasn't right to come without letting you know. I'm sorry." He wasn't making eye contact, just looking at his mug as he added sugar, too. "I've said that to you a lot over the years. I've tried to make things better between us. I don't know what else I can do."

"Why *did* you come on this trip?"

"I told you—I came for Rohan and Kamila, and for *Imani*. I wanted to be here for her first trip to East Africa. But also..." He finally looked up at Jana. He seemed...sad. Anil had extremely expressive eyes, but the expression in them was usually the same. Good humor. Cheerfulness. Often a bit of mischief. When she first met him, she assumed that was how he was always feeling. Later she'd learned that he had the ability to put on that face even when he didn't feel it. A talent she didn't have.

She *had* seen other expressions in those eyes. She'd seen this very sad, resigned look before—the day she refused his marriage proposal.

She bit her lip. "Also what?"

He took a mandazi from his plate and dipped it in his coffee. "Jana, for almost five years I've done what's best for Imani, but also for *you*. I know I messed up back then. I've apologized and I've tried to make it better. I referred you for jobs, I defend you to anyone who says any shit about you. And I've kept my distance from you to keep you comfortable. But I can't do that forever."

Did he expect a cookie? He'd been a complete and utter ass to her five years ago when he hadn't told her the true nature of his marriage before hopping into bed with her. She'd been incredibly hurt and betrayed, and she could not trust him. But she'd worked with him anyway. She'd never been petty. She'd never bad-mouthed him to Imani or to anyone else.

Jana's whole body tensed. "You won't keep your distance anymore?"

He took a deep breath and looked straight at her. His eyes were swirling with determination. "It's time for a change. I will *always* put Imani first. But this"—he indicated between them— "this can't work forever. As Imani gets older, we can't be the best parents possible without working together. Communicating better. I'm not saying I want to change our custody agreement, but wouldn't it be nice if we could work together because we respect each other instead of because the piece of paper the lawyers drew up tells us to?"

Jana blinked. It sounded like Anil wanted the same thing she did—to get over the past so they could co-exist more easily. But for some reason, having a common goal didn't make this any easier.

"I've gone along with everything you wanted," he continued. "I think it's time you gave me something *I* want."

Jana's teeth clenched. "What do you want? More custody?"

Did he want to take Imani away? Did he want primary custody so he could move to D.C. as he got his new nonprofit off the ground? That couldn't happen. Jana wouldn't let him.

Anil recoiled at her accusation, though. "No. *Of course not.* I said I didn't want to change the custody agreement. You're an amazing mother—I would *never* do anything to take that from Imani. I just..." He sighed. "There is something I want. Maybe I need to grovel more first...but I was hoping that—"

"Good morning, sunshines!" Nicole said, walking toward them. Shelina was close behind. "Jana, I'm to see if you are available for an impromptu Bridal Brigade meeting." Nicole smiled widely at them, which made Jana wonder if Asha had told her to rescue Jana from Anil. But Jana didn't want the rescue. She wanted to know what Anil was about to say.

"Oh," Jana said. "Sure. Just give me—"

Anil stood. "I'm done, anyway. I need to catch up on my email. You look lovely as always, Nicole. And Shelina, I had a rousing conversation with your sons yesterday. You're raising some lively boys! We'll talk later, okay, Jana?"

Jana nodded, her fists in a tight ball on her lap.

Once Anil was out of the dining room, Shelina sighed. "He gets hotter every year. You ever see that video of Stanley Tucci making cocktails for his wife? That's Anil's vibe. He's like...old-fashioned handsome. Such a DILF. I *love* a dad bod."

That was actually a common sentiment—Jana had overheard some playgroup moms calling Anil a DILF recently. "Can you not?" Jana asked. "I really don't want to hear about Anil's *bod* right now. What's this meeting about?"

Nicole indicated the banquet hall next door. "Asha said, and I quote, 'Jana looks like she'd rather pop a pus bubble on her own ass than eat a meal alone with that man, and we've left her long enough.'"

Jana rolled her eyes. "I was fine. I didn't need a rescue."

"That's what I said. If you wanted to walk away, you would

have. Anyway, we do need help reasoning with your daughter. She's picking animals for each place setting based on what the person looks like."

"She's giving Rohan's Nilufer Aunty a hippo because she has big teeth," Shelina added. "Somehow I don't think the aunty would appreciate that comparison."

Jana cringed. She may as well join the rest of the bridesmaids setting up the party. She could put that whole conversation with Anil aside for the sake of her friends. But she did need to finish the conversation—and soon.

She had no idea how she could pretend to be okay with the man now. Not when he clearly wanted something from her. Something that he knew Jana wouldn't want to give.

Jana was curious what that was. Terrified, but curious.

CHAPTER 9

"Daddy, when will we see gorillas?" Imani asked. They'd been driving through Serengeti National Park for close to an hour, and pretty much all they'd seen were wildebeests. Lots and lots of wildebeests.

"Sorry, sweets," Anil said. "There aren't any gorillas in Tanzania." He frowned. "I guarantee we'll see baboons, though. We will see baboons, won't we, Joseph?"

Joseph, their incredibly cheerful and patient tour guide/driver for the day, nodded. "I guarantee it, my friend." He said something in Swahili into his radio. Jana's Swahili was terrible, but she was pretty sure he said, "Who has seen baboons? A little girl wants baboons."

Despite the wildebeests, the incredibly bumpy road, Imani's boredom, Mom's lying, Kamila's meddling, and of course, Anil's presence, Jana was enjoying their first game drive. The scenery was breathtaking: Wide, open spaces as far as the eye could see, except for the many other tour vehicles around. Sturdy baobab and wispy acacia trees in the distance. Palms, shrubs, and more birds than Jana had seen in her life. Even without the primates (or any mammals other than wildebeests), the Serengeti was *spectacular*.

The vehicle slowed after they came around a bend. Jana remembered from her safari as a teen that slowing like this meant that the driver thought something worth seeing was nearby.

And yes. It was most definitely worth seeing.

It was a pride of lions. Three full-grown female ones, and one smaller young one—a baby.

"Simba!" Imani yelled out.

Simba was the Swahili word for *lion*, but Jana was pretty sure that Imani's outburst was more due to watching *The Lion King* at least thirty-seven times in the last two months than the Swahili words they'd been practicing at home.

The lions were majestic, lounging among the tall grasses. They looked regal and...content. Satisfied. Like they were exactly where they belonged in the world.

"Those are three lady lions and one of their babies," Joseph said.

"It's like the hashtag Bridal Brigade, right, Imani?" Kamila asked. She was in the Toyota Land Cruiser with them, along with Mom, Nicole, and Asha. The rest of the Bridal Brigade was in another Land Cruiser behind them, along with Shelina's kids. "All your aunties and you!"

"Where's the daddy lion?" Imani asked.

Jana turned to answer Imani. "The male lions don't live in the pack with the female lions."

"Mommy Lion doesn't like Daddy Lion. That's why Daddy doesn't live with us! That's why Simba needs aunties!"

Jana blinked at her daughter, not knowing how to respond to that. Especially with Anil sitting right there.

"Your mommy and daddy like each other," Anil said, patting his daughter's arm reassuringly. "And you live with me every other week."

"And I'm here," Mom said. "And Kassim Uncle, too. There is nothing wrong with being a child of di—"

"Look! There's another baby lion right over there!" Kamila broke in.

Clearly Jana needed to talk to her mother today. This charade had to end before Anil found out about Mom's little lie.

The following evening, Jana was in her room getting ready for a mehndi and spa night in Kamila's suite. When Jana got out of the shower, Mom was picking out jewelry in her room, and Imani was playing a game in the sitting room on her iPad with her big pink headphones on.

Finally, Jana could talk to her mother alone. Mom had been with the aunties all day.

"Mom, you can't mention *divorce* in front of Anil. He doesn't know about this little lie of yours." Jana sat on Mom's bed and started brushing her hair.

Mom waved her hand. "Beta, it's not a lie. You were with him, and now you are not."

"But we were never *married*."

Mom turned around to look at Jana with a pointed look. "So? No one needs to know that. No one even knows his family...all the way in Washington." Mom turned back around and looked in the mirror to put her earrings in.

Jana looked at her mother's face. If she studied her own features, Jana could see that her eyes were her mother's and her nose was her father's, but the whole effect wasn't either of them. In temperament, though, she was like her father, so she'd felt more connection to him. Her mother's idea of a perfect night was twenty of her closest friends and loud music, which was as enjoyable as a root canal to Jana. But also, it sometimes seemed like their relationship was surface-level only. Mom felt like just another aunty, not Jana's actual mother.

Mom took care of Jana and of Imani. She made their favorite foods and hadn't ever complained about Jana moving back home to have a baby. But she and Mom didn't *talk*. Did her mom ever think about dating again? Did she accept Jana keeping Imani but not marrying Anil? Was she proud of her daughter? But Jana didn't know how to ask these questions—her mother had never taught her that language.

Jana shook her head. She was expected to be in Kamila's suite in ten minutes for a private Bridal Brigade dinner before a team of aestheticians and mehndi artists were going to get the bridesmaids ready for tomorrow's sangeet party. Jana sighed. She didn't even want to go tonight, but she remembered her decision from a few nights earlier. She needed to enjoy, or at least pretend to enjoy, the things she didn't want to do.

Jana stood. "Just . . . please don't make things more complicated for me and Anil, okay? Stop telling people we were married."

Mom nodded as she put her necklace on. "Of course, beta. I always want things to be easier for you."

Another way that Jana was different from her mother—they appeared to have wildly different definitions of *easier*.

Jana brought Imani with her to Kamila's for the mehndi night, but after about five minutes, Imani complained that they were all being too noisy for her to watch *PAW Patrol*, so Jana set Imani up with her iPad in the extra bedroom of Kamila's suite. She put the last of Mom's samosas and a salad on a plate for Imani's dinner. Jana had no idea what Imani would eat for the rest of the trip.

"She can spend the night there if she falls asleep," Kamila said as Jana came back in the sitting room where the dining table had been set up. "That bedroom is empty. Rohan's parents insisted we needed two bedrooms because we can't share before we're married. Like we haven't lived together for three years now. But I don't care what kind of room we're in...as long as there's a bed. A big bed. And a bathtub. A stand-up shower. A—"

"Too much information," Shelina interrupted. "You're marrying my brother-in-law. This is gross."

Kamila grinned at her sister. "I would think that you'd be happy that both your sister and brother-in-law are being satisfied physically." Kamila took a bite of food and moaned with appreciation. Dinner was biryani, with fragrant chunks of goat and potato nestled in vibrant spiced rice. Kamila appeared to have given up on her fruit-only diet.

Shelina turned to Jana. "Why doesn't Anil keep Imani tonight? You should have brought an au pair like I did." Shelina flashed her smug mom smile. Being a stay-at-home mom had always been Shelina's lifelong dream. And yet it didn't surprise Jana that Shelina had a full-time nanny.

"She's not an *au pair*. She's a nanny from Newfoundland," Kamila said. "Not that there is anything wrong with Newfoundland, but *au pair* implies some European waif who's teaching your kids Parisian French or something. Your nanny is teaching them sea shanties."

Yuriko snorted a laugh. Kamila's suite was a bit more spacious than Jana's, so the table adorned with white roses and gold tableware fit nicely in the sitting room. Elsie and her team had transformed the whole space to resemble a luxury spa that rivaled the one in the Four Seasons in Toronto. Around them, small nail and mehndi stations were ready for their pampering, each with big flower arrangements and stacks of plush white towels. There was even soothing music coming from somewhere. But the effect was far from relaxing to Jana.

Shelina did have a point—Anil could have stayed with Imani tonight. But until Jana figured out what Anil wanted to say to her at breakfast two days ago, she wasn't going to ask him for a favor.

This whole trip had been minefield after minefield, but she was determined to appear like she was enjoying it. "Hey, can I ask you all something?" Jana said, realizing that these women might be just the ones who could help her. "If I wanted to try to be more...*social*, like, let loose a bit, how would I do that?"

Yuriko smiled. "You should come to my dungeon when we get home!"

Jana's eyes narrowed at her. *Dungeon?*

Kamila giggled. "No, what you *should* have done was come to Amsterdam with us. Pimping a dildo is the *definition* of letting loose."

At that, Jana spit out a mouthful of onion-cucumber salad. *What?*

"Easy there," Nicole said, handing Jana a cloth napkin.

"That reminds me, Jana—Nicole and I pimped a dildo for you," Asha said. "Since you couldn't be there and all. Nicole and I don't need two, so we had an extra. Kamila, what did you do with that dildo we made for Jana?"

"Ooh, it's in here somewhere." Kamila stood suddenly, briefly wiping her mouth with a napkin, and then rushed to her bedroom.

Jana took the opportunity to find out what the hell was going on. "Okay, what exactly did you make for me in Amsterdam?" Maybe a banjo? Bongo? Bilbo Baggins?

"A dildo," Yuriko said, chewing. "We did a 'pimp my dildo' workshop in the red-light district. It's a popular bachelorette party activity."

"What does that even mean?" Jana asked.

Yuriko grinned. "We painted phalluses. Glued some rhinestones on dicks. Glitter, too. You know."

Jana most definitely did not know. She'd never been happier to miss a party in her life.

"Don't be alarmed," Nicole said. "It's not a real dildo. It's not safe for human...use."

"As my gynecologist wife reminded us every thirty seconds while we were there," Asha said.

Nicole rolled her eyes and laughed at Asha.

Shelina giggled. "Did anyone find out what the men were doing while we were in the painting party? Did they have a 'pimp my vagina' session?" She wagged her brows suggestively.

Nicole cringed. "The word you're looking for is *vulva*...and the thought of any adhesive substance that isn't an FDA-approved sterile surgical bond coming anywhere near a vulva—real or simulated—reminds me too much of the vajazzle trend of the early 2010s. *No thank you.*" She shuddered just as Kamila returned to the sitting room with a paper bag that she handed to Jana.

"Your souvenir from the bachelorette party," Kamila said.

Gingerly, Jana reached inside. And there was indeed a painted penis in it. Tastefully decorated, at least, with crisp lines of muted gray and navy blue. They'd even added a few tiny rhinestones to accentuate focal areas. It was the most elegant penis Jana had ever seen.

Jana quickly put the penis back into the bag. What the hell was she supposed to do with this thing?

Kamila picked her spoon back up. "Want me to see if there is something similar to do here so you can let loose, too? I'm doubting it would be as good—Tanzania is a pretty conservative country. But Elsie can make anything happen."

Jana shook her head. "No! That is *not* the kind of letting loose I meant." Jana sighed, looking out the window briefly, then at the five women at the table. "Something more... I really need that job. Dr. Lopez is looking for me to be a team player. He said he wants to hire someone *vibrant*."

"So just be vibrant," Shelina said. She popped a potato in her mouth.

Jana exhaled. "That's exactly what my mom said."

Asha tilted her head at Jana. "It's okay that you're quiet. Quiet people make great employees."

Jana shrugged. "It's not that I'm quiet. It's that I'm grumpy. I want him to see me as easygoing, adaptable, and fun."

That was just one of Jana's objectives for this trip—to be seen as *fun*. The other objective, to be seen as *over* Anil Malek, she wasn't going to ask for help with because she didn't want anyone to know Anil still affected her so much. "I'm asking for some suggestions on how to seem more *dynamic*. Not racy. I want to let loose."

"We can totally help with that," Asha said. "We are the loosest girls in the Serengeti." She frowned. "That did not come out as I expected it to."

"We are the letting loosest?" Kamila suggested.

Nicole snorted. "Still not sure about that phrasing."

"What kind of person does he want on his team?" Yuriko asked.

Jana listed the traits Dr. Lopez mentioned in the interview. "A lively team player. Someone comfortable speaking in front of an audience. Someone willing to take risks. Someone compassionate. A good communicator."

There was a knock on the door of the suite then. It was Elsie, plus a hotel maid, the mehndi artist, and the aesthetician. While they efficiently cleaned up dinner and set up the room for the spa session, Jana checked in on Imani, who had eaten the samosas and was watching *The Lion King* again.

Later, as Kamila was getting her bridal mehndi on her feet, she clapped her hands together. "Okay, Jana, let's get back to your problem. Grab your planner and start a 'letting loose' list."

Jana frowned. "A 'letting loose' list?" Could someone change their entire personality using a to-do list?

Asha grinned. "Ooh, great idea. I have your first item!"

Jana wasn't sure about this idea but grabbed her planner and opened a blank page. She wrote *Let Loose in Tanzania* at the top.

"Okay," Jana said.

"Dance Bollywood style at the sangeet," Asha said, grinning.

Jana frowned. "How is that going to get me a job?"

"Lots of ways. We're at a wedding—a team player social person would most definitely dance at a wedding. Plus, dancing Bollywood will show the man you're in touch with your culture, and since he wants you as a South Asian development specialist, that's a good thing. And it proves that you are comfortable being on a stage."

Jana hadn't danced for years. But she had taken five years of Bollywood-style dance lessons as a kid with Kamila and Shelina. She was rusty but capable of this. She wrote *dance Bollywood style* as item one.

"I have one, too," Nicole said. "Sing."

"Sing what?"

"Sing anything…with the brigade. In front of others. Vibrant people always sing. I love karaoke."

Jana shook her head. "I'm a terrible singer."

Shelina snorted. "You don't want to do something you're bad at?"

Kamila glared at her sister. "You're a fine singer," she said to Jana.

"I'm really not," Jana said. Dancing she could do. But she sang like a cat with laryngitis.

"Just write it," Asha said. "You don't have to do everything on the list... It's just there as inspiration. Think of it like your vibrant mood board."

Jana reluctantly wrote *sing in front of others* on the list.

"Wear a color!" Shelina said. "Something you choose yourself, not something picked out for you for the wedding events."

Jana frowned, looking at her beige pants and black T-shirt. She added it to the list.

Yuriko grinned. "I have one! Go skinny-dipping!"

The entire brigade looked at Yuriko quizzically.

"Don't swim naked in Tanzania," Namrata, the mehndi artist, said.

"Seriously, listen to her," Kamila shook her head. "Any watering hole here is hippo infested. Those things are nasty. You know, there are more hippo-related fatalities in East Africa than any other animal."

Namrata raised one confused eyebrow at Kamila. "I meant because it's illegal? And wrong."

"Actually," Jana said, "there are more *mosquito*-related fatalities than any other animal in the world."

Nicole nodded. "True. Malaria. But... are mosquitos animals?"

Yuri shrugged. "Skinny-dipping was in the small-town romance I was reading earlier. That's how the main character let loose."

"Well, I'm not going to swim naked." Jana couldn't even imagine what her mother would say about that. Or the aunties. "I'm trying to get a job here."

"But you don't specifically have to do it. It's inspiration," Kamila said.

"I am *specifically* telling you *not* to do it," Namrata said.

"What about swimming in the bikini Kamila got you?" Asha suggested.

Jana shrugged. She wasn't really a bikini person and wasn't planning on using that swimsuit, but she added it to the list. As inspiration. It was better than skinny-dipping.

Shelina waved her hand in the air, which made the aesthetician, who was painting her nails, scowl. "I have another one! Hook up with a strange man."

Jana frowned. These ladies seemed to have missed the point of this list. "Um, no, thank you." Hooking up with a strange man was what got her into this mess in the first place.

"What about just flirt?" Asha asked. "When Sam Uncle isn't around, of course. You're single and carefree and on holiday... why not?"

Jana shook her head. She couldn't imagine flirting with someone in front of Anil.

"How about have a long conversation with a stranger? And not about the wedding or your work. Show you're personable and confident," Nicole suggested. Jana nodded, writing it down.

Namrata suddenly stretched her arms. "There. All done."

They all crowded around to look at Kamila's finished feet. "This is so beautiful," Jana said. The intricate, lacelike design on both of Kamila's feet was breathtaking. "I hope it wasn't a huge inconvenience to come all the way to Serengeti for this."

Namrata snorted. "Are you kidding? Serengeti weddings are the dream. It's worth the drive from Nairobi."

That led to a conversation about how far Nairobi was from the Serengeti. Then Asha told them about a club that served game meat she'd gone to as a teenager, which led to a discussion about the nightlife in East Africa. Jana tuned them out and nibbled on fruit. She had nothing to add in a discussion about nightclubs.

"I don't think we'll be going to any clubs," Kamila said, "but I have another item for your list, Jana. Be the last one up at night. I mean, obviously assuming your mother or Anil has put Imani to bed. But if you're able to, stay up late and close the bar with us."

Jana hated staying up late but wrote it down anyway.

In the end, there were six items on Jana's "letting loose" list. She was pretty sure she wouldn't end up doing them all, especially the singing, but this was just inspiration.

Something had to change in her life, and pretending to enjoy these things might be the way to jump-start that change.

CHAPTER 10

It was past ten by the time Jana left the mehndi party in Kamila's suite. The others were staying, of course, talking, sipping cocktails, and enjoying themselves. But Imani was exhausted, and now that Jana's own mehndi was done, it was time to get her daughter into her own bed. But with both Jana's and Imani's hands wet with mehndi paste, Jana couldn't carry her daughter back to their suite. She couldn't even hold the child's hand. Jana got about three doors from Kamila's, encouraging her sleepy daughter to keep walking, before Imani just stopped, whining for her mommy to pick her up.

"Baby, I can't. I don't want to smudge my mehndi before the wedding." It was already risky since Jana had so many bags hanging off her arms—her own purse, Imani's backpack with her iPad and headphones, plus the bag with the dildo in it. Jana had no idea why she agreed to take that thing with her.

"But I'm tired!"

Jana didn't blame her. She was also tired and cranky.

"Mini! Are you okay?" Someone came out of a nearby hotel room. Anil, of course. He was dressed casually in a green short-sleeve shirt that brought out the pale halo in the irises of his brown eyes.

Jana took a deep breath, ignoring the goosebumps on her skin. "She's fine. Just tired."

"Daddy, Mommy won't carry me," Imani whined, putting her arms up for her father to hold her.

Anil lifted Imani, arms barely flexing with the weight. Imani immediately rested her head on his shoulder but kept her hands in the air so she wouldn't smudge her own mehndi. He chuckled, rubbing Imani's back. "We were all in Zayan's room." He indicated the door he'd just come from. "I heard her."

Of course. He probably thought Jana was a terrible mother. She held out one hand to show Anil, which caused the dildo bag to slide to her elbow. "We have fresh mehndi. I couldn't pick her up."

He smiled. "No worries. I get it. You could have called me if you needed help."

No, Jana could not have. She wasn't going to go out of her way to spend more time with him.

"Where's your room?" he asked, then held out his empty hand. "Here—let me take your things."

Jana merely stared at him, knowing she'd say the wrong thing if she spoke.

"I can hold this," he said again, his hand on the handle of the bag with the dildo in it hanging off her elbow.

Dildo.

There was a painted, bedazzled dildo in the bag Anil Malek was trying to take off her arm.

"I'll hold it," Jana snapped, taking a step away from him.

Anil stared at her for several long seconds, eyes intense. She had no idea what he was thinking. She had no idea if he was going to try to take the bag from her, which could cause a bit of a scuffle and smudge her mehndi. And probably cause the penis to roll down the hotel hallway. Well, the testicles would probably prevent the rolling. It would likely just stand there erect on the floor. And Jana would be deader than dead.

Finally, thankfully, he turned and started walking down the hallway. "Where's your room?" he said curtly. Because now he was annoyed with her. Because Jana was incapable of having a normal conversation.

Jana had no choice but to guide Anil to her suite. He even had to take her key card out of her purse and open the door, since Jana was useless with her mehndi hands.

When they were in Jana's suite, Anil offered to get Imani ready for bed to preserve Jana's mehndi.

"Okay. Thank you. Imani can probably wash off her mehndi paste now." The color would be darker if Imani left the paste on overnight, but there was no way she'd sleep like that. Jana carefully took the bags off her arm, hiding the dildo bag with the souvenirs she'd bought the day before. She went into the bedroom to see if Anil needed help finding Imani's pajamas.

The door to the en suite bathroom was open, and Jana could see Imani sitting on the counter with her hands in the sink, and Anil gently rinsing off the paste while telling Imani about his night. Jana froze, mesmerized by their conversation.

Apparently, the Groom's Platoon had left the resort for dinner, and there had been monkeys all over the grounds of the restaurant they went to. Imani was listening intently to her father tell her about them, which made Jana wonder if Anil always spoke to her about his day this way.

It was strange seeing them carrying out what was obviously a routine for them. Jana was closer to Imani than anyone in the world, and Imani was clearly as close to her father as she was to her mother. But Jana was hardly close to Anil. As Jana watched him do something mundane and domestic with their daughter, it was difficult to feel detached from him.

Anil was such a doting father. He was so gentle with Imani. He loved her as much as Jana did and seeing that love in front of her made a warm glow spread through Jana, which was disconcerting.

She was supposed to be getting over this man on this trip. Seeing him daily certainly wasn't helping with that.

Thankfully, Anil didn't linger or expect Jana to talk to him after Imani was tucked into bed. Which was best. Being alone with him...in a hotel...was bringing back feelings Jana didn't want to revisit.

The sangeet party, which would include the puro and pithi ceremonies, was the traditional pre-wedding event in their culture. Jana had been to many, and they were usually exuberant, boisterous affairs with music, dancing, and lots of food. She dreaded them.

But Jana did concede that the bride looked utterly breathtaking tonight. For the marriage ceremony the next day, Kamila and the bridesmaids would be wearing simple Western dresses, so tonight the dress code was full-on Indian glam. Kamila was wearing an elaborate yellow-and-magenta lehenga covered with gold embroidery and finished with heavy gold jewelry. Her hair was in cascading curls draped to one side, and her makeup was done with shimmering jewel tones and a deep magenta lipstick. She looked better than any of the brides in the Bollywood movies she and Rohan showed at their weekly movie nights. Rohan also looked amazing in his fitted charcoal sherwani. Jana and the rest of the Bridal Brigade were in deep magenta geor-gette saris with open-backed blouses and wide gold embroidery on the hem. And the groomsmen looked dapper in their gray kurta sets.

But in Jana's opinion, Imani really stole the show. Her purple-and-yellow lehenga was like a miniature version of Kamila's, and her curly hair was down instead of in her normal braids. Jana was convinced that there was nothing cuter in Africa than her daughter and couldn't stop taking pictures of her while the guests were finding their way into the banquet hall.

"Mommy, you come be in the picture!"

"I'll take it," someone behind Jana said. She turned and saw it was Marc Ainsworth—one of Rohan's groomsmen. Jana handed him her phone and stood with Imani.

"I can't get both of your outfits...Maybe pick her up?" Marc suggested.

Jana shook her head. There were dozens of hidden pins hold-ing her sari together, and picking up a squirmy four-year-old could mean either a pin in her hip or a wardrobe malfunction with the whole sari ending up puddled on the floor.

"I got her," Anil said, hoisting Imani into his arms. Of course, Imani grinned as if Mufasa himself had lifted her. "Daddy!"

Anil kissed Imani's forehead and stood next to Jana, posing for a picture. Jana wanted to step away. This felt way too much like a family portrait for her taste. But there was no better way to show everyone she was fine with Anil, so she needed to grin and bear it. But still. His arm that was holding Imani brushed against Jana, making her skin pebble. She stood rigidly as Marc motioned them to get even closer. Anil had pushed up the sleeves of his kurta, a devastatingly handsome yet casual look that made Jana's knees weaken. She decided it would be best if she avoided more contact with that solid, bare forearm, so she didn't move.

"Smile!" Marc said.

Jana *did* smile—or at least she faked it, trying not to think about the fact that this would be the first picture in existence of just the three of them together. They didn't even have a picture together from the hospital—not that Anil was in the room for Imani's birth, but Jana did let him in once the baby was all cleaned up and wrapped in a blanket. He must have taken about five hundred pictures of his new daughter that day, but none of Jana. That had been one of Jana's rules. They were co-parents—not a family. No matter what Anil seemed to think.

But on this trip, they *were* a family. Or at least Jana was pretending they were.

The moment Marc was done, Jana took two large steps away from Anil. Imani was gleefully showing Anil the mehndi on her arm and pointing out all the cartoon characters Namrata had drawn on her.

"There's Peppa Pig, and here's Dora, and look, Daddy! Here's Minnie Mouse, like my name! I can show it to Minnie Mouse when I go to Disney."

Just like the night before, the two of them were focused only on each other. Anil was fully engrossed in his daughter's description of her mehndi. A lot of adults didn't really know how to communicate with four-year-olds. Even parents. They weren't quite toddlers, but not quite kids yet, either. One needed to come down to their level but not treat them like babies. Anil was so good at it.

Because of course he was. He was great at talking to anyone. But it was a weird, unsettled feeling seeing the person who sat in the villain or asshole category in Jana's mind being so patient with her daughter.

Whatever. Right now, she needed to get Imani and Anil separated because Dr. Lopez and Farzana Aunty were either already in this banquet hall or would be soon. And Jana assumed Farzana Aunty would love to meet Jana's friendly "ex-husband" and talk to him about their aspirational "divorce." This whole situation was a ridiculous balancing act. She wanted Dr. Lopez to see her as a vibrant, fun person, and she wanted everyone to think she was over Anil and the past. But she also needed to keep Farzana Aunty away from Anil so he wouldn't find out that everyone thought they were divorced and embarrass her mother. This vacation was far from relaxing.

Shelina came to the rescue. "There you are, Imani. Come— I need the photographer to get a picture of you with Adam— he looks so cute in his baby kurta!" Shelina beamed at Jana. "Wouldn't it be cute if one day we could show this picture at *their* wedding? We should make them get married."

Jana made a face. Why would anyone imagine the wedding of four-year-olds?

"We're not *making* Imani get married to anyone," Anil informed Shelina. "If she wants to get married at all, that is."

He looked very irritated at Shelina's comment. More than Jana, actually. Jana watched him curiously—*irritated* was probably too weak a word here. His hands were flexed, and his face had reddened.

"Mommy didn't get married, and Mommy is smart, so I'm not getting married," Imani announced. "Or I'm going to marry Thomas the Train."

Thank goodness Mom and the aunties hadn't heard that. Also, thank goodness for adorable little girls breaking tension. Anil laughed and rubbed Imani's shoulder. "I don't think you can marry a train, kiddo."

After Imani left with Shelina, Jana started to walk away when Anil put his hand on her arm for a half second. Maybe longer. It certainly felt like longer. Jana's eyes fluttered shut for a moment when his hand came in contact with her bare skin.

He gestured to Imani. "She looks so grown-up."

Jana watched Imani walking with Shelina, her long lehenga skirt skimming the floor. She did look older in that outfit. Not the baby she still was in Jana's mind.

"Not a baby anymore," he continued. He looked at Jana. "Still making that face like you smell a dirty diaper when I talk to you, huh?"

"I don't make a face." She wasn't even annoyed at him at this moment. Jana couldn't win here.

He snorted. "You do. You are now."

Jana tried to look pleasant but probably looked confused. "I'm not intentionally making a face."

Anil laughed then, which completely lit him up and made it hard for Jana to be mad at him. It would be hard for *anyone* to be mad at that smile. Maybe Jana should be trying to emulate Anil to be seen as *vibrant*.

"She wrote her own name last week," Jana said.

Somehow Anil's face got even brighter. "Her whole name?"

Jana nodded. "Imani Rosemin Suleiman Malek. She ran out of space halfway through so Malek is on the next page."

He beamed. "She's brilliant. I mean, I didn't expect anything else with you as her mother."

Jana didn't know what to say to the compliment, so she said nothing.

"Oh, I forgot to tell you," he said, "we went to this fancy

restaurant in another resort for a tasting menu last night, and the chef had made this peanut-coconut brittle with cardamon and chilies. I had them pack some up for you because I know you love anything peanut."

Jana frowned. She *did* love peanuts. Especially in desserts. But he'd already brought her that peanut butter candy bar... Was he going to continue to shower her with peanuts all over Tanzania? "Why did you do that?"

He shrugged. "Because it was easy to." He glanced around the heavily decorated hall. "Can you believe all this? I wonder how many mosquito nets they could have bought with the money this party cost."

Jana chuckled. "I was thinking the same thing. I guess it's good to pour money into the economy, though. Apparently, this hotel hires a lot of local villagers. I was chatting with a porter earlier—he's a warrior in his tribe."

"I do get how tourism is important for the local economy, and I know these places do a lot of good work for both conservation and human development, but it still feels jarring to be on the other side of it. Gorgeous wedding, though."

She agreed completely. On one hand, Jana knew logically that this one wedding wasn't having a negative impact on the big picture, but after working in development for so long, this felt strange.

And also? It was strange to be having a conversation like this with Anil again. For a moment, it felt like they were back in London talking about the economics of development. "Anil, the other day at breakfast, what were you going to say? You said you were hoping that..."

He looked at her for several long moments, but Jana couldn't read his expression. His mask was firmly on. "Let's save that conversation for later, okay?" He chuckled. "I don't want that look of yours to come back."

Jana didn't want to make that face—whatever it was—either. She wanted to talk about development and about Imani learning to do up her own shoes and ask him how that private dinner was. But what she wanted to say and what she actually said apparently weren't in sync.

She noticed Dr. Lopez and Farzana Aunty walking into the room.

Jana turned back to Anil and said, "I gotta go. Bridesmaid duties." She rushed to the other bridesmaids who were preparing for the events to start.

Kamila and Rohan had combined the puro ceremonies, which were traditionally done by the bride's side, with the pithi ceremonies, which were by the groom's side. Traditionally, the groom's family would bring in the bride's trousseau, but Jana knew the elaborately wrapped packages Rohan's parents were carrying into the hall were not filled with fancy Indian clothes and jewelry but instead hotel towels. Kamila insisted there was no point in bringing things to the other side of the world just to show off.

Jana's mother was standing in for Kamila's mother to welcome the Nasser family to the Hussain family since Kamila's mother had passed away years ago. This was funny to Jana because all three families had known each other for years. Long before Rohan or Kamila had been born. Plus, this was the second Hussain/Nasser wedding.

But Mom was in her element up there. Smiling in her sari. Talking and laughing with everyone. Belonging with the family. Weddings were Mom's happy place.

After the blessings at the door, the event dissolved into being like pretty much all of Kamila's gatherings—a boisterous party full of delicious food, loud music, and louder talking. Jana was determined to at least appear to enjoy herself.

After the dance floor had been busy for a while, Asha appeared next to Jana at their table.

"C'mon, Jana. It's time to check an item off your list."

Jana had no choice... She went with Asha, glad at least that they wanted her to dance, not sing. She could do a little Bollywood freestyle then escape back to her table.

But when the DJ put on the song "Mehndi Laga Ke Rakhna," Jana knew two things: one, Kamila was behind this scheme, and two, a little light Bollywood freestyle wasn't what they had in mind. Although this was a popular Indian wedding song, Kamila, Shelina, and Jana had been in countless competitions dancing to this very song with their dance troupe as kids. They'd spent months perfecting the choreography—and Kamila knew Jana would still have the moves memorized. Jana looked out and saw many guests had stopped what they were doing to watch them. Including Sam Lopez and Farzana Aunty.

Jana could do this. She took a deep breath, kicked off her shoes, and hiked and tucked her sari. She'd said she wanted to get out of her comfort zone, so she intended to do that. Jana stood next to Kamila and Shelina on the dance floor, closed her eyes, and let the fast beat pound through her until muscle memory took over.

With Kamila taking the lead, Jana stomped, twirled, and swayed to the music, shocked that her body still knew what to do. Shelina and Kamila remembered more of the moves, but the three of them were still mostly in sync. Jana was stiffer than she used to be, and definitely more out of breath, but with the music in her ears and the wood floor beneath her feet, everything else melted away. She'd completely forgotten how much she *loved* dancing. She didn't need to think about what to say, or worry about what people were thinking of her—she could just tune out the world and let the music control her actions. Jana was smiling when the song ended, and everyone gave the three of them a standing ovation. She laughed, hugging Kamila and Shelina.

There. The first item on the "letting loose" list easily checked off. And it felt really good.

Jana noticed then that Anil was looking at her with a curious expression. Like he had no idea what he was looking at. Or who. Jana glanced away quickly, finding her shoes.

When the DJ switched to the Macarena, Jana escaped the dance floor. There were limits to how much letting loose she'd do. She found a quiet corner to catch her breath.

"Enjoyable party," said a voice behind her. It was Dr. Lopez. Jana quickly put her job interview smile on.

"Yes! I wouldn't expect anything less from Kamila," Jana said.

"She's such a delight." He stepped closer. "I really enjoyed your dance. You have many talents!"

Jana smiled. "Oh, thank you. I really love Indian dancing. It's a great way to connect to my culture."

"I'm thoroughly impressed. Now that I finally have you alone, Dr. Suleiman, I wanted to reassure you that I haven't told anyone at the wedding that I interviewed you last week. Not even my Farzana knows. As you know, I am only one member of the selection committee at Think, and the board will have input on the final decision, so really, us being together here should have no bearing on your application."

"Thank you, Dr. Lopez."

He nodded. "I did inform the HR department that I was unexpectedly on holiday with one of the applicants when I first saw you. I don't want anyone accusing me of bias. Thankfully, I'd already given them my short list to start the process of getting references and background checks. Please, just think of me as a wedding guest, nothing else." He indicated toward Kamila on the dance floor. "I understand you grew up with Kamila and Rohan?"

Jana nodded. "Yes. Our fathers started a company together soon after moving to Canada. And we all used to travel together. We even came here to Tanzania when I was fifteen."

He smiled. "I don't know how I didn't make the connection when I first interviewed you. I remember meeting your parents around the time I was first married. And of course, I had just met your mother again several weeks ago. She spoke to Farzana more, though, and no one mentioned you were in development."

Jana smiled. "My mother said she enjoyed meeting you."

He said nothing for a few moments while they watched the dancers. Tim and Asha were patiently trying to teach Imani the Macarena.

"It's wonderful how they're all there for your daughter," Dr. Lopez said. "It takes a village, and clearly you have an extremely supportive one."

Jana nodded. "She's a lucky girl."

"I remember from your resume that you headed a project here in East Africa. It sounded like a fascinating endeavor. You were working with a hospital system, right?"

Thank God—work was one topic she could talk about without feeling like a fish flopping at the bottom of a boat. She nodded, and they spoke for several minutes about the sexual health project she'd helped launch in Kenya years ago.

"I have to say, I am impressed, Dr. Suleiman. I've never met someone as young as you who has already made such an impact."

This was going so well. Dr. Lopez may have said that their

being on the same trip would have no impact on Jana getting this job, but Jana disagreed. She *felt* vibrant, and she was confident that Dr. Lopez was seeing the dynamic, lively team player he wanted to hire.

Eventually, Mom took Imani up to their room to sleep. Jana even danced again—nothing fancy, but she joined the Bridal Brigade for a Taylor Swift song. After that, she decided she deserved a reward for all her letting loose and found herself a cup of tea and sat at her empty table.

She wasn't alone for long, though. Nicole was sitting with her in minutes.

She gave Jana a tired smile. "I'm too old for this. I thought my bridesmaid days were over when I turned forty."

Jana chuckled. She liked Nicole. Nicole was Black, with shoulder-length curls and warm brown eyes. Most of the time, Jana forgot Nicole was the oldest member of the Bridal Brigade, because Jana herself felt that way.

"This is my first time as a bridesmaid," Jana said.

"Where's Imani?" Nicole asked.

"Mom took her to bed. She has to be somewhat functional at the wedding tomorrow."

Nicole shrugged. "At least there won't be dancing, then. Just the ceremony, then dinner. Tame in comparison." Nicole's brow furrowed. "Tame . . . except that it will be in the middle of a game park surrounded by wild animals."

Jana shook her head. Why the ceremony was happening out in the wild was a mystery. Jana wasn't afraid of predators. She was more afraid of . . . chaos. Nasty vultures fighting over an animal carcass. Imani getting cranky. Being downwind of smelly wildebeests.

"It's certainly going to be memorable, though," Nicole continued. "Unlike my wedding. I don't think anyone remembers anything about that North Markham banquet hall." Nicole turned to look at Jana, head tilted. "You okay tonight? You don't seem yourself."

Jana frowned. Well, no—she wasn't herself. She was dancing and talking and trying to keep what Anil called her dirty-diaper expression off her face. She quickly changed her frown to a smile.

"I'm having fun." She chuckled a bit. "A little out of my element, but I'm trying."

Nicole laughed. "I'm a lot out of my element." She looked over to the dance floor, where Kamila, Asha, and Tim were holding hands and spinning in a circle with Jerome in the middle for some reason. "You know, I never would have imagined I'd end up with someone like Ash. I thought I'd be a single cat lady forever. It's amazing how when new people come into your life, they kind of change what your element is. The hardest part is taking that first step, though. Then everything is seamless." She shook her head. "Don't mind me—it's unbelievable that I'm here in Tanzania as a bridesmaid in this big wedding that's not even my family, or my own culture. You know half my family didn't come to my wedding? The 'Christian' half was not impressed I married a Hindu lesbian." Nicole made air quotes around the word Christian.

"Ugh. That's horrible."

"It is what it is." She paused. "What did you decide to do about your mother?"

"What do you mean?"

"About her telling everyone you were married."

Jana shrugged. "I told her to stop...and not to say anything to Anil. I doubt she'll listen, though."

"Can't you tell everyone the truth?"

Jana shook her head. "I can't break her bubble. She's not going to get this kind of wedding for her own daughter."

"She should be proud of you as you are."

Jana shrugged again.

The music changed then, and a slow song came on. It was "Can You Feel the Love Tonight" from *The Lion King*. Very cheesy, but Jana had to expect it, considering where they were. It was too bad Imani was missing it.

Nicole hopped to her feet. "That's my and Asha's song!" She was on the dance floor in seconds. Soon everyone was paired for the romantic dance—everyone except Jana. She picked up the elephant at her place setting. It was a beauty—smooth black wood and big ears. Jana had always loved elephants—probably because her dad had loved them. When she was little, he used to call her his tiny elephant because she loved peanuts. She still had several wooden elephants from Dad at home.

Anil suddenly appeared, sitting in the empty chair next to hers. Jana was exhausted, so she didn't even try not to make the dirty-diaper expression this time.

"Ah. The fifth-wheel table," he said.

Rohan also had a married couple among his groomsmen, Kamila's and his friends Tim and Jerome. And Marc was dancing with Yuriko (Jana wondered if he knew about her *dungeon*), so the entire Bridal Brigade and Groom's Platoon had been neatly coupled off...minus Anil and Jana.

"How are you enjoying the party?" Anil asked.

"It's fine."

He chuckled. "I had no idea you could dance like that. We

should put Imani into Bollywood lessons. Maybe she inherited your rhythm."

"Sure. I'll look for a teacher when we get home."

He smiled, looking at Rohan and Kamila, who were dancing cheek to cheek to the Disney song. "Did you think they'd finally go through with it? I feel like they've been engaged forever."

"It's only been three years."

Anil shrugged. "That's a long engagement. I was only engaged for six months. I assume *you'd* want a long and torturous engagement."

Jana hadn't known that he and Nadia had only been engaged for six months. If this were any other person in the world, Jana would ask what the rush had been. But also...why did he assume Jana would want a long engagement? And *torturous*? She was trying to be nice, and he was...baiting her. Like he wanted her to snap at him.

Was he still bitter she'd turned down his marriage proposal? She'd been four months pregnant when he asked her to marry him. And she assumed he would have wanted to marry before Imani was born. That would have been even shorter than his six-month engagement with Nadia. Would they have had the time to plan a big wedding like this? Would either of them have wanted one? But of course, they would have had to wait until he was divorced...They couldn't have had a fast wedding.

This. This was what was *torturous*...Anil making her think about things she hadn't thought about in years.

"Why would you think I'd want a long engagement?" she asked. "And *torturous*? Really?"

He smiled widely, and it was so charming and amiable and so...*attractive*. It took everything in Jana not to get up and walk away from him. "Are you kidding me?" he said. "I know you, Jana Suleiman. You're a little fussy, very hard to please, and most of all, you're *uncompromising*. You can't do anything if not perfectly. Your engagement would be long because you'd want the wedding just right. And it would be torturous for the person who was waiting for you."

Jana snorted, shaking her head. "Have you always been this cocky? You don't know me nearly as well as you think you do. Remembering that I like peanuts isn't *knowing* me."

Something flashed over his face that Jana couldn't decipher. He said he knew everything about her, and sometimes she felt like she knew everything about him. She knew where he was most of the time. She knew his homemade macaroni and cheese was creamier than hers and that he only ate fruit at home in smoothie form. She knew when he read books to Imani, he made silly voices and that he frequented garage sales when Imani wasn't with him to find books and toys for her. But all this information about him was filtered through a doting four-year-old.

She didn't *really* know him anymore. She had no idea what he was thinking or feeling inside. She thought she had once, but she'd been wrong.

"I'm sorry," he finally said, rubbing the back of his neck. "I think you're right. Maybe I don't know you. I didn't know you could dance like that. Let's start this conversation over. I want to make a request about Imani," he said. "I was going to wait until we were back home, but now is as good a time as any."

This was about whatever he'd been talking about at breakfast a few days ago. She braced herself. Did he want to take Imani to D.C. for a few months while he launched that start-up? Or maybe…was it possible that Anil was seeing someone, and he wanted to tell Jana before introducing the person to Imani? Her hands fisted.

"Okay, then. What exactly do you want?" she asked.

He looked straight at her. "Disney World."

Jana blinked. With the Disney song still playing, she wondered if she'd misheard him. "Did you say Disney?"

He nodded.

"You want to take her to Disney before me? You know I'm planning to next year."

He shook his head. "No. I want *us* to take her. I want to come when you go."

Jana's eyes widened. "What? Anil, that's ridiculous! We don't go on family vacations together!"

"It's not ridiculous. Look at us—we are *literally* on a family vacation right now. I want to be there when Imani sees Mickey, Minnie, and Darth Vader for the first time, just like your parents took you, and my parents took me."

"Disney didn't own Star Wars when we were kids!"

He ignored that very good point. "I want to be there to help you with her. Disney is a lot without another parent."

"There is nothing wrong with single parenting."

"Of course there isn't. But you know she can be challenging when she's overstimulated. And she'll be happier with us both there. You're an excellent mother, and you'd do fine, but this will make it easier for you."

Jana made a face then. Why was he complimenting her so much? He *had* to know she wouldn't appreciate it. And why was everyone trying to make things *easier* for her?

"I get it," he said softly. "I know I haven't earned your trust back yet. But Imani isn't a baby anymore. She *notices* that we don't get along. That we never talk. I don't want her remembering me as the absent father. The one her mother hates."

Jana gritted her teeth. "I have never *ever* bad-mouthed you to her. *Never*." They'd agreed on that as part of their deal, but also, she wouldn't do that to her daughter.

He sighed, fidgeting with Asha's gazelle at her place setting. "I *know* you haven't bad-mouthed me. I know." He looked up at her. "Do you have any idea how your utter perfection makes everything so much harder for me?"

Jana scoffed. So, he'd find it easier if she *were* a bad mother?

When Jana told Anil she was pregnant, he immediately insisted that he would be in the baby's life. Jana assumed that meant child support and some visits every couple of weeks. She'd thought Anil would treat being a dad the same way he treated everything: with charm, good humor—and no commitment. But that's not what happened. He'd been there for Imani. He bought a place near Jana's, and insisted on 50 percent custody. He'd dealt with midnight feedings alone, exploding diapers, vomit, tears, doctor's appointments, and everything else. He'd picked Imani up from daycare, taken her to playdates, and figured out kids' birthday party gifting etiquette. He even braided Imani's hair better than Jana had ever been able to do. Anil was the fun dad, but he was also the firm dad. The affectionate dad. The good dad. Imani was so lucky to have him.

Maybe this would be easier for Jana if *he* weren't such a perfect father, too.

But just being a good father wasn't enough for Jana to forgive the man for betraying her five years ago. He was Imani's father—he was *supposed* to be dedicated to his child. And being there for Imani wasn't the same thing as making it up to Jana.

But he'd tried to do that, too. He'd apologized, of course. He'd given her that job at Aim High when she'd needed it. He'd referred her to other jobs, too. He'd defended her and, most importantly, given her space and not insisted they get along.

Until now.

Pretending to move on was hard enough, but actually moving on was a whole different story. There was no way she could agree to a trip to Disney with this man. She didn't want to be *pretending* to be enjoying it. She wanted to make sweet memories with her daughter.

"We're not a couple," she told Anil. "We've never been a couple. Who even goes on holiday with their co-parent?"

He started counting off names on his fingers, some of whom were people Jana knew. It wasn't a surprise—this was the era of conscious uncoupling. Modern co-parenting. But just because all those people could spend time with their exes didn't mean Jana could.

She shook her head. "No. If you want to take her on a trip next year, too, fine. But not Disney before me." It was out of the question.

"Jana!" Kamila said, interrupting their conversation. She sounded like she'd had more than a little of the bottle of champagne from the head table. She was pulling on Rohan's arm, dragging him behind her. "Can you believe I'm going to be *married* tomorrow? Married! To Rohan! I can't even. Did you ever think this would happen when we were kids?"

"Technically, we're already married," Rohan said.

Kamila put her hand over his mouth. "Shhh...I told you that didn't count. *Kamila Hussain's* wedding wasn't at Toronto City Hall." Since they weren't Tanzanian, Kamila and Rohan had had a legal ceremony at home before this trip.

Rohan laughed and pulled Kamila into his arms, whispering something in her ear. Which made Kamila giggle, then blush, then grab her husband-to-be's butt. Or husband's butt, depending on one's interpretation of the situation. Jana shook her head.

Very weird to see her childhood friends groping each other in public.

Her arm still around Rohan's waist, Kamila smiled at Jana. "I want you to be happy like this one day, Jana. You deserve it more than anyone I know. More than me. After everything." She glared at Anil. Seems the champagne was reminding Kamila that she hadn't fully forgiven Anil for lying to Jana and getting her pregnant. Jana appreciated her friend's support.

"It's late. I'm going to get to bed." Jana stood, smiling at Rohan and Kamila. "Congratulations. Kamila is wrong—you two deserve happiness more than anyone. See you tomorrow." She turned to Anil. "Good night, Anil."

Jana left. She had done enough peopling for today.

CHAPTER 11

T hanks to Elsie's otherworldly planning skills, everything went without a hitch the next morning. After the brigade was all primped and primed—Kamila in a beautiful cream lace tea-length full-skirted dress with a wide rose-pink sash, and the bridesmaids in dusty-rose cocktail-length sleeveless crepe dresses—they met up with the Groom's Platoon outside the resort for pictures with the photographer.

"You look nice," Anil said to Jana while the photographer was taking bride and groom shots.

Jana smiled pleasantly at him. "So do you."

She was being honest—he did look nice. He was dressed the same as the rest of the groomsmen, in casual cream dress pants and jackets with white linen shirts and no tie.

Anil nodded toward the bride and groom. Rohan was currently tearing up after seeing Kamila in her wedding dress for the first time. "They look...nice, too."

Jana looked at him with one brow raised. "This conversation is...*nice*," she said.

Anil looked down, chuckling. Jana was glad to confirm he was finding this all as awkward as she was.

Rohan kissed Kamila's hand then, and the whole wedding party cheered, including Jana. After what felt like hundreds of pictures, the wedding party was guided to two Land Cruisers to take them to the wedding site. The rest of the guests would be brought in a tour bus.

The wedding ceremony was being held at two o'clock in a clearing in the middle of Serengeti National Park, about a fifteen-minute drive from the resort. When they got there, Jana looked out the window of the Land Cruiser. The weather was glorious—sunny with a warm breeze, and not a cloud in the sky. Jana was sure that Kamila had sacrificed something to a deity to get such a perfect day for her wedding. There was a large acacia tree in the middle of the clearing and tables scattered around it with white tablecloths fluttering in the breeze. A white tent was off to the side, where Jana assumed the caterers were getting the food ready. Buffet tables lined the perimeter with large silver platters with domed covers. The decoration was pretty much nonexistent—just some white flowers and a very minimalistic white tiered cake.

No other embellishments were needed—just the East African savanna spread as far as the eye could see. Umbrella trees and distant baobab trees. Short and tall grasses. And dust—which normally wouldn't be a welcome addition to a wedding but now only served to add a sepia-toned haze to the space. It was truly magical.

Jana wouldn't have wanted a wedding celebration anything like the sangeet yesterday. But this...the outdoor simplicity was exactly Jana's style. She opened the door to take a deep breath of the Serengeti air. Imani wasn't far from the vehicle, standing with Jana's mother. Jana waved.

"Mommy!" Imani came running to the Land Cruiser. Jana

almost yelled at her daughter to stop running so she wouldn't fall, but Imani was wearing her Minnie Mouse sneakers with her pink flower girl dress, so she'd probably be fine. The shoe choice was because no one wanted an adorable flower girl face-planting in the dirt during the ceremony. The bridesmaids, however, weren't so lucky. Kamila had chosen pink sandals with two-and-a-half-inch cork wedge heels for the brigade. Jana put her arms out for Imani, who hopped into her mother's lap.

"You look pretty, Mommy!" Imani said, hugging Jana. "They put flowers in my hair!"

"They're beautiful flowers!" Everyone in the vehicle cooed over how adorable Imani looked in her floral crown braid. Jana peeked out to scan the rest of the crowd. Her mother was with Kassim Uncle and Nadira Aunty. Dr. Lopez was across the space with some of Rohan's extended family. The groomsmen had gotten out of their Land Cruiser and were mingling. Anil was nowhere near Dr. Lopez, so that was good.

When it was time for the event to start, the groomsmen came to escort the bridesmaids out of their vehicle. Muslim weddings usually consisted of a nikah recitation and blessings, and an officiant had been brought from Nairobi for the ceremony. An acoustic guitarist played a slow tune as the wedding party started walking arm in arm between the tables in their assigned order: Marc and Yuriko, followed by Nicole and Tim, Shelina and Anil, Jana and Jerome, and finally Asha and Zayan. Jana was grateful she wasn't expected to walk with Anil, but she did slightly snicker to herself that none of the actual couples in the wedding party (Asha and Nicole, Shelina and Zayan, and Tim and Jerome) had been paired up. Finally, Imani walked toward the front scattering rose petals.

Jana saw the imminent disaster happening seconds before it

did. Imani had been instructed to walk toward Jana, dropping petals along the way, then give Jana the empty basket. Afterward, she was to sit at the table with Jana's mother. But Imani's eyes were only on one person as she walked down that aisle—her father.

Damn. She should have arranged for Imani to see her father at some point today before this. Imani was totally going to go show Anil her flower crown, or her pretty dress, instead of going to Jana or to Jana's mother. And Farzana Aunty would then mention the moment to him and gush about their amazing conscious uncoupling arrangement, because she was obsessed with divorce. Mom would be mortified, and Dr. Lopez would discover his new employee candidate's family had been lying to him and his partner.

Jana could feel herself sweating as she stood next to the other bridesmaids at the front. She smiled encouragingly at Imani, hoping her daughter would remember that she was supposed to bring Jana the empty basket, then go sit with her nanima, and not get distracted by her father grinning at his daughter like, well, a proud daddy.

Imani did seem to understand that her mother was trying to tell her something with her eyes, though, because she suddenly sped up, rushing to Jana. She upended the basket when she reached her, dumping the white rose petals in a mound right where Kamila and Rohan were supposed to stand for the ceremony. Imani handed Jana the basket and said, "Like that, Mommy?"

The crowd laughed. Jana turned bright red, embarrassed that her daughter had made a scene. Imani giggled, then buried her face in her mother's leg. Jana could feel everyone staring at her daughter. And staring at her.

What were they all thinking? *Oh, there's that little Suleiman-Malek girl. She's so cute. She's Jana Suleiman's daughter, you know... Poor Rashida, having to take in Jana after her divorce.* Or maybe some would think, *You know, that child is illegitimate. The girl's father had an affair with the mother. He was married.*

Jana's fingernails dug into her palms as she tried to calm her heart rate. She hated feeling so exposed. Nausea was building in her stomach, and she felt the prickle of sweat on her back. Jana looked away from her daughter, hoping the ceremony would continue, when she noticed Anil was watching her, and the expression on his face stopped Jana in her tracks. It wasn't, *Oh, look how cute our daughter is,* or, *Oh, how embarrassing,* or even, *You clearly didn't train Imani well enough for this.*

Nope. He looked... concerned. Supportive. He gave Jana an encouraging nod. It was a look that said, *You're doing fine. You got this.* She held his gaze, telling her heart rate to slow and the muscles in her body to relax. She took a breath.

What was he thinking? Jana had thought that this was what she'd want her wedding to look like... Was this also what he would have wanted if she'd said yes that day?

This was torture—being here at a wedding with Anil. Jana tore her gaze away, feeling a sharp prickle behind her eyes.

The guitarist changed songs then, so Jana shooed Imani to go sit with her nanima. It was time for Kamila and Rohan to walk down the aisle. Asha discreetly kicked the mound of flower petals out of the way.

Rohan and Kamila looked incandescently happy walking down the aisle arm in arm. Jana had always known that Kamila and Rohan were perfect together—even when they were all kids. It took them over thirty years to get to this point, and Jana was so thrilled for her friends. But also... Jana didn't think she'd ever felt so alone while surrounded by people. It wasn't that she necessarily wanted to be coupled off like her friends but more that Jana wondered if anyone would ever want to be with her like that.

After the blessings and the nikah recitation, Rohan and Kamila said a few words to each other. It was adorable—Kamila was as confident as ever, but Rohan was completely unable to speak because he kept getting choked up. There was hooting and clapping when the bride and groom kissed, until a giraffe strolled by in front of them and stopped to look for a moment before walking on by. Everyone laughed.

Trays of tropical juices were handed out by a waiter, and Asha made a quick toast, followed by Zayan. And then the wedding ceremony was done. Everyone could mingle, eat, and congratulate the happy couple.

Of course, the food was phenomenal. The previous night at the hotel, they'd been served high-end Indian food, and here at the nikah ceremony, it was casual but delicious Tanzanian nyama choma, which translated to grilled meat. Kebobs, skewers of beef mishkaki, and bright red pili pili chicken were being grilled over charcoal. Fresh masala fries were brought out from the tent in big silver bowls. There were green salads, fragrant spiced rice, and a dessert tray filled with pastries and fruit. Plus, a stunning white cake dotted with simple buttercream roses. Everything looked amazing and tasted even better.

"Isn't it kind of strange to be grilling all this meat in the middle of a game park?" Shelina asked while she and Jana were in line for more pili pili chicken. All the food was good, but this dish had always been one of Jana's favorites.

Jana shrugged. "I doubt the lions care for spicy chicken. Plus, I assume this spot doesn't have a lot of wildlife coming through it. That's why it's used for events."

Elsie, who was nearby, talking to one of the cooks, shook her head. "Oh, there *are* animals here. That's why we brought those guards." She pointed to one of several armed guards who stood around the perimeter of the space. "But we've been doing events here for years. Animals don't intrude on us. They might look, like that giraffe during the ceremony, but we are much too noisy for them to want to come closer. We do sometimes have to clear some animal dung before events."

Shelina made a sour face, then looked down at the ground. "Ew. That's gross." Then she yelled to one of her sons who was sitting on the grass to get up.

Jana wasn't afraid of a little dung. She'd encountered much worse when traveling. "What kind of dung?" she asked, curious.

"Elephant mostly," Elsie answered. "Sometimes herds use this as a corridor to the watering hole. But there's a shorter route that's much more common. You two aren't frightened of wild animals, are you? I can ask Mo over there to stay near you. He's a very sharp shot."

Shelina's eyes widened, clearly horrified at the thought of an armed guard following her. Jana knew the guns were loaded with tranquilizer darts. She also knew that the darts took too long to work to be of much use in a sticky animal-versus-human situation.

"I wouldn't mind seeing some elephants," someone behind them said. Jana turned, then cringed (internally) to see that it was Farzana Aunty with Dr. Lopez. She'd been avoiding them all day. She made a quick scan to see where Anil was. He was quite a distance away with Zayan and Jerome.

"Did you see any on your game drive a few days ago?" Elsie asked Dr. Lopez. Jana fully expected that if the answer was no, Elsie would whip out her cell phone and arrange for someone to take Dr. Lopez to see some pachyderms immediately.

He laughed. "No, none, but there will be opportunities later. I would love to get a picture of an elephant now in the dusk light, though."

"They are our daughter's favorite animal," Farzana said. "She wanted to come along on this trip, but she's planning her own wedding right now."

"Oh, congratulations!" Elsie said. Farzana Aunty and Elsie started talking about the upcoming wedding.

Jana stood awkwardly, smiling at Dr. Lopez.

He smiled back. "Did your daughter enjoy the game drive?"

"Oh yes!" Jana said. "But we didn't see any elephants, either. Poor Imani was expecting to see gorillas." Jana really needed to keep Imani out of her conversations with Dr. Lopez and Farzana Aunty.

Shelina clearly saw no risk in talking about her, though. "Wasn't Imani an adorable flower girl? I wish I had a daughter. But I've heard girls are easier to raise when they're kids but are absolute nightmares as teenagers. Zayan would totally be the dad with the shotgun interviewing his daughter's dates. So sexist, right? Imani's dad wouldn't…" Shelina's voice trailed off as she remembered she shouldn't be mentioning Imani's father in front of these two. Jana was about to steer the conversation away from her daughter and toxic masculinity, when Shelina decided to take the nuclear option and run away.

"I think my son is calling me!" she said, before bolting right out of the grilled-meat line without even getting any.

Awkward. Now Jana had no idea what to say. As usual.

"Those outdated patriarchal sentiments of the father needing to protect his daughter's virtue just won't die," Farzana Aunty said. Jana hadn't noticed that she was back with them. "Thank goodness you were never like that, Sam." She put her hand on Dr. Lopez's arm.

Jana shook her head. "My father wasn't like that, either." Of course, back when Dad was alive, no one would have thought that Jana's virtue was at risk.

"A lot of it is rooted in culture," Dr. Lopez mused. "Machismo in the Spanish-speaking world holds back progress in many ways."

"And in Indian culture," Farzana Aunty added. She smiled at Jana. "Hopefully your daughter isn't held to outdated gender expectations like that as she gets older." She looked toward Imani, who was sitting at a table with Jana's mother. "It's so lovely to see how much she is doted on by your friends and family. Rohan is smitten with her."

"She has amazing uncles and aunties."

Farzana Aunty smiled. "I'm happy that she has so many role models. Does her father live near you?"

Jana nodded. She really needed to change the subject before they asked any more personal questions. Thankfully they were at the front of the line then, so they were able to load up their plates with mishkaki and pili pili chicken. As the three of them walked back to the dining tables, Jana saw that Anil had moved—he was now at Mom and Imani's table, helping Mom encourage Imani to eat. Damn it. They would pass the table on their way back, and Jana had no doubt that these two would take the opportunity to chat with Imani and her father.

"Oh my goodness!" Jana said, pointing out into the distance. "I think I just saw an elephant between the trees there!" She didn't see an elephant, but hopefully they would follow anyway.

"Right there," Jana said, stepping farther into the tall grasses edging the clearing. She put her hand over her eyes to block the sun and pointed to the little grove of acacia trees in the distance. Dr. Lopez and Farzana Aunty followed her and looked where she was pointing. After a few seconds of searching, she shrugged. "It was probably a shadow. Oh well."

Farzana Aunty chuckled. "Oh, I'm sure we'll see lots on the safari. Hopefully there will be time to have a nice chat with you and your ex-husband, too! I'd love to learn more about how well you two cooperate!"

Ugh. How the hell was Jana going to keep this woman away from Anil on the safari? Jana was going to have to come clean about all the lies. Everyone would be talking about this for the rest of the trip.

Jana could feel her panic rising as her fists clenched. She took a step away from Dr. Lopez, and the next thing she knew, she was facedown in a pile of African savanna mud. Or…butt down, at least.

These stupid shoes were nowhere near appropriate for this terrain.

"Dr. Suleiman!" Dr. Lopez said, reaching for her with his free hand. "Are you okay?"

She was sitting in dirt. Yuck. This was *disgusting*. Jana wriggled her ankle. At least she was pretty sure she hadn't hurt anything. Except her pride. And her dress, which was now covered with pili pili sauce *and* mud.

Maybe a broken ankle would have been a good thing, because it could have given her an out for the safari.

"Mommy!" Jana heard Imani yell. "You fell down! Daddy! Daddy! Mommy fell down! She fell in the elephant poop we found before! You have to help her! Don't worry, Mommy. Daddy is going to take you out of the poop!"

CHAPTER 12

J ana closed her eyes and repeated her daughter's words in her mind. *Don't worry, Mommy. Daddy is going to take you out of the poop!*

Jana was in poo. It was the poo of her favorite animal in the world, but still...*poo*. And Anil was coming to rescue her. And Dr. Lopez and his wife were right here with Jana. Jana opened her eyes and tried to scramble to her feet before anyone could help her up, but Anil was already in front of her.

Damn it.

His strong arms were under hers in a second as he tried to lift her out.

"I'm fine, I'm fine. Shoo!"

Did she just shoo away Anil Malek?

"Are you okay? Here," Dr. Lopez said, moving in front of Anil to try to give Jana a hand again. Jana didn't want to be rescued by Dr. Lopez, either. She didn't need her potential new boss yanking her out of a pile of elephant turds.

And she was attracting a crowd. Mom was on her way. And Kassim Uncle, Nadira Aunty, Jon Uncle, the wedding party...everyone.

But maybe this wasn't poop? Why was she trusting a four-year-old to know the difference between dung and dirt?

"Jana!" Elsie said, rushing to them. She seemed to be able to navigate the Serengeti grasslands in stilettos just fine. "Are you all right? How wonderful that you found some elephant dung!"

Welp. So wonderful.

Jana waved away the crowd of people offering to help her and tried to get to her feet again. She needed to salvage some dignity here. "I'm okay." She stood. Or at least she attempted to stand. Because when she put her weight on her left foot, she almost fell to the ground again. Anil and Dr. Lopez both reached for her.

"Let me get Mo to come carry you," Elsie offered.

Jana kept her weight on her right foot and looked down, seeing two things. One, the cork wedge heel on her left shoe had come clean off. She wasn't hurt, but her shoe certainly was. And two, there was a mound of dried, fibrous dung in front of her. She hadn't actually fallen into elephant poop; she'd only tripped on it and fell into dirt.

Didn't feel like much of a consolation now, though.

"She doesn't need the man with the gun," Mom said. "Her ex-husband is right here. Anil can carry her. It will be like their wedding night!" She then looked at Farzana Aunty standing next to her. "They are still close, you know. You saw the picture from the airplane!"

Jana closed her eyes. She was frozen. Speechless. Standing on one foot. Near elephant poo.

Kamila and Rohan had arrived at her commotion by now. In fact, pretty much everyone was here. Staring at Jana and yelling suggestions. She even heard someone say that there was an old Sanskrit proverb that said falling in elephant excrement at a wedding meant you would be the next to marry. Jana doubted that proverb existed. The aunty was probably trying to make Jana feel better. Or Jana's mother feel better.

By then, Jana had been standing on one foot for too long. She started to stumble again, but Anil had his hand on her arm in a second.

"It's okay, Jana. Lean on me," he said softly. Kindly.

She did. She had no choice. She couldn't hear anything but her heart pounding in her ears. All her blood had swished down to her feet.

"I can get you out of here," Anil whispered in her ear. "Will you let me help you?"

She didn't want to think, so she just nodded.

"It's okay...I'm going to take her to the..." Anil paused.

"The Land Cruiser!" Kamila yelled. "Elsie hid flats for the whole brigade in there!"

If there were flats in the vehicle, why were they all still in these damn wedges?

Jana sighed, still leaning on Anil for support.

"Let's get you those shoes," Anil said. In one swift motion, Anil lifted Jana into his arms and started walking toward the Land Cruiser as the crowd parted in front of him like the Red Sea.

Jana had been carried like this by Anil before. In London. When he dropped her on the bed there, he proceeded to peel off her clothes. She hoped he couldn't hear her heart racing now.

He was still so strong. She pressed against his warm, firm chest. Her face was near his neck—and the scent of his sandal-wood cologne was all she could focus on. She felt like she was floating. At one point, he stumbled a tiny bit—as Jana had already established, the ground was unstable—and he tightened his grip on her at the same moment she squeezed her arms around his shoulders.

When he got to the Land Cruiser, he set her down gently, and Jana supported herself against the vehicle while he opened it. She climbed in, and he followed her and closed the door before she could stop him.

And then they were alone in the eight-seat safari vehicle. Jana ignored the large man and the vivid memories and climbed into the rear row of seats, reaching behind into the trunk space to the large duffel bags stashed there. One of these should have the shoes in them. And maybe a change of clothes, because she couldn't be sure there was no trace of poop in the dirt her butt had landed in. Thankfully, elephant dung had no smell. She found a towel and some baby wipes in a bag, but no clothes.

"Are you sure you're okay?" Anil asked. He'd sat on the seat directly in front of her. The scent of his subtle cologne was now filling the air inside the vehicle.

"I'm fine. I'm not hurt," she said, still rooting around in the trunk. She didn't even care that she was giving Anil a prime view of her rear end. It was probably covered with dirt, anyway.

"I don't mean physically."

"I'm mortified," Jana said. "And a little disgusted."

He turned so he was sideways in his seat and could face her. "I know you don't like crowds. And..." His voice trailed. Jana knew what he was thinking—he didn't need to finish the sentence.

Another memory from their past—the first time she saw Anil as more than just charm, charisma, and personality. The first time he'd rescued her when she'd almost had a panic attack in the middle of a meeting in Dushanbe. She'd been presenting her findings on the plausibility of adding a mental health unit to the medical clinic she was overseeing the opening of, and Anil had come to the meeting with his friend. Jana had presented in meetings many times before that, and she was sometimes nervous, but she usually did fine. But that day there was a man there who was constantly speaking over her, interrupting her and questioning pretty much everything she said. Jana was used to older men disregarding the importance of mental health, but something about his condescending tone and the way he talked down to her, even insulted her intelligence, triggered something. He wouldn't let up—and she felt so . . . exposed. Then the room went blurry, her heart started to pound, and Jana could no longer speak. She bolted out the door, and Anil followed her. She'd talked to him a handful of times since he'd arrived in town a few days earlier, and she'd thought he was handsome but kind of annoying. Basically, he was way too . . . *much*. In fact, she remembered thinking Kamila would love the guy.

But he sat with her and helped her calm down. He asked her about her idea. He even helped her flesh out her research into a workable plan. They continued talking about it for the next few days, and she realized that Anil *was* charm, charisma, and personality, but he was also intelligent, forward-thinking, and committed to the same issues as she was. And he *valued* Jana's knowledge and experience. She presented an actual plan that could be implemented in a similar meeting a few days later, this time anticipating the annoying man's objections, making it so ironclad that no one could say no. All while Anil sat with the others, smiling at her reassuringly, and giving her strength. At the time, it felt like Anil had rescued her.

And now he'd rescued her from an overwhelming situation once again. She hated that seeing him now had dusted off all the albums in her mind of the past.

"Anil, please." She found the shoes. They were in little fabric drawstring bags, each with a bridesmaid's name on it. The simple cream flats were exactly her size. She laid the towel down on her seat and sat to change shoes. Then she opened the baby wipes. Anil didn't say anything as she fruitlessly attempted to clean the dirt and pili pili sauce off her dress.

"If you're worried I'm mad about what your mother said, I'm not," he finally said. "I gathered she was stretching the truth a bit to her friends...Three aunties have already asked me to talk to their children about how to divorce properly." He smiled, but it was a different smile. Not cocky. Not fake. Personal. Real.

She'd been keeping Mom's lie from him since they'd gotten here, and he already knew? "I'm sorry. I tried to get her to stop."

"It's fine. I get it. Parents can be...difficult. You could have warned me, though. I'm not your enemy, you know."

Of course he wasn't her enemy. He was her co-parent. She looked down at her dress. Her cleaning attempts didn't seem to be making a difference.

She reached back and found some spot cleaner in the duffel. "I don't see you as my enemy."

"You're still irritated that I'm here, though."

"Here in this vehicle, or here in Serengeti?"

"Here in Tanzania."

Jana frowned, twisting to dab at the back of her dress with the spot cleaner. "I'm trying not to be irritated." Or at least trying to appear less irritated.

"Do you want some help with that?"

She glared at him. "What do you think?"

He chuckled. "I think I'm the last person in the world you'd want touching your rear end."

She couldn't help it. She laughed at the ridiculousness of this situation.

"What would you have done if you'd known I was coming?" he asked.

"I don't know." Jana would have still come on the trip—she wasn't that petty. Mentally preparing herself to spend this much time with him would have been helpful, though.

He sighed. "I apologize. I should have told you."

"You apologize a lot."

He shook his head. "You...I never know what to do when it comes to you. My instincts always fail me."

"You mean because I don't succumb to your charms like everyone else?" She sounded more bitter than she intended. The truth was she had no idea what to do or say to Anil, either.

He looked away from Jana, eyes focusing on the wedding outside.

He finally spoke after several long moments of silence. "What would our wedding have looked like?" he asked.

"We never would have lasted," she whispered. Was he really sitting here imagining their wedding?

Hadn't she been doing the same thing during the ceremony?

Neither of them said anything again for a while before he finally looked back at her. "All I'm asking...the reason I came on this trip...is I'm hoping we *can* be a family. Be the aspirational co-parents that all those aunties think we are. Not just for Imani, but also...for me. I don't want to brace for impact whenever we talk. I want to actually help each other. We even work in the same field...I want to talk to you about work, and about Imani writing her name, and about how happy our friends are. I want us to be there for each other."

Jana wanted those things, too. Honestly. But she was coming to wonder if they were even possible.

She ran her fingers through her hair, forgetting it was in an updo. Great. Now her hair was a mess, too. "There is another reason this trip is extra hard for me. It's Dr. Lopez. Sam Uncle."

Anil's eyes widened. "Wait…you have a *thing* with *Sam Uncle*? He's, like, what—your mother's age? Isn't he with Psychologist Aunty?"

Jana snorted. "No, I don't have a *thing* with Dr. Lopez. He is the executive director of Think Canada. I interviewed for a director position there. It would mean a lot less traveling and a stable job close to home when Imani starts kindergarten. I didn't know he was Rohan's uncle, and I didn't expect to see him here."

Anil beamed, his smile lighting up the whole vehicle. "I thought he looked familiar! I've heard him speak! Jana, this is good news—he'll definitely hire you now! Do you want me to give him a reference? I can tell him how great you were when we launched Aim High."

She tilted her head. "Anil, seriously? Do you think someone spending time with me in a social situation would make them want to *hire* me? I just tripped on a pile of elephant shit and almost had a panic attack. I'm awkward and grumpy. You know people don't like me *more* after hanging out with me."

He shrugged. "I did."

She shook her head. "Yes, well, you are not normal." She sighed. "He and Farzana Aunty think you and I were *married*. Mom went on and on about how amazing our divorce was before the trip. The whole wedding party has been helping me keep them away from you so they didn't say anything."

He chuckled. "That explains so much about the last couple of days."

Jana looked out the window. Outside, she could see the wedding celebration continuing, like she wasn't having a crisis with her ex in the middle of Serengeti National Park. "Mom is having an aunty one-upping crisis or something. But it's not right. I'll tell them all the truth."

"Your mother will be devastated."

"I can't keep lying to Dr. Lopez. I want him to hire me."

He shrugged. "It's not a lie that matters, though. I'm happy to go along with it if anyone asks. Then when you get back to the city, you can tell him that it's a technicality—we were together but not married. He's not going to pry, because it's none of his business. And I'll also do what I can to get you the job. Talk you up. Tell him how impressive you are. This will be good for you."

"Why would you do that for me? Lie for me?"

"It wouldn't be lying. You are impressive."

Jana scowled.

He stared at her before speaking. "You won't ever give me a chance to be anything but the bad guy in your life. If you'd asked me for help from the beginning, I would have said yes. And I think you knew that. Give me a chance, Jana. If everything goes well, and we can get along again, then maybe..."

She knew he'd want something in return. Forgiveness, probably. Or maybe he wanted her to take that board vacancy at Aim High. "What?"

"Disney," he said.

Fuck. Not that again. Jana opened her eyes wide. "That's all? You'll help me get this job just for Disney?"

He nodded. "I just want to come to Disney with you. But only if we're getting along."

Jana bit her lip. Was she willing to give him that? Not wanting him to come to Disney wasn't Jana being petty, or revenge, or anything like that. It was self-care. Being in this small vehicle with him now, or in her hotel watching him wash Imani's hands, or sitting next to him on a crowded plane had all been so hard. She couldn't think straight with all the memories coming back. With all the what-ifs. But at least here there were others around. Jana couldn't travel for two weeks alone with just him and Imani. His betrayal still hurt too much. She could finally take a trip with Imani, and this would taint it.

"Come on, Jana," he said. "I don't want to break your mother's heart, either. She's so great for Imani."

That's what would happen if Jana revealed to everyone that Mom lied. Mom's heart would be broken. Nicole had said Mom should accept Jana as she was because Jana was the only daughter she had.

But Jana saw it differently. Jana was the only daughter Mom had, so Jana shouldn't be a disappointment to her.

"Fine. It's a deal. We'll *pretend* we're friendly ex-spouses, and you'll pretend I'm pleasant to be around, and I'll think seriously about Disney."

He smiled. "I guess we were once married, then." He reached for the door of the Land Cruiser. "And you *are* pleasant to be around...sometimes. But I'd better get out of here, because people will definitely wonder what I'm doing alone with my ex-wife for so long."

He mock saluted, then flashed that knee-weakening Anil Malek smile before leaving the Land Cruiser.

Jana put her head back on her seat and sighed. What had she gotten herself into? By the end of this trip, she was sure that Anil would hate her as much as he seemed to think she hated him.

Or worse...maybe Jana would hate him less.

CHAPTER 13

B right and early the next day (well, not too early—after all, there had been a wedding the day before), everyone gathered in the lobby of the resort with their luggage, waiting for the Land Cruisers to pick them up for the safari trip. There was a nervous energy in the air, as this was the first ever safari for many of them.

Jana wasn't nervous—at least not about the safari itself. In Jana's mind, the danger of this trip wasn't malaria, lions, or even a sunburn. It was the deal she'd made with Anil the day before. That they were going to pose as amicable co-parents and exes for the trip. It was one thing for her alone to pretend she was over him and the past, but somehow it was even more monumental for him to be in on it. Pretending together they were once in love. Once *married*. And pretending they were still close friends. Jana honestly had no idea how she was going to get through it. And all this on top of her pretending she was enjoying this trip. Pretending to be social. Vibrant.

But she'd gone this far—she had to keep going now.

Eventually, five Land Cruisers pulled up in front of the Serengeti resort, and they all piled in for their weeklong safari, which would visit three more parks and resorts. Although Elsie had planned the trip, she didn't have as tight a rein on them anymore, so there were no assigned vehicles. Jana managed to get in a vehicle without

Dr. Lopez or Anil. She knew she wouldn't be able to avoid them all week, but she welcomed the break from the pretending for now.

Their first game park was the Ngorongoro Conservation Area, the site of the Ngorongoro Crater. The drive was long, bumpy, and uneventful, but being in the safari vehicle brought strong memories of that trip with her father years ago. Jana missed him. When he was alive, she had a constant reminder that being different—not being fluent in that secret code that everyone else seemed to have the key for—didn't mean she was an outsider. She could still be connected to people, like her father had been.

After everything that had happened to Jana in the last five years in both her personal and professional life, it was no wonder that deep inside, all she wanted was to chase that feeling of contentment that had always surrounded her father. But maybe it wasn't possible. What was it Nicole had said—that new people in her life made her *element* change? Jana wasn't the same person she was before her father passed, or before she had Imani—and maybe there was no way to get that back.

She was getting morose, which wasn't helping anyone. Instead of looking out the window for the rest of the trip, Jana opened her planner and stared at her "letting loose" list. Only one item had been checked off—dancing at the wedding. And unexpectedly, she'd loved that. Jana smiled. Maybe this strategy could work—maybe letting loose was the way to feel connected to the world again. She could do this.

After the three-and-a-half-hour drive, they arrived at the Ngorongoro hotel a little past two o'clock. This was another luxury resort, and it was situated at the top of the ridge around the enormous Ngorongoro Crater. Their rooms weren't ready yet, so the whole party was led out to a terrace behind the hotel.

The view was incredible. Almost the entire crater was visible all the way to the opposite ridge (thanks to the binoculars from the Bridal Brigade kit), and Jana could see forested groves, flat plains, and a large pond in the distance that was tinged pink.

"Mommy, are there animals down there?" Imani was scanning the crater with her plastic children's binoculars.

"Definitely." But even with Jana's better binoculars, she still couldn't see any.

"Hi, Mini!" Anil said. Jana hadn't realized his Land Cruiser had arrived.

"Daddy!" Imani said, frowning. "We can't find animals."

"Let me look," Anil said, taking out of his messenger bag an even more powerful pair of binoculars—not like the ones from the wedding party backpacks. He looked for a minute, sweeping his gaze across the whole crater. Jana was sure he wouldn't find anything. How would he even know where to look? She watched his face. Of course, she couldn't see his eyes, but she saw his jaw set and his mouth form a straight line. He was wearing a leaf-print linen shirt and tan pants that miraculously didn't look wrinkled after the drive. His brow was furrowed.

She needed to stop staring at Anil so much.

"There!" he suddenly said, brows shooting upward. "In that clearing in the trees!"

Jana looked where he pointed but couldn't make out any clearing. Imani complained she couldn't see anything, either. Anil passed his binoculars to Imani, trying to adjust them to her small face, but it wasn't working.

"Let's see if I can show your mother," Anil said, taking Jana's binoculars from her and looking into them. After a few seconds, his mouth widened. "There. Here—you look, Jana." He moved his head away from the binoculars but didn't move his hands, so Jana would have to squeeze between his arms to look.

Jana didn't like the idea of being shown this…whatever it was…with Anil surrounding her. But they had a deal. They were supposed to be amicable now. She squeezed between his arms and put her face to the eyepieces.

Before Jana saw anything, she felt Anil's warmth. He smelled like dust. A bit of sweat. Laundry detergent. The slightest hint of the same sandalwood cologne she'd smelled yesterday. Jana's throat went dry. She focused on the view through the binoculars, ignoring the feel of his breath on her neck. She could lean back half an inch and she'd be touching him. He could kiss her under her ear with barely any movement.

Jana balled her fists and squinted through the eyepieces. It was an elephant. And it was *enormous*. On the very edge of a small clearing in the middle of the trees, surrounded by bright emerald leaves contrasting with the animal's deep gray color. Its tusks were huge and gleaming white. The elephant was pulling leaves from a nearby tree with his agile trunk and eating them.

Elephants were Jana's favorite animal. Her hands rose to hold the binoculars herself, and Anil stepped away. She focused to see the animal clearer. Jana knew elephants were big. She'd seen them years ago on that first safari. And she'd seen smaller Asian elephants in India, of course. But this still took her breath away. It seemed broader, taller, and a richer shade of gray than any elephant from her memory. It was positively majestic, and Jana was rendered literally speechless.

"What is it, Mommy?" Imani asked.

Jana grinned, almost giddy from seeing her first elephant. "Here—let me show you." She knelt to Imani's level to show her daughter the animal.

Imani squealed. "Elephant! Daddy, it's an elephant! Is that a real elephant? Kamila Aunty, did you see the elephant?" Others joined them then, no doubt drawn to Imani's excited outburst. Soon, about half of the wedding party were passing around binoculars or using their own and excitedly laughing and pointing out the animal.

Jana took a deep breath. It felt like something unraveled in her. Or started to unravel, at least.

"Can we go down there, Mommy?"

Jana ran her hand over her daughter's braids. "Tomorrow, love," she said.

"With Daddy, too? We'll all be in the same car, right?"

"Hello! Attention!" One of the hostesses had stepped outside. "Anyone in the north wing of the resort—that's suites ten and up—your rooms are ready. You can follow me, please."

There was a bit of shuffling as people checked their room cards, then about half the party left the terrace, including Anil, but Jana and her mother's suite wasn't ready yet. Imani was now with Kassim Uncle at the railing around the terrace looking for more elephants, so Jana went to the nearby bar for a bottle of water. Her phone buzzed while she was heading back to Imani. She checked it—Asha had sent another dik-dik pic to the Bridal Brigade group chat. Jana snorted, shaking her head. She was starting to find these weirdos in the brigade kind of funny.

"Something wrong?" Dr. Lopez said. He was sitting at a table with Farzana Aunty.

She turned and put on her smile. "Nothing at all. I'm still buzzing from seeing that elephant."

"It was magnificent, wasn't it?" Farzana Aunty said. "Your daughter's enthusiasm was infectious. She is clearly very attached to her father."

"Yes. She's…" Jana hated the term *daddy's girl* but that's what Imani was. Especially lately. And Anil was a total girl dad.

"I think it's wonderful that you brought her here." Dr. Lopez smiled, looking in Imani's direction at the railing around the terrace. "Your daughter will thank you for this trip when she's older." He indicated at the empty chair at the table. "Join us."

Jana sat.

Farzana Aunty gave a warm smile. She was different from Rohan's mother. She was talkative like Nadira Aunty but seemed more thoughtful. Like she chose her words carefully. "May I ask how long ago you separated?"

Jana bit her lip—what was the best answer to this question?

"Oh . . . it was a long time ago."

"Your daughter doesn't have memories of the two of you together?"

"No," Jana said. "Imani has no memories of us as a couple. And we don't really talk about it to her. This is just how her family is. Mommy and Daddy don't live together but are both important in her life. I'd hate for her to think something is missing that was once there."

Farzana Aunty smiled. "That is a very interesting way of thinking about it."

"We shouldn't pry into her personal life, my dear," Dr. Lopez said. He was right—he shouldn't, because he was considering her for a job. But Farzana Aunty didn't know that.

"Jana!" Kamila said, pulling on Jana's arm. "You are needed. Sorry, Sam Uncle, I need my bridesmaids to help with a crisis!" Kamila looked somewhere between panicked and elated, and Jana had no idea if there was really a crisis or if she was trying to get Jana away from Dr. Lopez again.

"Oh, go ahead," Dr. Lopez said, smiling. "Duty calls!"

Jana nodded and asked her mother to keep an eye on Imani, then followed Kamila into the hotel.

This hotel was not as large as the Serengeti one, but it was also luxurious, with rich dark wood and East African tribal-inspired decor. Kamila hurried down a hallway, and Jana followed.

"Is there really a crisis? Because I was fine with Dr. Lopez."

Kamila turned sharply. "Of course there's a crisis," she said. Kamila turned down another hallway and slipped into a meeting room where the rest of the wedding party were already sitting.

It was about the size of the tiny elephant corner at the Serengeti hotel. This room was also African-animal themed. But instead of just elephants, the decor was of many animals—only in ridiculously bright colors. Green giraffes. Purple lions. Orange rhinos. It was quite psychedelic.

The crisis turned out to be about a private wedding party event that Kamila and Rohan were planning as a thank-you to the Bridal Brigade and Groom's Platoon. Clearly Kamila's definition of a crisis was vastly different from Jana's.

"You don't have to thank us," Asha said. "This trip to Tanzania is thanks enough. Plus, you gave us those backpacks."

"Yeah, but y'all are paying for your trip," Kamila said. "So—"

"Question," Tim interrupted. "Why was there a whole box of condoms in *each* backpack? Did you think this would be like spring break or something? We are almost all middle-aged and married."

Nicole shook her head. "You're never too old, or too committed, for safe sex."

Shelina snorted. "Yeah, but—"

"You can donate them," Nicole said. "Leave them with the front desk at the hotel and they'll give them to the local village."

"If we're going to donate, let's do it right," Asha said. "Giving them a handful of boxes of condoms seems cheap. I wonder if we can get a shipment here from home."

Finally, a topic that Jana knew how to talk about. "I worked with an organization that promoted sexual and reproductive health in Kenya. Maybe we can partner with them."

"Yes!" Anil said. "I know that clinic! They're based out of Mombasa, right?"

Jana nodded, and she and Anil told the others details about the sexual health clinic she'd worked with in Kenya many years ago. "Maybe they can help us find something similar here? We could make a donation in the wedding's name." Jana pulled out her phone to see if she had their contact information.

"What kind of work did they do?" Nicole asked.

After explaining the scope of the clinic and the tangible differences they were able to see in southeastern Kenya, Jana and Anil answered some more questions about the most effective ways to donate to reproductive health causes here. It was strange for them to be explaining their work together like this. Like a team.

Strange, but it oddly felt normal, too.

"You really are the coolest one here, Jana," Kamila said.

Jana shook her head. She was so far from cool. But then she noticed that Anil was looking at her with an unreadable expression. It was the same look he had after watching her dance, like she'd surprised him. Jana felt exposed. She looked down at her phone.

They got back to talking about this private party, and everyone agreed on going to another hotel for it—away from the parents, and children, for that matter.

Jana didn't have an issue with leaving Imani with her mother and Kassim Uncle for one night. And a night without her mother, the aunties and uncles, and the Lopezes meant Jana might be able to check more off the "letting loose" list. Weirdly, she was looking forward to that.

CHAPTER 14

The buffet dinner in the hotel dining room was loud and energetic but also delicious. Jana could have gorged on the nyama choma and casava stew all night. After dinner, Mom hopped out of her seat before Jana had even finished her chai and announced that she would take Imani so Jana could stay with the young people. Jana assumed it was because Mom herself was tired from staying up late after the wedding ceremony doing lord knows what with the aunties and uncles. Probably playing cards. But this was good—it was a chance for Jana to check another item off the list.

She ordered a drink from the bar and sat at a table with the rest of the wedding party. Anil was at the other end, talking to Marc and Jerome. Everyone near Jana was talking about Bollywood gossip—a subject Jana knew nothing about, so she couldn't join in.

"What about you, Jana?" Kamila suddenly said, perhaps realizing that Jana was the only quiet one there. "You seen any good movies lately?"

Jana shrugged. "Only kids movies."

Kamila grinned. "Yeah, but kids movies are great. Honestly,

any movie that breaks out into song works for me. I don't know why there aren't more English musicals. Superhero movies should have musical numbers."

Soon everyone was talking about their favorite English-language musicals, and Jana, again, had no idea how to even contribute.

This was a mistake. How could she expect that checking off a random item on a list could change her life? Trying to fit in was only making her feel more like the wedding party outcast. Dancing was fine because she was still in her own head then. This was impossible.

But Jana wasn't really getting out of her comfort zone if it was *comfortable*. She waited for an opening in the conversation. "I liked *Mamma Mia!*," she said.

"Yes!" Asha squealed. "Love *Mamma Mia!* And the sequel is even better!" She excitedly grabbed Kamila's arm. "You know what we should do? The Bridal Brigade should do karaoke to 'Dancing Queen.'" She looked at Jana, then Nicole, grinning, clearly remembering the *sing* item on the "letting loose" list. "Do any of the hotels have karaoke?"

"I don't know," Kamila said, picking up her phone. "I'll ask Elsie."

They started talking about other ensemble songs they could sing, and Jana only felt more detached as the night went on. She stuck it out, but she wouldn't call the night a success. But she supposed she'd at least tried.

The game drive through the Ngorongoro Crater was as spectacular as expected. Jana was in a Land Cruiser with Imani, Mom,

Anil, Asha, and Nicole. They saw gazelles, zebras, and giraffes, all within the first ten minutes of getting to the bottom of the crater. As the drive continued, they saw lions, eagles, and even a cheetah. The coolest sighting was a rhino (from a distance—Anil's powerful binoculars were useful), which their guide said was rare these days. And amazingly, the pond that looked pink from a distance appeared that color because of the hundreds of pink flamingos in it, which delighted Imani. The joy on her face as she furiously colored in her coloring book after seeing each new animal was priceless.

At lunch, they stopped at a picnic area, and their guide distributed boxed lunches that he'd brought from the hotel.

"The book is almost full!" Imani said, flipping through the pages.

"And we still have two more parks," Anil said. "Lake Manyara and Tarangire."

Imani frowned. "Are the same animals there?"

Jana shook her head. "It will be similar, but not exactly the same. Manyara is famous for being the only place in the world where people have seen lions sleeping in trees."

"Like the raccoon in the backyard!" Imani said. She was a true Toronto kid and very familiar with raccoons.

"And Tarangire is supposedly full of elephants," Anil said. "I think it will be your mother's favorite park."

Jana was particularly looking forward to that one. She heard laughing behind her. Turning, she saw that it was Mom and Kassim Uncle fumbling with a selfie stick.

"I think they're making a TikTok," Asha said as she unwrapped her sandwich.

Jana's eyes narrowed. "My mother's on TikTok?"

Nicole beamed. "I think it's great. Do you know how many

patients have found me because they saw me on doctor-tok? It's a valid way to make connections these days."

Nicole was popular on the social media platform for her "Real Talk about Vaginas" series. Jana agreed that someone dispelling myths about bodies for TikTok's young audience was a valuable service, but what exactly were Mom and Kassim Uncle planning to do?

She found out soon enough. Kamila played a lively Bollywood song on her phone, and Mom and Kassim Uncle did a choreographed dance to it with the East African terrain as their backdrop.

Imani squealed with joy and went closer to watch her nani and uncle.

"They're going to go viral with that," Anil said. "Boomer dance-tok is...well...booming." He started telling the others about an older man who gave out life advice on TikTok while riding a unicycle who was growing in popularity and even getting sponsorships at this point.

Jana plunged her straw into a juice box of mango nectar. "I don't think I understand the world anymore." Thank goodness no one had told her to be more active on social media for her "letting loose" list.

Anil laughed, nodding. "Honestly, everything changes so fast; most people can't keep up. Imani's world will be different from ours." He smiled that annoying Anil smile. "But social media isn't scary. It's just another medium for the same social interaction we've always had."

Was that a dig at Jana and her antisocial self? Jana's first instinct was to snap at him, but she tamped that down. Then she forced the scowl off her face. She smiled pleasantly. "True." Her eye twitched.

They finally saw their first elephant after they got back on the road after lunch. Actually, two elephants. They were standing together in the open air, just kind of…hanging out. And they were *magnificent*. Almost regal in their stature, with long white tusks and massive ears. Jana was entranced. She didn't know why, but she even felt herself tear up.

"Mommy, Mommy! Elephants!"

"They're beautiful!" Anil said. He stood to take pictures from the open top of the vehicle. Jana stood, too, so she could look at the elephants with no window separating them. She didn't take pictures, though. She could get the shots from Anil or Asha later. Right now, she wanted to stare at these with her naked eyes.

They were so conspicuous. But they were here. Not hiding in the forest. What would it be like to be so comfortable in your own skin? To have no urge to escape when others came close?

After another hour of driving around the game park, it was time to head back to the resort. Jana had heard that the drive out of the crater was a bit harrowing, and that turned out to be a massive understatement. The climb down in the morning had been steep, but nothing too extreme. The trip back up was a different road, though. A narrow, twisting path that zigzagged up the crater ridge with absolutely no barrier between dirt road and cliff wall. At one point, Jana swore the Land Cruiser was completely vertical.

"Only Land Cruisers can do this," Nelson, their driver, said. "This is why you don't see any other models down there."

Jana would prefer that Nelson would skip talking now and focus on driving. She hadn't been worried about physical dangers on this trip, but that was before she'd known that the Land Cruiser would be driving straight up a wall made of mud to get out of the crater.

Nelson didn't seem nervous, though, and he did this drive all the time. Imani was between Anil and Jana and was happily watching *Peppa Pig* on her iPad with headphones. Jana's mother was next to Nelson in the front, and Jana would bet she had her eyes closed praying. Asha and Nicole were in the seats in front of Jana and had their eyes glued out the window, seeming to love the thrill ride.

Jana glanced at Anil on the other side of Imani. All the color had drained from his face. He was clutching the side of Imani's booster seat with knuckles as white as that large elephant's tusks from the day before.

"You okay?" Jana asked him softly.

His head turned sharply to her, then he tried to chuckle. It came out like a weak grunt. "Yeah. This is steep."

She nodded. "It is. Reminds me of a drive through a deadly pass in the mountains of Pakistan," Jana said. "I almost kissed the driver when it was done for not killing us all."

His head tilted, looking at Jana. "You're quite a badass, you know that?"

Jana snorted, then cringed when they hit a bump.

"You know," he said quietly a few seconds later, "I always worry about you when you go off on those trips."

He didn't specify what he was afraid would happen, but he didn't have to. Treacherous truck drives were only one of the hazards Jana dealt with in her work. Political unrest, disease, terrorism…Jana had seen everything. Anil worked in non-profits, too, but he hadn't been to nearly as many potentially dangerous places as she had.

He glanced at Imani, who was oblivious to them all. Jana knew what Anil was thinking. That every risk either of them took could have a profound, lifelong effect on the lives of the three of them. This was why Jana insisted on knowing where he was at all times. To know he was safe. And so he would know she was safe. They passed over another large bump, and Anil's eyes closed briefly as his fingers tightened over the fabric of Imani's seat.

Jana didn't really think about it—she reached out and put her open palm on Imani's lap. Imani didn't notice—*Peppa Pig* was much too interesting. But Anil did. He put his hand in Jana's, and she squeezed it.

His trembles calmed as he squeezed back. She didn't know why she'd done it—maybe because he'd already helped her on this trip. It was Anil who had given her that look of understanding during the marriage ceremony when everyone was looking at her and Imani. And it was Anil who'd rescued her after she tripped on elephant dung. And finally, it was Anil who was helping her now—pretending their relationship was so much more than it ever was.

No matter how detached, bitter, or rude Jana was to Anil, she couldn't avoid the truth—her life was forever connected to this man's. And right now, he needed support, so she gave it.

Once they reached the top of the crater and were on safe ground, Anil took his hand away. Jana rubbed hers, trying to forget the warmth and solidity of his fingers. The rest of the drive back to their resort was uneventful and mostly quiet. Once there, everyone went to the hotel lounge, but Jana decided she was entitled to a break from being social. She took Imani for a bath instead. Imani fell asleep right afterward, so Jana herself was able to luxuriate in the enormous shower, washing off all the dust from the drive. She was brushing her hair when there was a knock at the door. She assumed it was her mother forgetting her room card.

But it wasn't. It was Anil. His face was back to his normal

expression—no sign of the fear in his eyes earlier. Just easy good humor.

Jana tried to keep her expression blank. "Yes?"

His eyes traveled down the plush hotel bathrobe that reached Jana's ankles to her bare feet. She wasn't concerned about him seeing her like this—this monstrosity covered her considerably more than the navy shorts and tank she'd been wearing for the game drive.

Still, she wrapped her arms around herself. "What? Why are you looking at me like that?" she asked.

He chuckled, running his hand over his chin. It wasn't as smooth as she was used to seeing it. Clearly, he was shaving less on holiday. "Just weird seeing you with wet hair and a bathrobe. I missed seeing you like this."

She raised one brow. "You missed seeing me in a bathrobe?"

He laughed. "No. You look great. Human."

She didn't know what to say to that. The look on his face was nothing like the look he'd had when he'd called her a badass earlier, but both comments were...complimentary? "What is it you want?"

"Right. Straight to business." He held out a thin book. "The hotel shop had this. It's a coloring book with safari animals—I thought since Imani's almost done with the other one..."

"She's sleeping." Jana indicated one of the bedrooms in the two-bedroom suite.

"Okay. I'll give it to her later. I grabbed this for you, too." He held out a second book—it was slim, with photographs of art pieces on the cover. Jana took it and thumbed through it. It was about a women's art collective that sold their pieces online and shipped them around the world. The book was filled with pictures and described how the women started their collective and how it was supporting local families. It was exactly the kind of book Jana would buy on holiday.

"Thank you. This is . . . thoughtful." She didn't know what to say. First peanut snacks, and now he was buying her books?

"No problem. Is this a good time to talk?"

"What do we need to talk about?" Jana tried not to sound curt—but she probably failed. Being pleasant with him was easier when others were around.

"You know . . ." He looked over his shoulder down the hall-way. No one was there. "Stuff." He leaned close. "I don't exactly know what your mother has told people."

He had a point. She stepped out of the doorway to let Anil in. He walked into the sitting room of the suite. It wasn't much—just a small area with a sofa and a table near a large picture window.

"I can't get over the views here," he said, walking toward the glass. "Love how every room faces into the park."

"Yeah. I guess if you're going to stay on the edge of the crater, a room with a view is a necessity." She didn't mention that moment when he'd panicked when they were climbing the crater a few hours ago.

He stopped at the window. "This trip really is a once-in-a-lifetime experience. Are you enjoying it so far?"

She nodded. "It's reminding me a lot of a trip I took here as a kid. My last holiday with my dad, actually." It was also reminding her of the trip to London with Anil five years ago, but she wasn't about to mention that.

"I hope the memories coming back isn't a bad thing." When Jana didn't say anything, he continued. "My most memorable trip with my parents was Disney."

"Ah. So you're here to try to convince me to bring you."

He chuckled. "No. That's completely your decision." He grinned his charming Anil Malek smile. "Maybe I wanted you to see how important it was to me."

Jana raised a brow. "So you're manipulating me? Is that why you keep buying me things?"

"No. Why do you always think the worst of me?"

She didn't, did she?

"This room is smaller than the Serengeti ones," he said, looking around. "Reminds me a bit of that place in London. Cozy."

So, traveling together was taking him down memory lane, too. This robe was almost the same as the one she'd worn there. She crossed her arms over her chest. He was breaking an unsaid rule again. They never ever reminisced about their past relationship. Fling. *Affair*.

"I don't know why we have to have this conversation *now*. Alone." That time she couldn't hide the annoyance seeping into her voice.

"Because Sam Lopez or his wife may ask me about our *marriage* at any point."

Jana sighed as she sat on the sofa. She wrapped the robe tighter around her chest. She wanted to get out of this ridiculous thing—it was much too warm, but Imani was sleeping where her clothes were. "I don't know details, but she said we were married but now we're good friends. I said Imani had no memories of us together."

He chuckled, running his hand over his head. "Okay. Easy enough. Who's in on it?"

"What do you mean?"

"I mean, Kamila and Rohan know we were never married. And I assume their parents do, too."

Jana shrugged. "The bridal party knows the truth. Beyond

that, assume everyone else thinks we were once married. Mom used to tell people this years ago, but I'd thought she'd stopped. And it doesn't really come up anymore. But that new aunty studies divorce outcomes in children, so either Mom or she brought it up."

He sat next to her on the sofa. "What about Nadia? Am I supposed to have married you after her?"

Unspoken rule number two broken. They did *not* talk about Nadia. *Ever.*

Jana felt a sourness in the pit of her stomach. She stared at him frowning long enough that she knew he'd say something to break the tension.

He sighed. "It's unlikely anyone will mention her. Rohan is the only one here who knows her, and he hasn't seen or spoken to her since college."

"Okay," Jana said.

"Do you think the aunty will ask why we split up?" Anil asked.

Jana cringed. "No. Why would she ask that? That's an incredibly intrusive question."

"I know. But she *does* study divorce." He paused. "I'm curious what you would say, anyway. At the wedding, you said we never would have lasted. Why do you think we would have split?"

She stared at him for several moments before speaking. "You don't seriously think we *would* have lasted, do you?"

He shrugged. "I have no idea. I hadn't really thought about it until you said that."

Jana blinked. "We barely knew each other. And we're much too different."

He tilted his head. "I disagree. We're both ambitious and passionate about doing our part to reduce the inequalities and injustices of the world. I think we're quite similar."

"Professionally we may be similar, but personally we are not."

"We're both committed to our daughter. We have the same parenting style."

"You love people. I...don't."

He shrugged. "So you're an introvert and I'm an extrovert. Lots of couples are like that. Look at Kamila and Rohan."

"You're...*nice*. You have lots of friends."

"So are you. Look at all your friends here."

"They're Kamila's friends, not mine."

"They're yours, too—you danced with them at the wedding. You were up talking about karaoke for hours last night."

Jana frowned. "Why are you arguing with me about this?"

He shook his head. "I'm not arguing. I'm *challenging* you."

"But why?" If he was trying to make her angry, it was working. Working very well.

He shrugged. "Because it's the only way we ever talk. And I'm trying to understand you. You've been a bit of a mystery on this trip. For years you've been running away from me, and now you're holding my hand on the safari and asking me to pretend we're friendlier than we are. Then you look at me like I killed your puppy when I gave you that book."

"I said thank you for the book. It was thoughtful." She paused. Maybe her face hadn't said that. "I don't understand why you care, anyway. Or why you keep bringing up the past."

Anil exhaled, frustrated. "Because..." He ran his hand over his face. "Because, Jana, you and I both know that this *friendship*, whether it's real or fake, will never work if we don't move on from the past. You'll never be able to *pretend* to like me— to decide to be friends and then just be friends. You need to feel it. That's the way you're wired. And I can't be civil...be cooperative, knowing you hate me."

Jana's eyes narrowed. "I don't hate you. Stop talking like you know everything about me. And I'm so sorry I can't be *phony* like you."

He shook his head, anger in his eyes. His voice was still controlled, though. "I am a lot of things, Jana Suleiman. And you seem to excel at finding every fault I have. I'm phony. I'm a liar. I'm a cheater. I'm arrogant. What else? I also don't always put my dishes in the sink, and I leave my taxes to the last minute. Go get your precious parenting app—we can make a list."

Jana stared at that stupid handsome face. He said he wanted to challenge her, and now she wanted to fight right back. To finally let out all the hurt, anger, and frustration she'd kept in for years. Jana was tired of being cool and dignified...She wanted to be hot and angry. She wanted to scream at him. For having it all so *easy*. For still winning, after everything. For keeping his reputation, for everyone liking him, and for never having a wrinkle in his perfectly tailored linen shirt. He'd brushed off all his mistakes with that idiotic charming smile still on his face. All the years of resentment building in Jana were bursting to get out. She gritted her teeth. "Do you really want to know what I'd add to that list?"

"Yes!"

"Okay. You're *likable*," she said with a snarl.

He frowned. "You don't like me because other people like me?"

"Yes. I'm contrary that way. When all those rumors were going on about us, did you lose any jobs? Your reputation? No, because you were so damn *likable* that your sins slid off that charming smile."

He shook his head angrily. "I *hated* what happened with that job of yours. I was very vocal to whoever would listen that it was complete bullshit. You didn't deserve that."

Jana knew he'd tried to help. She'd heard about his rants from many of her colleagues. But the damage had already been done. The sexist world meant the grumpy, antisocial woman was always more villainous than the charismatic man.

"It's not even just the job," she said low. "Everyone fucking loves Anil Malek. Even my oldest friends—they *have* to have you in the wedding party. Mom *has* to tell everyone we were married even though I said no to you. People *want* to be around you. You didn't have friends drop you because you reminded them of their own cheating partners. People don't feel the need to challenge you to have an actual conversation."

She narrowed her eyes. She didn't try to read his expression—she didn't even care what he was thinking. She wanted to let it all out. "I walked away from you years ago. I chose to raise Imani as a single parent. And everyone looks at me like I've made some huge mistake that made my life so hard. And they look at you like you're a saint for doing your damn job and being a good parent to your child." She said it quietly, with her jaw tight, even though she wanted to scream it. But Imani was sleeping.

He didn't say anything, just stared at her with wide eyes. This is what he wanted. *Communication.* And it hurt as much as she thought it would.

"Go ahead—call me a cold bitch for hating you because of *society*, instead of anything you actually did." Jana wiped a traitorous tear that was falling down her cheek. "I do sympathize over what Nadia did to you. I really do. You didn't deserve the way you were treated by her or her family. And maybe you don't deserve the way I've treated you over the years. But I didn't deserve to be caught in the cross fire of the implosion of your marriage. You *should* have told me you were still married."

He nodded. "Yes, I should have. I've apologized many times.

I own that." He sighed. "It felt good to forget about her for a little bit. I got so caught up in...you. But tell me this: What if I had told you the truth? That I was technically married only because I couldn't *find* my wife to serve her divorce papers? What difference would it have made? The marriage was just a technicality by that point."

Jana's teeth gritted. "I would have known what I was walking into!"

"Would you have walked in anyway?"

Jana closed her eyes. She was pretty sure he knew the answer to that question. Yes. She would have. And so would he, even if they both knew this is how they'd end up.

Their relationship had only lasted two weeks, but it was an intense, emotional two weeks full of potential for a future. She'd stepped so far out of her comfort zone, and she wouldn't have done that if she hadn't seen something different, something special in their connection. They were magic together. In bed, yes—that had always been good—but also...collaborating with him. Talking for hours about their visions for future projects. And going shopping and to museums and galleries, and discussing books, art, and movies over long dinners.

Jana rarely truly connected with people, and never with anyone that deeply. Maybe Anil didn't think it was a big deal, or a long-term thing, and clearly neither of them expected they would end up with Imani and a lifelong bond as co-parents, but it was still the most intense relationship of her life. Honestly, the best. And she'd really believed he'd felt the same way.

But the lie he'd told—that he was divorced—wasn't small. Maybe it *was* just a technicality, and maybe she didn't have the right to know everything about the trauma his wife was putting him through then. But he had to know that in their world, in their culture, in their profession, Jana would be the one who would pay the bigger price if word got out.

If Jana hadn't found out she was pregnant after learning about Nadia's existence, maybe his little ploy to get Jana back in Toronto would have worked. Maybe she would have understood and forgiven him. They could have continued their relationship after his divorce.

Or maybe she would have told him she never wanted to see him again. She would have been able to walk away, and move on from him.

But she *did* get pregnant. She'd had no ability to walk away.

And the baby meant it wasn't about just the two of them anymore. Imani meant everyone knew about his cheating and saw Jana as the home-wrecker.

Anil was still staring at her, his lips in a straight line. It felt good to see something other than his normal easy smile. He said seeing her in a robe reminded him that she was human—well, for her, seeing him with his good-humored mask chipped away made *him* seem human.

"I would have," she whispered.

"Would have what?" he answered, voice equally low.

"I would have still been with you. I would have liked to know what I was getting into, and maybe I would have been cautious and we would have gone slower. But I would have been with you."

If things had gone slower between them, if they hadn't hopped into bed every moment they could, would they even have Imani now?

Jana sighed, looking down at her enormous plush bathrobe. There had always been something about Anil. She'd done things with him in those two weeks that she'd never even considered doing with anyone else. He had a way of looking at her that made her feel...exposed. Undressed. Which, for those unforgettable two weeks, was exactly how she'd ended up when he looked at her like that.

Jana felt naked now. Being honest with him...him *challenging* her...made her feel more exposed than if she hadn't been wearing this blanketlike robe.

What did Anil think when she opened the door wearing this? Had he realized she'd been fully naked only minutes earlier in the glass-walled shower? Had he imagined the steaming water running down her body? Had he wanted to pull on the belt of the robe and relive their nights in that London hotel? She remembered it so vividly. The shower in that hotel had been smaller, but they'd fit together in it fine. This one would be a luxury. Jana could feel heat pool deep in her core.

Was his mind in the same place as hers right now? It didn't seem possible, but he was still staring at her. Just like he had back in London. Just like there, she wouldn't even have to take off the robe. She could just scoot to the edge of the sofa, and he'd kneel on the floor in front of her. Jana looked down.

"Jana," he whispered. His hand reached up, slow enough for Jana to turn away if she needed to, and he gently lifted her chin so she was looking into his eyes again. She could get lost in them easily. Deep, rich pools of the warmest brown imaginable with faint gold lines around the irises. Jana swallowed. His hand lightly trailed up and wiped a tear from her cheek that she hadn't even realized was there.

He could kiss her right now, and she wouldn't stop him. The longer they looked at each other, the more she was sure that would happen. Since she hadn't gotten over him like she should have years ago, she was going to fall into that trap all over again.

She couldn't do that to herself. Jana looked away, breaking the spell. She couldn't get sucked into his charms and have him blow up her life while she was still feeling the aftershocks of their last implosion.

"Daddy!"

Imani was awake. Jana exhaled as she shifted farther from Anil. Their child launched herself at him.

Anil's face changed in a fraction of a second to good humor and affection. It was so easy for him.

"Hi, Mini! I got you a new coloring book!"

Jana stepped into the bedroom to change while Anil showed Imani the pictures in the coloring book. She wasn't sure they'd resolved anything, but Jana was done with this conversation anyway.

No one ever claimed that they were only trying to make things easier for him, because things were already so easy for Anil Malek.

CHAPTER 15

Anil ended up taking Imani with him when he left Jana's room—offering a quick swim before dinner. He barely looked at Jana. She had no idea what he was thinking about the conversation...or whatever else their daughter had interrupted. Hell, Jana wasn't even sure she knew what *she* was thinking. What had compelled her to be so honest with the man? She almost let him kiss her, for goodness' sake.

Which meant he was still physically attracted to her, too. It was probably just chemistry. Unwanted, inconvenient chemistry. Eventually, Mom came back to the room, and they both started to get ready for dinner. Jana had just put on a muted green sundress when there was a knock on the door.

Jana opened it to see Kamila wearing an amazing white maxi dress with bright green-and-pink flowers on it and holding a silver tray containing a white teapot and cups and a small plate of mandazi. "I thought you'd like some chai before dinner, since you weren't with the rest of us in the lounge."

Jana tilted her head, smiling at Kamila. This was very thoughtful...and needed. Jana invited Kamila in.

"Mom's in the shower," Jana said.

Kamila put the tray down on the coffee table. "Good. We can talk." She poured Jana a cup of chai and handed it to her.

The two sat on the sofa, and Jana inhaled deeply from her warm cup. The rich, creamy scent of cardamom, ginger, black pepper, and tea soothed her instantly.

"Thank you," Jana said.

"For the chai, or for not bringing the whole brigade with me to deal with your crisis?"

Jana chuckled. "Both. And I'm not in a crisis."

"Rohan and I saw Anil and Imani in the pool. He said you were...frustrating."

"Did he—"

"No. That's all he said. But he looked miserable. I haven't seen him like that since..." Kamila's voice trailed.

"Since when?"

"Since years ago. Before Imani was born."

Jana knew when Kamila meant. "When I refused to marry him."

Kamila nodded. She curled her feet under her on the sofa. "So you two had a fight?"

Jana took a mandazi and inspected it in her hand, picking at the black cardamom seeds poking out of the dough. "I'm not sure that's what I'd call it."

Mom came out of her bedroom then, already dressed for dinner. She quickly greeted Kamila, then rushed out, saying the others were waiting for her.

Jana looked at the door after Mom left. "She didn't actually say goodbye to me, did she?"

Kamila frowned. "Are you two fighting, too?"

Jana exhaled. "No. Mom and I never fight. Things are as they've always been."

Kamila looked like she wanted to ask more. She knew Jana's mother well. She'd been Kamila's Rashida Aunty forever—the one who gossiped with her father, always made the best dhokla, and who was like the universal aunty in the crew. But Jana doubted that Kamila ever really thought about who Rashida Suleiman was. Or ever noticed how distant she was with her own daughter.

Kamila must have read Jana's mind, because she changed the topic away from Jana's mother. "So what was the complicated not-a-fight discussion, anyway?"

"We're trying to be friendly on this trip. It's taking some negotiating. He's pushing hard for forgiveness or something. He says it's for Imani, but I'll bet it's more for his own guilt."

"I don't know what he's thinking, but I will say that man is very motivated by his daughter's needs."

"Don't say that's admirable," Jana warned.

Kamila raised a brow. "Okaaay..."

"I mean, no one ever says that about a mother. *She's so admirable...she did her kid's laundry.*"

"I fully agree with you. There is a ton of sexism in the way we see parenting."

"We're shamed for having the baby," Jana said. "For choosing not to have the baby. For working. For not working. We're shamed for having sex. For not having sex."

Kamila nodded vigorously. "Yes. Women can't win. Is that why you're salty with him?"

Jana nodded her head. "Yeah, partially. The man has had life so *easy*. Don't get me wrong—I adore Imani and have no regrets at all, but he hasn't seen nearly the fallout from our affair as I have. I lost a ton of respect, an actual job, and even friends."

Kamila's eyes widened. "You lost *friends*?"

Jana nodded. She wasn't sure why she'd never told Kamila

this. "My friend Jess from uni. After all the gossip came out, she said that supporting me reminded her too much of her cheating husband. And my other school friends went with her, too."

Kamila shook her head. "Unbelievable. That's not really a friend, you know."

Jana did know. When Rohan and Kamila found out about Jana's pregnancy, neither of them showed even a moment of judgment. They fell right into supporting her. Jana sighed, taking Kamila's hand and squeezing. "I know. And I know what Anil's ex did to him wasn't fair to him, but..." Jana's voice trailed.

Kamila looked at Jana curiously, probably shocked that Jana was being open about her life for the first time. "Jana," Kamila said slowly. "I don't actually know the whole story with him and Nadia. She left him?"

Jana sighed. She didn't even know *why* she'd kept it from her friend for so long. "Just between you and me?"

"Of course."

"Okay. Remember years ago when he followed me to Toronto after I left him in D.C.?"

Kamila nodded. "Yeah. That's when I first met him. That was right after you two broke up, right?"

"No, actually, it was a few months *after* we broke up. I left him when I found out he was married, and then I discovered I was pregnant a few weeks later. I stayed in D.C. a few months wrapping up my contract and figuring out what to do."

Kamila frowned. "Oh, I thought you were only in D.C. a few weeks."

Jana shook her head. She'd lied to everyone when she got to Toronto and said she was only in D.C. a week, mostly because she was ashamed that she'd left her post in Tajikistan so early into her contract. Jana hated thinking about those months—she'd felt so alone, and she'd had no idea what to do with the mess she'd turned her life into. Eventually, she decided to keep the baby, leave her job, and move back to Toronto. "Apparently after I left him, he finally tracked down his wife and told her it was beyond over and that he'd fallen in love with someone else. Then when I moved to Toronto, he followed me to apologize and win me over. But I refused to hear him out."

Kamila sat up straight. "Wait, Jana—he had to *track down* his wife? He didn't know where she was?"

Jana shook her head. "When I told him I was pregnant, he finally told me everything about his marriage. He hadn't seen or heard from Nadia for six months by then. He traveled a lot for work, and she was apparently hooking up with her high school boyfriend whenever he was gone. Anil suspected as much but had no proof. He came home from a trip one day and she wasn't there. He went to her family to see if they knew where she was, and they insisted he not say anything, and they'd find her. They threatened him, telling him they'd say he'd been mistreating her or something if he told anyone she'd left him. They were very traditional and were worried about saving face. So, he carried on with his life. He traveled a ton and came to Tajikistan to see a friend while I was working there."

"And that's where you met him."

"No, we'd met a few times before that. But yeah . . . that's when we got together. He told me he was divorced. A nice, amicable split, not a messy one with a missing wife and threatening in-laws."

"What a mess. But then he found her?"

Jana nodded. "Yes. And he told her he wanted a divorce. But all hell broke loose with her family. It was apparently a shit show. And it got worse when they found out I was pregnant, because they couldn't force him to stay with her anymore. They were the ones who spread the word that the split was because of *his* infidelity, not hers. They started the rumors about me, that I was a home-wrecker who knowingly split up his happy marriage and trapped him with a baby."

Kamila's eyes were wide. "Holy macaroni. That's how that job of yours found out?"

Jana nodded. "Nadia's family actually called the donors of the project. Anil stood up for me, telling everyone who would listen that Nadia left him a long time ago, but it didn't help much."

Kamila shook her head, frowning. "That's *horrific*. Poor Anil."

Jana looked at Kamila, annoyed. "Yeah, but he *told* me he was divorced. If he had told me his marriage was a mess, I could have decided whether I wanted to step into that mess or not. Plus, don't you remember how he tortured me back when he chased me to Toronto? Before I told him about the pregnancy? Teasing me and trying to make me jealous by flirting with *you*? It was vile." Jana suddenly remembered the comment he'd made earlier—that where Jana was concerned, his instincts always failed him. Seemed he had that issue five years ago, too.

Kamila was silent a moment. "Okay, yes, that was bad. He should have been straight with you. It took me a while to forgive him for that. But I feel like..."

"Like what?"

Kamila sighed, looking at Jana. "I'm not going to tell you to get over it. Be angry forever. I think you're totally justified. What's his rationale for wanting to suddenly be friends? You've seemed to be working well together as parents for a while now."

"He said Imani is starting to think that I hate him."

Kamila cringed. "Is that true?"

Jana exhaled. "Probably. Lord knows I'm terrible at hiding my feelings. It's just...it's hard for me. I've *tried* not to be mad at him."

"I know it's hard. Jana, you're a bit...fussy, and I love you for it." She frowned. "Is there a positive way to say that someone always holds a grudge?"

"And why shouldn't I? You said I was justified."

Kamila put her hands up. "That's my point. You *should* hold a grudge! I love how principled you are. You don't let people walk all over you, and it takes work for you to trust someone after they betray you. That's a good thing! That's why it took so long for you and me to be friends. You're not a doormat. That's an amazing example for your daughter."

Jana scowled. It didn't sound like a good thing. Easygoing people were happier.

"One question," Kamila said. "You don't have to answer if you don't want to... Do you think you and Anil would still be together if you had agreed to marry him?"

Jana snorted. "Anil asked me the same question earlier. Of course, I have no idea—we were only together two weeks. How could we know?"

"What did you tell Anil?"

Jana sighed. "I told him no. We're too different."

Kamila shrugged. "There are lots of reasons why relationships fail, but that's not a good one. Lots of couples are different. Look at me and Rohan."

"That's what Anil said." Plus, there were Jana's own parents. They'd had a happy, loving marriage, even though Mom was the social one and Dad was the introvert. He was sweet, quiet, and thoughtful. The one who sat silently at the table while everyone talked over one another. What would Dad say now about Mom's TikTok? Jana knew what he would say. *Let your mother be herself, because that's what we love about her.*

Jana took a long sip of her chai. "It's all a moot point anyway," she said. "Hypotheticals don't help anyone, because he had too much baggage. Maybe the baggage wouldn't have been such a big deal if I hadn't gotten pregnant, but I *did*."

Kamila nodded. "True. But remember—you don't have to forgive him or get over it enough to have a *relationship* with the man. Just enough so you can be friends. Maybe he's done enough groveling for that?"

Jana closed her eyes. She didn't know. The last week of Anil helping Jana when she was stressed and anxious; getting her socks, snacks, and that book; talking about development; and taking care of their daughter together—all that had *already* changed things between them. They'd held hands in the safari vehicle today. And they'd fought...quietly, but with more passion and emotion than they had in years.

They'd maybe almost kissed.

And there was still almost a week left of this trip.

Jana didn't know how she was going to survive it. Or if even more things would change between her and Anil Malek while they were in Tanzania.

"I want to," Jana said. "I want to be okay with him." She chuckled. "I decided that was my goal for this trip after I saw him. It's time to get over Anil Malek and the past. Or at least pretend to be over him. He's right—Imani sees my issues."

"How's that goal going?"

Jana shrugged.

Kamila frowned. "Between you pretending to let loose and pretending to be over the past, you're going to be a whole new pretend person by the time we get back to Toronto. Or a new real one."

"What do you mean?"

Kamila shrugged. "What's the saying? 'Fake it till you make it'? I think all this faking it could make a new Jana."

Jana didn't know if that was a good or a bad thing.

CHAPTER 16

Early the next morning, the whole party packed into the Land Cruisers for the drive to Lake Manyara National Park. Imani was clearly not loving another long trip and insisted they stop several times along the way because she had to go to the bathroom, or because her legs hurt, or because she wanted a samosa, but only one of the cheddar potato ones Mom made. Nelson was a pro, because every time Imani whined that she wanted to stop, he was at a clean, kid-friendly rest area within twenty minutes. Jana was genuinely grateful that Anil was with her, because he took half the complaints from Imani and half the attempts of diverting her attention from samosas. Neither of them said anything about their discussion the day before, but the tone between them had changed. They seemed kinder to each other. Or maybe it was only Jana who was kinder. She wasn't entirely sure if she was overcompensating, or if she'd made actual progress in getting over him. But it was easier to be with him, and Jana was glad for that.

They finally reached Lake Manyara National Park and took a shortish game drive before heading to the hotel. Jana was immediately struck at how different this park felt compared to the Serengeti and Ngorongoro. The Serengeti seemed vast—almost too vast. Dry and arid, and so, so flat. Ngorongoro was like an enormous bowl that contained every terrain possible in Tanzania—some forested areas, some arid spots, some wetlands, plus that pond stuffed full of flamingos.

But this didn't feel anything like the others. It strangely felt like they were driving through a tropical rain forest. It was so much lusher…so much greener than the other parks.

"Lake Manyara is a bird-watchers' paradise," Nelson said as they passed a pond. This one was also full of flamingos, but the guide pointed out a sacred ibis and even a black heron. They passed through an enchanting forested area thick with twisty, lush trees.

"Look, Imani," Anil said, pointing to the left when they'd stopped. "In that tree."

Imani turned to where Anil was pointing. She eventually squealed, "Lion!" Asha and Nicole excitedly started taking pictures. Jana tried, but she couldn't see any lion. Just trees.

"Here," Anil said, coming up behind her. She was standing at her seat to look out the roof of the vehicle, and she tensed when Anil came so close.

He bent to her level and reached around Jana's shoulder to point to the trees. "See the tree right in front of us?"

"Yes." She squinted, trying to ignore the warmth radiating off him. Was he going to notice that she was covered with goosebumps even on a warm day?

There was most definitely *not* a lion in that tree. Lions were big. That tree was small. If there was a lion, she'd see it.

"There is a smaller tree directly behind it. The lioness is on a branch about halfway up that tree."

Jana leaned forward, looking where he was pointing, and

finally saw it. She didn't know how she'd missed it before. A full-sized lioness lounging in a tree like she was a house cat instead of an apex predator.

"I see her!" Jana excitedly took a step back so she could tell Imani she saw the lion, forgetting that Anil was there. *Right there.* Behind her. She just backed into his whole entire body, and she was now pressed up against him. He was warm and solid, and his sandalwood and soap scent filled her nose. Jana closed her eyes as every nerve ending in her body came alive. He was going to step away from her now. He didn't want to be this close to her.

But he didn't move away. They stayed that way for a second or two. Or longer. Neither of them moved a muscle... They just looked at the lion in a tree with their bodies pressed together.

"Mommy!" Imani squealed. "Can you take a picture?"

"Yes! Excuse me!" She moved forward, trying to put some distance between her and Anil.

"Sorry!" he said awkwardly, moving back to stand on the other side of Imani.

The rest of the game drive was uneventful. They saw more birds, including a flock of vultures feasting on a gazelle carcass, which was pretty cool. They didn't see any elephants, though.

The vehicle was mostly silent on the way to the Manyara hotel after the game drive. Jana couldn't stop thinking about how firm Anil's chest felt when she crashed into it. Or how he managed to still smell like soap even after the long drive. She tried so hard not to think about how much she'd wanted to lean into him for even one more second and let them just be there in that moment. No past baggage, no family complications, nothing but the two of them.

What was going on with her? She knew she'd never stopped

being attracted to the man...but first that little daydream yesterday in the hotel, and now she'd practically swooned after he showed her a lion in a tree?

This had nothing to do with her *pretending* to be okay with him. It was completely because of his ploy—or maybe *efforts* was a better term—to patch things up between them. The moment he stopped giving her space, Jana just got caught in his charms all over again. But like Kamila had said, Anil's goal was to build a *friendship* between them. But of course, leave it to Jana Suleiman, always the overachiever, to skip over friendship and instead imagine him on his knees pleasuring her in her hotel suite.

Jana was pulled out of her unwanted train of thought when the Land Cruiser suddenly stopped short. Her hand reflexively shot out in front of Imani to protect her, and Anil's did the same thing.

His eyes widened when their hands touched in front of Imani. Or maybe his eyes were wide because of the scene in front of the Land Cruiser.

"Mommy! Daddy! *Zebras!*"

That was why Nelson had stopped. In the middle of the road in front of them were two zebras. Two zebras who would probably prefer privacy for their carnal adventure.

Asha and Nicole in front of them started laughing, while Nelson honked the horn. The loud noise interrupted the amorous zebras' coital activities, and Jana swore they glared at the Land Cruiser before strolling out of the middle of the road.

Jana put her hand down awkwardly, hoping Imani didn't ask about the scene in front of her.

"Mommy, were the zebras fighting?" Imani asked. Asha giggled.

Jana bit her lip. She had no idea what to say here—she looked to Anil for help. He looked like he was straining hard not to laugh, too.

He reached over and patted Imani's knee. "No, they weren't fighting, Mini. They were playing a game."

Imani turned to Jana. "What game?"

Jana asked Nicole for help, who had turned to look at the child. What was the point of having an ob-gyn in the vehicle if she couldn't help explain the birds and the bees to the pre-schooler? But Nicole shrugged, still chuckling.

"Leapfrog!" Anil said.

Imani frowned. "What's that?"

Nelson started driving again, and the rest of the trip was spent giving Imani a verbal lesson on playground games from her parents' generation until she forgot all about the zebra copulation in front of her.

Thank goodness.

When they got to the hotel, Anil insisted he would take Imani for the evening again. He said he would give her a bath, then put her down for a nap in his room while he caught up on some emails. Jana agreed. She had no idea how long this truce between them would last. Or if soon he'd start being cocky and *challenge* her again, and she'd become grumpy and bitter, so she thought it was best not to press their luck and spend the evening together. Everyone else said they were going for a swim, so Jana agreed to join them.

This was an opportunity to check off another item on her "letting loose" list. Dancing had helped loosen her up. Staying up late hadn't really done much, but maybe swimming in a bikini would give Jana some confidence. Jana headed to her room, which, for this hotel, was the bottom level of a small hut with a thatched roof. In her room, Jana slipped on the bright pink two-piece from the brigade backpack. She hadn't worn a two-piece in years—not since before Imani was born. She'd never been ashamed of her body—but she did grow up with religious Muslim parents who didn't like her revealing so much skin. But of course, they never minded her Indian dance costumes.

Jana looked in the mirror—something she didn't do often in swimwear. Usually because she didn't like to study all the changes in her body since giving birth. Maybe it was Kamila's preternatural shopping ability, but in this swimsuit, with its push-up bra cups, high waistband, and neon pink color, Jana looked...fine. Actually, better than fine. Jana turned in front of the mirror. She looked *good*. Fierce. This wasn't the same body she'd had as a twenty-five-year-old, but there was nothing wrong with it. And the color of the fabric—so much brighter than anything Jana ever wore—brought out the pink in her cheeks. Jana looked carefree, easygoing, and fun. *Vibrant*. She wrapped a pink, green, and black kanga around her waist, popped the bottle of sunscreen in her bag, and headed to the pool. She didn't even know if Dr. Lopez would be there, but she felt different in this suit. She felt like the person she wanted Dr. Lopez to see in her.

The whole Bridal Brigade, minus Shelina, was already at the pool. Kamila was applying sunscreen at a lounge chair, while the others were already in the water but near the edge so they could talk to Kamila.

"OMG, Jana," Asha said. "Look at you, you hot mama. You look *spectacular*."

Jana smiled as she joined them. Everyone was in swimwear, of course, and their kangas were draped over the nearby chairs, but

Jana was a little surprised that none of the other suits matched hers. "You all aren't wearing the swimsuits from the brigade backpacks?"

Kamila nodded. "They are. I picked out different suits for y'all based on your personalities. We don't have to be matchy-matchy anymore now that the wedding is done."

Jana frowned. Apparently, Kamila thought Jana's personality was a flirty hot-pink bikini?

"We've had a day and a half," Kamila said as Jana rubbed sunscreen on herself. "Shelina's kids were a *nightmare* on the drive. Remind me not to sit for three hours in a car with three boys under ten. We had to stop at a rest stop so the kids could be separated into the other Land Cruiser." She looked at Nicole. "I need to schedule an appointment to get my tubes tied."

Nicole raised a brow. "Rohan had a vasectomy last year." It was no secret that Rohan and Kamila weren't interested in having children of their own and that they were happy being dog parents and everyone's favorite aunty and uncle.

"I'm not taking any chances."

"Imani was a bit fussy on the drive, too," Jana said. "We had to stop for three bathroom breaks."

"Ha!" Kamila said. "Only three! The luxury! Jana, you did the right thing by having only one child. They feel like exponentially *more* when they increase in numbers. Like puppies, really."

Jana shrugged. She'd always assumed Imani would be her only child—and now that Imani was four, she'd pretty much missed the boat to give her a close-in-age sibling. Jana herself was an only child, and it suited her. She couldn't imagine having to share her life with brothers and sisters. Of course, Anil might give Imani a sibling one day. He may be older than Jana, but thirty-eight wasn't too old to have more kids.

Jana pushed the thought out of her head and took off her kanga. The to-do list said to swim in a bikini, so that's what she had to do. She dove gracefully into the water, resurfacing a few seconds later, her hair pasted to her head. The sun was low in the bright sky and gave everything a hazy sepia tone that made this whole scene feel so surreal. Peaceful.

She waded over to the edge of the infinity pool, where the water seemed to disappear into the horizon. It was an unbelievable view. Soon the others joined her, and they all looked out at the grasslands and baobab trees in the distance. It was like a postcard. There was just the right amount of breeze in the air. It was quiet, despite the increasing number of people in the pool area. The green dappled views stretched as far as the eye could see.

"I'm happy to be here," Jana said quietly. And she meant it. This trip had started so chaotic with Jana being tossed into one uncomfortable situation after another. But right now, here in this beautiful infinity pool, Jana was content. Almost happy.

Nicole must have heard Jana's silent proclamation because she squeezed Jana's hand under the surface of the water for a moment. "I'm happy we're both here."

Dr. Lopez and Farzana Aunty came to the pool area then. A group of aunties and uncles were with them, including Mom and Nadira Aunty. It appeared the pool was the party spot this evening. This was good. Now Dr. Lopez would see a fun, frolicking-in-the-pool-with-her-friends Jana. She smiled and climbed out of the water as they came toward her.

But Mom was not smiling. "Jana! What are you wearing? You can't wear a bikini like some—"

"I bought her that," Kamila interrupted. "She looks amazing,

right, Rashida Aunty? Jana should always wear Barbie pink."
Kamila was also wearing a two-piece, but the family expected it
of Kamila. Not of good-girl Jana.

Jana grabbed her kanga and wrapped it around her chest
because she didn't want to argue with her mother in front of
Dr. Lopez.

"Where's Imani?" Mom asked.

"Anil has her."

"You should bring her. She loves swimming."

Nadira Aunty nodded. "Yes, Anil had her yesterday, too. He
needs a break." Nadira Aunty looked at Farzana Aunty. "Jana's
such a good girl. She's not into partying like the others. You can
always trust her to make the right choice."

Mom nodded. "And so smart! Always reading a book. She
never gave us problems, this one."

Jana didn't love that Dr. Lopez was here to see her mother and
aunty treat her like a rebellious preteen in a skimpy swimsuit
one moment, then a one-dimensional good-girl the next.

"There she is!" Mom said.

Jana looked over, and sure enough, Anil, Imani, Rohan, and
some of the groomsmen were joining them at the pool.

"Mommy!" Imani was positively vibrating in her purple sea-
shell-print bathing suit, and she already had her floating swim
trainer around her chest and arms. "Are you going to come
swimming with me and Daddy?"

Jana grinned. "Yes, absolutely." It was a much-needed escape
from Mom and the aunties. And a chance to show Dr. Lopez
and Farzana Aunty how aspirational this broken family was.

Jana took off her kanga again. And Anil . . . stared at her.

"I thought you were going to put Imani down for a nap,"
Jana said.

"She insisted that we had to try every pool on this trip." He paused. "You're wearing a bikini," he stated.

Jana rolled her eyes. "Don't tell me you have a problem with my licentious swimwear, too. I've already heard it from my mother." Her choice of the word *licentious* was completely because Imani wouldn't understand it.

He snorted. "No issue at all. You look…great."

"Mommy looks pretty," Imani agreed. "Barbie has that swimming suit."

Anil laughed, then peeled off his T-shirt.

And he looked great, too. She hadn't seen his bare chest in years. True, his body wasn't the same as before, either, but that didn't mean it didn't look good. Very good. Jana turned away quickly. "C'mon, Imani. Jump in and I'll catch you." Jana lowered herself into the water and put her hands out to catch their daughter.

"Both you catch me!" Imani squealed. To Imani, having her parents together like this was just about the best thing that had ever happened to her.

Anil slipped into the water and stood next to Jana, and they each held out one hand for Imani to hold. After taking her parents' hands, Imani jumped, then proceeded to show off to everyone how well she could swim.

"She's a fish, right?" Anil said, watching their daughter.

"She's amazing." Jana stepped closer to him, smiling proudly.

Standing side by side, Jana and Anil watched their daughter swim. Jana tried not to think about how they were very close in the crowded pool, or that she could feel his bare leg against hers under the water. Or even about how strong his arms and legs looked later as he did a lap across the deep end. All Jana focused on was how much fun she was having with Imani and Imani's

father in the pool. It wasn't pretending, or for anyone else's—
including Dr. Lopez's—benefit. It was just a completely lovely
way to check off an item from her list. Wearing the pink bikini
was a totally effective way to let loose.

Later that evening, Shelina insisted Imani join her boys for
room service and a movie in their suite with their nanny. Imani
was excited to go, since they would be watching *The Lion King*.
After dropping Imani off, Jana went back to her own room to
shower, then changed into a pale tan maxi dress and sandals. She
brushed her hair and even put on some earrings. She had the
night off, and she was feeling good. The Serengeti was intense,
and Ngorongoro was chaotic. But here in Manyara, Jana was
feeling serene. At peace.

After another amazing dinner, most of the party moved to
the poolside lounge for drinks. Jana quickly checked on Imani
to find her daughter fine, then headed to the pool as well. She
didn't really have to—she'd already checked off the *stay up late*
item on her list—but this time, she was doing it because she
wanted to.

Everyone was crowded around one long table in the poolside
lounge, many with drinks in front of them. Jana joined them,
sitting across from Anil.

Anil smiled at her as she sat. She smiled back and gave a
slight nod to let him know Imani was fine. He dipped his head
in gratitude.

"Great news," Tim said. He was sitting right across from her
and holding the brightest green drink Jana had ever seen. "They
have a karaoke machine here. They're pulling it out of storage
right now."

"Jana," her mother said. She was sitting on the other side of the
table with Kassim Uncle, Rohan's parents, Farzana Aunty, and

Dr. Lopez. "Did you know that Sam works for an international nonprofit? Maybe he could help you find a job."

Dr. Lopez smiled. "I work mostly in policy and planning. I'm happy to talk to her about it later, though. This is a vacation. Let's put work behind us."

Jana tried to smile at him, but she was terrified—now that Mom knew he worked in her industry, would she talk about Jana even more?

"Oh," Kassim Uncle said. "I thought you were a professor like Farzana."

Dr. Lopez nodded. "I'm that, too. Part-time at U of T."

"Jana was thinking of being a professor," Mom said. "She taught at Cambridge when she was in grad school. They wanted to keep her, but she insisted on moving around to different places. But now she wants to stay in one place for Imani. So selfless."

"I would love to explore teaching more," Jana said, looking at Farzana Aunty. "You said you teach in addition to your research?"

"Yes, undergraduate developmental psychology. I do find it rewarding, but research is my first love."

"Teaching would be a breeze for Jana compared to the kind of fieldwork she's done," Anil said. He looked at Dr. Lopez and Farzana Aunty at the end of the table. "Honestly, I know I'm biased, but I'm in complete awe of the scope of her past work. And of course, I saw her talent firsthand when we started a nonprofit together a few years ago."

Jana looked at him. This was just him helping her get the job. Or maybe he meant it? He'd been complimenting her a lot lately.

Or maybe Jana should stop analyzing his every word?

"You should look into teaching. Campus life is so inspiring," Farzana Aunty said. "That's where Sam and I met, you know." She told the story of them locking eyes in a café on a crisp fall day. She neglected to mention that he was a professor and she was a student, though. Talk about a relationship with a problematic foundation.

But here they were, thirty years later, and they were clearly as in love as they were when they were married. Even after being divorced, they found their way back to each other.

Farzana Aunty's story led others to talk about how they'd met their partners. Mom talked a bit about meeting Dad—Jana's grandparents had arranged the meeting after prayers one day, and Mom's first thought was that there was no way she'd marry a man with ears that big. Asha and Nicole talked about how Kamila had set them up but tried to make it seem like a random encounter.

"So what if I'm not good at stealth matchmaking," Kamila said. "I was right about you two being perfect together."

The bartender came to the table then to tell them that the karaoke machine was ready if they wanted to use it.

For the first song, Mom, Nadira Aunty, Jon Uncle, and Kassim Uncle got on the stage to sing "Malaika," a famous Swahili song written in the forties that pretty much everyone who'd ever lived in Tanzania knew by heart. They sang it well—Jana did not inherit her mother's singing voice.

"Did you know 'Malaika' once hit number one on the Swedish pop charts?" Anil said. "It was recorded in the sixties by the Hep Stars, which was Benny Andersson from ABBA's first band."

Jana raised a brow at Anil. Since when did he know music trivia?

Anil shrugged. "I like ABBA. My mom's influence."

Asha clapped her hands together, looking at Kamila. "Love ABBA! We're still going to do 'Dancing Queen,' right?" The Swahili song was done, and Mom and the others were climbing off the stage.

Nicole shook her head. "Let's do 'Waterloo'!"

Kamila took Yuriko's arm in one hand and Shelina's in the other and pulled them onto the stage. "Nope. It's got to be 'Mamma Mia.'"

Jana waved her hands in front of her. She did not want to sing. The "letting loose" list was supposed to be there for inspiration—they said she didn't have to do everything on it. "No... I'm not really—"

"C'mon, Jana," Kamila said. "The brigade is supposed to be together! Let's go be... vibrant!"

Everyone was here tonight. Dr. Lopez, Farzana Aunty, Anil. She was just not comfortable singing in front of all of them. But... that list was about doing things that were *uncomfortable*. To show Dr. Lopez how she could be part of a team.

After dancing, and swimming in the pink bikini earlier, Jana had realized that the list—and *pretending* to be vibrant—was shockingly working. Stepping out of her comfort zone was awakening something in her. She felt closer to the person she used to be... or at least the person she wanted Dr. Lopez to see.

She finally nodded. As the rest of the brigade climbed the small stage in the lounge, Kamila grinned at them. "I just realized that life is imitating art! A destination wedding with my favorite friends? Just like the movie *Mamma Mia!*"

Yeah... except Tanzania instead of Greece, and unfortunately, no Colin Firth here.

But as the song started, Jana wondered if she'd ever really listened to the lyrics of it. Despite the upbeat tempo, "Mamma Mia" was about feeling bitter and angry after a failed relationship.

About not figuring out how to stop loving the person who'd broken your heart.

The lights were bright in Jana's eyes, and her legs were getting wobbly. Jana barely sang with the others. The lyrics were hitting too close to home. She closed her eyes as a prickle stung behind them.

She was being ridiculous. This wasn't her life imitating art. She and Anil were friendly. That's it. She was physically attracted to him, but that didn't mean she had *real* feelings for him. Just chemistry.

She looked out at their table...Mom was watching. Dr. Lopez. Her aunties and uncles.

And Anil was there, watching her sing about being broken-hearted.

Could he see that she was freaking out? See the torrent of confused emotions swirling through her? The loud music. Everyone staring at her. Singing about pain, about not being able to move on after falling in love so fiercely.

Jana squeezed her fists as the brigade sang—rather badly, honestly—until Jana reached her breaking point. She slipped behind the stage through the mosquito net walls covering the lounge area the moment the song ended. Everyone was clapping when she sat on one of the chairs near the pool.

Rubbing her temples, Jana heard the next song cue up and start. It seemed, hilariously, Farzana Aunty was going to sing an ABBA song, too—"When I Kissed the Teacher."

Jana wasn't alone for long. Rohan soon sat in the chair next to her.

"You okay?"

Jana looked up at him and smiled. "Yeah. Needed some air. I'm not much of a singer."

"Neither were they, if you ask me."

Jana chuckled.

"You... seemed different today. Until..."

"Until I had a panic attack because the lyrics from a seventies pop song were hitting close to home?"

Rohan paused, eyes wide. "I just remembered that movie is about a second-chance romance. Did something happen between you and Anil?"

Jana sighed. She'd never told anyone that she was still attracted to Anil. Because why would she? Jana was a private person. She didn't talk about things like this.

But this was *Rohan*. He was one of the first people she'd told about her pregnancy. He knew even before her mother or Anil. Rohan had kept her secret, helped her find a family lawyer, and had been a shoulder to cry on while she sorted out what to do.

She shook her head. "No. Nothing happened. I'm just confused. I'm not used to spending so much time with him." She paused. "Hey, Rohan, do you happen to know if..."

Rohan shook his head. "He's not dated anyone seriously since Imani was born, if that's what you're asking."

Jana chuckled. "Maybe it would be better if he had. Want to ask your wife if she'll find him someone?" Saying those words felt like a punch to the gut. Anil *would* move on one day. Jana had no doubt about that. He was a great guy. He deserved it. And it would destroy Jana's heart all over again.

"It can't be easy dating as a single parent," Rohan said.

There was that word again. *Easy.*

Jana shook her head. "I'm losing my mind. I am *not* interested in *dating* Anil. I've barely even forgiven the man! Plus, why the hell would he want to get involved with me? I'm the one who—

and these are his words, by the way—'has been torturing him for years.'"

Rohan didn't say anything for a while. Jana knew she didn't have to fill the silence with him. She didn't even have to ask him to keep this conversation to himself.

"I'll probably be single forever," Jana said suddenly. "I'm probably too fussy to fit someone in my life. But...seeing you and Kamila so happy, I admit I'm a little jealous. Maybe I need to find me a Rohan."

He snorted at that, shaking his head. "Nah, you need to find yourself a Kamila." He looked at Jana. "You do deserve it, you know. Whatever the aunties and your mother say, you aren't a fallen woman. You have as much value as anyone else. More, actually."

"I haven't internalized their judgments, if that's what you're thinking."

He shrugged, then stood, holding out a hand for Jana. "Let's go back inside. I'd prefer the safety of the mosquito netting. We can sit at the bar away from the others—I'll even buy you a drink."

Jana smiled and took his hand. "I'll take the drink, but we can join the others. I'm ready to socialize again." As they slipped through the netting, Jana took Rohan's arm and leaned on him. "Thank you."

He kissed the top of her head. "Anytime."

The table had discovered the Bollywood selections on the karaoke machine while Jana was gone, but at least no one insisted she sing again. After many songs, several of the older generation left, Mom included. The remaining group continued to chat aimlessly. Jana didn't exactly join the conversation. But she still sat with them. The tropical breeze passing through the mosquito netting was making her feel serene again. It was pitch-dark—darker than it ever got in Toronto. Eventually, the party had whittled down to just her, Anil, Tim and Jerome, Rohan, Kamila, and Farzana Aunty and Sam Uncle.

"Such a beautiful place," Dr. Lopez said. He looked at Rohan. "I am selfishly pleased that I came back into your life in time for this wedding."

Rohan chuckled. "We're glad you were able to join us. My summer trips with you in California were some of my favorite childhood memories. That and the big holidays with the rest of you." He smiled at Kamila and Jana.

"I find it so strange," Jerome said. "You, Kamila, Shelina, Zayan, and Jana grew up together, and now four of you are married to each other."

"I've always been the odd one out," Jana said. "I don't really fit."

"Nonsense," Kamila said. "You *fit*. You're one of us forever."

Jana smiled. That wasn't how Kamila used to feel about Jana.

Anil looked at Jana. "I remember being so sure you were an only child when I met you. I'd recognize one anywhere."

Jana frowned. "Why?"

"I'm an only child. And you're like me."

Jana shook her head. "I don't think we're that alike."

"I disagree. We've never had to compete with limited parental resources, so we haven't learned toxic methods of fighting for them, but we're both still driven. We're both a little stubborn and maybe not great at compromising, but we understand the value of seeing other people's points of view. And we're both terrible at communication in our relationships, despite being excellent at professional communication. Relationships with other only children are challenging for us."

Jana blinked, looking at him. Was he saying this to give

Dr. Lopez and Farzana Aunty a reason for why she and Anil divorced? Or was he being honest? Jana had no idea, but she decided to play along.

"I suppose you're right." She let out a nervous laugh. "We were doomed to fail."

He smiled before taking a long sip of his beer. "Nah, we didn't fail. We're friends now, aren't we? Unless you count the sunk cost of our wedding."

"Did you have a big wedding?" Farzana asked. This was a question that Jana didn't have an answer to.

"Not huge," Anil said without skipping a beat. "If it had been up to me, we would have run away to Vegas and eloped. It was certainly a memorable night, though." He looked around the table. "I don't think I'd ever been as nervous as I was on my wedding day. But that's weddings, right? You all know what it's like."

"Oh yes, I remember it well," Dr. Lopez said. "My stomach was in knots. But then I saw my beautiful bride waiting for me, and all the nerves fell away. It was like there was no one in the world but the two of us."

"That's beautiful," Kamila said. She looked at Rohan. "Is that how you felt?"

"I wasn't nervous," Rohan said. "I'd never been surer of anything in my life."

Tim snorted. "Is that why you bawled through the ceremony?"

Kamila glared at Tim. "You shush, mister." She put her hand around Rohan's neck and pulled him in for a kiss. He whispered something in her ear, which made her giggle, then stand. "Well, would you look at the time. We're going to call it a night. See you at breakfast." And they left the lounge, clearly eager to be alone.

Tim chuckled. "Newlyweds," he said. "I'm surprised they lasted this long."

Jana smiled. They were all silent for a few moments. Jana wondered if she should escape, too. She didn't need to be here until the end tonight—she'd already checked that item off her list. But she couldn't quite find it in herself to leave the table.

"I wasn't nervous on our wedding day," Jerome said, looking at Tim. Jana didn't know either man well, but she knew they were Kamila's friends before Rohan's. She assumed the two ended up on Rohan's side of the wedding because Kamila had so many more friends than he did.

Tim smiled. "Me neither." He looked at the others at the table. "We *did* do the speedo-wedding-in-Vegas thing, and they don't give you enough time to get nervous."

Anil snorted. "*Speedo* or *speedy*?"

Tim laughed, blushing. "OMG. I meant speedy. *Speedy*."

Jerome snorted. "Technically, it was both. And a bit *seedy*, too."

Everyone laughed. After Tim and Jerome told everyone about their wedding a decade ago, there was another lull in the conversation. Jana again considered if it was time to leave.

"I was sure, too," Anil said suddenly. "I mean, on my wedding day. She was the most beautiful person I'd ever seen, and it felt like time stood still whenever we were together. But I was nervous because I *felt* the fragility of the moment. Like maybe it was all an illusion." He chuckled, rubbing his face. "And considering how my marriage ended, my nerves were warranted. Maybe I knew."

Jana looked at him. He said *how my marriage ended*. He was talking about Nadia, not about his marriage to Jana, which never existed anyway.

Anil's carefree smile returned to his face. "But look at us now.

We're closer than we've ever been. The best of friends. We're so much better for Imani like this. And we're happier, right?"

He said *happier*. Not happy.

Why was she reading into everything he said?

"Well," Dr. Lopez said. "I, for one, admire you both for your maturity. It's no wonder you both work in development. Isn't that what we do? Work for the greater good? I love to see that you practice that in all areas of your life." He looked at his wife. Or ex-wife, technically. "Shall we turn in, too, my dear? Another long day tomorrow."

CHAPTER 17

Anil walked Jana back through the curving paths to her hut. "Thanks," Jana said as she reached the doorway.

He smiled. "I couldn't let you walk alone. There could be lions around."

She snorted. From this vantage point, she could make out the armed guard who patrolled the resort at night. They were safe from lions. She tilted her head. "What would you do if I was attacked by a lion?"

He shrugged. "I'd probably run like a scared squirrel. But I could at least tell the others what happened to you."

She chuckled. "That's not what I was thanking you for, anyway." She was thanking him for...letting them be closer today. For not mentioning their argument yesterday. For playing in the pool with her and Imani. For not questioning or chasing her when singing ABBA gave her an anxiety attack. For continuing this farce, or whatever this was.

And she was thanking him for challenging her. For forcing her to admit all the things that were so hard to say yesterday.

She didn't want to voice any of that out loud. But she was pretty sure he knew, anyway.

"Did it bother you? The stuff I said about weddings?" he asked.

"No. We need to make this lie believable, right?" She cringed at the word *lie*. She wanted to ask him if that was really what his marriage to Nadia had been like. Did he know it was fragile even at the beginning? But Jana didn't ask. That was breaking their unsaid rule.

Actually, she should be honest with herself. It was breaking *her* unsaid rule. Because he'd mentioned Nadia several times. Jana wondered if that rule had held her back. If they'd talked about what he'd gone through, about how he'd felt when Nadia abandoned and betrayed him, maybe Jana would have been able to forgive him sooner.

"Are you going to speak to your mother?" Anil asked. "I mean later. After we're home. If you get this job, then eventually Sam Lopez will learn the truth, won't he?"

Jana cringed. Yes, there was no way she'd keep lying to him if he hired her. "Yeah, but it will *crush* Mom. She's going to see him around socially." Jana sighed. "I hate disappointing her, but Mom's being so weird with me lately. Like what she said about my swimsuit. Why are families so complicated?"

Anil chuckled. "Our parents are immigrants. They literally came from a different world than ours."

"Yeah, and I guess it's hard to make the jump from seeing your daughter as a child to a fully independent person." Jana knew she would struggle when Imani started school in a few months. "Anil, promise me you'll knock me upside the head if I don't let Imani grow up."

He nodded. "That goes for me, too. I'd hate to become one of those fathers who talk about protecting my girl with a shotgun. But I get it. I kind of want her to be my little princess forever."

"I want her to be strong and independent and smart but still need me." Jana smiled. "Maybe the fact that we're having this conversation means we'll be good parents? Better than ours?"

"We are *already* good parents, Jana. And I think we will be no matter what happens in the future."

Jana agreed with that. Anil may not have been her favorite person for years, but honestly? There was no better father for Imani—and Jana was grateful she'd had her baby with this man.

They were both silent for a while. She wondered if Anil realized that was one of their first ever face-to-face conversations about parenting.

"Jana, you may not believe this," Anil said softly, "but I'll always want what's best for you. And not just because you're Imani's mother."

"I do...I mean, I do believe you."

He didn't say anything for a few seconds and looked at her with an unreadable expression on his face. Finally, he spoke. "Do you think you'll ever feel like that?"

"Like what?"

"Do you think you'll ever want the best for me, too? Like real friends?"

Jana didn't know. She'd been angry for so long. Maybe she'd been justified. Or maybe she should have let it go years ago. "Of course I want the best for you. You're Imani's father."

"Yeah, I am." He smiled.

"And I think..." She hesitated. "I *do* think you're a good man. You deserve to be happy." She looked up at the dark night sky. There weren't even any stars there. "Another long drive tomorrow."

He was quiet for a few moments. "Will we be in the same vehicle?"

Jana nodded.

A slight smile snuck onto his face. "I'm looking forward to it."

"So am I." Before Jana could think about it, she reached up and gave him a hug. Anil stiffened a fraction of a second before hugging her back, his strong arms tightening around her as his hand rubbed her back. It was so . . . comforting. Jana didn't want to let him go.

But she did. A hug was fine. Friends hugged all the time.

They all woke early for yet another long drive the next day. This trip, from Lake Manyara to Tarangire National Park, would take a little less than three hours. Jana was seriously starting to hate these long, bumpy journeys in the Land Cruiser. As they loaded their luggage in again, she said a silent wish that Imani would bring less drama than she had in the last trip.

And apparently, it worked because her daughter slept soundly for the entire drive, which gave Jana the chance to look out her window at the Tanzanian countryside.

Something had definitely shifted in the last day. Maybe the change of scenery, spending time in the place that meant so much to Jana, and seeing animals like she had with her father so many years ago had worked to change Jana's outlook. Or maybe it was checking off all those items on the "letting loose" list that had changed her. She felt . . . well, looser. She'd already stayed up later than ever, she'd danced, she'd worn a hot-pink bikini. She'd even sung.

Or maybe it was all Anil. He'd been pushing her since they got to Africa. Challenging her. Making her talk. But also, being *him*. Kind. Intelligent. Generous. Charming. He'd been chipping away at her defenses.

She had no idea if her new contentment would last beyond Africa. Was this her element yet? Did she want it to be?

They took their lunch break once they were close to their destination, stopping at a dusty picnic area inside Tarangire National Park. The other vehicles were on pace with them this time, so the whole party was able to eat together.

"Why are the lunches pretty much the same every day?" Shelina asked as she opened her white box. Jana knew what it would be—either a sandwich or a chapatti roll, a chicken drumstick wrapped in plastic, a hard-boiled egg, a banana, a box of mango juice, and a little packet of cookies. Whatever hotel they were leaving in the morning provided the box lunch for the day, and they seemed to have all read the same memo on what to put in it.

Jana unwrapped her chapatti roll in today's box. "I don't mind," she said. The dinners and breakfasts at the hotels were all amazing and varied. It was nice to have something a little predictable, stable, and guaranteed to be tasty on their travels. Plus, when they left the Serengeti with no more cheddar-and-potato samosas, it had been such a relief to discover that Imani *loved* the box lunches. A bit of predictability in a chaotic world was comforting

Shelina snorted. "*I'd* prefer more variety. We're adventurous, right, boys?" she said to her kids, who were ignoring her and eating their cookies anyway.

Jana understood the subtext here. Jana wasn't *fun* enough to be adventurous. She was the boring bridesmaid. The one who liked vanilla ice cream. Jana took a bite of her chapatti.

"Hey, Kamila," Asha said. "The next hotel is the tents one, right?"

Kamila finished chewing, then grinned. "Yep. I'm really excited about it. A friend of mine went and said it was stunning."

"I can't believe you're making us sleep in tents," Shelina said, scowling.

"They're luxurious! We need at least one tented camp on this trip, or it's not really a safari. Apparently, the food is phenomenal, too."

Shelina was still scowling. Jana wasn't worried. She'd slept in tents without running water enough times that this would be no issue. She turned to Shelina. "You don't like the predictability of the same lunch every day, but you'd prefer to stay at another hotel just like the three we've stayed in?"

That shut Shelina up. Good. Jana was more than a little over the woman's passive aggression.

"I was looking at the pictures," Anil said. "The rooms all have spectacular views. It'll be like when we went camping last year, right, Mini?"

Imani grinned. "Can I sleep in your tent, Daddy?"

"Oh," Anil said. He looked at Jana. "If you don't mind, I'd love to take her for the next few days. You've had her every night so far."

Jana nodded. "If that's what you want, Imani."

Kamila picked up her phone. "I'll text Elsie to call ahead and have them move the children's cot from your room to Anil's." She frowned. "Or have you switch rooms. Tents. Whatever. Elsie will take care of it."

Jana's gaze wandered to the grasslands near the picnic site and she nearly squealed like Imani at what she saw in the distance. An elephant. Just hanging out while they were all having lunch. "Look!" Jana said, pointing.

It was beautiful. No barrier between them—no wall, or window, or vehicle. Not even a crater ridge, like there was at Ngorongoro when they saw that first elephant. The animal turned toward them, and Jana swore it made eye contact with her for a few seconds. Then it turned and walked away, completely unconcerned about the humans picnicking in its habitat. It was happy to share its space.

"Thank you," Jana said under her breath. This was the perfect start to this leg of the trip.

She finally turned back to her lunch, and that's when she noticed that Anil was looking at her curiously. "Elephants really are your favorite animal."

He probably didn't remember it specifically, but she'd first told him that back when they were together five years ago. They'd been shopping in London—and she'd found a little painted ceramic elephant from India in a gift shop. She'd excitedly bought it and told him all about the elephant collection her dad had started for her.

That was the night they'd tried out that hotel shower together. They'd spent hours wrapped around each other. Talking. Always connected. It was the first time Jana had fallen asleep in someone's arms. And it was the night where she'd first thought that the relationship could have been the beginning of forever.

Sometimes Jana's memory was a curse.

"Well, you're in luck," Nelson said. "Tarangire is the elephant park." He looked at Imani. "How high can you count?"

Imani beamed proudly. "Eighty-seven."

"Okay, msichana mdogo, I want you to count the elephants you see today, all right? Then later you tell me how many there are."

Imani looked at Jana, eyes wide. "Are we going to see eighty-seven elephants, Mommy?"

Honestly, Jana doubted it. But she didn't want to crush Imani's hopes. "Maybe! Finish your sandwich, then we'll find out, okay?"

After lunch, they started their first game drive in Tarangire National Park. They were staying nearby for two nights this time, so there would be another game drive the next day through a different part of the park.

Within about ten minutes of driving, they saw their second elephant. Then their third. At a lush pond covered with greenery, they saw two more. They also saw the most amazing sight of the entire trip so far.

"Daddy, that elephant is little!"

It was a baby elephant. Staying close to its mother and frolicking and splashing water on itself. Jana was on her feet to take pictures of it before Nelson had even stopped the vehicle. It was the cutest thing Jana had ever seen. She lifted Imani in her arms to see it better. Everyone in the Land Cruiser was in awe, giddy with excitement. As the drive continued, they saw gazelles, the most vibrant striped zebras yet, and some giraffes. But Jana understood why this was called the elephant park. There were so many elephants. On their own, in herds, at the watering hole—everywhere. Anil kept pointing out new ones, and Imani eventually stopped counting (she really couldn't get past forty, anyway). But they definitely saw more than forty elephants. More than eighty-seven.

Jana had never imagined a more perfect game drive. There was an intoxicating energy in the air. Everything seemed to shine so much brighter. The leaves were greener, the sky bluer, and somehow, the animals were even more alive. This place was magical. Jana hadn't remembered smiling so much in her life.

After that amazing first drive in Tarangire, the Land Cruisers made their way to the new resort. Their vehicle was a bit behind the others, and when they finally got out, Asha's, Nicole's, and Jana's phones all started buzzing at the same time. Must be the Bridal Brigade group chat. Jana looked at the message.

Kamila: I'M IN HEAVEN. THERE ARE SO MANY DICKS HERE.

Jana snorted audibly.

Asha: I think we just found the quote for Kamila's tombstone.

Kamila: Stupid autocorrect. Dik-diks. I want to take one home.

Then about three pictures of the adorable antelopes flashed across their screens. Jana, Asha, and Nicole all crowded together, cooing.

"What is it?" Anil asked.

Jana smiled. "Bridal Brigade stuff." She slipped her phone into her pocket.

The resort was perched at the top of a high bluff overlooking Tarangire National Park. With light cream walls and a thatched roof, the main building was less ornate than their previous hotels but fit into the surroundings well. The main lobby area was a large circular room, with two other circular rooms off of it.

After getting their tent assignments they were given a list of rules for the facility. "We ask that you don't walk alone on the property at night. We have several guards patrolling who would be happy to escort you wherever you need to go. Or you can call here to have someone come. Electricity is available in rooms six through nine only. Please zip up your tent when you are in it, and use the monkey lock when you are leaving the tent or when you are sleeping."

"Why do we need an escort?" Shelina asked.

"Unlike the other hotels in the area, this property has no fence around it," the hostess said. "The patrols are to keep you safe from all wildlife."

"Wildlife!" Shelina exclaimed. "Big animals just wander around? Like…freely?"

"It's perfectly safe. Nothing to worry about. Emanuel here will show you to your tents."

They were taken to a path behind the building that led to the tents. "Mommy, Daddy, look!" Imani squealed. Their daughter had seen her first dik-dik.

The small animal was so much cuter in person than the pictures the Bridal Brigade had been sending each other. About the size of a golden retriever, the antelope had enormous eyes with thick black lashes, tiny little horns, and a sweet little heart-shaped nose.

Imani chased it as it bolted off the path.

"What is that?" Imani asked.

Emanuel, the porter, explained to Imani that they were called dik-diks, then told her about all the animals they could expect to see on the hotel grounds, including vervet monkeys, superb starlings, and others.

"Mommy, Mommy, he said sometimes elephants come, too! And that thing is called a dick!"

Jana snickered, because apparently being in the Bridal Brigade had given her the brain of a thirteen-year-old boy. Anil turned and looked at her with a raised eyebrow. Which only made Jana laugh harder.

The tents were lovely but small. Made of heavy canvas walls with thatched roofs, they each had a covered veranda with two safari chairs in front. The tents all faced the same direction, with sweeping views of Tarangire National Park in front of them. After Emanuel showed them how to use the monkey lock, Jana looked around the room she'd be sharing with her mother. Facing the tent opening there was a large four-poster bed with a mosquito net draped over it, plus a small dresser and a chest at the edge of the bed. In the back was a bathroom with a solar shower, a composting toilet, and a small wash basin. It was just the right balance of luxury while feeling like they were a part of the park.

"These tents are amazing," Jana said as she put her bag on the chest.

Mom frowned. "They're so small. Oh. They brought Imani's bag here."

As far as Jana knew, Anil's tent was a few down. "I'll bring it to Anil."

She found Anil and Imani sitting on the little veranda in front of their tent. Imani's feet dangled off the safari chair, not reaching the floor, but she looked so grown-up sitting there talking to her daddy.

"Mommy! Did you see? They brought me a bed!" She pointed inside. Jana peeked into Anil's tent, which was pretty much the same as hers, except the large bed was pushed against the side of the canvas so there was room for a small cot next to it.

"Daddy says we're going to watch the sun in the morning."

He nodded. "The sunrise over the park must be incredible. Imani and I have decided to wake up early to watch it from bed."

"Daddy's going to set an alarm. Did you know that monkeys can use zippers here?" She frowned. "They're smart. Zippers are hard."

Jana laughed. "I have your bag. Want me to help you get ready for dinner?" She looked at Anil, fully expecting him to say that he was capable of getting Imani cleaned and changed for dinner. And Jana knew he was capable. That's not why she asked.

But he didn't object. He just smiled and stood, taking the bag from Jana's hand. "That works. I'll unpack her things while you two pick something out. C'mon."

Together they went into the tiny tent and got their daughter ready for dinner.

Dinner was served in an open-walled thatched-roofed room,

with white tablecloth–covered tables and dark furniture. The food was delicious—maybe even better than the other hotels. Jana even had seconds of the ndizi na nyama. After dinner, everyone went to the lounge to talk and play cards. Jana was delighted to learn that there was no karaoke machine here—she had no interest in singing again. But she wasn't really a card player, either, so she sat back while the others played. She and Yuriko talked about houseplants for a bit after Jana admired the large ZZ plant arrangement in the lounge. It seemed Yuri had a somewhat secret houseplant Instagram account. Jana wondered if that had anything to do with her dungeon, but she didn't have the nerve to ask.

Soon, Imani was yawning, so Anil took her to bed. Jana offered to come help get her ready, but he said Jana could stay and enjoy herself. Jana almost insisted—she wasn't used to being around Imani and not being the one to take her to bed—but she just smiled and said good night to them both.

She was learning to get used to all sorts of new things in Tanzania. Like saying *good night* and *sleep well* to Anil Malek…and meaning it. And also, feeling a genuine sense of loss when he wasn't with her.

That was new, but somehow, it didn't feel strange.

CHAPTER 18

Jana had the guard walk her to her own tent soon after Imani went to bed, since she would rather read than watch others play cards. She changed into sweats to sleep in and had just brushed her teeth when her phone buzzed with a message.

Anil: Imani's not feeling well. She's asking for you.

Jana's fists clenched. She knew everything had been going too well. She closed her eyes a moment, then slipped on her sandals and opened the monkey lock. The armed guard was a few yards away. "Excuse me! I need to go to another tent!"

The guard rushed over to escort her to Anil's tent. Jana could hear Imani crying loudly before she stepped onto the deck in front, so she asked the guard to find their party in the lounge and bring Nicole because a child was unwell.

When Jana stepped inside Anil's tent, she found Imani sitting on the edge of the bed almost convulsing with sobs, and Anil next to her rubbing her back. Imani had a white washcloth in her hand.

Jana rushed to her, crouching in front and putting her hands on Imani's knees. "Imani, baby, what's wrong?"

Imani looked up at Jana, eyes wide. "Mommy, I threw up!" She hiccupped, then whined a bit.

"Oh, sweetheart." Jana looked at Anil.

He nodded. "She was fine. Brushed her teeth and was about to put on her pajamas when she suddenly felt sick. We were already in the bathroom, thankfully. Then she asked me to call you."

Jana ran her hand over Imani's head. She didn't feel particularly warm. "I'm so sorry that happened. How's your tummy now?"

Imani shrugged. Her big eyes were glistening with tears. Imani didn't get sick very often, and whenever she did, it completely terrified her that her body wasn't operating the way it was supposed to.

After she'd been sitting with Imani for a few minutes, there was a noise at the front of the tent.

"Jana, what's up?" Nicole asked.

Anil told Nicole to come in. "Imani threw up."

Nicole tilted her head sadly at Imani. "Oh no. How are you feeling now?"

Jana stood quickly. "I'm sorry. I didn't know what was wrong, so I had the guard get you—"

"Jana, it's totally okay. What's the point of traveling with doctors if you can't call them when a kid's sick? Jerome wanted to come, too, but I told him I'd text him if we needed anesthesia. Let me go get my bag so I can examine her, okay?"

Jana nodded. While waiting for Nicole to return, Jana wiped her daughter's hair with the damp washcloth. Imani was still sobbing while Anil was rubbing her back. Jana was sure the sound would keep any wild animals far away.

"Mommy?"

"Yes, baby?"

"You stay here even though Daddy is here?"

Jana looked at Anil. Why would Imani think Jana wouldn't stay if Anil was here?

"Of course, love. I'm not going anywhere," Jana said.

Nicole was back then with her carry-on bag. She sat in front of Imani and started pulling things out of it. After squeezing hand sanitizer in everyone's hands, she handed Jana a little packet. "Mix that into a bottle of water. It's an electrolyte solution."

Jana found an unopened bottle in the bathroom and sprinkled the powder into it. She could hear Anil telling Nicole about what happened before Imani threw up. When Jana returned, she saw that Nicole had put a thermometer in Imani's mouth.

The thermometer beeped, so Nicole took it out and looked at it. "Her temperature is fine. Okay, kiddo, here's what we're going to do. I want you to drink all this drink here." Jana handed her the bottle. "It tastes like cherries, but it also tastes a little bit like medicine, so you might not like it. But drink it anyway, okay? If you feel like you need to throw up again, you tell your mommy or daddy. Same if you feel like you need to go to the bathroom. Make sure you sleep a lot, and I will come see you in the morning. Sound good?"

Imani nodded, then choked back a sob. She looked exhausted to Jana.

Anil took out Imani's pajamas and helped her change while Jana went with Nicole to the bathroom so Nicole could wash her hands and Jana could talk to her without Imani hearing.

"She probably had some tap water...It's almost impossible to avoid it completely. A random ice cube, a piece of fruit washed with tap water instead of bottled. Her tummy is young, so it's a bit more sensitive."

"Do you think it was something she ate today?"

Nicole shook her head. "No. Probably not. No one else is sick. I'm not too worried about a single vomiting incident. This, too, shall pass—but I'm only a phone call away if anything else happens. If I don't hear from you, I'll call you in the morning, okay?"

Jana nodded, then impulsively hugged Nicole. "Thank you. Seriously."

Nicole hugged her back. "It's no problem. That's what friends are for. You're doing great with Imani. Seriously." She lowered her voice. "I know you two are doing a lot of pretending on this trip, but neither of you are pretending to be amazing parents. She's a lucky little girl to have you both."

Jana exhaled. "Thanks."

Nicole shrugged. "Like I said at the sangeet...sometimes it's hard to tell that you're in your element...but everyone else around you can see it crystal clear. Get some rest, okay? Call me if she gets worse. I know you'll worry, but to put you at ease, we're not *actually* in the middle of nowhere. There are excellent medical clinics a half-hour drive from here and a hospital only two hours away. Your daughter's got a hell of a lot of people looking out for her." She glanced at Anil, who was tucking Imani into the cot. "Seriously. Lucky girl. Lucky mama, too."

Nicole said goodbye to Anil and told Imani again to try and get some sleep, then left the tent. Jana stood by the bed. Anil was rubbing Imani's back, the same way Jana herself did when Imani was having trouble sleeping. Because of course he knew all the tricks to get Imani to calm down just like Jana did.

It was so strange. They had joint custody. He'd spent as much time with Imani as she had. Jana had never doubted that Anil was a dedicated and devoted father. As Nicole had said, Imani was thriving because of her father as well as her mother.

But joint custody meant one of them or the other. Not *both* of them. For more than a week now, they'd been parenting Imani *together*.

Imani shifted, getting more comfortable in her small bed. "Both stay?" Imani said weakly. Like she was afraid to ask for it.

Anil looked up at Jana. Okay...this was awkward. It was a very small tent, and there was only this one queen bed and Imani's cot. Not even a chair. "We'll stay if you want us to, baby," Jana said.

"Okay," Imani said softly. Jana squeezed in and sat next to Anil on the bed and put her hand on her daughter's head, gently running her fingers through her daughter's curls in a way that she knew would relax her.

"Sleep, baby, okay?"

Anil and Jana stayed like that, each with one hand on their daughter, until Imani stilled, her gentle breathing filling the small tent.

The night was so dark. No matter what Nicole claimed, it really did feel like they were in the middle of the wilderness. Anil's phone light was still on—the only light in the small tent. Even outside, Jana couldn't see or hear anything. She could only hear the soft breathing of her daughter.

They had been like that for a while, maybe twenty minutes, when Anil whispered, "I think she's asleep." He turned off his phone flashlight.

Jana moved her hand to her daughter's back. "I'm sorry she freaked out on you," Jana said. "I swear, for Imani, her emotions about being sick are always worse than the illness itself."

"You don't have to apologize, Jana. I'm her father. I know," he whispered. He shifted, straightening from being crouched over Imani. "That is not a comfortable position for so long. This place is amazing, but it's tight for three of us."

Jana took the hint. "You're right. She's asleep—I'll go." She started to get up.

A hand on her knee stopped her. "You *can't* go. You promised her you'd stay. What if she wakes up and you're not here?"

"I didn't mean all night!" Jana whispered. "Where am I supposed to sleep? In the shower?" Jana couldn't see him, and it was very strange to have a whispering argument in the dark. She couldn't sleep in the same tent with Anil. Not when her past feelings for him were crashing back like a tsunami.

He turned his phone flashlight back on. "Jana, you're being ridiculous. The bed is plenty big enough for us. I can even put one of my bags between us. Let's get some sleep, okay?"

He tossed the Groom's Platoon backpack to the middle of the bed. Jana wondered if he'd taken the box of condoms out of it.

Jana sighed. He was right, of course. This was the perfect test of the new truce between them.

"Okay. Fine," Jana said, standing. "I'm going to use your bathroom."

When she came out of the bathroom, she saw that Anil had gotten the bed ready, removing the bedspread and turning down the blankets. "Do you really want the bag between us?" he asked.

"It's fine. We're not twelve."

She heard him snort under his breath. "Okay. Do you want to be on this side closer to Imani?"

"Yes."

When Jana got into bed, she turned toward her daughter and stretched her arm out so she could rest it on Imani's back. She tried her very hardest not to pay attention to the feeling of someone sliding into bed behind her. At least it was dark. She wasn't forced to have any visual confirmation that she was once again sharing a bed with Anil Malek.

She didn't think she'd sleep, though. Because what was once

an eerily silent night suddenly got very loud. She heard a shrill cry from outside.

"What the hell?" she said, rubbing Imani's back so she wouldn't wake.

"It's a bush baby," Anil said. "I was chatting with Nelson earlier, and he said we would definitely be hearing them tonight. They live in the trees on the grounds, and their cries carry in the night. They're called bush babies because they sound like a baby crying."

"Wow. I'm glad I'm with you, because I would definitely have thought that was Imani crying if I were in a different tent."

He snorted. "Yeah, no. You are *not* glad to be with me."

She turned so she was lying on her back instead of her side. She wasn't going to face him or anything, but she wanted to make sure he heard this. "Are we going back there again? I don't hate you. Honestly."

He was silent for a few seconds. "Yesterday you said you were looking forward to spending time with me, but you sounded horrified at the thought of spending the night here. Be honest—if we didn't have Imani, you'd hate me."

Jana rolled her eyes. She'd had a great day yesterday, until her panic attack singing ABBA. But now Anil was picking a fight again. She didn't know why she'd been worried that spending the night with him would increase her pesky little attraction for the man—because clearly spending time alone with Anil Malek would only increase her irritation at him. "But we *do* have Imani, so that's a bit of a moot point, isn't it? Does it bother you that much that there might be someone who doesn't think you are Prince Charming incarnate?"

"I don't give a shit what anyone thinks of me. I care what the *mother of my daughter* thinks of me." Charming Anil was angry, despite his voice being no louder than a whisper.

Jana sighed. This wasn't the time for this. "We shouldn't be having this conversation. Imani is right here."

He exhaled. "You're right. But, Jana...I think it's high time we actually *have* this conversation. Soon. If we're going to move on, we *need* to clear the air about the past. For Imani."

"There is no air to clear!" Jana whispered as forcefully as she could. "We've talked enough. I know your justification for starting our relationship when you were still married. I know the fault wasn't all yours." He'd groveled. Hearing it again wouldn't make a difference. "And I know the sexist backlash I've faced also wasn't your fault and that you did what you could to stop it. What exactly are you hoping that more talking will accomplish? Are you looking for complete forgiveness so you can let go of your guilt?" She could hear her bitterness.

"No." His voice was a low rumble. "I'm not asking for forgiveness if you can't give it, but...maybe I'm asking you to stop punishing me with this hot-and-cold attitude of yours. It's been *five years*. Also..." His voice trailed.

"Also what?"

"Also, it would be nice to be able to think back to those weeks and remember the good parts."

Jana snorted. She turned away again to face her daughter.

Jana spoke quietly after they had both been silent for a while. "I know it's been a long time. And believe me, I know life would be better—for both us and Imani—if I could move on."

"But you're not willing to try," he said. It was a statement, not a question. There was something in his voice...resignation? Acceptance? If they weren't in a tent in the dark in the wilds of Tanzania, then maybe she could *see* how he was feeling. See why he was so determined to push the buttons that were probably rusted stuck.

"I *am* trying. But this is me. I'm fussy. Unwavering. I *want* to get past it all, but it's hard. I didn't *choose* any of this."

"You chose to have Imani." He said it so quietly—probably to make sure Imani didn't hear.

That was true—she did. She'd found out about the pregnancy with enough time to terminate. Jana was a staunch advocate for reproductive rights for all, and she'd defend a pregnant person's right to make their own choice until her dying day. And *her* choice had been to have her baby. And when she told Anil, he said they could be together. Get married and be a family. But she chose not to. Jana didn't regret either of those choices. Maybe it was unfair to put all the blame for the negative repercussions of them on him, though.

But despite the fact that his voice was barely a whisper, Jana *did* understand what he meant when he said, *You chose to have Imani.* He wasn't regretting Jana's choice. There was no bitterness. It was just gratitude. "And you chose to let me be in her life," he added. "That was so brave, Jana."

Jana didn't say anything, mostly because that statement made her eyes fill with tears. Everyone saw her getting pregnant as her biggest mistake. And not marrying Anil as her second biggest. But Anil understood.

"Okay," he said after a while. "This isn't the right time. We should be enjoying our holiday. We'll keep pretending to be friends. But later, before you make your decision about Disney, we need to have a serious talk, okay?"

Jana was terrified of that conversation. She exhaled. "Okay. I'm going to try to get some sleep now."

"Okay. Good idea."

Jana closed her eyes, hoping that sleep would save her from this awkward, painful night.

But she wasn't so lucky. Jana lay in that too-small bed wedged between her daughter and her daughter's father, thinking about all the things that were really scaring her about continuing this talk. She wasn't afraid of bringing her feelings of shame, betrayal, and disappointment to the surface. Those feelings had never left the surface to begin with. She wasn't afraid of Anil challenging her again. She was more afraid of what was happening now as her feelings of resentment and bitterness were waning. She was afraid of what moving on would look like for her.

Because without resentment, without betrayal, what was Anil to her? During this trip, they had been closer than they had been for years—both physically and emotionally. All those game drives showing their daughter animals and counting elephants. Playing in the pool together. Taking care of Imani when she was sick. Now they were sharing a bed like a family, with their daughter next to them.

In many ways, Jana's anger, resentment, and bitterness had become like a security blanket. Or a shield.

If she let it go, all that would be left would be the heartbreak.

But it was late and pitch-dark, and they were in the middle of nowhere with their sick daughter. Maybe now was not the time to put up her walls. Without turning, Jana reached behind her and put her hand out for him. She had no idea how he saw it, but his fingers intertwined with hers in seconds. She gently pulled on Anil's hand, and he maneuvered so his arm rested on Jana's waist, the big spoon to her little spoon. Jana felt safe and comfortable and thought she might be able to fall asleep now.

"Good night," Anil whispered.

"Good night, Anil."

CHAPTER 19

A faint light from outside woke Jana. She listened for Imani's slow breathing, telling her that her daughter was still sleeping soundly. Jana looked through the clear window on the tent door. The subtlest orange color had started painting the sky. Jana turned and propped herself up to watch the sunrise.

The sun wasn't hitting all the plains yet; most of the trees and hills were still darkened. But as she watched, the orange glow slowly illuminated the landscape. The clouds shifted from pale to brighter shades. Soon, dappled rays of red and purple started painting the vast terrain in front of the hills, bringing it out of its shadowed slumber. Were there animals out there taking this in, too? Maybe an elephant mama, lying near her baby, smiling to herself as the warm sun roused her from sleep?

The beauty on this trip had exceeded Jana's wildest expectations. The elephants, the baobab trees, the glorious panoramas. Even with all the frustrations, awkwardness, arguments, and feeling like an outsider, at this moment, Jana felt...whole. And assuming Imani next to her was fine, she felt content.

"It's beautiful, isn't it?" Anil said next to her.

Jana chuckled softly. Of course, she hadn't forgotten that she'd fallen asleep in his bed last night. Literally in his arms, which had probably been a mistake. But with the glorious Tanzanian sunrise in front of her, it was hard to feel regret about anything.

But she didn't exactly want to turn around to face him, either. It wasn't dark in the tent anymore. She didn't want the intimacy of seeing Anil's face before he put on his good-natured mask. Now he would have pillow creases and warm, sleepy eyes, and the private expression that was still burned into her memory from their past.

What would he see in her face? The grumpy mother of his child? Or would he think the fact that Jana slept in his arms meant she wanted this relationship to be *more* again?

"It's the most beautiful sunrise I've ever seen," Jana said. "Imani slept all night. She's still out."

"She's probably okay, then," he said. "When she had that stomach bug last year, she was up every twenty minutes."

Jana had only heard about the stomach bug after the fact since Anil had Imani then. She watched their daughter's sleeping face for a few seconds, then looked back out the window. The colors seemed to swirl in the sky even more now. She could feel the cool nip lessening as the sun's rays warmed the air.

She should get up. Sneak back to Mom's tent and take a shower. Did she still need an armed guard now that it was daylight?

"Don't leave yet," Anil said quietly.

"How did you know I wanted to go?"

"Because you're you. Stay and enjoy this sunrise with me. Just the three of us right now, okay?" He put his hand on her arm, and she felt the warm weight of it down through her toes. She rolled over to look at him.

He was *right here*. Next to her, under the same sheet as her. And it felt so... *familiar*. And normal.

She knew what he meant. *Just them*. A little family on holiday, like they were normal, functional, and *together*. Happy. Without all the baggage, lawyers' agreements, resentment, hurt feelings, and everything that Jana wouldn't let go of. Just them.

He was close enough that she could feel his breath against her cheek. His eyes were slightly hooded, but long lashes fluttered as he blinked. His jaw was scruffy again. His expression was soft. Kind.

Sexy.

They stared at each other for several long seconds, neither of them making a move. This time, it was clearer than that day in the Ngorongoro hotel—he *was* going to kiss her. Ignoring the chemistry between them was like ignoring a tornado right in front of her face. His hand on her arm moved slightly, fingertips barely brushing against her sensitive skin.

"Jana," he whispered.

Jana shook her head. She couldn't get caught in a moment with Imani next to her. Letting loose was apparently chipping away her sense of self-preservation.

She turned away from him and propped herself up on the bed to watch the sunrise over the East African plains. She couldn't get sucked in by Anil's charms again. No matter how much part of her wanted it, no matter how comforting and *right* it felt now. The risks were too big—she couldn't let herself get hurt all over again. And this time, Imani could get hurt, too.

But this, watching the sunrise together, was okay. It didn't scare her. And it also felt right.

Imani woke up energetic, giggling, and seemingly fine. She was utterly delighted that both her parents were with her, and she didn't appear to have any memory of throwing up the night before. Or her emotional breakdown because of it.

"Your tummy isn't hurting anymore?" Jana asked as she came out of the bathroom and looked for her sandals. She needed to get back to Mom's tent to shower and change for breakfast.

That reminded Imani of what had happened the night before. "Daddy!" she squealed with the same voice she used when she saw a giraffe. "Remember when I throwed up? You told me that lions can't smell puke so they won't eat us!"

Jana raised a brow at Anil.

"I was trying to ease her anxiety," he said.

Jana rolled her eyes. Now that it was morning, she could see Anil clearly. He was currently sitting on the middle of the bed with his legs crossed, braiding Imani's hair. And he was in his pajamas—which were thin athletic shorts and...

Holy crap—he wasn't wearing a shirt. She'd slept next to him all night while he was *topless*? How hadn't she noticed that? Not just next to him, but literally in his arms. His chest hadn't been touching her when they'd spooned, but still. There had been nothing between them all night but her thin T-shirt.

Jana hadn't wanted to be sharing a bed with him at all, let alone sharing a bed with him while he was half-undressed. True, she'd seen him without a shirt when they'd been swimming the other day, but this was different.

Last night, she could have buried herself into his strong, warm chest to sleep like she had five years ago instead of just holding his hand on her waist. He could have wrapped his arms tightly around her, and she could have heard his voice through his chest. And this morning, when they almost kissed while watching the sunrise, they could have been skin to skin, and they—

"Daddy, can I wear my leaves dress today?"

"Sure thing. I'll get it when I'm done with your hair."

Jana was still staring at his bare chest, horrified. "You're not wearing a shirt."

One eyebrow rose. "Uh...I literally just woke up? Here, Mini—hold this." He handed Imani the braid he'd been working on and hopped off the bed. After rummaging in his duffel bag a second, he pulled on a gray T-shirt, climbed back up behind Imani, and took her hair again.

Jana still couldn't look away. He was completely focused on their daughter's hair. Jana was mesmerized as he finished the first braid and started the second, first gently combing, then gathering small sections of hair and adding it to the French braid he was forming. When he was done, Imani wordlessly handed him a hair tie, which he wrapped around the thin end of the braid, twisting twice to secure it. Such delicate work for his big hands. The shirt he'd put on was thin—she could see his solid biceps and broad chest. She'd known Anil could braid Imani's hair, of course. Imani had come home with perfect French braids after a week with her dad enough times. But Jana had never actually *seen* him do it.

Attractive men braiding their four-year-old's hair was an untapped market for calendar pictures. Ovaries would explode on sight.

It was getting hot in this tent. Jana scowled and turned to the door. She needed to get away from this little domestic tableau. "I'm leaving. See you at breakfast, Imani."

Jana fumbled with the monkey lock but eventually was able to get the tent open and left quickly.

Mom was slipping on her shoes when Jana stepped inside the tent.

"Ah, there you are! I was just coming to see you. Do we have to take Imani to a doctor?"

Jana waved her hand. "No, no, she's fine. She threw up last night, but she slept well, and she seems totally okay today. We'll keep an eye on her, but I think it passed."

"Oh, shukar. That's good. Where is she?" Mom frowned. "Where did you sleep?"

Jana rummaged through her bag to get clothes. "Imani's with Anil. They're fine. Everything is fine. I'm just going to take a shower."

"But where did *you* sleep?" Mom asked again.

Jana did not want to answer the question. She did not want to say she slept with Anil Malek's arm around her. Or that he wasn't wearing a shirt. Or that they weren't sleeping at all early in the morning and were instead watching the most beautiful sunrise Jana had ever seen and maybe thinking about kissing. Or not thinking about it.

"Jana, where did you sleep?"

Jana turned to look at her mother. "I stayed with my daughter. She was sick."

"Anil went somewhere else? With that other single man... Marco?"

"It's Marc, and no. Anil stayed with Imani, too."

"Beta! You can't sleep in the same tent with him!" She put her hand to her forehead, scandalized. "What will they think of you? You are her mother—you should have stayed but sent Anil off somewhere else!"

Seriously? Was Mom really going all puritan now? First the bikini and now this?

Jana barely dated and certainly never spent the whole night with a man since moving home. She didn't do anything that would give Mom a reason to judge. Since getting pregnant, at least.

"They'll think a mother and father were staying with their sick child!" Jana snapped. "You're the one telling everyone we're friends!"

Mom smiled. "You're right. It should be fine. I am so glad she's okay... It's so dangerous out there."

Jana didn't know what to say. She exhaled. She didn't want to deal with this right now. She picked up her clothes. "I'm going to shower. I'll see you at breakfast."

The second game drive through Tarangire National Park was similar to the first. Breathtaking views that Jana couldn't believe were real. Elephants... everywhere. According to Anil, who was the only one still counting them, they'd seen more than two hundred elephants now. They also saw lions, zebras, hippos, giraffes, wildebeests, and water buffaloes. It was their last game drive in Tanzania, and it was a memorable one. Imani still seemed fine. Nicole was keeping a close eye on her, but the child was energetic and ate her box lunch with no complaint.

Jana was in a Land Cruiser with Anil and Imani again, since that was what Imani wanted. Thankfully, Mom was in another vehicle this time, which was good, because Jana had no idea what to say to her mother after her judgmental comments this morning.

But maybe she should have separated herself from Anil, too, because he barely spoke directly to her. In fact, he barely looked at her. And his smile—the charming Anil smile—was back. Not the private... *real* look that he'd been giving her for the last few days. Anil was pulling away from her.

Maybe he was just better at self-preservation than she was,

because whenever Jana's mind wandered, it settled on their weirdly *domestic* night together in his tent. Seeing him tenderly caring for their sick daughter. Each of them having a hand on her as she fell asleep. Then Jana falling asleep with the warm weight of Anil's hand on her hip. And of course, the morning, when they watched the breathtaking sunrise together. And *almost kissed*. Also, she thought of his naked chest, which had no business making her feel the way it had.

She was so confused and unsettled after it all. Was he feeling the same way? Did he have regrets?

At lunch, Dr. Lopez and Farzana Aunty joined the table with the wedding party. "I heard your little girl wasn't feeling well last night." Imani was sitting at another table with Shelina's sons and their nanny.

"She had a bit of an upset stomach, but she's fine now, thankfully," Jana said.

Dr. Lopez looked over to Imani. "Glad to hear that. It's always hard when kids get sick. She must have been happy you were with her."

Jana wondered if Mom was telling everyone how sick Imani was and how admirable Anil and Jana were for caring for the child all night together.

Anil nodded. "Plus, her Nicole Aunty was around, too."

"You know, it just occurred to me," Farzana Aunty said. "Would you two be interested in being interviewed by one of my grad students? They are compiling a series of surveys and case studies on family outcomes after divorce and are always looking for study participants."

Jana's eyes widened. Of course, she couldn't be interviewed by a researcher about her aspirational divorce—namely, because the divorce never happened. But...she cringed. She had to say yes, didn't she? She wanted Dr. Lopez to like her—to *hire* her. She couldn't refuse to help his wife—ex-wife—could she? "I . . . uh . . ."

"My dear, she's on holiday," Dr. Lopez said. "Let's keep work behind us . . . Perhaps you can speak to them after we're back home."

Jana gave him a thankful smile.

"I'm not sure our story would be that interesting, anyway," Anil said, not even looking at Jana. "Co-parenting hasn't always been smooth."

"Nonsense," Kamila said. "These two could write a book on conscious uncoupling."

"You should make videos!" Kassim Uncle, who was sitting at a nearby table with Mom, said. "On TikTok!"

"Dad," Shelina said. "Stop trying to get everyone on TikTok."

"They could put their wedding videos up and talk about their life now," Mom said. "I saw some other content like that—"

"Mother," Jana said, interrupting her and trying not to sound as irritated as she felt. *What wedding videos?* The last thing Jana needed now was Mom and Kassim Uncle fueling the fire.

"My organization has an active TikTok account," Dr. Lopez said. "We keep it professional, of course, but it's quite an effective way of connecting with younger donors. Speak their language, you know?"

Thankfully, that pushed the conversation away from Jana's supposed marriage and divorce and toward how social media can increase engagement in fields that aren't traditionally customer facing. Jana didn't have a lot to say about the topic, but at least they weren't talking about her.

That evening, Jana didn't just *suspect* Anil was avoiding her— she was sure he was. He sat at the clear other end of the table at dinner instead of sitting with Imani and Jana. And he didn't join the others for a drink afterward, saying he wanted to get Imani to bed early since she'd been ill the night before. Imani seemed fine and wanted to stay up, but Anil was firm. Jana told him to text her if there were any issues, and he said he would, but he also curtly told her that he was more than capable of taking care of their daughter alone.

Clearly, Anil had given up on his determination that they be friends. Had he decided Jana was just too hard a nut to crack? This was *good*—Jana had been scared they were getting too close. Too attached. This distance was what they needed.

But a part of her wanted to chase after him. To grab him and make him explain why he was giving her this cold shoulder. She wanted to challenge him like he challenged her. How could he sleep with his arm around her, then ignore her today?

Jana didn't chase him, though. She just sat in the lounge, swirling her mango punch in her glass, half-heartedly chatting with the Bridal Brigade about Asha and Nicole's upcoming kitchen renovation. This was why getting close to him had been a mistake. Jana was miserable.

Kamila got a phone call. Whoever it was made her smile widely. "Fabulous," Kamila said once she disconnected the call. "That was Elsie. There was a cancellation. The bridal party appreciation night is happening." She looked at Rohan. "She got six rooms."

Rohan smiled. "Which hotel?"

"Hatari Lodge."

"What are you talking about?" Shelina asked.

Kamila grinned. "Remember we were trying to organize one more bridal party get-together? It's all finalized. We'll have a final private party at a very cool hotel." She looked at Shelina and then Jana. "No kids."

"What are we going to do with the boys?" Shelina asked, seeming to forget that she'd loved this idea when Kamila had first told it to them.

"They'll have three grandparents and one nanny. And Imani will have her nanima, and my dad, too." She looked at Jana. "Or we can uninvite Anil so Imani can stay with her dad. Your call, Jana."

Clearly Kamila had noticed the coolness between Jana and Anil today.

Jana shook her head. "It's fine. I'll need to check with my mom, but if she's fine with it, so am I." Jana might be irritated at her mother right now, but she did trust her completely with Imani. "I guess I have to ask Anil if he's okay with it, too." She could call him. Or even go to his room to ask—but he probably didn't want her there.

Rohan was texting on his phone. "I just asked him. He said he's fine with it. He's heard of Hatari. Supposed to be amazing."

Kamila clapped her hands together. "Yay! The place looks *darling*. It's a small resort with all sixties modern design. It's named after a John Wayne movie! Very swanky."

Where the heck had Kamila found a midcentury modern hotel named after a movie starring a famous cowboy actor in the middle of Tanzania? Or in the northeast of Tanzania, specifically.

"Doesn't *hatari* mean danger?" Asha asked.

"The place is named after a *movie* called *Hatari!*," Kamila said. "It's not an omen or anything. It was filmed near there."

Jana sighed. She was inclined to think the name *could* be an omen. Because after things had been going somewhat well between her and Anil Malek for the last few days, they'd taken a definite turn today. All Jana could think about was what could happen at a small, stylish, private party with Anil Malek. And without their child.

Jana was pretty sure she was in danger, in one way or another.

CHAPTER 20

The following morning, a bus arrived to take the wedding party to Hatari while everyone else headed to a hotel in Arusha, a town near Kilimanjaro Airport. Jana and Anil said goodbye to Imani and promised they would FaceTime her that evening. Shelina's nanny was planning a pajama movie party, and Jana's mother told them not to worry at all and to have fun.

It was yet another three-hour drive from the Tarangire resort to Hatari, and Jana spent the trip as distanced as possible from Anil. If he was going to pull back from their *friendship*, then so be it. Their daughter, the aunties and uncles, Dr. Lopez, Farzana Aunty, and Mom weren't here—so there was no reason to pretend anymore.

Hatari Lodge turned out to be even cooler than promised. Secluded and very private, it was both quirky and extremely stylish. The lobby/lounge area was decorated in a bold color scheme with plush cushions on low seats. Paper lantern animal heads hung on the white walls along with tribal artwork and sixties movie posters. There were more tassels and sequins than Kamila's own living room. It somehow felt modern and trendy, while also feeling like they'd stepped back in time. The rooms were in a separate building from the lobby. Jana had agreed to share a double with Yuriko, and when they were led to it by the porter, they were greeted with a beautiful table with full glasses of champagne and the word *karibu* written in rose petals on the surface.

Jana looked at the porter. "Um, is this the bridal suite? Are we supposed to be getting this?"

He smiled. "This is for all guests at Hatari. Everyone should feel welcome." He showed them the luxurious room with two four-poster wood beds, crisp duvets, and a bathroom with a soaker tub. "Dinner will be served in the dining room at eight. Tonight, you have a choice of roast beef, coconut fish, or vegetable terrine. Do you know what you would prefer?"

"The fish, please," Jana said.

After Yuriko requested the vegetables, the porter left, and Kamila, Nicole, Asha, and Shelina came in.

"Your room is nicer than mine and Zayan's," Shelina said.

Kamila glared at her sister. "That's because your room only has one bed. Jana and Yuri need two." Kamila sat on the chair near the window. "Impromptu hashtag Bridal Brigade meeting. Isn't this place *amazing*? We need to take a ton of pictures. Tonight's hashtag is 'Rohan Kamila at Hatari.' Word of advice—don't bring your father, aunties, uncles, and in-laws with you on your honeymoon. Not that I don't love them all, but…"

"You should have come to Hatari alone," Nicole said.

Kamila shook her head. "Nope. Y'all are my ride-or-die crew, and this is all for *us*. Besides, this isn't really our honeymoon. Rohan and I are headed to a beach in Barcelona with no one to entertain but each other when you all go home. I'm kind of sad it's our last night together. This was my favorite wedding ever, and not just because it's mine."

Tonight was the official last night of the wedding, and guests would be leaving Tanzania on their own over the next few days. Some wedding party members were on a flight out tomorrow night, but Jana and her mother were leaving in two days, since Jana wanted to give Imani an extra night in Arusha to rest after the safari before the long trip home.

"So, what's the plan tonight?" Asha asked.

"Nothing really. We can hang out in our rooms this afternoon or go have drinks outside. There's no pool here—but I'm pooled out. Basically, we can do nothing. No game drive, no entertaining children or, worse, entertaining our parents. A four-course meal is being prepared for us, and apparently, there's a bartender here who knew John Wayne and loves to talk. Put on your sexiest dress for dinner. Tonight, we party in style." She stood suddenly. "I, for one, am going to test out the tub in the bridal suite. I'm hoping there will be a groom nearby to wrangle into it with me. See ya soon, ladies!"

Everyone left Jana and Yuriko's room, including Yuriko, who readily accepted Asha's invitation to join them for a drink in the lounge with the platoon. Jana declined. This was her chance to do whatever she wanted. She didn't have to be social or a team player, so she took her book out of her backpack and curled up on the window seat.

But after about half an hour, Jana found she couldn't concentrate. She kept wondering what the others in the lounge were up to. Was she wasting her only day in this special place? She didn't know where this was coming from—this was her first moment alone on the whole trip, and all she could think about was what she was missing. Maybe all her efforts to be more social had changed her. She remembered Nicole's comment at the sangeet—that when you step out of your element enough, you don't even notice when your element just changes.

Were Tim and Jerome finishing each other's sentences? Was Shelina not so silently judging the others? Was Yuriko giving any clues as to what she did with the dungeon in her house? Was anyone sending anyone dik-dik pics?

And what about Anil? Jana had no doubt he was with the rest of them. He was probably laughing. Maybe talking to Tim and Jerome about their plan to come back next year to climb Kilimanjaro. Or silently rolling his eyes to Marc about Shelina. Maybe he was playing chess with Nicole like they had in the Serengeti. Or maybe he was sitting at the bar with a beer in his hand, chatting with the storytelling bartender as if they'd been friends for years.

He'd always been like that. Standing out and yet fitting into a crowd. Being so damn personable that people just brushed off his past mistakes and he still came out on top. Jana had *noticed* Anil long before ever getting involved with him. Partially because he was extremely attractive in the exact way that appealed to Jana. Popular, charismatic, intelligent, and magnetic. He'd always seemed so much more...*alive* than anyone else in any room. It was like seeing one lone lily in a field of wild grasses. You couldn't help but see Anil in a crowd. Or at least Jana couldn't.

They may have been mismatched personality-wise, but once upon a time, Jana had been so sure she'd found something special with Anil. Her soul mate. She'd talked to him about things she rarely talked to anyone about. About her relationship with her parents. About feeling like the odd one out with Kamila, Shelina, Rohan, and Zayan. She'd even told him about being alone with her father when he'd had a heart attack. He'd wiped her tears when she cried about it, remembering that awful day.

Jana sighed. She didn't need to be dwelling on the past now.

She stood, looking out the window at Mount Meru in the distance. Jana was restless—maybe she could check something off her "letting loose" list. She pulled out her planner. There were two things left: have a long conversation with a stranger and wear a color. She had worn colors here—the sari at the sangeet, for example. Plus, the hot-pink bikini. Although technically, those didn't count because the list said to wear a color she picked herself, and she had not picked those clothes herself.

Where was she supposed to find a stranger to talk to? Her mind wandered again to what the others were doing in the lounge. For the first time in probably Jana's whole life, she felt a bit of FOMO—fear of missing out—about a social situation. She wanted to be there with the others. Maybe not to join in the conversation but to witness it. She wanted to be with them all.

And she wanted to be in Anil's orbit the most.

But that was preposterous. This is what she'd been afraid of—that being around him would bring up everything she'd buried beneath the hurt and resentment. Feelings that were more than just the physical attraction she'd had for years. She wanted to talk for hours about their work or Imani, or she wanted to sit in awe of him as he explained to others why it's important to educate girls in villages first. She wanted to watch him braid their daughter's hair.

But based on the way he'd been avoiding her since she left his tent in Tarangire, he didn't want any of that. Maybe he realized Jana's feelings for him were changing, and he was wisely keeping his distance. Anil wanted to repair their relationship so they could be better parents. He wanted to be *friends*—not more. And if he realized that they were getting too close—holding hands, sleeping in the same bed, even reminiscing about the past—maybe avoiding Jana was his way of putting a stop to all that.

If so, he was right. Whatever path they were on right now was *dangerous*. She wasn't sure she'd forgiven him for the past. The last thing she needed right now was a crush on her daughter's father. She'd been beyond destroyed when she'd lost him last time. She couldn't let that happen to her again.

Eventually, Jana turned off her brain and took a long bath, hoping to wash off this unsettled weirdness. She scrubbed, shaved, and moisturized, luxuriating in the ability to take more than ten minutes to bathe for a change. She blow-dried her hair, giving it a healthy shine instead of the frizz she'd sported for most of this trip. She put on the nicest dress she'd brought— a thin-strapped cream belted dress covered with vibrant flowers and leaves, with a full skirt and a long slit going up one leg. This would be the last night the wedding party would be all together. Jana wanted to make it a night she wouldn't forget.

She found the party in the lounge area near the front desk of the hotel. Jana wasn't the only one who'd put on her nicest clothes for this last night. Kamila looked stunning in a jaw-dropping magenta-and-teal dress with her hair cascading in loose waves down her back.

"Yay!" Kamila said, hugging Jana. "Look at you, Jana! That dress is to die for. Come—let's get you a drink."

Jana smiled, joining the table. Yuriko and some of the others left to change for dinner, and Jana ordered a drink from the waiter and sat with her friends. Jana noticed Anil, of course. She always noticed Anil. He was in a pale green dress shirt and charcoal pants, and he didn't even look at Jana when she sat at the table. Things were back to how they were before—back to their nonrelationship.

That was fine. Jana didn't need the attention of Anil Malek to feel like she belonged in this group. She sipped on her cocktail and chatted. Eventually, they were all brought outside to a beautiful gazebo walled with mosquito netting. A fully decorated table was set there with glimmering china, sparkling crystal glassware, and candles with flames dancing in the light tropical breeze. Jana found herself seated with Yuriko on one side of her and Nicole on the other. Anil was not sitting near her. He was smiling and talking to Jerome, and it looked like he was having a great night. The waiter came with the first course—a pureed potato-and-spinach soup, which was delicious.

"This was such a wonderful idea," Asha said. She was wearing a bright orange belted jumpsuit with her wild curls pulled back from her face. "Hey, Jana, did you see the giraffe outside your window?"

Jana shook her head. "I was in the bath."

"Mmm . . . the bath in our room was spectacular," Kamila said. "Right, Rohan? Big enough for both of us."

"The last few days have been so chaotic I was glad to have some alone time," Jana said.

"Just like old times, then?" Anil said, finally looking at her.

She raised a brow at him. "What do you mean?"

He smiled, swirling the wine in his glass. "I mean, you've always preferred to be alone."

She didn't take his bait. Didn't glare, frown, or scowl but put her new smiling, social face on instead and asked Marc if he'd ended up taking a walk on the grounds.

The rest of the meal was delicious. Jana thought the fish she chose looked the tastiest, but the real standout was the ginger-cinnamon Napoleon pastry for dessert. And the Tanzanian coffee served with it.

After dinner, Jana escaped for a moment to call Imani, who was having fun watching movies with Shelina's kids. After the call, Jana considered just going back to her room. Everyone had gone back to the lounge for drinks, but she was feeling off. It was Anil's comment about her preferring to be alone. Why bother finding a new element if people wouldn't let her change? Wouldn't let her find a new normal?

She'd been having a great night until he said that and sabotaged everything. But she wouldn't let him win. She joined the others on the low, plush seats in the lounge and ordered another old-fashioned, determined not to let her overthinking get in the way of having fun.

"We should play a drinking game," Kamila said.

"No thank you," Jana said. She did not play drinking games.

"Yeah, I agree with Jana," Anil said. "We had enough of that in college." He grinned at Rohan. "Hey, remember that guy everyone called the 'game master'? What was his real name . . . the one who used to wear that velvet blazer everywhere? We played that drinking game about slasher movies with him." He looked at the others. "You had to take a drink whenever the pretty girl did something stupid."

"Ugh," Asha said. "So sexist and juvenile. Let me guess—this 'game master' guy wore a fedora."

Jerome chuckled. "Come on, Asha. Should you be judging others on their misspent youth? I've heard your stories. What about that time you got drunk and stole a tiger?"

Asha tilted her head. "We *freed* a tiger. Not stole. I have done plenty of stupid things in my youth, but *that* was justified."

"Tell them about the time you streaked through physiology class in university," Nicole said.

Asha laughed. "It's a bit scandalous for this crowd, don't you think?"

"Nothing is too scandalous for this crowd." Kamila looked

around their group. "I happen to know at least one scandalous thing every person in this wedding party has done. More than one for most of you."

Zayan snorted, shaking his head. "My perfect big brother has never done anything resembling scandalous."

"That's what you think." Kamila pointed a finger at Zayan. "He did something rather scandalous only a few hours ago. In our Jacuzzi tub."

Shelina put her hands over her ears and looked at Zayan. "Who let your brother marry my sister, anyway?"

Rohan laughed. "No one *let* me do anything."

Kamila giggled. "*I* let you do lots of things to me. In fact, I encourage you. I beg you. I—"

"La, la, la," Shelina sang, her hands still on her ears. She turned and looked at Jana. "Anyway, not everyone has a scandal. I certainly don't. Jana doesn't, either. We're mothers."

Kamila snorted loudly. "Y'all have scandals. Just because you squeezed out babies doesn't erase the stuff that happened before that. Let's not forget about your pothead days when you were eighteen, Shelina. Remember when you asked Dad to water that 'plant' in your room for weeks while you were in school?" Kamila then looked at Jana and laughed. "And Jana arguably has one of the biggest scandals here in her past. One I *know* she regrets."

Jana blinked at her friend. Jana didn't have a lot of scandals in her past—at least not compared to Kamila herself, who was once a bit of a wild child. In fact, she had only one major scandal in her life. *Anil.*

Jana could feel her heart rate speed up. Kamila was a great friend. Even if they weren't always as close as they were now, Kamila had been there when Jana's other friends ghosted her when they found out she was having a married man's baby. Surprising Jana more than anyone, Kamila ended up being the most nonjudgmental, accepting person she knew.

But now Kamila was calling Imani's birth a scandal? Laughing at it? Even after Jana told her the truth about Anil's marriage?

Jana felt betrayed.

"That wasn't only *my* scandal. It takes two to tango," Jana spat out angrily. She glared at Anil.

Kamila frowned. "Jana, no. I'm sorry...I wasn't talking about...I was talking about that guy from high school we were both hooking up with at the same time. Remember?" Kamila smiled awkwardly, clearly regretting her words. "God, I was such an idiot back then." She looked at Rohan. "I hope you know you married someone who used to fog up windows with a stoner who had an Indian-girl fetish and used to play with devil sticks behind the school."

Rohan laughed.

Jana looked at the others. She'd read that moment wrong and felt terrible. She should apologize to Kamila. She glanced at Anil, but he wasn't even looking at her. The conversation had moved on. People were laughing and teasing Marc now—something about throwing up on the biggest roller coaster in Toronto. Then Tim was teased about the time his dogs were kicked out of a major dog show because he had used an illegal shine-enhancing shampoo on them. Everyone was poking fun at each other. They could laugh at one another and still be friends.

They knew what to say.

Jana's mood had completely soured. She pushed herself off the low seat. "I need another drink."

Mostly, she needed to get away from this crowd. All her past feelings of not fitting in were back. She walked over to the bar in the other room. "May I have an old-fashioned?" she asked. "Room one twenty-six."

"Of course," the bartender said. A few moments later he slid the drink along the smooth wood surface as Jana perched herself on the barstool.

"Asante sana," she said, thanking him in Swahili, then looked at his name tag. "Ayubu. I'm Jana."

He smiled. "Karibu, Jana. You are not going back to your friends?"

She shrugged, taking a small sip of her drink. "Needed a breather."

"Have you been traveling for a long time with them?"

Jana nodded. "Feels like forever. It's been almost two weeks."

Ayubu whistled low. "I could not manage being with so many people for so long."

Jana raised a brow. "You're a bartender."

His head tilted. "Ahh, but the difference is I only meet people as they are passing through. And they usually learn nothing about me when they are here. I never have to let others in, but I am welcomed into their lives." He leaned close, conspiratorially. "In this industry, you learn that the listeners are as important as the talkers. Even more important."

Jana smiled, swirling the drink in her hand. "I heard a bartender here knew John Wayne. I assume that wasn't you," she said. Ayubu looked to be about Jana's age.

He chuckled. "I sometimes feel like an old man, but I'm not *that* old. That is my uncle...He does still work here—sometimes. But not often—he is a relic of the past. Have you seen *Hatari!*? The movie that was filmed in the area?"

When Jana said she hadn't, that prompted a conversation with Ayubu, who turned out to be a major film buff, about

Hollywood-produced films set in East Africa and how those movies brought a lot of tourism dollars and recognition to the area but also gave Westerners a false idea of Africa. "It's unfortunate that the most famous film to come from East Africa is about a white woman named Karen," Ayubu said.

"*Out of Africa*, you mean," Jana said. It had been years since she'd seen it, but she remembered watching the movie with her father as a kid. "It would be amazing if a local filmmaker could make something that would get that kind of reach."

Which got them talking about the African film industry and stories being told through the African lens instead of the white colonialist one. It was fascinating. Jana forgot she was in such a bad mood.

"They should film a remake of *Hatari!* right here in this hotel," Ayubu said. "All these little details in design should be seen by the world, don't you think?"

Jana smiled in agreement.

"You don't seem very enthusiastic. Are you not having fun at Hatari?"

"Oh, no. I am definitely enjoying myself. This place... and the hospitality are amazing." She looked over at the wedding party. "I'm just not someone anyone would describe as... fun."

Ayubu made a disparaging sound. "People aren't fun or not fun. Moments are fun. Experiences are fun. Places. Some people adapt to those moments better than others—that's all. I'm sure when you are in your moment, people have a lot of fun with you." He shrugged. "And anyway, give me intelligence, a good conscience, and excellent conversation over fun any day. Even those *fun* people need someone thoughtful to remind them of that sometimes." He glanced at something over Jana's head for a second. "I suspect your friends are drawn to you for a reason."

He smiled, then spoke to a person behind Jana. "Another beer, my friend?" Jana turned to see who it was. Anil, of course.

Anil nodded. "Asante," he said when Ayubu handed him a glass moments later.

"Karibu. And"—he looked at Jana—"karibu to you, too. Nina furaha kukutana, my friend. I am very glad to have met you. Talking with you has been *fun*." He smiled widely, then walked away, whistling.

Anil looked at Jana. "You okay?"

"I'm perfectly fine," she said. "Just talking to the bartender." She chuckled as she realized that she could tick another item off her list. She'd just chatted with a stranger.

"Needed to escape the crowd, did you?" Anil sat on the barstool next to her. Now this was the second time he'd said that. Maybe it *was* passive aggression. Or maybe support. Jana wished she understood people better. Anil *had* rescued her from a crowd at the wedding ceremony. That was four hotels ago now. It was true what she'd told Ayubu—this trip had felt like a lifetime.

A lifetime that was no longer than her relationship with Anil in the first place. They'd been together for two weeks then. And her entire life had been turned on its axis. And now, almost five years later, they were together for two weeks again.

"Why do you people make me feel terrible for not thriving in groups?"

He shook his head. "*You people* . . . Who are you talking about?"

She took a sip of her drink before answering. "You. Extroverts. People who know how to talk to others."

Anil chuckled as he set his beer down. "Ah. Well, right now I feel like I don't have the faintest idea of how to talk to a particular person."

Jana put her glass down. He meant her. "We keep going in

circles, Anil. You said I was hot and cold, but you've barely acknowledged my existence since we woke up in that tent together. Except to throw some passive-aggressive nonsense at me. Why are we even bothering to fix this between us? We can keep going the way things were before. Maybe have lunch together with Imani once a month so she thinks we get along. There is no need to force something that won't work."

He stared at her for several long seconds, then looked in front of him at the bottles stacked behind the bar. "My ego was bruised. I saw the look of disgust on your face when you left the tent. You bolted out of there as fast as you could."

That wasn't because she *hated* him. It was because seeing him braid Imani's hair had made her want him *so much* that she couldn't think straight. Things were easier when they barely saw each other.

She turned away from him, also staring straight in front of her. "If your precious ego is so easily bruised when you're around me, then why are you here? Go sit with the others. Unless there is something else you'd like to say?"

"Yes. I wanted to tell you my flight out of Africa is tomorrow evening," he said, his voice flat. "I know you like to keep tabs on me all the time. I have a three-hour stopover in London, then I'll be in D.C. I'll be staying with my parents for two weeks while working on the start-up for the new foundation, then I'll be back in Toronto in time for Rohan and Kamila's Toronto wedding reception, and for my week with Imani." He stood, picking up his beer. "I'm sure you won't be home when I come to pick her up. And I'm sure you'll make yourself scarce when I bring her back a week later. You won't have to see me for any prolonged period of time again."

He walked right outside instead of heading to the other room where the rest of the party was. She watched him go.

CHAPTER 21

He was leaving Tanzania the next day. And she was leaving the day after that. Everything would go back to how it was before. That's what Jana wanted. To barely see Anil anymore. To barely be in each other's lives.

But wait. What about the Disney trip? Was he implying he didn't want to go anymore? And what about Dr. Lopez—was Anil angry enough to tell him that the Jana on this trip wasn't real and that she and Anil had never been friends? That she wasn't *vibrant*? Jana drained her glass in one gulp, then rushed out after Anil.

"Wait," she said when she caught up to him near the rooms.

He turned and looked at her. Anil seemed to think that *she* hated *him*, but that look on his face told otherwise—he was the one hating someone here.

"For someone who doesn't want to be bothered," he said, "you sure haven't left me alone on this trip." He continued walking toward his suite.

She followed him. "What does that mean?" What exactly was he accusing her of, anyway?

He shook his head as he fumbled in his pocket for his key

card. "Everywhere I turn, you're there. At the wedding, all the parties, all my game drives, every dinner, in the pool. *Everywhere.* Imani gets sick, in seconds you're there."

She blinked, staring at him. "We're on the same trip! You chose to come knowing I'd be here. And you insisted we be together for all the game drives and that I sleep in your tent that night! It's not like I *want* to be near you or anything... It's for—"

"Imani. I know." He unlocked his room. Before stepping inside, he stood at the door with his arm out as if to welcome her in.

"You want me to come into your room?" Jana asked. What was happening here?

His nostrils flared. "You want to have this conversation out here with wild dogs around?"

Jana winced and stepped into Anil's room. It was a smaller version of hers. Same beautiful, welcoming decor—only one bed.

He threw his room card on the desk, put his beer down, and turned to look at Jana. "I *know* you being everywhere I turn isn't because of *me*. I know I've been the one pushing for this... reconciliation. And I know we're only doing it for Imani. I decided to come because I thought this could be our chance to fix things. But I can't pretend it's been easy for me. That it doesn't sting to be facing you everywhere." She could see a throbbing vein in his forehead. His teeth were gritted.

"Why, because I won't stroke your ego like you want everyone to do?"

He stared at her, blinking. She'd gone too far. She didn't mean that comment... mostly. He'd said he always said the wrong thing to her, and she was realizing she did the same.

"Why did you follow me here, Jana?" he asked.

She leaned back against the door. For some reason, she felt if she stayed in contact with the exit, she wasn't really alone in this room with him. "At the bar, you said I wouldn't need to see you after this trip. Does that mean you don't want to go to Disney anymore?"

He stared at her for several seconds, face still blank. "No. You win," he said. "Have a good time."

Jana didn't know why that made her feel sad; it's what she'd wanted. "Are you going to tell everyone that we've been lying? That we've never been married, never been friends?" She cringed thinking about how upset Mom would be. Would this be a problem with Dr. Lopez?

"No, of course not. I'll go along with whatever you want. Pretend we were married. Pretend we are best friends. Whatever."

"But without Disney."

He sighed. "Yes, without Disney. If you don't want me there, I won't push it."

He wasn't going to fight to crack through her anymore? To challenge her? "Why? You've been pushing me for two weeks to talk, and now you're giving up on me?"

He gritted his teeth. "Because believe it or not, Jana, I do want you to be happy. And I clearly still make you very, very unhappy." She'd never heard anyone say they wanted her to be happy with so much venom in their voice before. She didn't understand it. She didn't understand him. "If you want that job, I'll do whatever I can to help you get it. If you want references, I'll give them. If you want to go back to avoiding me for the rest of your life, I'll deal." His voice was low. It scratched like fingernails on granite. "If you want to regret me every day, go ahead. I won't fight you."

He sounded nothing like himself. This was no easygoing

Anil, her amicable co-parenting partner. His constant charm had made him more frustrating than anyone else in the world to her. He made her want to scream.

She didn't *want* him to surrender. She didn't want him to give up on her. She couldn't imagine going back to how they were before, but she couldn't imagine anything else, either.

She should leave. Fighting wasn't helping anyone—it was only making her feelings for him more complicated.

Jana turned and put her hand on the doorknob, ready to open it and go back out into the Tanzanian wilds, when he spoke again with a low voice. "When Kamila was talking about scandals and regrets, your mind went to me immediately, right?"

She didn't turn to look at him. And she didn't wipe the tear that was making a trail down her cheek. "Why are you asking?"

He snorted. "Because I'm a glutton for punishment."

She turned sharply. "Why are you doing this to me, Anil? Why do you insist on talking about this and rehashing it forever? Why can't we just—"

He put his hands up in frustration. "I don't know how long you're going to torture me for a mistake I fucking regret more than anything in the world! I *need* to move on. I need to *live*...I can't exist in this purgatory you've left me in forever!"

"I haven't left you in purgatory! You've put yourself there! You walked into our relationship with open eyes and didn't give me the same luxury!"

"You're right! But you can't have it both ways, Jana! I can't be both the villain in your life and your savior when you need me! I can't be both a regret and a friend you hold hands with when you sleep. You don't have to like me. You don't have to forgive me. Just..."

"Just what?"

His face fell. "Just *release* me."

They stared angrily at each other for several seconds. "That's what I want," he finally said. "I want to be allowed to move on from you and the past... *finally*. I want to not be torn up with guilt and regret and the knowledge that I hurt the person I..." He paused, rubbing his hand over his face. "I want to be able to be in the same room with you without all this...tension. Emotions. For Imani, yes, but for me. Tell me what else I can do...or tell me now if it will never be possible."

She didn't say anything—just stared at him. Was it possible? Could she be in the same room with him and feel nothing? Not be overcome with feelings so strong they scared the crap out of her?

"What about you, Jana?" he finally said. "What do you want? If you could snap your fingers and have anything, what would you and I be?"

Another tear escaped. It was made of anger and resentment and so much more than she knew how to deal with. She wanted what he wanted, too. To set him free. But she was afraid if she set him free, then she wouldn't have him anymore. She leaned her head back on the door. "If I could snap my fingers and have anything, I'd want things to go back to how they were before."

He snorted with derision. "You mean back to us never seeing each other and sending barely professional messages back and forth about our daughter?"

"No." Her voice cracked. "No. Before that." She looked up at the ceiling, blinking away the tears. She couldn't make eye contact with him right now. "I'd go back to those two weeks. Back to when you made me feel things I'd never felt before. When you made me believe I was enough just the way I am." She looked at him finally. "I'd go back to when I fit somewhere. In your arms."

He blinked, looking at her, face still unreadable. Then in two long strides across the room, his lips were on hers.

And he was back. Anil Malek was kissing her. Filling in all the empty parts of her. Making the world turn on the same axis as her again. His lips pressed onto hers as he poured all that pain and anger and resentment into her, and she just let him. Hell, she practically rolled out a welcome mat for him.

His kiss was furious, tongue sweeping through her mouth, his hands tightening on her cheeks. He tasted of dark beer and danger. *Hatari.* The charming easygoing Anil was long gone—this was barely contained primal energy. He suddenly pulled away, hands still on her cheeks, fire in his eyes.

"Jana," he whispered. She had to close her eyes, overwhelmed with the intense emotions. This was Anil—the only person who made her feel like this. Ever. They'd had two weeks then, and the shock waves from the intensity still echoed through her core.

"Jana," he whispered again. She opened her eyes to look at him, seeing a question in his expression. *Is this okay?*

Because he was Anil. Because even before, when they were in the throes of passion, he put her first. Her comfort. Her needs. Her *pleasure.*

But since she'd never made things easy for him, she needed to be crystal clear now. She slipped one arm around him and pulled his head down to mouth a kiss into his neck, lingering to suck in the sweet sandalwood taste of him and loving the gasp that escaped his lips. She inhaled deeply to drink in more of his scent, of his heat, of him, then answered his wordless question. "Please," she whispered softly into his ear. "Give that to me again."

He crashed into her with another bruising kiss, and this time she let her hands roam over the solid body that had left a permanent imprint on her memory. None of this should have felt new to her—she'd been kissed by these lips and touched by these hands before—but this was different. More urgent. It was like they were both desperately trying to fill in the holes left behind after they exploded into each other's lives five years ago. His leg pressed between hers, the soft cotton of her dress luxurious against her sensitive skin.

He eventually pulled her away from the door and gave her a firm nudge toward the bed. She let herself fall back, pulling him on top of her. She needed his weight on her. Crowding her. Blocking out everything that wasn't Anil Malek. He looked down at her, the pad of his thumb trailing slowly over her cheekbone. His eyes were so beautiful—the richest brown imaginable. Like the dark beer he'd been drinking. And as usual, Jana had trouble reading the expression in them.

"I don't know if we should talk about this," he finally said.

Jana didn't want to talk. Words were difficult for them. Bodies had always been easier. She tightened her hold around his waist, and felt his erection, hard and insistent on her leg. Smiling, she reached down to stroke the thick length of it through his pants, watching his eyes roll back. "Not really feeling like conversation right now," she responded. "And I don't think you are, either."

He chuckled, shaking his head. "You've always been the smarter one." He leaned down and kissed her again.

Jana couldn't believe how good it felt. And it felt even better when he reached down and grazed her leg with his hand, following the slit in her dress with a determined touch that sent all her nerves into overdrive. She gasped in his mouth when his roaming hand traveled from her thigh to her hip, and she curled one of her legs over his. She wanted to drown in this man all over again.

A whimper escaped her lips when he pushed her underwear to the side and slipped fingers inside her with no preamble. She broke the kiss, holding on to the back of his head, moaning as he went deeper. Good lord, why... *how*... had she ever walked away from this man?

"Is this good, Jana?" he asked.

"God, yes. Please. Don't stop." She clutched him as his magical fingers and thumb brought her sensations she forgot she could have. Jana's mouth was open against his cheek as her pleasure crested, clumsily searching for his lips. He kissed her again, swallowing her screams as her pleasure seemed to go on forever.

He pulled back to look at her as her orgasm subsided. Jana felt wrung out and recharged at the same time. And this time, she *could* read the look on his face... He looked like he'd conquered a mountain bigger than Mount Meru.

"What are you thinking?" he asked.

"That I can't believe that just happened."

His forehead furrowed. "You said it was okay."

She grinned and pulled his face down to hers. "It was way, way better than okay," she said against his lips, then reached for his belt.

"Are you sure, Jana?"

She knew why he was asking her—this would change *every-thing* between them. But honestly? That ship sailed one orgasm ago. And maybe *she* should be the one to ask, because she was the one who walked away last time. "Are *you* sure?" she asked.

He didn't answer. And his hesitation gave her time to think... Was this a mistake? Some excellent orgasms tonight (and they *would* be excellent—they always had been) were one thing, but was she willing to face whatever this would do to their relationship? She'd been so furious when she walked into this room, and he'd been even angrier. And taking this step while already in a heightened emotional state could be dangerous.

"You're thinking too hard, Jana. Tell me what you're feeling, not what you're thinking."

She smiled. The truth was, Jana was feeling more alive than she had in years. She took his cheek in her hand, loving the light stubble, and trailed her thumb down it. It was amazing to be able to do this now. Touch the face that had occupied a permanent place in her mind for years. "I...I need this tonight. Just one night. No promises, no holding back. What about you?"

He nodded, leaning into her touch. "I feel the same way. Just one night."

Jana smiled, putting her hands on his belt again, then paused. "Um...I'm not on the pill." Not that that had helped much five years ago. Back then, she'd been on antibiotics for a sinus infection, so they'd used condoms. Most of the time.

He got up quickly, holding his open pants so they wouldn't fall, returning a few seconds later with a condom. "We can thank Kamila and Rohan for their backpacks," he said, unbuttoning his shirt. Jana laughed. But then watched him undress, because this time she could.

Anil was still a beautiful man. A little less firm and a little thicker in the waist than five years ago, he still had a broad chest and solid legs. When he rejoined her on the bed wearing nothing but his boxer briefs, he slid his hands over Jana's legs again, this time slipping her underwear down. Then he pulled her dress over her head.

Jana felt self-conscious suddenly, covering her stomach with her hands. She didn't mind the changes to her body—she'd been playing in the pool with him only a few days ago. But that high-waisted push-up bikini covered things. Her stomach was nowhere near flat anymore. "I...I have stretch marks..."

He tugged her hands away and sat her up to take her bra off. When she lay back down, he sat next to her and looked. Jana wanted to curl up into herself. To hide. What was he thinking right now?

"You're beautiful," he whispered. With barely a touch, he ran his fingers lightly over the silvery lines on her stomach. She shivered as his fingers caressed her skin. He then dipped his head to plant kisses on her belly. "So beautiful," he said again, a little tremor sneaking into his voice. She stroked the back of his head, grateful. These marks on her body were from growing and feeding Imani. And Anil was the only person who loved Imani as much as she did.

He moved his mouth up to her breasts, first kissing, then following the trails of the stretch marks with his tongue. When he took her nipple in his mouth, his tongue flicking the tip, she moaned again, arching her back.

"Now. Do it now, Anil. Condom." She pulled on the waistband of his briefs.

"Yes, ma'am." He rolled off her and out of his briefs, then made quick work of putting on the condom. When he was back on top of her, he propped himself up on his elbows. This time, he didn't have a serious or emotional question in his eyes, but instead his smile was all Anil Malek charm. "Ready?" he asked.

She nodded. She'd never been more ready in her life. Taking him in her hands, she guided him into her body.

When they were joined again, Jana could feel it all slip away. The resentment. The bitterness. None of that could survive when it felt so perfect. He knew exactly the right angle, the right pace to make nothing but this moment matter. He knew how to make her scream. She arched her back, curling her legs around his hips. They were nothing alike, but like this, with him deep inside her, it felt like they were where they were supposed to be. Jana held him tight as he moved inside her, and when his breathing sped up, she put her hand down to where they were joined, pressing hard to make sure they reached their peak at the same moment. She wanted to give them that.

They were kissing when she came, and his mouth tore away when he reached his peak seconds later. He clutched her tightly, calling her name as the shudders of pleasure passed through him.

It was him saying her name that made her eyes water. Because her name on his lips felt like a promise this time, just like it had last time.

Eventually he pulled out, and after rolling off the bed to dispose of the condom, he came back and lay next to her. She held him in a tight embrace. They lay like that for a while, unspeaking, as their breathing returned to normal. And all Jana could think about was how fitting it was that this place was called Hatari.

Because now that she'd been reminded of how perfect she and Anil were together, she knew she was most definitely in danger.

CHAPTER 22

One weird thing Jana hated about herself, something she hoped Anil didn't remember, was that she often cried after an orgasm. The bigger the orgasm...the more tears. A small self-given orgasm might make her eyes well up a bit, but an intense, toe-curling one triggered by some partner activities could make her shake with a sob. It was mortifying.

The tears weren't because of sadness, happiness, or any other emotion. It was just an annoying reaction of her body. One that had her hiding in the bathroom after sex with most of her small number of past partners. A bonus was the bathroom trip after sex helped prevent UTIs, but still.

Just once she'd like to have some after-sex closeness and snuggles without feeling the urge to run away.

She wriggled free from Anil's grip and rushed to the bathroom. She didn't dare speak, because that was an orgasm unlike any she'd had in years, so he would definitely hear her voice crack. But hopefully he'd understand she needed to regroup after that mind-blowing experience.

After cleaning up, she looked at herself in the mirror. The tears hadn't stopped and her eyes were puffy. Her skin reddened.

Makeup a mess. And this time, there *were* emotions behind the tears.

She was overwhelmed. She was terrified. She was amazed. And she weirdly felt more alone and isolated than ever.

She was feeling everything right now. She choked back a sob.

Stepping out of her comfort zone was one thing, letting loose another...but what had compelled her to *have sex* with Anil Malek? It didn't matter how good it felt to be close to someone again—not just anyone, but the one person she'd felt the most at home with ever—this could be a *huge* problem. For their future, and for their present. For *Imani*. Their daughter was thriving— why would Jana do anything that could jeopardize that?

Jana didn't know what to do with herself, so she turned on the stand-up shower. There was a knock at the bathroom door seconds later. She quickly wiped her face with a towel and wrapped it around herself before opening the door.

"Can I join you?" Anil said, indicating the shower.

Part of her wanted to say no. She wanted to be alone to wash away the torrent of emotions so she could move on after what they'd done. But then she remembered a similar moment way back in London. She'd been feeling this same feeling...the simultaneous sensation of too many emotions mingled with emptiness. Along with a whole lot of fear that a connection that intense could only end in disaster. She'd let him into her shower then, and he'd washed her tenderly, filling in all the nooks and crannies that felt depleted after sex.

She ached for that sensation again—that feeling of belonging somewhere, even for only one night. So she nodded and quickly dropped the towel and stepped into the steaming shower before he could see her eyes. She let the hot water run over her face and hair.

Anil stepped into the large shower enclosure and immediately pulled Jana into his arms. He was the opposite after sex. Still hungry for contact. His impulse was to get closer while hers was to run away. She didn't exactly relax into his embrace, but she stayed in his arms, his body engulfing hers in warmth while the water poured over her.

"You okay?" he asked, his voice barely audible over the sound of the water hitting the stone base of the shower. She nodded but stepped out of his hug and picked up one of the little bottles of soap from the ledge.

"Here, let me," he said, putting his hand out for the soap.

She let him wash her, and she didn't know why. She knew it was wrong—that sleeping with him hadn't solved anything between them. But being taken care of like this was so...soothing. He poured the sweet tropical-scented soap onto a washcloth as Jana turned. He gently but firmly swiped it over her back. Closing her eyes, she let her senses fill with steam and the warm, coconut-and-papaya scent of the soap.

The scent prevented her from feeling like they were back in London. Back then, he'd always come looking for her when she ran away after sex. He got used to her quirks and never made her feel like less for having them. Jana wondered if he was thinking back to that now. He turned her and started soaping up her front, all the way from her feet and up her shins and thighs. She didn't hide her body this time, trusting that he didn't mind how it had changed. And his expression was readable now—a mixture of tenderness and awe.

"Thanks," she said after he'd lathered every inch of her. She stepped under the stream of the oversized rain showerhead. "Want me to do you?" she said, hand out to take the washcloth from him.

"No," he said. "I got it." He started soaping himself up. "So..." he said after a few seconds. "I know I said we would hold off on major conversations until after this trip..." His voice trailed. Jana was not used to Anil not knowing what to say.

"But that was before we had sex," she said. There was no point in speaking around the facts here.

"Yeah," he said. She watched him as he lathered up his muscular calves. "I didn't expect that to happen, by the way."

Jana snorted. "No...can't say I did, either. Look, Anil, maybe I shouldn't have had those two...three drinks, and yeah, it's been kind of weird to be traveling with you again and—"

"And that didn't mean anything?" He wasn't looking at her. He was washing his calves.

She put her hand on his arm. "No. That's not what I was going to say. It *did* mean something. I was going to say that *this*, you and me, we're complicated."

He moved onto soaping his forearms. "That we are."

"And I don't know what you're expecting. Or wanting—"

He stopped her by putting his arm around her waist. It occurred to Jana that maybe conversation would be easier if they weren't naked right now. Or at least it might be more productive. She couldn't help herself—her hand wandered to his backside. It wasn't fair that he still had such a nice butt after all these years. She squeezed it.

He chuckled, then leaned his head down to kiss her neck. "We said one night, Jana." He was still kissing her in between saying the words, and her knees were threatening to stop holding her up. "I'm just...I need you to understand that *one night* doesn't mean there are no...feelings here. I know I've challenged you a lot lately, but I will *always* be there for you. It's our last night in Tanzania. Let's make it memorable—I have no expectations. We can talk later."

She would probably agree to just about anything if it meant he'd keep his lips there, but the part of her that was still thinking logically wondered if his insistence that he had no expectations was for *her* benefit or for *his*.

She pushed the thought aside because there was one thing she fully agreed with . . . might as well make this night as memorable as possible.

For the second time since they'd been in Tanzania, Jana woke up in bed with Anil Malek. This time, though, they were in a proper hotel room—not a tent. And their sick daughter wasn't in a cot next to them.

But it still scared the crap out of Jana. When she opened her eyes, she saw Anil next to her reading something on his phone, as if being together like this were the most normal thing in the world. She wondered for a second if this is what her life would have been like if the last five years had happened differently. Just waking up next to her partner after a party celebrating their closest friends' wedding.

But no. This was not her life. It could have been if Anil hadn't been married when they met.

She shouldn't be here. She sat up.

"Oh, good—you're up." His grin told her that he was hoping for one more roll in the hay before they went their separate ways this morning. But they'd agreed on one *night*. It was no longer night.

"Morning," Jana said. She swung her legs out of bed, taking the bedsheet to wrap around her body and started looking for her clothing.

"You're leaving?"

"Yes." She found her underwear.

"Just like that?"

Her strapless bra was near her dress, thankfully. Even though it was unlikely that anyone would see her as she snuck out, Jana didn't want to be in public wearing this dress with no bra.

Holding her clothes close to her chest while clutching the sheet in an attempt to stay covered, she headed to the bathroom.

"Jana, wait," he said. He'd sat up. He wasn't covered at all. Which made sense because the only sheet on the bed was currently wrapped around Jana like a kanga. But still. She didn't know where to look when he spoke to her. "Should we... debrief?" he asked. "About last night?"

She raised a brow. "Um, I think you're already 'debriefed.'"

He laughed, looking down at his naked body.

She pointed to the bathroom. "I'm going to go in there to put my dress on. Then I will come out here, where hopefully you will have at least *re*briefed. Then I'm going to my own room, and ideally not wake my roommate. I'm going to shower, then get dressed so I can be in the dining room on time for breakfast."

"And we will never speak of this again?" he asked, resigned.

She shook her head. "We *will* talk, just not now." She couldn't sweep this under the rug. Her life was too enmeshed with his. But she needed to think first. "I need time. Can you give me some space for now?"

He nodded. She couldn't read his expression again, but that was probably because he was naked, so her eyes kept traveling downward. She waved awkwardly and stepped into the bathroom.

When she came out, Anil was thankfully in briefs again. Nothing else, but at least he'd taken that hint. Jana headed straight for the door. "Okay, I'll see you at breakfast," she said. Very awkwardly.

"Yep. See you then!" He sounded just as awkward. She left the room.

Yuriko was thankfully still sleeping when Jana quietly snuck into the room. Not bothering to find clean clothes, she stepped straight into the bathroom and took another shower, happy to wash Anil Malek off of her.

What. The hell. Had she done?

As she scrubbed her hair, she thought about how on earth they could possibly move on from this. Clearly, Jana had to go back to avoiding the man. Going to Starbucks when he came to pick up or drop off Imani. Making sure all her communications with him were distant and through the app only. She most definitely was not going to go to Disney World with him. Nope. He said he'd come if this trip brought them closer. Well...the trip definitely brought them closer. But that wasn't necessarily a good thing.

Because that—having sex with Anil—had been a mistake. It was an enjoyable mistake (slight understatement—it had been freaking mind-blowing), and it certainly scratched an itch that she maybe didn't know was irritating her so much, but it had not been a *healthy* decision. There was already too much...stuff between them, and they had no choice but to be in each other's lives. Now there was even more for Jana to overcome.

After her shower, Jana put on one of the plush white hotel robes. When she opened the bathroom door, she was met with not just Yuriko, but the entire Bridal Brigade. All in robes like the one Jana was wearing. Except Yuriko, who was in her bed in her satin floral pajamas. Nicole and Asha were both on the bed with her, propped up on Yuriko's headboard. Kamila and Shelina were on Jana's unused bed.

"Um," Jana said awkwardly, taking the towel turban off her head. "What's going on?"

"Emergency Bridal Brigade meeting," Kamila said. "Sit." She scooted closer to her sister and patted the space next to her on the queen-size bed. Jana wasn't sure she wanted to know what the purpose of this meeting was.

The moment she sat, there was a knock on the door. Jana looked at Kamila. Was the Groom's Platoon joining them for this meeting? In other words, was Anil at the door now? Shelina got up to answer it.

"We ordered a continental breakfast," Asha explained.

That was thoughtful. And helpful, because she didn't want to see Anil in the dining room.

After a waiter wheeled in a tray with a carafe as well as some pastries and fruit, Shelina started pouring coffee and serving the brigade. The fact that no one had said why they were here yet gave Jana a good idea what the purpose of this impromptu meeting was, but she waited until someone else divulged—just in case she was wrong.

She really hoped she was wrong.

"So…" Kamila said, stirring the sugar into her coffee and looking at Jana. "Here's the thing. I know today is *officially* the last day that the hashtag Bridal Brigade is a thing, and we will disband this afternoon, but as of now, you all are still my bridesmaids. And as a group, we all agreed that we are entitled to know about any major changes in anyone's lives. If for no other reason than so we can support our sisters in the brigade, but also so we can avoid any awkward comments and moments when we're in larger company."

Yep. Jana was right about why they were here. This was an interrogation.

Jana looked at Yuriko. "You *told* them I didn't come back to the room?"

Yuriko nodded. "If you'd asked me to cover for you, I would have kept your secret. But for all I knew, you'd been eaten by lions."

"Yuri was worried," Kamila said. "I asked around, and the bartender said he saw you leave with Anil while we were playing FMK in the lounge."

"What's FMK?" Jana asked.

Asha grinned. "Fuck, marry, kill. By the way, you were voted least murderable in the wedding party because we decided the negative impact to the world would be the greatest if you died. When we moved on to who was the most fuckable, we decided to stop playing with people we knew and focused on prime-time news anchors and FoodTV personalities. Did you know that Kamila has a bit of a Guy Fieri thing?"

Kamila waved her hand. "He's a champion of small businesses. I like that. But that's not the point right now. Jana, has your relationship status changed?"

"Since when?"

"Since you left the bar last night with your ex. Is he no longer an ex, and now a current?"

Jana sighed. So much for not speaking about this. "No. He's not my anything."

"So you didn't spend the night in his room?" Shelina asked. "See, Kamila? I knew there had to be an explanation. She was probably—"

"No," Jana clarified. "I *did* spend the night in his room."

"Oh." Shelina frowned. "For Imani? Oh my god, is she okay? Were you on the phone with her all night?"

"No. Imani's fine, as far as I know. Haven't spoken to her since right after dinner last night."

Kamila glared at Shelina. "Shelina, I'm trying and failing to guess why you're attempting to find any explanation possible for Jana to be in Anil's room other than the obvious—that they were testing out his bedsprings."

Jana raised a brow.

"Doing a two-person push-up," Asha suggested.

"Ooh, that's a good one," Nicole said, laughing. "I've always liked 'threading the needle.'"

"Filling the cream donut!" Yuriko exclaimed. The rest of the Bridal Brigade all looked at her.

Kamila cringed. "Thanks, Yuri. I'll never be able to get a Tim Hortons Boston Cream again." She looked at Jana. "So it's true, then? You had sex with Anil?"

Jana sighed. "Yes."

"But you're not back together?" Nicole asked.

Jana shook her head.

"Was this so you could check off that *hook-up* item on your to-do list?" Asha asked.

Jana frowned. "I didn't even add that item!"

"Yeah, and you did it anyway because you're such an over-achiever," Kamila snorted.

"Thank you all for your concern," Jana said, "but this isn't something I want to talk about right now."

Kamila slapped Jana's arm. "Okay, but tell us how to support you! Do we need to *hide* this information? Keep the Groom's Platoon from finding out? Or should we be keeping Anil away from you? Get you out of this country without seeing him? You name it, girl—we're here for you."

"You're not going to ask *why* I slept with him? Or ask for...details?"

Kamila shook her head. "No. Of course not. You don't want

to talk about it, so we won't talk about it. I wouldn't say no to details, because I've always wondered about him. I assume he's generous but an absolute *beast* in bed. But one-night stands can be awkward. Especially with an ex-whatever-you-two-are. You're a brigade member. We got you. Tell us what to do to make this easier for you."

Jana wanted to be upset that the whole brigade had barged in on her like this... but they were being supportive. It felt good to have them on her side.

But she had no idea how to make this easier. "Nothing. Don't do anything. Don't tell anyone, don't speculate, don't try to influence anyone. I stepped into this mess, so I'll figure out how to deal with it."

"Okay. Sounds good. Ladies, we're going to support Jana by giving her the space she needs to work out her interpersonal problems. Now, eat up so we can go pack. Our bus to Arusha will be here in a few hours."

CHAPTER 23

With the support of the rest of the brigade, Jana added *pretend I didn't sleep with Anil* to the list of things she was pretending in Tanzania. She'd meant it when she said she fully intended to talk to him about it—just not yet. After breakfast, Jana dressed and packed her things to leave Hatari. The drive to the luxury hotel in Arusha where the rest of the wedding guests were staying would be short, and when she climbed into the van, Anil was already sitting in a window seat with Jerome next to him. He didn't look at her as she passed him. Which was fine. She'd asked for space, and he was apparently willing to give it.

Of course, during the drive, Jana's mind wouldn't stop replaying what had happened in his room. If she was honest, the fact that she'd let it happen wasn't really that big of a surprise. She'd been fighting the return of her feelings for the man since they'd arrived in Africa. No, the surprise was that *he* let it happen. Because honestly, she assumed that she'd angered him too much, been too bitter, been too *Jana* for him to even think about getting back into bed with her.

He'd said he didn't have expectations—but what *expectations* did he mean? A relationship? He'd wanted to marry her once, but that may have been out of obligation. This whole trip, he'd been talking about *friendship*. He wanted them to cooperate better as parents. But friends didn't normally do what they had been doing a few hours earlier in his hotel room.

Maybe sex didn't have to mean a relationship, though. Last night, Jana had been emotional and lonely and needed an outlet for her pent-up energy and, yes, maybe a bit of sexual frustration. All the memories of the past were invading her brain in the worst way, and she was confusing her past feelings with the present. She'd needed to feel light, carefree, and *desired* the way she had five years ago. Sleeping with him had been about *letting loose*—that was it.

This could be a turning point for them—maybe now they could actually *be friends*. Jana decided to be mature and explain that she was grateful he'd been there when she needed him, and that he was right—it was long past time for them to get over their history, but there didn't need to be more than that. Sleeping with him seemed to have dissolved the last lingering traces of her resentment. She felt optimistic that a better, cooperative relationship could be possible now.

When they got to Arusha, they found most of the guests in the pool area. Imani rushed over to give Jana a hug when she saw her. "Mommy!"

Jana hugged her tight, then held her in front of her to watch her expression as Imani told Jana all the things she had done since they'd seen each other the day before.

"We watched three movies but I fell asleep before the second one, but then when I woke up there was chocolate in my hair because I was eating it before so Nanima had to give me a bath before sleep so my hair was all messy this morning but Nanima said we'd leave it and maybe you would fix it but I said I wanted Daddy to do it because he's better at braids and…" She paused, "Is Daddy coming?"

"I'm right here, Mini," Anil said behind Jana. Jana stepped aside so Imani could hug her daddy.

One more meal together had been arranged in Arusha before people started leaving in the evening. Everyone was at one long table, and big plates of scented rice, chicken curry, and vegetable bhajias were in the middle. Jana sat near the rest of the wedding party. She smiled and said hello to Anil when she sat, but he only briefly looked up at her, then went back to talking to the others. Kamila was showing everyone a picture she'd received of her dogs. Her friend Maricel was taking care of them at home since she was too pregnant to travel.

"Ugh," Kamila said. "I miss my babies. Look at Potato's new sweater. And Darcy had a haircut! Whoever is going to Toronto in the next few days, can you go hug my doggos for me? Oh, that reminds me! Jana, is it okay if Elsie sends the souvenirs to your place instead of mine? Our concierge gets annoyed when packages come when we're on holiday."

Kamila had arranged to have the wedding things plus the wedding party's souvenirs shipped directly home so they wouldn't have to worry about taking them on the plane. Jana nodded. "Sure, no problem. I'll be home."

"Don't remind me we're leaving," Nicole said, spooning rice onto her plate. "The hospital is restructuring, which means I'm going to have to break in new staff." She shuddered.

"You're going back to Washington, right?" Marc asked Anil.

Anil nodded. "Yeah. I'm launching another Aim High in D.C. Getting it off the ground has been challenging since I'm not there often. But the region needs it—the services for newcomers aren't anything like they are in Canada." Jana wasn't sure, but she thought she detected something in his voice. Almost...bitterness? Or maybe it was exhaustion. They hadn't slept much the night before, and they were...energetic. She didn't want to study his face to gauge his expression, though.

"Thinking of relocating for good?" Jerome asked.

Anil shook his head. "Nope. Until Imani is grown, I'm destined for a double life." He glanced at Jana a second, then looked back at his plate. "But maybe I'll go for longer stretches—there is nothing but Imani keeping me in Toronto at this point."

Jana looked at him, her spine straightening. That was the first time she'd ever heard him express any displeasure about being tied to Toronto. She'd always assumed he'd been happy to stay for her and Imani.

Wait. For *Imani*. He wasn't in Toronto for Jana. She looked away quickly. She wished she could see inside his brain. He hadn't said a word to Jana all day. True, she'd asked for space, but he hadn't even said hello when she sat down. Was he having regrets over last night? Or was this because Jana refused to talk to him when she left his room?

Jana could feel nausea building in her stomach and a prickle behind her eyes. Why was she reacting this way? She was getting what she wanted, right? She didn't want a relationship. She said she wanted space, and that's what she was getting. But being with him here, at this table where he seemed fine and unaffected by last night, was torture. It physically hurt her. He was talking to Jerome now about some hiking trails near his parents' place. He was laughing. And Jana couldn't take it anymore. Couldn't take his carefree attitude, his ability to not be affected by last night and casually talk about the part of his life without Jana in it.

The moment her plate was empty, Jana rushed from the dining

table before anyone could see her tears. She sat in a low wooden chair in the lobby of the hotel, willing her body to return to normal. This hotel, maybe because it was in a city instead of a national park, didn't look like any of their safari hotels. It was clean and minimalist, with gleaming tile floors and white walls. If it weren't for the few framed pictures of animals on the walls, no one would even know they were in East Africa.

It didn't look like the rest of the trip, and it didn't feel like it, either. Jana covered her eyes with her hand. All that letting loose had been a disaster. It hadn't changed anything—she was still as awkward and as out of place as ever. Except now she had a boatload of problems she didn't have before.

"You okay?" a voice behind her said. Jana looked up to see Yuriko, Shelina, and Nicole.

Jana sighed. She was starting to love this crew, but she was also looking forward to having her crises in private again.

She wiped her eyes. "I'm a wreck."

Nicole nodded sympathetically and sat next to Jana. "You have a lot going on. There is nothing wrong with feeling it. You're doing fine—a little breakdown is nothing to be ashamed of. Have you spoken to him yet?"

Jana knew Nicole meant Anil. She shook her head. "I asked for space...He's giving me space."

"But you maybe don't want that anymore?" Yuriko asked gently.

Jana shrugged. She had no idea what she wanted anymore. Or what he wanted.

"C'mon," Nicole said, standing. "Let's talk somewhere else. There's going to be a bit of chaos here soon. Everyone flying out tonight is coming to wait for the van to the airport."

Jana nodded. The last thing she wanted was for people to see her this way. The four of them headed around a corner toward the pool and outdoor lounge area.

"I'm not surprised you have regrets," Shelina said. "What would even compel you to *sleep* with Anil, anyway? I mean, yeah, I know you were pretending you were married once, but after he cheated on his wife with you last time, I'm surprised you'd go there again." She snorted. "It's all so...*juicy*. Like a—"

Jana closed her eyes. Did Shelina think she was helping at all here? Jana suddenly opened her eyes when she felt an arm on hers. Nicole. She was stopping Jana from walking farther.

Because right around the corner, Rohan's parents, Mom, Kassim Uncle, Dr. Lopez, and Farzana Aunty were standing together, seemingly posing for a giant group picture. From the wide-eyed look on all their faces, it was clear that they'd heard what Shelina had said.

Jana wanted to fall into a hole. Or a crater. The Olduvai Gorge wasn't far—maybe Jana could hide in there for the rest of her life.

"Oh my god, I am so sorry!" Shelina said, cringing at Jana. "I...I'm so sorry. I should have kept my mouth shut."

Shelina looked genuine in her apology at least. But the damage had already been done.

Jana froze a few long seconds, then turned and rushed back around the corner to escape them all.

"Jana—wait!" Her mother rushed after her. Jana turned and looked at her.

Mom's face was sour. Angry. "Did Shelina say you went to *bed* with Anil? Have you no shame? What will people think? All my friends heard! I thought you were better than this, Jana."

Jana blinked at her mother. Did Mom care at all about what Jana was going through? About how terrible it felt to be exposed like that? Or did she only care about what others thought?

After Jana said nothing for several long seconds, tears falling down her cheeks, she turned away, not wanting to look at her mother.

"It's okay, beta," Mom said, maybe finally feeling some compassion. "We can tell everyone Shelina was making a joke. Don't worry. We can say—"

Jana shook her head. "No. Enough. I'm *done* lying for you to save face." She took a deep breath. "I was *never* married to Anil. We were *never* divorced. And we have *never* been friends. We've barely spoken to each other unless we needed to for the last five years, and *you know that*. You know he was married to *someone else* when Imani was conceived, and it's time you stop lying about my past." She wiped away a tear. "All you do is tell people how amazing your daughter is... how proud you are of me. But you're lying about who I am. You really think I'm a disappointment." She finally turned and faced her mother. "I don't care if you're proud of me or not. I just want you to *accept* me. Why aren't I good enough for you?"

Jana's voice cracked when she saw the gutted, destroyed look on her mother's face. How could Jana have said all that to her? Mom was a widow. She took care of Jana. She cared... in her own way.

And that's when Jana noticed Dr. Lopez standing behind her mother. He'd heard Jana's outburst. He knew they'd been lying from the beginning. Jana shook her head and walked away.

Jana's knees were shaking as she wobbled out of the lobby. Nicole took her by the arm and guided her to Asha's and her room. Jana hid there while half the party, including Anil, Dr. Lopez, and Farzana Aunty, left for the airport. She did not want to watch Anil say goodbye to Imani. She'd had enough heart-warming father-daughter moments burned into her memory for a lifetime. And she had absolutely no idea what to say to Dr. Lopez—so she decided to say nothing.

Jana might have just lost everything. She'd upset her mother. Embarrassed herself in front of everyone. And worst of all, she'd lost the respect of Dr. Lopez and Farzana Aunty. They knew that it had all been a lie now. The divorce. Her and Anil's amicable co-parenting relationship. All of it. He said he wasn't the only one making the decision for the job, but she assumed he *did* have the power to veto whatever decision the board made. She had no doubt she'd lost a lot of integrity in Dr. Lopez's eyes.

Did he think all those lies were to get the job? To make her stand out to him by impressing his divorce-researcher wife? To hide the truth that she'd slept with a married man?

Jana wanted that job so much...especially after getting to know Dr. Lopez on this trip. She couldn't believe that going along with her mother's lies might have cost her the opportunity. And she hated the fact that she'd disappointed a man she'd come to respect so much.

And then there was Anil. Had anyone told him what Shelina had said? How did he feel about everyone talking about him again?

While Jana was hiding in Asha and Nicole's room, Rohan and Kamila came in to check on her.

"I can't even believe Shelina said that," Kamila said after they were all sitting with steaming mugs of chai. "She's always got her foot lodged firmly in her mouth. She says sorry, by the way, but I wouldn't let her come up."

Jana shrugged. She didn't really blame Shelina...that much. The lie would have come out eventually.

"Did you talk to Anil before he left?" Kamila asked.

"No."

"Are you going to talk to him?"

"Of course. I talk to him all the time."

Kamila tilted her head with a knowing glare. "I mean talk to him about filling your cream donut at Hatari."

Rohan huffed a laugh at his wife's choice of phrase.

Jana's eyes widened. "You told *Rohan*?"

Kamila shook her head. "*I* didn't tell Rohan what you did at Hatari. *Anil* did. The Groom's Platoon had a little chitchat at breakfast. They are very open with each other. I'm not even allowed to look at their group chats."

"Really?" Jana cringed. What kind of *details* had Anil told the others? She could feel her face redden.

"It was all a part of our promise to be fully authentic with each other," Rohan said.

Jana raised a brow. *Authentic?*

He chuckled. "Yeah. I easily had the most emotionally intelligent groomsmen in existence. When the women weren't around, it was all talk about self-awareness, genuine communication, and recognizing toxic masculinity. Very open group. We tell each other everything."

Meanwhile, the ladies were fond of playing fuck, marry, kill and sending each other dik-dik pics.

Kamila snorted. "Y'all would have giggled like schoolboys if you came to the penis-painting party."

"Probably," he said. He looked at Jana. "Anyway, Anil didn't say much, but he seemed pretty shaken up."

Jana exhaled. She was a *private* person. She wasn't used to everyone being up in her business. She took a sip of her tea.

Kamila and Rohan stared at Jana. Waiting for her to say

something. Jana knew her friends. If she said she didn't want to talk about it, they would respect that and let it go.

Jana sighed. "I'm impossible. I don't know why he wanted to be friends at all. I'm not exactly a friendly person."

"*We* want to be friends with you," Rohan said.

Jana shrugged. "I've known you two since birth. You're stuck with me."

Kamila shook her head. "*Wrong.* If I didn't *want* to be friends with you, I wouldn't be. Heck, we *weren't* friends for years. People misunderstand you, but you are a freaking delight."

Jana snorted. *Misunderstand.* "Come on, guys—you two know me better than most. I never know how to act or what to say in groups, so people always think I'm a stuck-up snob." She wasn't sure she'd ever said that aloud. Kamila and Rohan both had looks of pure compassion on their faces, which somehow didn't really help Jana feel any better.

"You've lost some confidence lately...but you are still you in there. Anil sees that," Rohan said.

Jana shook her head. "I've been terrible to him. All he wanted was for us to be friends, and I didn't give him a chance." She remembered that conversation they'd had before having sex— that Jana would never see anything but his flaws.

Kamila snorted. "I think he wants to be a lot *more* than friends with you."

Jana shook her head. "I doubt it."

"You had sex."

"Yeah, but that was letting loose for a night. He said he had no expectations. Didn't you hear what he said at lunch? Imani is the only thing holding him in Toronto. He doesn't want to be with me. He wants things to be easier between us—that's it."

They were all silent for a while.

"He does," Rohan said suddenly.

"Does what?" Jana asked.

"Want to be with you."

Kamila turned to him. "He told you that?"

Rohan shook his head. "Not in so many words, but yeah. Anil cares about you. A lot. But he gets how complicated it is, and he doesn't want to get burned. And he wants to protect Imani above everything else."

Jana didn't know what to say. Part of her believed Rohan, but it terrified her to think that Anil could care that much. It also terrified her to think that he might not.

"Jana, what do you want from him?" Kamila asked.

Jana shrugged. Then took a long sip of her chai. She honestly didn't know.

"I think you have a lot of thinking to do," Rohan said.

Later, when she knew he'd be at his gate waiting for his flight, Jana texted Anil.

Jana: I didn't see you before you left.

Anil: Did you need to? I said goodbye to Imani.

Jana had no idea what to say to that. It was clear that he didn't really want to talk. After she stared blankly at her phone for a few seconds, another message came through.

Anil: I'll let you know when I'm in D.C.

She exhaled. She'd asked him for space, and maybe he wanted the same thing.

Jana: Okay. Have a safe trip home.

Anil: You too.

The trip home tomorrow couldn't come fast enough. Jana was about done with Tanzania.

CHAPTER 24

Shockingly, Mom apologized to Jana for her gross judgmental comments before they boarded their flight at Kilimanjaro Airport the next day. It wasn't a long apology, but Jana supposed it was better than nothing.

"And I'm sorry for exploding, too," Jana said. "I was...stressed."

"Nah, beta. It's fine. We can move on, okay?" Mom patted Jana's arm.

Jana was pretty sure "move on" meant sweep the issue under the rug in true Suleiman-family fashion, but Jana was okay with that. She didn't really want a long conversation about their lack of a mother/daughter relationship in public, anyway. They didn't speak about it again for the rest of the trip back home. They didn't really speak about anything at all. Mom was the same, happily chatting with her friends and being a little annoying about making sure Jana and Imani had enough to eat. Jana just read her book.

After getting home, Jana pretty much did nothing but sleep and laundry for a few days. Imani bounced back to Toronto time easily, but jet lag was kicking Jana's ass, so she relied on autopilot.

Despite wishing she could put off dealing with her problems until her body caught up with the time zone, Jana did apologize to Dr. Lopez as soon as she was home. He was a kind man—and Jana was a professional. It was possible he didn't think less of her after everything that happened in Arusha, but Jana needed to set things right. In an email to his Think address, Jana apologized for not coming clean about her marital history the moment she'd discovered Mom had told him that Jana was divorced. She apologized for her mother's boasting, and she assured him that her mother had no idea he had interviewed Jana, so none of that was an attempt to influence him. Finally, she apologized for her outburst on the last day of the trip. She also admitted she wasn't really a people person and that all those wedding events were way out of her comfort zone. And she shared that she and Anil weren't really friends.

She added that she knew that this wasn't a good way to start a professional relationship—and she understood if he wanted her to step away from her application at Think. There would be no hard feelings at all, and she would wish him and Think Canada well for the future.

She didn't get a response. And she had no idea if she was still in the running for the job.

Jana busied herself after that by getting everything ready for the start of Imani's school year in a few months. Her daughter needed new clothes, shoes, a book bag, and other school supplies.

Mostly, Jana admitted to herself, this was busywork so she wouldn't think too much. Because she'd prefer to avoid thinking, or overthinking, right now. When Jana stopped focusing on how many pairs of sneakers Imani would need, or on how to make an Instagram-worthy bento lunch for a four-year-old in less than fifteen minutes, or if ergonomic backpacks for four-year-olds were a thing, her mind wandered to where she preferred it wouldn't go.

Like wondering if she could have hacked it as a director at Think anyway. Or if Imani's social and intellectual development would be on par with her classmates at school. Or if not hiring someone because they lied about their marital status or because they pretended to be an extrovert was discrimination.

Or even worse, she'd think about Anil.

Because when she lay awake at night, her mind was a continuous loop of Anil. It wasn't just replaying that night in Hatari when he'd taken her places she'd honestly forgotten were possible (although that particular reel was on replay often), but other memories of the two weeks they'd traveled together in Africa. Like when he lifted her in his arms in the Serengeti after she tripped on dung. His expression when he showed Imani that first elephant in Ngorongoro. When they'd put their hands out together to encourage Imani to jump into the pool at Manyara. When they'd watched that sunrise together in the tent in Tarangire. She almost wished he'd done at least one horrible thing so she'd remember that she was supposed to dislike the guy.

He'd, of course, texted Jana when he arrived in Washington. Just a short message on the parenting app to let her know where he was. And he'd FaceTimed Imani with his parents the day after Jana and Imani got home, so Imani could tell her dadima and dadabapa all about her trip. Jana had said a quick hello, but that was it. They were still giving each other space.

Jana spent some time looking for new jobs, too. But prospects in her field were few and far between. There was definitely nothing else in Toronto right now.

Feeling dejected, Jana headed into the kitchen on Thursday afternoon to get a snack. Imani was in the corner, reading a book about animals to her dolls. Or rather, making up a story based on the pictures.

"You okay, beta?" Mom asked. The smell of fried onions and spices filled the room.

"Yeah, fine." She took her snack, Mom's dhokla and red chutney, to the dining table and sat where she could still see Mom cooking. Watching her mother cook had always been comforting to Jana.

"I'm making biryani and taking it to Kassim's. I'll leave some here for your dinner," Mom said.

"Okay. Thanks." There was still tension between them. Jana could feel it. She didn't argue with her mother often—but the few times they did, they never talked about it. Things were usually a bit awkward for a while, then went back to how they were before. Jana kind of figured that that cycle would go on forever.

But awkwardly, this time, Mom *did* want to talk about it. "I meant to ask you—did Anil hear about what Shelina said in Arusha? He didn't say goodbye when he left."

Jana frowned. "It wouldn't surprise me if he heard. He was probably embarrassed everyone was talking about him. Maybe if people would stop telling lies about him at parties, then he would be more polite when he left them."

Mom blinked. And again, Jana felt terrible for snapping at her mother. Jana was all her mom had. So what if Mom embellished her life a bit...told some tales so she could keep up with her friends? Who was she hurting?

Jana. That's who Mom was hurting.

Jana stared blankly at her mother, having no idea how to have this conversation, when the doorbell rang. Saved by the bell.

Jana opened the door and was greeted by a stranger in a blue uniform. "I have a delivery for Jana Suleiman."

Jana nodded. "That's me."

"Sign here, please, then I'll get it out of the truck."

Jana signed where he indicated, assuming the delivery was the box of souvenirs from Tanzania. She stepped back into the house to tell Mom, who was now spooning the biryani onto a large serving platter.

Jana headed back outside to find three boxes on the porch. Jana looked on in horror as the delivery person brought even more boxes out of the truck and stacked them up. Clearly, everyone had done a lot more shopping in Tanzania than she had. She started taking the boxes, eight in all, into her house one at a time.

Jana was on the porch grabbing the second-to-last box when suddenly and unexpectedly, Dr. Lopez was in front of her.

"Hello, Dr. Suleiman. Can I help you with that?" Dr. Lopez said.

What was he doing here?

Jana put on her professional smile. "Dr. Lopez! Hello! Nice to see you! I was just…The souvenirs from Tanzania just got here. And you don't need to call me Dr. Suleiman! Jana is fine. I'll just get these boxes here. It was a big delivery. My mom's inside. Cooking." Jana clamped her mouth shut so she'd stop rambling.

"Oh. I'm sorry it's a bad time," he said. "I probably should have called first. Farzana is in the car—we're on our way to a dinner party at Kassim's house, but I wanted to offer to drive your mother since she's bringing the food." He smiled. Because of course he was offering to pick up Mom. He was a kind man.

Jana had always been struck at how much Dr. Lopez's eyes

reminded her of her father's. In other circumstances, she would have been delighted to have him and Farzana Aunty as members of her aunty-and-uncle circle. But she'd rather have him as her boss. "Oh, okay, I'll ask her. She's packing up the food." Jana turned to put the box down, when he put his hand on her arm, stopping her. "May I speak to you for a moment first? I won't take much of your time."

Jana nodded. She was nervous . . . even shaking a bit. She took a deep breath, put the box in her arms down, and motioned for him to join her on the two little wrought-iron seats on the covered front porch of the house.

After they were both sitting, Dr. Lopez smiled. "I hope you're not embarrassed about what I happened to overhear on our last day in Tanzania," he said. "We should know better than to lurk around corners. And Farzana sends her love, by the way. She wanted to tell you there is nothing for you to worry about, and she's sorry she didn't get the chance to chat before we left."

They were accepting and not judgmental? They didn't think less of her for all the lies? These people were too good. She felt like she was letting them down. True, the lie that had sanitized her relationship with Anil into something more acceptable to the community was Mom's doing, but Jana should have corrected her. She'd been afraid Dr. Lopez would see her differently if he knew the truth about Imani's birth. She hadn't wanted him to know about her scandal.

"I'm so sorry I wasn't honest to either of you. I emailed you . . ."

"I saw that, but I wanted to wait to respond until I'd spoken to my colleague in HR. It was always a risky situation—you and I being on holiday together. I thought I could keep things professional and distant between us so it wouldn't affect your application, but I didn't take into account that Farzana would be so delighted with you. Or that seeing you with your daughter and friends would make me see just how intelligent, thoughtful, and *real* you are. I called HR immediately after getting home to tell them that you were who I wanted on my team. Today I received word that the rest of the board also wants you."

Jana blinked, speechless.

He smiled. "Your references had nothing but praise for you, so I have been given approval to officially offer you the position of director of research and programs at Think Canada."

"But... I lied to you."

Dr. Lopez shook his head. "I know your personal life being exposed at the hotel was embarrassing, but please don't let a little embarrassment stop you. And as for your mother telling me and Farzana you were married—your marital status has no bearing on your employment, of course. Neither does a little parental... gloating. I'm a parent—I do it all the time, too."

The job was hers. Jana's hand reflexively went to her mouth. "Oh my goodness. Thank you!"

He smiled widely. "I think we are going to work very well together."

Once Jana was able to communicate through the shock, they discussed terms and salary, which was more generous than she'd expected. He said the paperwork and a formal offer would be in her email the next morning. Her start date would be a week from Monday, and she could come into the office and meet everyone before then.

"Thank you again," she said. "For being so... understanding about my personal life."

He gave a warm smile. "Dr. Suleiman, *Jana*, you know the story about how Farzana and I got together, right?"

"You were a professor, and she was a student."

He nodded. "She was a graduate student. I wasn't her supervisor, but it was still inappropriate. I was an assistant professor at the time, and I resigned my position, and we moved across the country and eloped. Her family didn't approve, because I was older than her and not Muslim. My family were mad because she was a student and I gave up an excellent job for her. I lost most of my friends."

"But love conquered all?"

He snorted. "Hardly. I think the love lasted about five years. The marriage lasted eight." He sighed. "It took a certain amount of psychological fortitude to come to terms with what we'd done, and I'm not sure I was ready. I felt so much guilt—I should have known better. And Farzana was feeling so isolated from her family. I took out my guilt on her, and she took out her resentment on me. I regret that we didn't give each other a real chance. Or give our family a chance. We were both so stubborn." He smiled at Jana. "A funny thing happens with time, though—old scandals become just that. *Old*. People still talk about us. There are some in my family, and in hers, who don't approve of our reconciliation. But when people see how happy we are and that we don't hide from our past, they realize that judging us does nothing. You should be living for *you*, not for others."

Jana smiled, remembering when Farzana Aunty sang "When I Kissed the Teacher" at karaoke. Farzana Aunty was *owning* her past scandals. She was truly a legend.

"I consider myself lucky every moment of the day that I was given a second chance. Farzana and I are happier than we've ever been. Our kids are *delighted*. I'm so grateful we were able to get out of our own ways. But enough for now. We have plenty of time to get to know each other." He smiled and looked at the boxes on the porch. "You said these boxes are souvenirs from the trip?"

Jana chuckled, then told him about Elsie shipping all the trinkets the wedding party had bought.

"What an excellent idea. My suitcase was so full—we really should have had things shipped. Did you buy a lot?"

She told them about the animal figurines she had bought, including one from a vendor in the Serengeti that was made of bent wire and cut-up soda cans.

"How unique! I'd love to see it—after you've opened the boxes."

"Oh, I can get it now." One of the boxes still on the porch said SERENGETI on it. Jana used her key to open the box and dug out a wrapped package with her name on it. She unwrapped it in her lap to show Dr. Lopez.

Only...it wasn't an elephant.

It was the penis Nicole and Asha had painted for her in Amsterdam.

Her boss had just seen her blinged-out dildo.

Mom came outside then, holding the platter of biryani. "Oh, Jana, what's that?"

CHAPTER 25

Later that night, after Imani had gone to sleep and Jana had hidden away the dildo, she heard her mother come home from Kassim Uncle's. Strange. Mom never came home from one of Kassim Uncle's parties so early. Maybe it was because she'd ridden with Dr. Lopez. Jana didn't go downstairs to greet her, because she didn't want to continue the conversation from before Dr. Lopez arrived earlier, but when Mom didn't come upstairs to bed, Jana went down to see if she was okay. She found her mother sitting in the living room, a decorative box that looked vaguely familiar at her feet. Jana frowned, sitting next to her. Mom had a photo album on her lap. That's what that box was—it held all the family albums. Jana hadn't seen it in years.

"You're home early," Jana said.

Mom nodded. "Everyone was talking about the wedding, and about how well Kamila and Rohan have done with their lives. Successful, and so happy." Mom looked at Jana. "I know what you're thinking. I didn't talk about you."

Jana blinked. Was that because Mom didn't think Jana was successful or happy?

"Let me show you something," Mom said, flipping the pages

of the album. Jana had seen it before—it contained vacation pictures from Jana's childhood. There were pictures from their trip to Disney World, Muskoka, Quebec City, and even Tanzania. Jana, her dad, plus all the other kids, too—Kamila, Shelina, Zayan, and Rohan.

"You notice anything about these pictures?" Mom asked, pointing at a few specific ones.

Other than Jana's frizzy hair, there was nothing out of the ordinary. There was one of her and Dad on a ride at Disney. One where they both had binoculars in their hands looking out the roof of a safari vehicle. One where they were in side-by-side tubes on the rapids in a river.

"It's me and Dad in all of them."

Mom nodded. "I took all the pictures when we were on holiday. In other families, the father takes the pictures, but not in ours. You and he were always together—not noticing the world around you. So, if I didn't take pictures, no one would."

Jana didn't remember that.

Mom flipped to the next page. "I never felt like we were like the other families. They had two kids...I just had you." She smiled. "I thought you were better than those kids. Smarter. You never gave us any trouble." Mom closed the album and picked up another one from the box. "In this album, your daddy took the pictures."

Jana hadn't seen this album before. It was filled with pictures of Jana. In her ornate Bollywood dance costume at a recital. In her fifth-grade speech competition where she won first place for her speech on the economics of war (Jana had *always* been Jana, apparently). There were pictures of cupcakes she'd baked as a kid, of her winning academic awards, and even pictures of her straight-A report cards.

"Dad made this album?" Jana asked, tearing up.

Mom nodded. "He was so proud of you."

Jana tried to remember if he'd ever told her that. But even if he'd never said it, Jana *felt* her father's pride. He'd come to all her recitals and clap from the front row and put her A-plus essays on the fridge. Mom flipped to the next page, halfway through the album. There was only one picture on the page...a shot of Jana accepting an academic award—the history award—in grade eleven. There were no more pictures after that.

And Jana knew why. Her father passed away about a month later. Jana closed her eyes. She didn't want to think about that terrifying day.

"I should have kept the album going," Mom said. "Things were never the same after that."

Jana shook her head, wiping the tears from her eyes. She'd gone to university just over a year later. At first, she was only a few hours away, but after her first year, Jana transferred to the UK. And she hadn't ever really come home after that—until she was pregnant with Imani.

"Do you..." Jana paused. "Do you think Dad would still be putting pictures in here?" Parents were proud of their adult kids for different reasons. Jana wasn't running her own company, like Kamila, Rohan, and Zayan were. She wasn't a yoga mom and head of the PTA with a nanny and housekeeper like Shelina. Jana didn't own a home or have a husband.

She was a single mom living with her parent, bouncing from job to job.

Mom turned sharply to look at Jana. "Nah, beta. Don't *ever* think he wouldn't be proud of you. If he was still with us, this album would be full. Pictures of your university graduation, and of the good work you've done around the world. He'd frame every article about you. He would tell everyone about his brilliant daughter."

"Okay," Jana whispered. "But what about Imani? Dad was so...*traditional*."

Mom shook her head. "We grew up at a different time. In a different place. I don't think we realize how damaging the things we were taught were." She sighed. "No one ever prints pictures to put them in albums these days," Mom said, picking up her phone and launching the photos app. She opened an album that was all pictures of Imani. Some had Jana in them, too. Some of the pictures were from a long time ago—Jana nursing baby Imani. Holding her hands while she was learning to walk. Pushing Imani on the swings.

Jana could feel herself tear up again.

Mom smiled at the pictures. "I wish your father were here. He would have been such a loving nanabapa. He would have had albums full of pictures of Imani. And of you with her. I should have done that for him."

Jana didn't say anything, just sat with tears flowing down her cheeks. Dad would have been the *best* grandfather.

Mom put her finger on a picture of Jana and Imani from the sangeet in the Serengeti. "My mother *hated* it when people took pictures of her kids. There are hardly any of me or my brothers and sisters. She said it would promote vanity. She would scold anyone who said we were smart or beautiful...She said our heads would get too big. She wanted us to be pious and humble."

Jana's maternal grandmother died when Jana was quite young, but Jana remembered that she hadn't been a very nice woman.

Mom suddenly looked at Jana. "That's why I took so many pictures of you on holiday. I didn't want to be like my mother. But I should have done more. I *am* proud of you, beta. So proud of you. Your father was better at showing it. I'm sorry I said those things about you and Anil. I wanted life to be *easier* for you. I never wanted you to suffer." She held Jana's hand. "And when everyone talked about their kids and how proud they were, I didn't know how to say that even though you took a path that we were taught was wrong, I *still* think my child is the best one. People talked and gossiped, and I thought I was helping."

Jana didn't know what to say. She blinked.

"Your father always said, 'There is no limit to what my Jana can do.' But…after he passed, you weren't the same. It was so hard for you…And whenever you came home, you seemed…"

"A little lost," Jana said. She felt a lot lost after Dad died. Like she didn't have an anchor at home anymore.

Mom nodded, her eyes glistening. "I think I forget that what *I* think will make your life easier, or what our culture says will make your life easier, isn't the same as what *you* feel will make it easier. I promise, beta…I will try harder. I will *listen* to you. And I am *very* proud of you, beta. Always."

With tears streaming down Jana's face, she hugged her mother. "Thank you, Mom."

After Mom released Jana from her tight hug, she looked into Jana's eyes. "I…don't know what happened in Africa with Anil—"

"Mom, I—"

"No, wait. Let me speak. I know it's not my business, and I know that you will do what you feel is best for you and Imani…but I just…" Mom exhaled, clearly not sure how to say this. "I hope you're not staying away from something that can make you and Imani happy because of what other people think. Or even what I think. You should live for *you*, not others."

"That's what Sam Lopez just said."

"He's a smart man. PhD, like you. You should listen to him, not me."

Jana laughed. "Thanks, Mom."

"I will accept whatever choice you make. And if it's a choice that makes you and Imani happy, I will be happy, too. I love you, beta."

Dr. Lopez's and Mom's words wouldn't leave Jana's mind. Was Jana letting other people's opinions get in the way of her own happiness? She still hadn't really talked to Anil since getting home. Little contact was normal between them—but Jana *missed* him. A lot. She'd grown used to being around him again. At Hatari they promised they'd talk once they were home, but they were clearly both avoiding it.

But before anything, Jana needed to figure out how she felt about him. She'd finally forgiven him—that much she knew. *Releasing* him . . . moving on from her anger and resentment felt like removing a stone she'd worn on her shoulder for five years. She hadn't even noticed the weight until it wasn't there anymore. But under the anger was a boatload of heartache and lingering romantic feelings that really should have faded a long time ago.

Heartache and pain. At times when they were in Tanzania, it almost physically hurt her to see him. To wonder what could have been if she hadn't run away that first time. But other times, she felt joy like she hadn't known in a long time. When they played together in that beautiful infinity pool, when they watched the sunrise together, and when he tenderly washed every inch of Jana's body. She'd felt wanted, valued, and a lot less lost when she was with him.

But they were so different. Were they even compatible?

She knew so many happy couples were made up of contrasting personalities. Rohan and Kamila, Mom and Dad, even Asha and Nicole. At the end of the day, social, or private, or whatever in between didn't matter. That was just window dressing. There was so much more to who they were than what people saw on the surface.

And who Anil was under the surface was generous. As committed to bettering the world as Jana was. An excellent father. Better at braiding hair than her. Jana *did* know who Anil was. She closed her eyes, remembering the torrent of emotions that made her ache when she was with him that night at Hatari. The way that every look, every touch made her feel things... *everywhere*. It had *never* felt casual with Anil. Even way back. She had lied to herself for a while that it had just been a fling, but at the time, those two weeks had felt like the beginning of forever.

A relationship with Anil Malek would be complicated, difficult, and maybe even frustrating. But what would no relationship with him be like? Could Jana go back to how things were before Tanzania? The memories would fade eventually, and maybe she'd see something other than Anil braiding Imani's hair when Jana brushed it, or she'd feel something other than his hands all over her when she took a shower.

Jana closed her eyes for a second, feeling a sharp prickle behind them.

Jana couldn't go back. She was in love with him.

The realization hit her like a tsunami. She wasn't ready for these feelings, but she couldn't sweep them under the rug anymore, either. It was time for Jana to be the one to push. To *fight* for him. But fighting for a man was way out of her comfort zone. Jana chuckled to herself, wondering if she should add it to her "letting loose" list.

Jana decided to start by inching out of her comfort zone this time. She'd found some cute school clothes online for Imani, but they were from a store that didn't have a Canadian shipping option, so she texted Anil to ask if she could have them sent to his parents' house and he could bring them when he came home. It was late, so she didn't expect a response.

In the morning, he texted that he'd bring the clothes but didn't say anything else. She resisted the urge to write back. She wanted to go slow to gauge how he was feeling.

That night, Jana was doing some reading on Think projects around the world when she noticed she'd missed a text from Anil an hour earlier.

Jana: Sorry, I missed your message. I assume you wanted to FaceTime with Imani?

Anil: No worries.

Jana needed to keep the conversation going. They'd had hundreds of these little two-word conversations over the years. They never went further than that. But Jana needed to take it further.

Jana: I got the shipping notification for that clothing order. You should get it tomorrow.

Jana cringed. That had to be the most unromantic text in existence.

Anil: Okay. I'll look out for it.

Jana put her phone down. She had no idea what she was doing.

The following evening, Anil FaceTimed Imani at bedtime. Jana didn't interrupt but stayed close so she could hear his voice telling Imani about his day and reading her a story. He sounded so soft and gentle when he talked to their daughter. Loving. The voice gave Jana full-body shivers while also being the most comforting sound in the world. Jana had to figure out how to make this work with Anil or she'd never survive Imani's calls with her father.

After their daughter had gone to bed, Jana texted him again.

Jana: I found my mom's mandazi recipe. Do you want me to send it to you?

He responded right away.

Anil: No thank you. I have my own mother's recipe.

Jana: I really loved your mom's mandazi when I went there for brunch back then.

He didn't respond.

The next evening, she tried again. She texted him the most adorable picture of that frolicking baby elephant they'd seen at the watering hole in Tarangire.

Jana: I was looking through pictures and found this one! I should enter this in a photo contest, shouldn't I?

He responded that yes, she should, and that it was a great picture.

Jana had noticed an ad online earlier about a touring production of *The Lion King* musical coming to Toronto in a few months, so she suggested they get tickets when they went on sale in three weeks.

Anil: For all of us?

Jana: Yes, all of us. We should both be there for Imani's first musical, shouldn't we?

Anil: It's your turn. I took her to see the Nutcracker in December.

Jana: I think we should go together.

Anil: Why? That's not necessary. You go ahead.

Jana blinked at her phone. This wasn't working. Either he wasn't taking her hints that she wanted to spend time with him as a family . . . or he was and had no interest.

Jana needed to rethink her strategy.

A few days later, Jana went shopping to get new clothes for work. On the way home, she noticed a new restaurant. She looked up the menu once she got back to the house and then sent Anil a link to its website.

Anil: Did you mean to send me that?

Jana: It's a new pili pili restaurant! We should take Imani when you're back. The food looks spicy, but there should be something there for her.

Anil: You want to go to dinner together?

Jana exhaled. Clearly, she needed to be more direct.

Jana: In Tanzania you said we needed a reset on our relationship, and it would be easier if we were friends.

There was no answer to her text. With her heart pounding in her chest, Jana watched the three little dots appear, then disappear several times. Finally, she texted him.

Jana: If that's not what you want anymore, okay. I'll step back. I'm sorry.

This time there were no three dots. Just nothing. It was time for Jana to take the big risk. She took a deep breath and typed before she lost her nerve.

Jana: Or maybe that place will be too spicy for Imani. We could leave her with Mom. Have a date just the two of us. It will give us a chance to talk.

There was no response for several seconds. Jana would have taken the text back, but it was showing as read on her screen. She was about to make a bad joke so he would think she was kidding, when her phone rang—and Anil's name flashed on her screen. She had no choice but to forge ahead, even though it felt like a whole flock of butterflies weren't just fluttering in her stomach, but headbanging to death metal. She accepted the call.

"A date?" Anil said immediately after Jana said hello.

Voice shaking, Jana answered. "Yeah, no worries if you say no, and I promise no hard feelings."

"Like a *date* date?"

"Yes."

"Like a romantic date?"

Maybe this was a mistake. Maybe Rohan was wrong and Anil wasn't interested. Jana's hands were sweating. "Say no if you don't want to, or say yes. But let's not overthink this. Keep it simple. Just a dinner. You said we needed to talk when we were back in town."

"I never said a *date*, though. A date as more than friends?"

"As two people who are open to figuring out if they *can* be more than friends. But if that's not what you want, then—"

"I didn't think that was what *you* wanted, Jana. I didn't think you wanted that in a million years."

"Did you forget what happened at Hatari?" Jana asked.

He chuckled low, sending a shiver down Jana's spine. What would his face look like if he were here with her right now? Would he have a private smile? Or would his brows be furrowed in confusion? "I've honestly thought of little else," he said.

And there it was. He'd been as preoccupied with thoughts of that night as she'd been. Jana could feel a heat burning inside her. He still wanted her. "So then…"

"My answer is yes. Let's have a date. Me and you," he said. Jana could practically see the smile in his words.

"Okay. That's good. I'll ask Mom what evening she's free next week to babysit. You'll be back Friday, right?" Jana sounded awkward, but she wanted to scream with joy.

"Yes. I'll be by to pick up Imani around four. I was thinking I would take her to see that new movie with the trolls…since I know you won't want to."

Jana chuckled. "Appreciated. Mom will be here on Friday, but I'll be out. I have an orientation meeting at Think."

There was a pause before he spoke. "Jana, you *got* the job?"

She grinned. "I did!"

"That's . . . that's *amazing*. Congratulations!"

"Thank you. So, I'll see you at Kamila and Rohan's wedding reception on Saturday?"

"Yes. Babysitter is lined up."

"Okay. I need to go now."

"Good night, Jana."

He disconnected the call, and that was it. She knew that they would talk more later, and they would say everything that needed to be said in person . . . but that felt a tiny bit . . . anticlimactic. But later, when Jana was about to get ready to turn in for the night, a text came through.

Anil: You still up? I have something I need to say.

She tensed, worried. Was he going to give her hell for torturing him for so long then simply asking him out? Or was he going to back out?

Jana: I'm here.

Anil: Okay. Thank you.

Anil: That's what I needed to say. Thank you for giving me this chance. I hope you never regret it.

Jana smiled as she curled her feet under her.

Jana: I don't think I will.

Anil: I'm looking forward to coming back. Good night, Jana.

Jana: Good night, Anil.

She turned off her light. She wasn't sure she remembered what it felt like to go to sleep smiling, but she was all about the new experiences lately.

CHAPTER 26

The next few days were...strange. She texted with Anil pretty much daily, although they didn't talk about their upcoming date. Jana told him that Imani's daycare teacher had called her to say that Imani had told the whole class that her favorite animal was a dick. Thankfully, their daughter then showed the class and the very disturbed teacher a picture of a dik-dik. Jana and Anil laughed together at that. Overall, everything seemed normal, which was what was weird, because they had never been normal before.

On Thursday, Kamila and Rohan returned from Spain, and the #BridalBrigade group chat immediately resurrected. After a few cheers and *I miss you all* GIFs, dik-dik pics started filling the feed again. Jana laughed, then placed the not-safe-for-use dildo from Amsterdam on her coffee table and snapped a picture of it. She sent the group chat a warning message that she was about to send a NSFW pic, then sent a picture of the dildo. That had been the ongoing joke while they were in Tanzania—threatening to send a dick pic, then sending an adorable dik-dik pic. But Jana upped the ante and sent an actual dick. Or, at least, the painted dildo.

After laughs, cheers, eggplant emojis, and a lot of innuendo, Kamila called Jana asking if the dildo meant the shipment from Tanzania was in. Jana said yes and told her she could bring her the boxes Friday evening. Jana knew Kamila wanted some of the souvenirs to decorate the wedding reception on Saturday.

On Friday around three, after giving Imani a big hug and kiss since she would be at Anil's for the week, Jana headed over to the Think Canada office to meet with Dr. Lopez and the rest of her new colleagues and to sign her offer letter. It was a warm day, so Jana was wearing cropped black slim pants with black heels and a cream blouse.

Jana was nervous but also excited when she walked into the converted Victorian mansion housing the Think Canada office in Midtown Toronto. After she greeted the friendly receptionist, she sat in the lobby, waiting for Dr. Lopez.

"Jana, welcome! Wonderful to see you!" Dr. Lopez said as he came down a hallway. He looked so different here in an office setting instead of in Tanzania, or on her front porch. Still tanned from the trip (like she was), he was in his nonprofit executive director outfit instead of the *boomer on safari* look. Chinos and a tweed blazer complete with elbow patches.

"Hi, Dr. Lopez!"

He greeted her with a warm handshake. "I do hope you'll call me Sam now. Come. Let's get the boring paperwork out of the way, then I'll give you a tour and introduce you to the team. We're a small group, which makes us so much like a little family. I think you're going to fit right in."

Jana followed him to her future office, a modern, sleek space on the second floor with a window overlooking the road. After Jana signed the necessary paperwork, he took her around the building to meet her new colleagues. The handful of friendly fundraisers, assistants, researchers, and managers seemed very nice and welcoming. She knew she'd need time to remember everyone's name and role, but most were about her age, except for two women who were about a decade older. She did recognize a few names from papers she'd read. Overall, she was confident that she'd enjoy working with them.

This had been her last worry—would she get along with her new colleagues? Would they judge her? So far, no one seemed to know about Jana's past reputation. Or if they knew, they didn't care. She met her new research assistant, Andrew, a friendly man probably a bit older than her. He was from the Philippines and had worked for many years with an NGO there before moving to Canada. Personality-wise, he reminded Jana a bit of Tim, but with Nicole's dry humor. Jana could already tell she would love working with him.

She sat with Sam and Andrew in an open meeting space to go over the current projects for an hour before they walked her back out to the lobby. A few other staff members were there with the receptionist, and they asked Jana her impression of Think so far. They were all still talking in the lobby when a man about Sam's age and a younger woman came into the office.

"Zachary! Maria!" Dr. Lopez gave the man a handshake and kissed the smiling woman on the cheek.

Sam introduced the pair to Jana. Zachary Peterson was apparently one of Sam Lopez's oldest friends. They were coming to collect Sam because they had plans in the evening. Jana knew Dr. Peterson by reputation—he was the head of international development at the University of Toronto and had been a top researcher in the field for years. Maria Peterson, his wife, was considerably younger than him. Maybe in her late thirties.

She was effervescent and chatty and was clearly also close to Dr. Lopez.

"We want to hear all about your trip!" Then she smiled at Jana. "Oh, this must be your new second-in-command! I'm so glad you found someone!"

After some small talk, Maria looked back at Dr. Lopez. "I cannot wait to hear about Tanzania. I can't believe I didn't realize I *knew* the groom when you told me about this wedding! When I saw that picture Farzana posted on Facebook, I nearly screamed. I haven't seen Rohan in eons!"

"You know Rohan?" Jana asked, surprised.

"Yes! From college! You know him, too?"

"Yes, he and the bride are old family friends."

"Dr. Suleiman was at the wedding, too," Sam said. "In the wedding party. It was quite the coincidence. The ceremony was spectacular. Imagine, the Serengeti sun shining on us all. There was even a giraffe watching the ceremony with us!"

She clapped her hands together. "A giraffe! How . . . immersing!"

"Here, let me show you." Sam took out his phone and scrolled. Then he handed it to Maria. Jana didn't see it—but she'd seen pictures of the giraffe at the wedding ceremony before. She'd seen the giraffe in person, too. "The flower girl is Dr. Suleiman's daughter."

"Oh, she's just darling! Oh my god," Maria said suddenly. "Is that Anil Malek?" She was pinching to zoom into the picture. "I knew him in college, too. I had no idea he and Rohan were still in contact."

Sam looked briefly at Jana. "Yes, he was in the wedding party."

Maria tapped the phone with her finger. "That's a surprise! He married my friend Nadia right after college but he was unfaithful and got the other woman pregnant, if you'll believe it." She looked up at Sam. "It was quite the scandal in our college friend group."

Jana's fists clenched. She needed to get out of here before everyone discovered she was the *other woman*. She took one step backward.

"I need to have a talk with Nadia, though," Maria said, not noticing Jana freaking out. "Last I heard, she was back with Anil. I suppose it's romantic, like you and Farzana. Still, it's so *messy*, you know? He'll be stuck with that *other woman* in his life forever because of that poor child. I'm sure nobody wants that."

What?

Sam put his hand on Jana's arm briefly.

Voice shaky, Jana asked for clarification. "What did you say about Nadia and Anil?"

"Oh, they're back together. I saw a picture of them on her Facebook yesterday. I really should call her and say, *Girl...what are you doing?* Hey, maybe Nadia was at the wedding. Do you know her? Tall woman. Really beautiful."

Jana's knees shook. She took two more steps back. "No, Nadia wasn't there. But the *other woman* was. And their child, too. She was the flower girl." Jana took a breath. "I'm the other woman." Jana's eyes went blurry. She turned quickly. "I need to go. I'm just...goodbye."

And she walked right out of the Think office.

One five-minute conversation with a "desperate housewife" of academia gossiping about her college classmates had blown everything Jana had been happy about to smithereens.

Jana's knees were shaking as she wobbled to her car several streets away from the mansion. This was all unreal. What were the chances that someone who knew Anil and Nadia back in *college* would show up at Think while she was there? Probably the same as the likelihood that Rohan's uncle was the executive director in the first place.

Wait. Rohan had first told Jana about this job because he heard about it on a college friend's Facebook post. That friend must have been Maria. *Fuck.* Sometimes the world really was much too small for Jana's likings.

Now the gossip…Jana's past…was known by everyone she would be working with. She had no doubt that the staff that had heard Maria would talk to everyone else at Think. Her colleagues. Her staff. Jana reached her car, got inside, and sat, putting her head in her arms on the steering wheel to think. She was literally shaking. Her breathing was heavy. She was in no condition to drive right now.

And what about Anil? Were he and Nadia back together? It couldn't possibly be true. Clearly, Maria only knew Nadia on social media and hadn't actually spoken to her—she could have been mistaken about the picture she saw.

Jana had just learned to trust the man again, and she knew that everything that had happened in Tanzania would not have happened if he was in a relationship with his ex-wife the whole time. But Maria *had* seen pictures of Nadia and Anil together, so even if she didn't know the nature of their relationship, it was clear Nadia *was* in Anil's life in some capacity. And Anil hadn't told Jana that.

Jana had never, not once, asked Anil if he still spoke to his ex-wife. She should have asked questions before getting involved with him again. The events of five years ago should have taught her better. Five years ago, she'd believed him when he said he and Nadia were divorced. She never pressed, never insisted on more details about his wife or why his marriage had ended. She'd been so caught up in the passion and stepping out of her comfort zone that she missed all the warning signs.

History was repeating itself now. *Hatari*. The Swahili word for danger. Only helpful if Jana would actually listen. She felt a tightness in her throat.

She should ask him. Figure out if what Maria had said was even true—that he and Nadia were speaking again. Or if they were back together. It was only fair to Anil to ask him before jumping to conclusions.

She picked up her phone to text Anil, but Jana noticed then that she still had her notifications on silent from when she was at the Think office. And she had a missed message from Anil from about an hour ago.

Anil: Taking Imani to see a movie and then dinner, but can you call me later tonight? Just need to talk to you about something. Don't worry, it's not about Imani.

Jana reread the text three times. She didn't respond to it—he was at the movies, anyway, and she couldn't exactly accuse him of lying to her while he was out with Imani.

But what could he possibly need to speak to her about?

Was he going to tell her about Nadia? Maria said she saw a picture of them together on Facebook *yesterday*. Maybe Anil wanted to tell Jana that he had reconnected with his ex-wife and wanted to put the brakes on whatever was starting between Anil and Jana. Or maybe he was going to confess that when he'd slept with Jana in Tanzania, he was cheating on Nadia.

Bile rose in Jana's stomach.

She couldn't put herself through all this again. She tossed her phone to the passenger seat. It was easier to walk away now before things got even messier.

Jana put her head back in her arms and let herself cry. It was over. After everything had been going so perfectly for the first time in her adult life, she'd lost it all.

CHAPTER 27

J ana finally pulled herself together and drove to Kamila's place
instead of going home. She told herself it was because she
had all those boxes from Tanzania in her trunk, but really, she
couldn't bear the thought of being alone. Of not being able tell
a friend what had just happened.

Kamila and Rohan lived in a tall condo building in Midtown
Toronto surrounded by amazing restaurants and several dog
parks. When Jana got there, Rohan came down to help bring
up the boxes to their unit on the fifteenth floor, telling Jana that
Kamila was at the animal shelter.

Their unit was bright and sunny with a huge window overlooking the city, and all the colorful touches you would expect
from Kamila Hussain's home (now Kamila Hussain-Nasser). But
it wasn't without Rohan's touches, either, like the heavy wooden
bookshelves and sleek gourmet kitchen. Once Jana and Rohan
had brought all the boxes in, Jana fell heavily on a sofa, exhausted. The moment she sat, Kamila and Rohan's energetic dogs
attacked her with love. Darcy, a small bichon frise, was getting
on in years, but she would probably have puppylike enthusiasm
until her last day. And Potato, an enormous, affectionate beige

Lab mix, was exuberant and loved people more than anything in the world. Jana wasn't a dog person, but these two were hard not to love. Jana rubbed the dogs' heads as they settled at her feet.

Rohan's eyes were knit with concern as he handed her a glass of water. "You okay? You look…"

Jana sighed. "Like I've been crying?"

He frowned. "Kamila told me you went to your new job today… What happened?"

There was no point keeping this in. Jana had no idea if Sam would tell Rohan, or, hell, if that Maria woman would. Jana took a deep breath, mortified when she choked back a sob.

In seconds, Potato was on his feet. He rested his face on her knees and looked up at Jana with his big brown eyes. Seriously the sweetest dog in existence. Jana scratched his ear.

"Potato knows when someone needs him," Rohan said.

Jana let the dog nuzzle into her hand. "Smart boy." She rubbed the dog's head for a few seconds before speaking again. "Yeah, something happened at the Think office. Some friend of Sam Lopez showed up who knew Anil. From college. She knew you, too. And Nadia," Jana said.

Rohan frowned. "Who?"

"Maria something. I don't know her maiden name. She's married to a professor—Zachary Peterson."

Rohan frowned. "Maria Lima. Yeah, I know her." He put his hand to his mouth. "Shit. It was from *her* Facebook post that I heard about the job in the first place. I wasn't thinking. What did she say?"

"Dr. Lopez showed her a wedding photo and when she saw it she proceeded to announce to everyone in the lobby that her friend Nadia's husband, Anil, got another woman pregnant while they were married. She was shocked you were still friends with him."

"Oh my god. Why would she say that?"

"Gossip? She didn't know I was the woman." Jana swallowed. "She said Anil probably *hated* that he was stuck with the *other woman* in his life forever because of the *poor child*."

Rohan picked up his phone. "I'm messaging her. How dare she—"

"Rohan, no. She didn't know it was me."

"Did Sam Uncle say anything?"

"No. I did, though. I told her the cute flower girl was the *poor child* in question, and that *I* was the other woman." She leaned down to rub behind Potato's velvety ears. Jana knew she should ask Rohan if he knew anything about Anil and Nadia being together again, but honestly, it hurt too much to even think about it now. And she wanted to wait until she had spoken to Anil later. "Then I left. I may resign Monday."

Rohan shook his head. "What? Why?"

"You don't understand, Rohan." She looked down at the dog. Dogs had life easy. All they wanted was a scratch on the head. "So many people heard her. Dr. Lopez, plus Dr. Peterson, who is the head of international development at U of T, but also the receptionist and a few other Think employees. Even my new research assistant. Sam Uncle might be *understanding*, but you know how much people love dirt like this. I...just can't handle everyone talking about me anymore."

"Oh, Jana." Rohan's voice was soft. Gentle.

She focused on the dog, who loved Jana no matter what she did. "I feel like...no one sees me. They only see this thing that happened to me. They either think my life is *so hard*, and I need to be pitied, or they think I'm a home-wrecker who split up a marriage. I can't go to work if that's all they see." She sniffed loudly again, and Potato tilted his head with concern.

Rohan got up from the armchair and sat next to Jana, putting his arm around her. "I'm sorry everyone was cruel to you back then. You didn't deserve that."

Jana leaned into her friend and let her tears come.

Now that Jana was properly crying, Potato climbed on top of her, and Darcy joined him. Potato was a little heavy to be on her lap.

Jana chuckled. "You all are pretty good at comforting, but it's a little crowded."

Rohan laughed. He sat up straight and lifted Darcy onto his lap. Potato jumped back down to the floor and resumed his position facing Jana with his chin on her knees. She scratched his ears.

"We've known each other a long time," Rohan said.

She nodded. "All my life."

"And I think you and I are more alike than different. We've both always strived to be the best, and our professional image is important to us. For years, I struggled with a corporate shark reputation—I was nothing to some people but a heartless executive."

That was ridiculous to Jana. Rohan was a bit buttoned up, but he was the most generous, giving person out there.

"Then I realized it was because I kept my personal and professional lives too separate. I never let anyone see any side of me but the professional one. People I work with needed to see me as a person—otherwise, all they'd see was a corporate shark. I know you're private, but maybe letting people get to know the real you will help them see that you are a lot more than this reputation."

"Yeah. Well, you know it's hard for me to open up to people. That's why they don't like me."

He shook his head. "*You* know that's not true. Look at the wedding party. They all liked you. You enjoyed being with them, right?"

"Yeah, I guess I did." She sniffled. "Too bad there's not a Bridal Brigade party right now to take my mind off all this."

Rohan frowned. "You know there can be, right? One text to Kamila and she can have a party here in less than half an hour."

She'd been kidding when she'd said that. The last thing Jana wanted was a house full of people judging her for thinking about quitting her dream job. Jana had had enough of stepping out of her comfort zone for now—she'd been happier when she was lonely and bitter.

Jana shook her head. "Kamila is good but not that good. She can't get a party together in half an hour."

Rohan took his phone from the coffee table. "Shall we test her?"

Jana raised an eyebrow but then nodded. Mostly because she wanted to see if Kamila could really do it.

Rohan smiled as he texted his wife.

Within the next half hour, one by one, the Bridal Brigade started showing up at Kamila's house. First, Yuriko arrived with a block of aged cheddar and a wheel of Brie. Then Asha and Nicole with grapes, dried apricots, dark chocolate, Gruyère, and aged Gouda. Then Tim and Jerome with the most enormous wood board Jana had ever seen, along with a baguette and some crackers. And finally, Kamila arrived with bottles of wine, some Turkish pastrami, and beef soppressata, along with cured olives and some Quebec washed-rind cheese.

Jana stood back in awe as everyone set up the most epic cheese tray she'd ever seen, arguing about what should go where on the big board.

"I don't understand how you all happened to have this stuff at home," Jana said.

Asha snorted and turned to look at Jana. "We didn't. Kamila gave us strict orders on what to buy at what store on our way here. She's a one-woman well-oiled machine. Working with Elsie really made Kamila level up her event-planning skills."

Jana stepped back to watch them set up this little impromptu get-together. Wine poured, charcuterie arranged, small plates distributed, and they were ready. They all sat around the living room with plates perched on their laps. The group was still making small talk—first, a little about Rohan and Kamila's honeymoon in Barcelona, then Tim and Jerome had some funny stories about their fact-finding trip to Moshi to learn more about the Kilimanjaro climb. Neither Jana nor Rohan mentioned Jana's crisis, which she appreciated. Jana didn't really join in on the conversation, but being with friends...not being alone, felt comforting.

They started talking about the Toronto wedding reception, which would be the following night. "The restaurant has a karaoke machine," Kamila said. "We should have a *Mamma Mia!* revival show!"

Jana shook her head. There was no way in hell she was going to sing at a party again. Especially that song. She redirected the conversation by suggesting they open the boxes from Tanzania. As they sorted the souvenirs into piles, Jana told them about Dr. Lopez showing up while she was bringing them into her house.

"I can't believe you opened that box in front of Sam Uncle!" Kamila said. "You knew the dildo would be in it."

Jana shook her head. "Why would I think the dildo would be there? The box was labeled Serengeti. You made those in Amsterdam."

"Maybe because we gave you the penis in Serengeti?" Asha said.

Jana stopped folding the kanga fabric in her hand and glared. Kamila blinked, then burst out laughing. "It's hilarious, though. I would have loved to see your mother's face. I wonder if they told my dad? Or Rohan's parents?" She shrugged. "I guess now I'm good to display my penis art on a shelf the next time my Dad or in-laws come to dinner."

Nicole and Asha nearly fell into the pile of folded kangas laughing. Jana shook her head, imagining Nadira Aunty's face if she came over to her son's house to see a brightly colored penis on a shelf.

Jana chuckled. Her friends *were* making her feel better, even without them knowing why she was upset. She pulled another box in front of her and used a small knife to cut the tape off. She started dividing up the contents, each item labeled on either the paper or plastic wrapping. There was a stack of woven bowls for Yuriko, a whole bunch of soapstone figures for Marc. And another heavy piece that was probably also soapstone. It was wrapped in paper and had Anil's name on it.

"What's that?" Yuriko asked.

"It's for Anil." She added it to his pile. Anil had purchased mostly wood pieces, but there were a few rolled-up art canvases, too.

"Open it. I want to see," Kamila said.

They'd been opening the packages of anyone who wasn't here to snoop at their purchases. Kamila said it was her prerogative, since she paid for all this stuff to be shipped to Canada.

"I'm not opening Anil's stuff."

Kamila snorted. "Why is it different from anyone else's? Rohan opened Marc's."

Jana rolled her eyes. After she'd slept with him, then asked him on a date, then freaked out when she discovered that he was still talking to his ex-wife and maybe actually even back together with her, it felt weird to be opening the man's knickknacks. But she knew if she didn't, someone else here would. So, Jana unwrapped the paper. Inside was a creamy tan carving of a family. Jana had seen statues like these in most curio shops in Tanzania. Made from smooth carved soapstone, they depicted minimalistic figures of people. Often, a mother and child. Jana had also seen some of families—parents and two or more children.

Anil had bought one of a family of three—two parents and one child.

Jana ran her finger over the smooth stone. The adult figures each had one arm around the other and one around the child, which was reaching for its parents.

"Wow," Tim said. "That's a little on the nose, isn't it?"

She started tearing up, looking at the little soapstone family.

"Jana," Nicole said. "Are you okay?"

Jana nodded, putting the soapstone carving on the coffee table. "You guys...I'm sorry. I'm bringing you all down. Just ignore me. Had a rough day." She sniffled loudly. Embarrassing. Potato was by her side in seconds.

"We can't ignore you," Asha said. "The brigade never leaves a wounded soldier down."

"Is that what I am? A wounded soldier?"

"I wasn't in the Bridal Brigade," Rohan said.

Tim nodded. "Yeah. Technically, Jerome and I were in the Groom's Platoon."

Kamila glared at them. "We're all in this together. *Including* you, Jana. We've even giving Anil a dishonorable discharge for you."

"You don't even know what he did," Jana said.

"Doesn't matter," Kamila said. "Friends before dudes." She frowned. "That doesn't sound right."

"Chicks before dicks?" Asha offered.

"Hoes before bros," Tim suggested. "More inclusive language."

"Thank you," Asha said.

"Sisters before misters," Rohan said. Kamila beamed at him, proud of her husband.

Jana shook her head, amazed that these were the people she wanted when everything was falling apart. She sighed. "I can't dishonorably discharge Anil from my life—he's Imani's father."

After a pause, while everyone awkwardly ate their charcuterie, Nicole turned to Jana, her face in that trademark no-nonsense look. "You do know that telling us what he did is an option, right? It might make you feel better. I know we're a bit extra, but even Asha and Kamila can be grown-ups sometimes."

Asha nodded. "We can be mature—we promise. What happened?"

Jana took a deep breath. These were her friends. And Rohan was right. Maybe she needed to let people in if she wanted them to understand her.

She told them about Maria telling everyone in the Think office that Anil had cheated on his wife with some woman. Kamila inhaled sharply after hearing the story. "Rohan, you're *friends* with this person?"

"Not really. We were in the same friend group in college, but now we're just Facebook friends."

Asha looked at Kamila. "We need to ruin her. Glitter bomb? Back in school, I replaced half this girl's coconut shampoo with coconut *oil*. It still lathered up and looked the same, but she had stringy hair that wouldn't dry right for weeks. That might be too complicated—Rohan, do you have a phone number for her? We could put a fake ad on Craigslist offering her service as a—"

"I thought you were going to try to be adults?" Rohan asked.

Asha nodded. "The Craigslist thing was going to be *very* adult."

Jana shook her head. "I don't want revenge. She didn't mean harm to me; it was just gossip. It's always just gossip." Jana felt a headache coming. She wanted it all to go away.

Back at Hatari, Anil had asked her what she really wanted, and she had said she wanted to go back to their two weeks. Back to when she felt like she belonged somewhere. In Anil Malek's arms. Now she'd like to go back to the shower in Hatari. When he'd cared for her so tenderly after she felt emotional after sex. "She also said she thinks Nadia is back together with Anil," Jana added quietly.

Everyone was silent for a few seconds. Finally, Kamila spoke slowly, voice tight with anger. "What the MacGyver's muffins did you say?"

Rohan's eyes were huge. "You did not tell me that part."

Jana sniffled, nodding. "She said she saw a picture of them on Nadia's Facebook, and they're together. In D.C."

Rohan shook his head. "That cannot be true." He glanced at Tim and Jerome. "He would have told us. Did you ask him?"

Jana shook her head. "No. I will, but he's out with Imani now. It is possible, though. Did he think to tell any of us the truth about his marriage five years ago?"

Kamila looked at Asha. "Forget this Maria—we're sending Anil a glitter bomb."

Nicole shook her head. "He has a four-year-old daughter. I'm pretty sure his house is already covered with glitter."

Asha scowled. "The shampoo trick won't even work on the stupid bald man. And I'm not putting coconut oil in his body wash, because then he'll have soft, moisturized skin, and he doesn't deserve that. Can we dull his razor blades so he has red bumps on his head?"

Jana couldn't help it—she snorted a tearful laugh, almost

sending a snot bubble on poor Potato, who was still staying close to her. "You are all *ridiculous*. You don't have to do this for me."

Rohan looked around. "Has anyone else seen this picture?"

Kamila shook her head. "Facebook is the root of all evil, so no. It's been months since I've been there."

"I canceled my account," Tim added.

Jana had never even had one.

"Rohan," Jerome said. "You used to know Nadia. Send her a friend request and then you can see her pictures. What's her last name?"

"Nadia Jivani. Or Malek, I suppose," Jana said.

Rohan shook his head. "I'm not snooping...Why don't we just wait to ask Anil?"

"It's true," Nicole said. Everyone turned to look at her. How could Nicole know this? "I mean," Nicole continued, "there are pictures of them on her social. I figured if someone was going to post a picture on Facebook, they would probably put it on Instagram, too. Her account is not private." She held out the phone for everyone to see.

Jana didn't want to, but she looked at the picture. It had been posted a few days ago and was of four people who looked like they were on a hike. Rocky terrain, lush trees. All of them were in hiking clothes. Jana didn't recognize three of them—a tall South Asian woman, a Black woman, and a Black man—but the fourth person was Anil.

Kamila looked at Rohan. "Is that her?"

He sighed, nodding. "Yeah, that's Nadia. I don't know who the other two are. But this doesn't mean they're back together, though. Just that they're hiking."

"Nicole, what's the post say?" Kamila asked.

Nicole looked back at her phone. "Hiking Rock Creek with my love."

Jana inhaled sharply. It was true.

"She hasn't tagged anyone," Nicole continued. "She's got a pretty minimalistic account. Lots of scenery. Woman of few words." Nicole looked at Jana. "There's another picture from a few months ago." She held out her phone.

It was Nadia and about eight people sitting at a long table in a restaurant. The Black couple from the last picture was there, and so was Anil. The caption was something about Nadia celebrating her birthday with those closest to her.

Everyone started talking at once again, analyzing the body language in the pictures. Tim mentioned that Anil had told him that he'd recently gotten into hiking in D.C. with new friends.

But Jana couldn't process what they were saying, thanks to the hammering of her heart. Anil was with Nadia only a few days ago. And also with her before they'd gone to Tanzania. Jana felt like she was going to throw up.

This didn't mean Anil and Nadia were together—Nadia could have meant one of the other two in the hiking picture when she said *my love*. But either way, he'd kept this from Jana.

Jana's phone buzzed then. She checked it—it was Anil.

Anil: I just got home. I made reservations at this gorgeous Peruvian place for us Wednesday. I wanted to ask if you liked South American food, but they had a cancellation so I needed to act fast.

Jana stared at the text. He was just going to carry on like everything was normal. But of course, he didn't know Jana'd seen pictures of him and his ex-wife. With shaking hands, Jana texted back.

Jana: No. I'm sorry, but I won't be going to dinner with you.

She didn't want to talk to him. She didn't want to be in Anil's life if Nadia was there, too.

Anil: Do you need to work that night? I can see if they have a table Thursday instead.

Jana: No. I changed my mind. I can't go to dinner with you. I don't think we should complicate our and Imani's life right now.

Anil: What happened? Can I call you after Imani goes to bed?

Jana: My job might be at risk. Someone was gossiping about us again. I need to focus on work and keep my life simple for a while.

Anil: Oh no. Who was gossiping? I can speak to them. Let me help you. As a friend.

Jana closed her eyes for a moment before writing back.

Jana: I'm not looking for a friend right now. Or anything. Please leave me be. Have Imani call me tomorrow.

Anil: So that's it? You're pushing me away again?

Jana: One question for you. Are you back with Nadia?

She stared at her phone for several long moments, but he didn't respond.

"Did you ask him?" Kamila said, startling Jana. Jana looked up. "Yes. He hasn't responded."

Rohan pulled out his phone. "Let me ask him."

Jana put her hand out and shook her head. "No. Please." She closed her eyes and took a breath, then looked at Rohan. "I just...I want it to go away." Her voice cracked again. "I need to focus on work right now. I don't need this in my life."

Kamila put her hand on Jana's. "Okay. We got you. Tell us when you want us to get revenge and we're there. I can't believe that he'd do this again. Honestly, we should have known better than to trust a bald man. I thought he was a Jean-Luc Picard...not a Lex Luthor."

While everyone discussed whether they believed Anil was with Nadia or not, Jana looked up Nadia's Instagram on her own phone. And there she was. *Nadia*. Even the name was like a punch to the gut for Jana. For years, Nadia had been like an illusion to her. Not a real person. First, she was the person whose marriage Jana thought she'd ruined. Then she was the villain who'd left Anil. Then the person whose family had tried to ruin Jana. Now she was the one who had ruined Jana's chance at happiness.

But seeing her pictures, Jana realized that Nadia may be those things, but she was also just a person. One with laugh lines, maybe from squinting in the sun too much. A woman who didn't seem to mind taking pictures with her hair blowing in her face. She had warm eyes and a wide smile.

She was a human being.

"It isn't possible they're together," Yuriko said, pointing to the statue on the coffee table. "Why would he buy a carving of a family of three if that's not what he wanted? He's not with his ex."

Kamila slid the big box the carving came from in front of her and read the label. "It's from Hatari. Wasn't the gift shop there only open the day we left? He bought this after you had sex."

Jana frowned. "We don't even know if he bought this for himself. And if he did, how do we know this isn't to represent Nadia, him, and Imani?"

"Because Imani is *your* child," Rohan said. "We still don't know for sure that they are together."

"Don't you all see?" Jana said. "It doesn't *matter* if they are together. He didn't tell me he was even talking to her. Just like he didn't tell me about her five years ago."

Kamila held out her hand to Jana. "Here—let me see the pic."

Jana handed her phone to Kamila, who started scrolling the feed. "She's cute, isn't she?"

Jana raised a brow.

"I mean, not as cute as you, but Anil has such good taste. She's very...*wholesome*. I'll bet she always has a bag of homemade trail mix in her backpack. And sunscreen. Doesn't seem like the type who would cheat on her husband, honestly. But I mean, people don't always look like what they are...Oh fudge." Kamila suddenly tossed the phone down like it was a hot potato. She looked at Jana, eyes wide. "She just requested to follow your Insta."

"What?" Jana took the phone "Why? And why now?"

After looking at the phone a second, Jana realized the answer. "Jesus, Kamila. You were *liking* her pictures?" Kamila had hearted pretty much all of Nadia's feed. And the phone was logged into Jana's account—with her first and last name.

Asha threw a decorative cushion at Kamila. "Kamila! You're not supposed to *like* posts if you're online stalking!"

Kamila nodded. "I know, I know. I'm an idiot. The double tap is a habit when I'm on Instagram. Her pictures are pretty. I'm sorry. Just ignore and block."

Jana stared at her phone. Ignore and block...but why? Jana hadn't done anything wrong to the woman. "Or I could...accept?"

Everyone was silent awhile, before Asha smiled widely. "Yes. Do it. Ask *her* if they're together. That's going on your 'letting loose' list."

Jana nodded. With a pounding heart, Jana accepted the follow request and followed Nadia back, too.

And in seconds, she had a direct message from her. "She just messaged me."

Everyone was silent. Jana opened the message and read it.

Nadia: Hi Jana.

"What did she say?" Kamila asked.

Jana motioned Kamila to lean closer so she could read the messages.

Jana: Hi.

Nadia: This is strange. Thanks for responding, though. I figured you hated me, lol.

Jana had no idea what to say, but she had to say something.

Jana: I don't really know you.

Nadia: No, you don't. But...we could get to know each other.

"Ask her if she's sleeping with Anil," Kamila suggested.

Jana didn't ask that. She didn't know what to say, so she said nothing. But Nadia kept writing.

Nadia: I am so sorry for everything. For what I did. For what my parents and sister did. I never expected Anil would speak to me again. And I never expected I would ever speak to you. I told him that one of these days I'm going to try to get the four of us in one big group therapy session together to clear the air.

Jana: Four of us?

She had better not be thinking Imani was the fourth. Jana's fist clenched.

Nadia: You, me, Anil, and Darren. My partner. He's the one I left Anil for...we've been off and on since high school. He's in the picture you liked. We all went hiking together a few days ago. That's Darren's sister with us.

Jana stared at the message, hands shaking.

"She's *still with* the floozy she cheated on Anil with!" Kamila said. "What's the male version of a floozy?"

"Forget floozy," Tim said, looking at Nicole's phone. "He's a hottie!"

Jana exhaled. Anil *wasn't* in a relationship with Nadia. Jana had no idea how tense she'd been for the last few hours thinking of the possibility of that. But now, Jana just...released. And unfortunately, releasing meant crying. She choked back a sob, mortified. The dog whimpered again.

Without skipping a beat, Kamila put her arms around Jana and rubbed her back. "See? What did I tell you? He wants *you*," Kamila said.

After Kamila let her go, Jana wrote back with tears still running down her face.

Jana: Oh. Okay. Thank you.

Nadia: I wish things had been different. But I've always wanted to tell you one thing: Anil always belonged with you, not me. I'm so happy that you two are giving it a shot.

Jana didn't respond.

Nadia: I'll leave you alone now. But if you're willing, I'm here to talk anytime. Answer any questions you have. I'm rooting for you and Anil forever.

Jana didn't know what to say, so she just wrote Thank you.

"She seems nice," Kamila said.

Jana looked around. She'd forgotten everyone was here. She choked back another sob.

Kamila stood. "All right, I think on that note, this party should wrap up. Jana clearly has some thinking to do. Put all your stuff in a box...I'll hang on to Shelina and Zayan's, and Rohan can take Marc's to work next week. Who needs help carrying things? Jana, take Anil's and tell him you have it—You'll speak to him soon."

Jana was about to snap at Kamila for meddling since she had no idea what she was going to do with the information that Anil was definitely single. But then she remembered that she *would* be speaking to him soon—when Imani called the next day.

Jana nodded and started collecting her souvenirs. She did need to think...and that was best done alone.

CHAPTER 28

With her mind racing, Jana took her and Anil's boxes back home. She had no idea what she was going to do—there were too many emotions swirling through her at the same time. But the strongest one was relief. Anil was not *with* Nadia again. Also, Nadia had *apologized* for what she and her family had done in the past. And she *wanted* Jana and Anil to be together.

But the relief Jana felt the moment she learned that he and Nadia weren't a couple told Jana she didn't trust Anil as much as she claimed to. And that Jana had a lot of repressed shame over possibly being the other woman again. It had partially been the shame that had made her push him away.

But shame over the past wasn't worth giving up happiness now. Nadia had figured that out—she was still happy with Darren and had made amends with Anil. Farzana Aunty and Sam had figured it out, too. Now it was Jana and Anil's turn. The image of the statue wouldn't leave her head. He bought a carving of a happy family of three. They could *maybe*, miraculously, be that.

Jana needed to do something. Apologize to Anil for not trusting him first. And then... what? How could she fix this family?

When Jana got through her front door with one box balanced on top of the other, she was surprised to see a light on in the kitchen. She set the boxes near the steps and took her shoes off. Mom was cooking? At nine o'clock at night?

"You okay, Mom?" Jana asked, walking into the kitchen.

Mom looked up and smiled at Jana. "Oh good, you're home. Come, beta."

Frowning, Jana stood next to her mother at the kitchen counter. Mom was mashing a bowl of potatoes, and there was a package of samosa wrappers and a bowl of shredded cheese nearby.

"Why are you making samosas now?" she asked.

Mom smiled. "When Anil came to get Imani today, he said something that made me think... You should bring some samosas over there for her."

"Why?"

Mom shrugged as she dumped the bowl of grated cheddar cheese into the warm potatoes, along with some ginger-garlic paste and chopped cilantro. She mashed it together with the potato masher. "To make things easier for him in case Imani doesn't want to eat. There is no reason for the two of you to be managing Imani separately—why not be a team? You can bring these to him before the party tomorrow."

Jana smiled. Mom was matchmaking.

"And maybe," Mom said as she opened the pack of samosa wrappers, "it's time you learned how to make these yourself. Because you won't live here forever, eh, beta?"

Where exactly did Mom think Jana was going? They hadn't really talked much since they'd looked at photo albums together that night, but things were... good. Maybe not perfect, but much better than they had been in a long time. Jana trusted that her mother really was trying to be less judgmental.

Maybe these samosas were her way of giving Jana her blessing for whatever Jana decided to do in the future.

Mom handed Jana the potato masher and the bowl. "You mash."

Jana took over from her mother, combining the filling ingredients for the samosas while Mom mixed a paste of flour and water that she would use to glue the samosa wrappers closed after filling them.

Jana had fully intended to call Anil tonight and try to repair what she broke. But first, she wanted to repair this with her mother. Jana complained that she and her mother never had a close relationship, and she blamed her mother for her judgments and boasting, but when had Jana ever opened up about what was going on in her own life? When had she ever paused and made samosas with her?

"Something happened at the Think office today," Jana said.

While Jana and her mother cooked together for the first time in Jana's memory, folding the samosa wrappers into perfect triangles stuffed with the potato-and-cheese mixture and deep-frying them in hot oil until they were crisp and golden, Jana did something else that she wasn't sure she'd ever done before. Told her mother about her problems and asked for advice.

"I don't think people will talk about you, beta, at work. Not when they see how amazing you are at your job. Maybe they will gossip a little bit, but you just have to be better at the job to get above that."

Jana sighed as she turned over the samosa frying in the deep pan. That had always been the answer. Do more. Achieve more. Be better than everyone...because then no one would notice the real messiness inside.

A popping sound startled Jana. "Damn it, the samosa exploded."

Mom laughed and looked at the carnage in the pan. The samosa filling had blown out of a hole on one side. "I think you filled this one, beta. I told you not to wrap them too tight." She took the samosa out and put it on a small plate. "If you try to make it too perfect, there is no space to breathe. The pressure is too much and they explode."

Jana chuckled. She had no idea if her mother knew how profound that statement sounded right now. Neither of them said anything for several moments as Jana continued to fry the samosas. A few more of Jana's exploded, but her mom's expertly filled ones looked perfect. After Jana dropped two more triangles into the hot oil, Mom smiled at her.

"Jana, do you remember when you were eight and you stole a nail polish from the dollar store?"

Jana frowned. "I did?"

Mom nodded. "I wouldn't buy it for you, so you put it in your pocket. But your father found it, and he was so disappointed. He grounded you. I think that was the first time we punished you. Maybe the only time. You were the good girl. Kamila and Shelina were holy terrors back then. It was just nail polish, but you were so . . . ashamed. You promised Daddy you would never be bad again."

Jana vaguely remembered that shame. She'd been bad—taken a risk and been burned for it. She'd disappointed her parents. She remembered feeling like she destroyed her good-girl image.

Jana chuckled. "I still don't wear nail polish."

"Beta, don't worry about what people think about you. The only person you need to impress is *you*." Mom frowned. "Don't break the law again, but it's okay not to be perfect."

Jana smiled, looking at the mess around her. She would need to learn to embrace the mess if she wanted to make samosas.

"Thanks, Mom. Hey, can we put chilies in some of these? Anil likes more heat."

One thing was crystal clear now—it didn't matter what her mother, her culture, her coworkers, Nadia, or even Dr. Lopez thought about her past and present. All that mattered was what Jana thought.

Jana was tired of things being *easy* if they didn't make her happy. She loved Anil Malek, and if Nadia and Rohan were right that he wanted to be with her, too, this could be the beginning of the rest of her life.

A life of happiness. A life less alone.

But what she did need to think about was how exactly to proceed. Maybe she should just show up at his condo. She could apologize for canceling their dinner and beg him to hear her out—she could explain all her past hurt and feelings of betrayal that came to the surface when Maria told her that he was with Nadia again. Or maybe she could do a grand gesture—have a dozen roses sent to him. Or better, she could just show up wearing nothing but a trench coat.

Jana laughed to herself. None of those things were remotely Jana-like. Jana had been stepping out of her comfort zone— letting loose—for weeks now. And it had worked—her element *had* changed. She was more than willing to take risks that she wouldn't have even a month ago.

But she couldn't just show up at Anil's—namely, because Imani was there. It was funny—she would have thought starting a relationship with Anil would be convenient because they already had a child together. Dating as a single parent had always been complicated. But dating the father of her child was extra complicated—because whenever she didn't have Imani and was free to be alone with him, he would have their daughter.

It was late—past eleven o'clock. She should probably wait until the morning to do anything. But she'd already let this go on too long.

She texted him.

Jana: I'm so sorry about before. Can we talk? I had a rough day, and I'd love to explain why I was so curt with you earlier. I hope we'll still be able to go to dinner. That Peruvian place sounds lovely.

Jana kept her phone by her bed all night but didn't hear back. Maybe she'd ruined things with Anil before they'd even started.

It was past noon and Jana still hadn't gotten a response from Anil. She finally texted him again, asking if he'd gotten her message the night before and telling him she needed to speak to him.

Anil: No need to explain. I spoke to Nadia this morning. She heard from Maria. I know what happened at Think and why you pushed me away again.

Jana: If you knew, why didn't you respond to my text?

He didn't answer right away, but eventually a new message came through.

Anil: You told me to leave you alone. And that's what I did. What I've always done.

She couldn't hear or see him, but there was bitterness dripping off his words.

Jana: What do you mean?

Anil: You pushed me away. Again. You even asked if I was with Nadia again. Seriously? Come on, Jana. How could you think that after everything that's happened in the last few weeks?

Jana: But you didn't tell me that you were even talking to her! What was I supposed to think after I saw that post on Instagram? You weren't honest with me, even though you said we were friends.

Anil: I didn't tell you because I was afraid you would do this exact thing. And let's be real here—Nadia has been a better friend to me lately than you have.

That felt like a knife to her chest. But the truth was, he was right. When Jana didn't respond, he continued.

Anil: It hurts that after everything, you still don't trust me. I can't keep doing this—fighting for you and walking on eggshells. I don't want to tiptoe around your hot-and-cold attitude forever. All I wanted was a chance to get to know each other again. I was planning to tell you all about Nadia coming back into my life as soon as I saw you. Jana, you know how I feel about you...and if that's not enough to make you want to fight for us, then I don't see how this can ever work.

Jana stared at the phone. He didn't want her anymore. Jana had ruined it. She'd run away from him twice now. And she'd treated him horribly. Anil had had enough.

But he'd never really been open with her, either. She didn't actually know how he felt about her. Because he'd never told her. Rohan and Nadia said that he cared about her, and yeah, maybe this argument was proof that it was true, but it had been *Jana* who'd proposed going on a date. It had been Jana who'd said she wanted to see if they could maybe be together. He claimed he had, but he'd never really fought for her, either. Buying her socks and chocolate bars wasn't the same thing as telling her how he felt.

Jana closed her eyes, leaning her head back on the sofa. There was no point. They were terrible at communication, and maybe there was too much damage. Jana let herself wallow in what could have been for a few seconds, before she sat up with a start.

No. He wanted someone to fight for them. They both deserved that. Their family deserved that. It was time for Jana to do the most "letting loose" thing she could think of—to knock that damn comfort zone so far off its axis that she could never go back there again.

It was time for Jana to be bold. Jana quickly opened the #BridalBrigade chat group.

Jana: I need to make a grand gesture. Kamila, are you still open to some karaoke at your wedding reception?

It was a few long moments before anyone responded, and Jana was worried she'd overstepped. This was Kamila's wedding reception—why would she want anyone stealing her thunder? Even if this was now the fourth official event for this marriage, it still wasn't Jana's to hijack.

But then a series of exclamation points and hearts filled Jana's screen.

Kamila: YES

Kamila: A thousand yesses. Let's do this!!! Grand gestures are my favorite thing in the world! Let's put a big, Bollywood-style ending to this wedding and get you your man! I can talk to the restaurant and they'll set it all up.

Everyone else in the brigade started cheering and lighting up the chat with emojis and throwing out song ideas. Jana laughed. She loved this crew so much.

Jana: No, not Bollywood. I know exactly what song.

Over a video call, the Bridal Brigade planned and rehearsed the song. Jana would be in the middle this time—whether her voice could manage that or not. The center of attention. In front of her friends, family, and even her boss. She was ready to put herself on the line for her own happiness.

CHAPTER 29

After rehearsing with the Bridal Brigade, Jana had just enough time to rush to the mall and get a new outfit for the party. Her muted beige cocktail dress wasn't right for this gesture, so she bought a rich fuchsia formal jumpsuit to wear instead. With its plunging neckline, it was bolder than what Jana usually wore, but tonight, Jana wanted to be noticed. Before leaving for the party, Jana put the small, wrapped soapstone carving in her bag.

Finally, she drove downtown for Rohan and Kamila's wedding reception. Since their wedding had been on another continent, and they both had a ton of Toronto friends, clients, and colleagues, they'd booked a large Harbourfront restaurant for this last party to celebrate their marriage. It was a stylish, laid-back event rather than a formal wedding reception. The brigade had no specific duties and had been told to just enjoy themselves.

Jana's mother and all the aunties and uncles would be in attendance, but this was a child-free event. Jana and Anil's regular babysitter, a local college student, was with Imani at Anil's condo. Jana should have been nervous about seeing everyone again. All the aunties and uncles and, of course, Sam Lopez and

Farzana Aunty. She had no idea if he would mention what had happened at the Think office the day before. Either way, Jana knew it would be awkward. But she didn't care. A week earlier she would have cared. But it appeared that Jana's element had changed.

All her nerves were saved for Anil and the song she had planned. Jana insisted that they sing later in the night so most of the party was focused on Kamila and Rohan first. Jana was afraid that Anil would want to speak to her before her performance. She was afraid he would ignore her. She was afraid of his reaction to her song. And she didn't know if it was futile, if there was no longer anything between them to fix. But Jana was determined. She wasn't going to let fear guide her life anymore.

The restaurant had a vast indoor space with wide-open doors at one end and a large patio illuminated with twinkle lights and flickering candles on the other. Kamila's stamp was all over this party. It was tasteful, elegant, and the right amount of over-the-top.

Jana found most of the wedding party at the bar. There were several others who weren't at the wedding there, too, including one of Kamila's close friends, Maricel, who hadn't been able to travel because she was due to give birth any day now.

"Jana!" Asha said. "Come—we're showing Maricel all the dik-diks she missed. Ooh, love that outfit! That's the last thing on your 'letting loose' list—a bright color you picked out yourself!"

Jana laughed. Asha was right. The "letting loose" list was officially complete.

The party was lively. Jana stayed close to her friends, although she did see Sam Lopez across the room with the aunties and uncles. And of course, Anil was there. He didn't greet Jana when he saw her. Not a smile, nod, or anything. But he did look at her for a moment longer than usual. And, if she wasn't mistaken, she saw his gaze travel down her body in the bold jumpsuit that showed off her curves, and there was heat in his eyes. His brain might not want Jana anymore, but she'd bet his body did.

But all she needed to know was how his heart felt.

The food was all served tapas style, with servers bringing around little plates of pili pili chicken and mishkaki as a nod to the East African wedding, but also other Kamila and Rohan favorites like biryani, coconut shrimp, fish pakoras, and samosas. Plus, fresh vegetable rolls and ceviche. Jana mingled, laughed, talked, and pushed her nerves to the bottom of her stomach where they wouldn't get in her way. She was still determined. She was going to do this—she was going to fight for her family. Whenever she felt afraid, she put her hand on the soapstone carving in her bag, reminding herself why this was important.

Finally, after the party had been in full swing for many hours, Kamila climbed the stage decorated with twinkle lights and big green floral arrangements and took the microphone. She and Rohan had already made a speech together earlier thanking everyone for coming and showing some pictures and video clips from Tanzania on a screen.

Kamila smiled. "I know my closest friends and family are probably tired of me and Rohan by now. I dragged y'all all the way to Africa and back to celebrate us. But since I have the absolute best friend squad in history, I knew they'd do anything for me, just like I'd do anything for them. And that's why when one of my favorite people in the world told me she needed the hashtag Bridal Brigade's help with something tonight, I gave a big, resounding yes. So, my amazing bridesmaids and I have one last performance for you, led by my incomparable, brilliant, gorgeous friend, Dr. Jana Suleiman, PhD!"

As they had discussed, Jana and the brigade joined Kamila on the stage. Jana's heart was beating so hard she was sure it was louder than the cheers of everyone at the party. She was glad she'd worn flats because there was no way she'd be able to stand now in heels.

Jana said a silent prayer and took the microphone from Kamila, thanking her, as the rest of the brigade stood on either side of her.

She looked at the crowd from the stage. Her mother was there, smiling. Dr. Lopez and Farzana Aunty. Kassim Uncle, Jon Uncle, Nadira Aunty. Rohan and Kamila's professional colleagues. Other friends and family. *Everyone* was about to see her put her heart on the line.

But Jana's eyes were only on one person—Anil. He had a surprised look on his face—like he couldn't believe Jana was in the middle of the stage. Well, neither could she.

"Okay." She put on a smile. Focusing only on Anil instead of everyone here helped. "Today, someone—he knows who he is— told me that I knew how he felt about me. Well, I *don't* know. And I can't really blame him for not telling me when I haven't told him how I feel either. So...here goes." She looked at the others on the stage. "Let's do this, girls."

The ABBA music started, and Jana began singing. The audience burst out into applause when she got to the title line of the song, "Take a Chance on Me."

With the brigade singing with her, Jana belted out the lyrics with feeling, emotion, and, more than anything else, joy. She let go of all her inhibitions, didn't think at all about how terrible she sounded or what the aunties and uncles were thinking right now. Or about Dr. Lopez. She didn't care that everyone in the room knew she was groveling to the man she loved, begging for another chance.

She watched Anil the whole time, and she saw the moment that the song did what it was supposed to do—and his expression went from skepticism and surprise to joy. He laughed and cheered with the others, and Jana could swear she saw tears in his eyes.

Jana pointed right at him when she sang the words *I love you so*, and she swore his face almost split with the size of his grin. And everyone in the room cheered even more.

While Jana was still singing "take a chance on me" as the song was ending, Anil crossed the room and climbed the stairs to the stage. She didn't even get a look at his expression before he took Jana's face in his hands and kissed her the moment the song ended. The brigade cheered loudly on the stage, high-fiving each other. Anil looked at Jana's eyes, and now she could see that there were tears there.

He wrapped her up in a hug and whispered in her ear, "I love you, too."

Jana hoped they wouldn't stay long after her ABBA song. They were arm in arm, climbing down the stage stairs, when he whispered into her ear that he hoped she would come home with him. Jana knew they needed to talk, that even if those ABBA lyrics were pretty close to how she felt, not talking is what had gotten them into this mess. And this would never work without communication.

But when they were on their way out of the restaurant, Jana was stopped by Sam Lopez, asking her if she had a minute. Anil said he'd go ahead and meet her at his place. She had her own car here, anyway.

Jana sat with Dr. Lopez at a table near the back of the room. He smiled widely. "That moment was so romantic. I don't think there was a dry eye in the room. Farzana was entranced with your song."

Jana laughed. "You didn't think it was a bit over-the-top?"

He waved his hand. "Nonsense. I admire your bravery in going after what you want. I just wanted to speak to you alone about what happened at the office yesterday. Maria was mortified. She wanted to call you and apologize directly, but I told her I'd speak to you first. She's a bit of a gossip, but she wouldn't have said such things if she'd known your history with Anil. She learned a hard lesson yesterday. I wish it hadn't been at your expense, though."

"Thank you, Sam. I should apologize, too, for storming out of there."

"There is no need. I felt it was important to let you know, now that you've signed the employment contract and are stuck with me, that I was aware of your personal history before I interviewed you. I didn't know your connection to Rohan, or who your parents were, but I had heard gossip through the grapevine in the development community before your resume ended up on my desk."

Jana blinked. Dr. Lopez *knew*? He knew she was the other woman, that she had never been divorced, and that she'd lost a job after being labeled a home-wrecker?

He knew all that and he interviewed her anyway? And he didn't say a word in Tanzania about being well aware that Mom and the aunties were all lying?

Jana didn't know what to say.

"As I mentioned earlier to you, I am no stranger to professional scandals. Your personal life should have no impact on your employability, but I know that others hadn't always given you that grace. I was determined to give you a fair chance precisely because others hadn't. But then after interviewing you and getting to know you, I wanted to have you on my team solely because of your skills, education, and professionalism. And the rest of the team who you met yesterday all agree. We are all looking forward to seeing you in the office on Monday, Jana."

Jana couldn't believe it. This man was everything. She was thrilled she would be working with him. Instead of shaking his hand, she gave him a hug and told him she was also excited to start working at Think on Monday.

When Jana finally walked out of the elevator onto Anil's floor in his condo building, she found him waiting for her in his doorway, still wearing the suit and tie from the party but without a jacket. He looked…intense. Certainly not as joyful as she'd left him earlier but instead serious. The second she was at his unit, he pulled her in by the arm and closed the door behind her. She didn't even have a chance to look around the condo before his mouth was on hers.

And it was like everything was right again. This kiss wasn't like the relatively chaste but joyful kiss after she'd sung the song earlier. This was all emotion and passion and heat. And having Anil back in her arms was…amazing. She'd had several moments of extreme relief today. When Kamila agreed to help her get Anil back. When Anil's face broke out into a smile while she was singing. When Dr. Lopez said his team was looking forward to seeing her at work.

But they all paled in comparison to this. This…*unraveling* as they were once again the way they were supposed to be—with his lips on hers. She could never get enough of him. The feel of his big, hard body against hers. His sandalwood scent. His stubble against her face. Everything. She eventually pulled away. "This . . . this is breakable," she said, putting her bag that still had the soapstone carving in it gently on a nearby table. Then she reached up to put her hands around his neck and pulled him down for another consuming kiss.

She held on to him hungrily as his tongue swept through her mouth. Her eyes were pressed closed and she didn't think—she just felt . . . everything. She felt like she was back in Tanzania, at Hatari, like she was in the shower stall in London, and like she was in bed with him in D.C.

She felt like she was home.

Eventually, the kiss slowed into something else. She was pressed against his condominium door, and she could feel his hardness against her. She ground into him, considering stripping her jumpsuit off right there so he could worship her body with no barrier between them. Or better, unbuckling his belt and sinking to the floor so *she* could worship *him*. But she needed another door between her and her sleeping child for that. She pulled away from the kiss, but kept him close, and opened her eyes to look at his.

His big brown eyes were glassy. His lips were swollen. He was so, so gorgeous. She was never going to walk away from him again. She smiled lightly. "Hi. Can I assume the babysitter left?"

He dropped a kiss to her forehead. "Hello. Yes. I paid her for the whole night even though I'm home way earlier than I thought I'd be. I didn't know you could sing."

She laughed. "I can't really. Did you like it?"

He chuckled. "Yes. Very much. I especially loved the lyrics."

She looked at his beautiful face and took a deep breath. "Song lyrics are great, but…" She bit her lip. "You and me, we haven't communicated very well on our own. I think we should have that talk before we get carried away."

His eyes closed a second, then he wrapped Jana in a full-body hug. If she'd thought the kiss was emotional times one hundred, this hug was emotional times a thousand. "Thank you, Jana."

She smiled as she hugged him back, feeling a comfort and contentment like no other. When she pulled away, she asked if she could look in on Imani first.

Anil led her to Imani's bedroom—a room that Jana had seen many times when she'd FaceTimed their daughter to say good night. The walls were painted pale lavender, and there was a white four-poster bed in the middle of the room with a mound of stuffed animals on the end of it. Imani was sleeping deeply. Jana leaned down to kiss her daughter's head. When she stood back up, Anil wrapped his arms around Jana from behind, resting his chin on her shoulder. Jana had never felt so content— wrapped in the arms of the man she loved, together watching the little human they'd created and shaped sleep soundly. Jana blinked away a tear. She didn't think she'd ever been so happy in her life, and she made a promise to herself that she would fight to keep this family like this forever. They watched their daughter sleep for a few more moments before heading out of the room, closing the door softly. It was time for them to talk.

Anil guided her into the living room and onto a plush gray sofa. Jana had never seen the condo in person but had seen it countless times on video calls. It was weird to be here in person. Like walking onto the set of a favorite TV show—a place that looked familiar but didn't *feel* familiar. She hoped it soon would.

"Can I get you something to drink? Tea? Wine? Water?" Anil asked.

"Wine, if you have it."

He nodded, then disappeared into the kitchen. She pulled the soapstone carving out of her bag and put it on the coffee table. Anil's apartment was very... Anil. Masculine but not devoid of personality or color. Lots of art from his travels juxtaposed with pale cream and gray furniture. Plus, toys, games, and coloring books everywhere. Unlike Jana's house, where Imani's things stayed in her room, here there was no hiding their daughter. It reminded Jana that any relationship between them was really between the three of them.

He came back into the living room and sat next to her, handing her a glass of red wine. Jana took a sip, then placed it on a coaster on the table. It was clear they were both nervous.

He spoke first. "I've been thinking about our argument this morning, and you were right—I *should* have told you I've been speaking to Nadia again after we got closer in Tanzania. But you were finally... tolerating me, and I thought it would make you run away again. But I should have been honest, especially considering our history. I'm sorry."

Jana shook her head. "I'm supposed to be the one groveling here. I was the one who shut you out the moment I heard gossip instead of speaking to you about it. *I'm* sorry."

"I think we've both done things we shouldn't have. Did you really think I would get back together with Nadia?"

Jana sighed. This was harder than letting their bodies do the communicating. "No. not really. But I was scared. All the pain from the past came right back. I think I was more traumatized by what she... well, what her family did to me than I realized."

"Yeah, I can understand that. That must have felt horrible when Maria said those things in your office."

Jana nodded. "She basically said I was a floozy who broke up her friend's marriage. Everyone was looking at me. My boss. Even my research assistant. And then she said you and Nadia had reconciled. Logically, I knew it couldn't be true. But you hadn't told me you were even talking to her again, so I thought I couldn't trust you. And I really *didn't* know how you felt about me. About us. You said yes when I asked you on a date, but you also said Hatari was just for one night. You kept saying you wanted us to be friends."

He nodded. "I did just want to be friends. This isn't at all what I expected from you...I just wanted to be able to co-exist better. I thought you hated me—the last thing you needed was me telling you that I'm still in love with you."

It was like a bomb had gone off. At the party, he had said he loved her, not that he *still* loved her. "Still?" Jana whispered.

He smiled. "Yes. *Still.* I've been in love with you for almost five years. I fell in love with you when we were first together, and I've never stopped."

She had felt everything for this man in the last five years. Hatred. Resentment. Anger. Even attempted indifference.

But he was loving her through all that. Loving Jana. Bitter, grumpy Jana. She didn't know what to say. "Say it again," she whispered.

He smiled and pulled her close. She went willingly, settling herself against his strong body. He was solid and warm, and she fit right here. He put his big hand on her hip and looked into her eyes. "I love you."

"I love you, too."

He smiled, shaking his head. "I can't believe it."

"It's true." Jana said. "Maybe not at first...I don't know if I was in love with you five years ago, but I was on the way there.

And now…Tanzania changed everything. I finished falling in love with you."

He'd always been the kind of person who smiled a lot, but she wasn't sure she'd ever really seen him smile until this moment. He tried pulling her in for another kiss, but she stopped him. Mostly because she knew if they started again, they wouldn't stop. And she meant it—they needed to talk to each other this time.

Jana curled up against his side. "I wish you'd told me how you felt before now. When you said things had to change between us, I thought you meant you were leaving town."

"I did think about leaving. Many times. But I'm also in love with Imani, and I can't be away from her." He shifted Jana so he could look at her face. "I don't think you understand, Jana. I didn't *want* to be in love with you. It hurt too much. I felt like my life was in…"

"You used the word *purgatory* before."

"Yeah. I felt stuck. I was miserable. So I went to Tanzania because I knew you didn't want me there. I thought spending time together might help me stop seeing you as this mythical perfect being. I wanted to spend time with you to fall out of love with you."

"Did it work?"

He huffed a laugh as he pulled her into his lap, settling her on his firm thighs. His head dipped down to kiss her neck. "No. Not even close."

Jana had mountains of things she wanted to say. That she was sorry she was stubborn for so long. That she forgave him. That she was tired of running away from her feelings. And she wasn't going to let other people's judgments get in the way of her doing what would make her happy anymore.

And that his little push—him challenging her to get out

of her comfort zone—was the best thing he could have ever done for her.

She didn't know what to say, so she indicated toward the wrapped carving on the table. "Open that," she said. With her still sitting sideways on his lap, he pulled the paper on the soapstone sculpture, revealing the sweet family of three inside. "You and me," she said, "we can never be just us. I was always afraid of letting myself get close to you. Afraid that letting go of my resentment would unearth... *this* underneath it."

"What is... *this*?"

"These strong feelings. You know I don't warm to people easily and that it's hard for a lot of people to like me. But with you, things were so easy. I felt like we were on the same wavelength when we were together—and I haven't been on the same wavelength with anyone in a long time."

He didn't say anything, just let one hand trail up her back and into her hair.

"Back then it was only two weeks," she continued, "but I'd thought it would be forever. And then when it all fell apart, I was so incredibly hurt. But blaming you completely, even after I found out what you'd gone through, wasn't fair. You tried to make it up to me. You offered me the Aim High position, you referred me for other jobs, and you supported whatever I needed. I should have forgiven you a long time ago, but I was afraid that if I did, I'd remember that I haven't fit with anyone in my life the way I fit with you. And I didn't want to get hurt again. We'd found balance with Imani. I didn't want to risk ruining that. And... I admit I was afraid of what people would say."

With one hand still in her hair, Anil looked down at the carving of the family in his other hand.

Jana kept talking, wanting to let it all out now that she'd been brave enough to start. "I don't think I realized how much I'd internalized stuff from my mom. But I can't let my image...or shame, get in the way of my happiness anymore. I can't go into this relationship worrying about what others will think, or about what will happen if it goes bad. Because despite everything that went wrong before, we've still been great parents. And we'll still be great parents no matter what happens because we're both good people."

He nodded, burying his face into her neck. Anil had always been a very affectionate lover. She'd missed that so much. "Imagine how great it would be for her if it *does* work," he said. "She'll have *both* of us, not either-or."

Jana touched the carving in his hand, letting her finger trail the smooth arms of the adult figures around the child. "Watching you with her helped me fall in love with you."

"Seeing you with her always made me love you more." He put his finger on the carving. "I bought one of these in Africa, too."

Jana frowned. "I know. This is yours. The souvenirs from the trip got here."

He chuckled. "Okay, that's good. I thought it was too much of a coincidence if you had bought the same one. Same color and everything."

"I don't know why you bought it, but—"

He squeezed her tighter. "I bought it because I wanted *this*. You, me, and Imani. A team. It was the morning after that night in Hatari, and you had just run out of my hotel room looking like you never wanted to see me again. And I thought that was it. It was just a one-night stand that had no hope to continue. But when I saw this figure in the shop, it felt like a good omen. I decided then that I would give you space until I was back in

Toronto, but then I would fight for you. *Us*. Slowly, without scaring you away, I was going to make you realize that we can have this. But then you went and asked me on a date before I could." He shook his head, smiling. "*Overachiever*. Always with that perfection, Jana."

She smiled. "I want to be a family, too." She rested her forehead on his.

That was enough talking. He reached down and put the carving back on the table, then took her face in his hands and kissed her. She soaked him in, turning so she was straddling his thighs. He held her tight, locking her to him. As if she would even think of leaving again.

This connection that had knocked her off-kilter five years ago, and scared the crap out of her since then, was back and better than before. She wasn't going to run anymore. Before long, he led her to the back of the condo to his bedroom—the only room in his home that she hadn't seen on a video call before. It wasn't big but had a floor-to-ceiling window with a breathtaking view of the Toronto skyline. She wanted to sit there and stare at it. Later, though. Anil used a remote control on his nightstand to close a gray roller blind over the window. He tossed a condom on the bed, and Jana noticed right away that it was another one from the bridal party backpack.

He stood next to her. "I..." He grinned. "Not just one night this time, right? We're dating?"

She took his hands in hers. "We skipped dating. We're in love." She lifted one of his hands and kissed the back of it. "I've walked away from you twice. That first time...that was your fault."

He nodded. "I agree."

She kissed his other hand. "The second time—yesterday— that was my fault. I'm sorry."

He smiled. "But you're here now."

She kept his hand and kissed his wrist. She let her tongue play with the tender skin, feeling him shudder. "I'm here now," she whispered. Her mouth was still on his forearm. "I don't want to run from you anymore. I love you."

"I love you, too," he said. He stepped around her and ran his hand down the middle of her back. "How do I get you out of this thing?"

She laughed, unzipping the hidden side zipper and stepping out of the jumpsuit. She watched him remove his dress pants and dress shirt. They climbed into bed, and after he rolled on the condom, he guided her on top of him.

She leaned down to give him a long kiss, then lifted herself onto her knees before lowering herself onto him.

And they were joined again. He was warm and hard, and Jana felt complete. She lay on him, her entire body covering his. With one arm around her back and the other on her head, he kissed her while he moved inside her. He felt so, so good. How had Jana walked away from this? This is where they made sense. This is where they fit.

They reached their peaks within seconds of each other, Anil clutching Jana's hips and murmuring her name like a mantra. And she followed, looking at him the whole time. Telling him she loved him.

After cleaning up in his en suite bathroom, Anil loaned Jana some flannel pants and a T-shirt (if Imani woke up, Jana would figure out how to explain she was having a sleepover with Daddy, but she didn't want to have to explain a naked sleepover). They climbed into Anil's very comfortable bed, wrapped themselves in his satiny-smooth sheets, and talked. Really talked. She told him all about her conversation with Dr. Lopez, and about the Bridal Brigade charcuterie party.

He laughed. "Those people. I can't believe Kamila *liked* Nadia's pictures."

Jana shrugged. "It contributed to me getting here, though. Kamila even said Nadia seemed nice. It was so...mundane."

He chuckled. "I'm not entirely used to her being back in *my* life. Super odd to have her in yours."

"Why did you let her back in your life?"

"I wasn't sure I wanted anything to do with her when she first called me a few months ago. But she wanted a chance to apologize. She's a different person from before. I hadn't realized how much her personality was because of trauma from her parents. She's so much more carefree now."

"So, all of it was because her parents didn't approve of her partner?"

Anil nodded. "Apparently, before I met her, they'd even sent her off to some relative overseas who'd basically kept her on house arrest. Nadia didn't tell me any of this back then. Darren isn't Muslim. Or Indian. But also, he's Black. And only a mechanic. Not good enough for their lawyer daughter."

Jana cringed. Poor Nadia.

"They are happy together now. And she has no contact with her parents or sister. After she apologized and explained everything to me, we kept talking, and we got together a few times. I like Darren a lot."

"It's so strange, you two being friends after what she did."

"You don't think I should have forgiven her?"

Jana sighed. "I don't know. I'm not sure I would have."

Anil raised himself on one elbow to look at her. "It's not worth holding on to it anymore. Nadia is happy. She's working through her trauma. And me?" He leaned down and kissed Jana. "I'm happy, too. Yeah, I can wish things were different back then, but now is what matters, right?"

They looked at each other for several long seconds. And Jana realized that as much as she loved this—being alone with him in his bed right now, just talking—they could never really be free of their baggage, their past and their differences. Plus their parents, Kamila and Rohan, their friends, and most importantly, their daughter would always be there, too.

Nothing would be easy. Nothing would be uncomplicated. A life with Anil Malek would always be full of lots and lots of mess.

But none of those people had any say—any *influence*—on whether Anil and Jana would be happy together. That was only up to the two of them. She pulled him down and kissed him. They may not ever be truly alone, but right now, this was the closest they were going to get. And Jana wasn't going to waste that.

CHAPTER 30

Six months later, Disney World, Florida, USA

"Daddy, can we have breakfast with the princesses tomorrow?" Imani asked. Jana really hoped Anil would say no this time, but she doubted it. They were all having lunch in the park at Disney World, and Jana had learned that Anil was not capable of saying no to any question that included the word *princess* that Imani could throw at him. They'd already gone to three princess breakfasts. Jana adored her own daughter, but another roomful of screaming five-year-olds who weren't hers before she'd had her morning coffee wasn't her idea of a relaxing holiday.

Then again, no one had promised this vacation would be relaxing. Energetic, entertaining, and loud, but not relaxing. Honestly, not that different from the last vacation this family had taken together.

"Oooh, I have a better idea!" Kamila said, flipping through a brochure. Kamila was still wearing the mouse-ear hat she'd bought earlier that day, and every time Rohan looked at her, he seemed like he was either holding back an eye roll or a laugh. "There's a safari breakfast in the Animal Kingdom."

Asha looked at Kamila with one brow raised. "Really? Do you

think *this* group in particular would enjoy a fake safari after our real one only a few months ago?"

"It will feel nostalgic," Kamila said. "But with no delirium from the malaria pills, and we can eat and drink without asking what the ice cubes are made of, or what the fruit was washed in. And no mosquito nets."

Nicole and Rohan chimed in with their thoughts on a Disneyfied safari. Soon, the discussion turned into an argument, as it often did when traveling with close friends who had strong opinions about everything. Jana sat back on the edge of the discussion as always. Despite her objection to another princess breakfast, she really didn't care what they decided. She was happy to be on the edge— she belonged here just as much as if she'd been in the middle.

When their small family trip to Disney grew to include Rohan, Kamila, Asha, and Nicole, Jana was surprised at how much she didn't mind the new plan. Seven people was nowhere near as big as the giant thirty-plus-person group for the wedding. And thankfully, there were no aunties or uncles here. Or bosses, for that matter. But still. Jana would never have imagined that she would willingly travel with a group again so soon after that trip.

But nothing in Jana's life was what she'd expected lately. Her element had changed so thoroughly she barely remembered what her life was like before Tanzania. Jana was now the director of research and programs at Think Canada, managing the research department and working closely with Sam Lopez to develop new Think projects around the world. She was also about to teach some seminars at the University of Toronto, working with Dr. Zachary Peterson. She loved her new job so much more than she thought she would. She still felt like she was making a difference, but she was doing it by creative planning, as well as by helping to mold young minds so they could have their turn at changing the world. She'd even taken a seat on the Aim High board of directors, happy to be involved with the organization again.

Imani was in kindergarten, and watching her walk into school with her tiny Lion King backpack broke Jana's heart a tiny bit every day, but Imani was thriving. The #BridalBrigade chat continued, and they still sent each other dik-dik pics, and they also had regular outings, too. The last couple of them were, strangely, playing Dungeons & Dragons in Yuriko's basement. That was what her secret dungeon had been the whole time—she was apparently a high-demand game master who hosted popular role-playing nights with mostly men players in her home. Jana had never been more social in her life. She'd even kept in touch with Nadia and was planning to get together with her alone when Anil took Jana and Imani to D.C. next summer to see his family. Jana's life was chaotic, social, and busy. She loved it. Most of the time.

Later that night, they escaped the more outgoing members of their group after dinner. Once Anil and Jana had put their over-sugared and overstimulated daughter down to sleep in her own room in their two-bedroom suite, Jana sat on the couch and put her head on Anil's shoulder.

"Tired?" he asked.

She nodded.

"We can ask Kamila and Rohan to keep Imani for part of the day tomorrow. I doubt they'll mind. If you want a bit of a break from the park."

Jana took her head off his shoulder and smiled. They'd been officially a couple for six months now. Six months that had easily been the happiest of Jana's life. After being alone for so long, it had been an adjustment to let someone into her life. But being with him was also the easiest thing ever. Their old connection was still there. She could talk to him for hours about her work or about his. And when things became too much for Jana, he was always willing to whisk her away so they could be alone.

And Imani was positively ecstatic to have her mommy and daddy together at the same time so much.

Jana took his hand. "Thanks, but seriously, it's fine. As long as I get some alone time at the end of the night."

He chuckled as he leaned down to kiss her neck. "I think alone time benefits us both." This was where they had always been the most compatible. Things in the bedroom were still very, very good.

He suddenly raised his head. "I forgot—I have news. I got a call while you were giving Imani her bath."

"Who was it?"

"The real estate agent. I know I'm supposed to list next month after I clean out some more, but she got an inquiry. If I list now, we'll probably get a lot more than we thought."

"Like how much more?"

He named a generous number. Generous even by Toronto real estate standards. Jana laughed. With that, plus the down payment she'd saved, they'd be able to get the three-bedroom house near Imani's school that they dreamed about. Jana was ready. Ready to move out of her mother's house, ready to put down her own roots. And ready to make a future with Anil and their daughter.

"That's amazing." Jana grinned.

"You sure about this? We've never lived together."

Jana nodded. She looked into his beautiful face, still not really believing that this was real and that they were finally happy after so many years. "I'm ready. Completely ready. I love you."

"I love you, too, Jana."

And she kissed him. Because this was exactly where she belonged.

DON'T MISS FARAH'S NEXT NOVEL

COMING SUMMER 2024

RECIPES

RASHIDA AUNTY'S CHEDDAR-AND-POTATO SAMOSAS

These samosas are a little unconventional but delicious. Use this basic recipe as a starting point—they are just as yummy with more spices (try garam masala and cumin), vegetables (try peas or finely chopped sauteed cabbage), and/or chilies added (finely diced jalapenos or serrano peppers would be amazing).

Makes 15 samosas

INGREDIENTS

- 1 ½ lb potatoes, peeled and cut into 1-inch cubes
- 4 oz shredded old (aged) cheddar cheese
- 2 green onions, sliced finely
- 1 tsp grated ginger or ginger paste
- 1 tsp grated garlic or garlic paste
- 1 tsp amchur (dry mango) powder (optional)
- 2 tsp coriander powder

- ¼ tsp Kashmiri chili powder
- ½ tsp salt
- 2 tbsp flour
- 3 tbsp water
- 1 pkg 10 x 10 in. spring roll wrappers (or samosa wrappers)

DIRECTIONS

1. Steam potatoes over simmering water for 10 minutes or until tender when poked with a knife.
2. While potatoes are steaming, mix grated cheese, green onions, ginger, garlic, amchur powder, coriander powder, Kashmiri chili powder, and salt in a large bowl.
3. Top cheese mixture with hot potatoes, and using a potato masher, mash the potatoes with the cheese and spices. The heat from the potatoes should melt the cheese. Once mashed, stir with a spoon until filling is fully combined. Cool filling slightly.
4. Make a paste by mixing 2 tbsp flour with 3 tbsp water. Stir until smooth.
5. Cut each spring roll wrapper into thirds lengthwise so they are approximately 3 x 10 in. Scissors work well for this. Cover wrappers with a damp towel.
6. Important: wrap the samosas loosely! The potato filling will expand when fried, and the samosas will explode if there is no room for expansion. Leave an air pocket inside if possible.
7. To wrap samosas: Place one wrapper on a cutting board with the long side facing you. Measure 2 tbsp of the potato filling and place it near the bottom of the right end of the wrapper.

Using your fingers, shape the filling into an equilateral triangle that sits near the bottom of the wrapper, with the tip of the triangle about half an inch from the top. Fold the top right corner of the wrapper over the triangle.

8. With your finger, spread a little of the flour-water paste over the folded-over edge.

9. Fold the triangle upward and to the left so you have an equilateral triangle with the filling surrounded by the wrapper, with a point facing downward and a flat edge facing up. The remaining wrapper should be to the left of your triangle.

10. Spread the end of the remaining wrapper with the paste, then fold the triangle downward and to the left. The flat edge is now down, and the point is facing up. Fold any remaining corners of wrapper down, sticking with the paste. Seal up the corners, if necessary, with the paste.

11. If wrapping the samosas this way is too complicated, roll them up spring roll– or burrito-style. They will still be tasty!

12. Deep-fry over medium-high heat for a few minutes, turning often on each side until golden and crisp. If any explode, eat them yourself.

13. Enjoy warm!

Note: Spring roll wrappers are readily available but are thinner than real samosa wrappers, so these samosas are crisp but a little delicate. If you have access to an Indian or Asian store, you can find real samosa wrappers about this size (3 x 10 in.), which are a little sturdier, and result in fewer explosions.

MANDAZI

These East African fried donuts are traditionally eaten for breakfast or as a snack with chai or filter coffee, or with an East African stew made with pigeon peas called bharazi. For more coconut flavor, add a tablespoon or two of grated coconut to the dough.

Makes 2 dozen mandazi

INGREDIENTS

- 2½ cups all-purpose flour
- ¼ cup sugar
- 1 tsp active dry yeast
- ¼ tsp salt
- ½ tsp roughly ground cardamom seeds (break open green cardamon pods to get the seeds, and crush with a mortar and pestle)
- ½ cup coconut milk
- ½ cup warm water
- Oil for frying

DIRECTIONS

1. Mix the flour, sugar, yeast, salt, and cardamom seeds. Add coconut milk and water. Mix to form a soft dough (add more flour if necessary, but you want a soft, slightly sticky dough). Knead by hand for 5 minutes or with a mixer until dough is smooth and elastic.

2. Place the dough in an oiled bowl, cover, and let rise in a warm place until doubled in size (1–3 hours).

3. Knead dough again and divide into 6 equal pieces.

4. Roll each ball into a 5 in. circle. Cut each circle into 4 wedges. Let rest for 15 minutes.

5. Fry in small batches in hot oil. When one side has puffed up, flip over. Continue to cook, flipping until they are golden brown on all sides.

ACKNOWLEDGMENTS

A few years ago, before my first book was published, I was sitting in a Tanzanian national park with my husband, children, and my parents, with a tablet on my lap and a breathtaking vista in front of me. I was attempting to write a book. I'd hoped that being in such a picturesque, magical spot that has such a special place in my heart would tap into a new creativity well deep inside me. I was wrong. I couldn't write anything. My time was much better spent taking in my surroundings and enjoying my vacation with my family. I took lots of pictures, thinking that one day I would write a story set in Tanzania using all the memories from my trip as inspiration.

And here it is. *Jana Goes Wild* is my sixth published novel and my love letter to Tanzania, the country where my parents and grandparents were born and raised, and the country where I have spent some of my most memorable holidays. But it truly takes a village to birth a book, and this one is no different.

Huge thanks to my editors Leah Hultenschmidt and Sabrina Flemming, who took my hot mess of a draft, figured out what I was trying to do with it, and guided me to get there. And who didn't complain when I added more ABBA to the book with each draft. To my amazing agent, Rachel Brooks, whom I can't imagine navigating this career without. To Kristin Nappier for the excellent copyedit and reminding me how commas work. To everyone at Forever, including production editors, the sales team, the art team, and more—it's always so comforting to be in all your capable hands. To my incomparable publicist, Estelle Hallick, whose contagious enthusiasm for my books makes me love them more. And to Caitlin Sacks for making my dream of publishing a book with an elephant on the cover a reality.

To my beta readers for this story, Namrata Patel and Lily Chu. I am so, so indebted to you for helping me figure out how to get two unlikable side characters from my last book, *Kamila Knows Best*, and make them fall in love. And make me fall in love with them, too.

To my writing friends, specifically Roselle Lim, Lily Chu, Namrata Patel, Nisha Sharma, and Mona Shroff for being there for me as I struggled to get this book out.

To my parents for taking me on that trip to Tanzania in the first place. To my kids for their patience and understanding. And as always, to my husband, Tony, for supporting me in every possible way.

Also, to ABBA—thank you for the music.

ABOUT THE AUTHOR

After a childhood raised on Bollywood, Monty Python, and Jane Austen, **Farah Heron** wove complicated story arcs and uplifting happily ever afters in her daydreams while pursuing careers in human resources and psychology. She started writing those stories down a few years ago and never looked back. She writes romantic comedies for adults and teens full of huge South Asian families, delectable food, and most importantly, brown people falling stupidly in love. She lives in Toronto with her husband, her two teenage children, an elderly rabbit, a fish, and two cats who are in charge of the house.

To learn more, visit:
FarahHeron.com
Twitter: @FarahHeron
Instagram: @FarahHeronAuthor
Facebook.com/FarahHeronAuthor